# Bloodstream

Emilee Carter grew up in a seaside town in the south-west of England and has remained there into her twenties, using her media degree to pursue her journey as an author.

Emilee joined the Bookstagram community while writing her debut novel and found the courage to share her fictional worlds with the real world.

When she isn't writing or reading, Emilee can be found watching nineties and early noughties romcoms in her PJs, with a jar of Nutella and a spoon.

# Bloodstream

## EMILEE CARTER

PENGUIN BOOKS

PENGUIN BOOKS

UK | USA | Canada | Ireland | Australia
India | New Zealand | South Africa

Penguin Books is part of the Penguin Random House group of companies
whose addresses can be found at global.penguinrandomhouse.com.

First published 2024
002

Set in 12.5/14.75pt Garamond MT
Typeset by Falcon Oast Graphic Art Ltd
Printed and bound in Great Britain by Clays Ltd, Elcograf S.p.A.

The authorized representative in the EEA is Penguin Random House Ireland, Morrison Chambers,
32 Nassau Street, Dublin DO2 YH68

A CIP catalogue record for this book is available from the British Library

ISBN: 978-1-405-95805-9

www.greenpenguin.co.uk

For anyone who has never really felt like they belong.
You'll find your place.

# I

The incessant buzzing of Faith's phone on her desk was merely background noise to her at this point. This was her fourth missed call today from an unknown number, but she was so wrapped up in editing this week's podcast that she hadn't let herself stop working long enough to pick up. She hadn't even paused to eat despite it being hours past her standard lunchtime. As she edited another clip and zoomed in on her special guest's facial expression, she made a pact that if the number called once more, she'd answer.

Sure enough, right when she was stood with her head buried in the fridge looking for smoothie ingredients, her phone rang.

'Hello?' Her throat was dry, and she realized she desperately needed to invest in one of those big water bottles that had gone viral recently.

'Good afternoon, is this Faith Jensen?' A man's voice came through the speaker, his French accent obvious.

'Yes, it is. Speaking?' She tried desperately to work out who it was.

'This is Gabriel Lopez, CEO of the International Endurance Championship. Do you have a moment to talk?'

'Absolutely. What can I do for you?' Faith was a professional. She carried herself well, and although she was passionate, she always kept her composure. However, if anyone was looking through the window of her London flat right now, they would see that her jaw was practically on the floor.

'I'm going to cut right to the point, Faith. I know that you haven't applied for a job with us, nor have we advertised any roles, but I've been tracking your career for the last couple of years, and I would like to bring you on board within the organization as a social media manager. Your motorsport podcast is a hit not just with fans but within the industry too, and I think you could provide us with a fresh take on social media. The online world is changing constantly, but you've impressed me with your ability to keep up and forge your own path into the world of racing. You would be responsible for creating and implementing the new social media strategy for the entire championship. That means you, alongside a colleague, would be in charge of all our interns. We would also expect you to run the organization's main social media channels in addition to the accounts of one of our top racing teams. It's a lot to take on, but we think you're the perfect person for the job considering your history. So, are you up for it?'

'Wow. I'm – I'm stunned. This is an incredible opportunity, Mr Lopez. Thank you so much. I'd love to take you up on it.' Tears immediately sprang to her eyes. A job within a motorsport organization was something she had been working towards for years. This was *it*. Her big break.

'The lack of hesitation is precisely what I expected from you. I understand you must have a million questions for me, and we'll get to those in a face-to-face meeting next week, perhaps? I know your social media experience doesn't begin and end with the podcast, so I would love to discuss your other work in further detail. Can I add you to my calendar for Monday afternoon?'

'Absolutely. It's safe to say you've made my week, sir. I appreciate you reaching out, and I look forward to meeting you.'

'See you soon, Miss Jensen.' If she wasn't mistaken, his voice picked up at the end as if he was even close to being as excited as she was.

Faith had been working on her *Across the Line* motorsport podcast for four years. What had begun as a shared hobby with her ex-best friend, Bea, had turned into a real career for Faith. In the year or so since Bea had left to join the IEC as a photographer, Faith had been working ten times as hard on it. She had guest stars every week, ranging from fans of the sport to caterers, media personnel and ex-interns, and she'd even managed to snag a few drivers lately. Their endorsements never failed to give her an extra boost.

She ran social media alongside the podcast, which was where the brand deals came from, and each podcast was published in both video and audio format to maximize growth and engagement. Faith had built a big enough following that she had been able to open an online store and sell her own-brand merchandise. From tote bags, water bottles and key rings to T-shirts, baseball caps and sweaters, she did it all. She used to hand-make everything using various machines she'd invested in, but as the podcast grew, so did her workload.

Due to the lack of stability and the fact Faith had naively decided to move to London, the most expensive city in the UK, her main job was as a freelance social media manager, although her client base had reduced significantly as her own social media presence had grown. Her clients were one of the best parts of her job. She taught them how algorithms worked, how to use hashtags to their advantage and how to target their audience. Faith knew what she was doing in all aspects of branding, especially her own, and she knew how to do it without manipulating her followers into thinking she was someone she wasn't.

As her final stream of income, which she deemed necessary as a backup with today's cost of living, Faith worked as a journalist for a popular motorsports website. That had come after the podcast, because she had started out on social media when she was still living in her mum's caravan in Cornwall when she was sixteen, and built enough of a fanbase just from *being* a fan. She was still in contact with the friends she'd made on the internet ten years ago.

Flying around the world with a racing organization and sharing it with people just like her was a dream. She had grown up wishing she could be trackside, stayed up into the early hours watching races live with a dodgy internet connection. She owed this job to her younger self.

Faith wasn't much of a risk taker. In fact, the only big risk she'd taken was saving up the money from her part-time job as a waitress and moving to London to study marketing at King's College. She hadn't been popular with her mum for that, and she still wasn't, but look where it had got her. She didn't live with many regrets these days, because how could she when at the age of twenty-six everything she'd dreamed of was right in front of her?

'Faith!' The gentle tap on her door and the sing-song voice behind it was a welcome sound. She wandered over and opened it without checking to see who it was. Amina from across the hall came over at the same time every night. She moved like clockwork.

'Hello.' She grinned at the older woman's slightly frazzled expression and her good mood skyrocketed when she saw what she was holding in her Mickey Mouse oven gloves.

'Still your favourite? Shakshuka.' Amina beamed.

'Yes, thank you!' Faith stepped aside so her neighbour could come in and place the dish on the kitchen counter.

'You look very happy today, dear. Something worth sharing?'

'Actually, yes. You might want to sit down.'

'Ooh, this sounds serious!' Amina hurried over to the worn green-velvet sofa and made herself comfortable, oven gloves still on, and that was when Faith felt a pang of guilt for what she would be leaving behind. Her neighbour had stepped in to fill a maternal role the day Faith and Bea had moved into this flat, and she relied on Faith's babysitting services two evenings a week.

'I got a job offer.'

'Another brand deal?! You're doing so well with those lately!'

'Not exactly . . .' Faith bit her lip. 'You know the IEC?'

'Oh yes. That's the big racing championship, right? Not with that lovely *Ricciardo* man I like, the Australian, but the other one? With the twenty-four-hour race every summer.'

'I mean, there's *loads* of racing championships, but yes, that's the one that's offered me a job. The one my podcast is primarily about.'

'Faith, that's amazing!' Amina leaped up and wrapped

her in a warm embrace. 'I'm so proud of you. Wow, no wonder you're bursting at the seams!'

'It's a lot to take in and I have very few details at the moment, but I'm meeting with the head of the organization next week. I don't know the salary yet, but maybe I'll be able to afford to stop the journalism side of things, and the client work. My time in between races will have to be spent on the podcast and my own social media, because while I'm on the road with them I'm going to have to focus solely on my work for the organization. I can't get distracted by everything else I have to do.'

'Darling, your entire life is about to change. Don't limit yourself, Faith. You won't need all those streams of income any more. If you want to see the world and take every opportunity this job gives you, whether that's socially or career-wise, you need time.'

'That would just feel like I'm giving up on everything I've built.'

'But this was always your end goal, yes?' Amina raised a perfectly shaped eyebrow, challenging Faith to tell her she was wrong.

'Of course.'

'You already outsource the online store, and you don't need as many new product releases as you've been doing. The podcast can be filmed and edited as and when you have time, because if you keep up vlogging, your followers will *love* it. In fact, you might even gain more from that than from the podcast. The journalism, yes, is a conflict of interest, but this job is taking you down a different route. The client work, well, the organization, is now your sole client.'

'You're right. You're so right. This job is the priority, the big dream. If other things have to be placed on the back burner, so be it. I can't believe this.'

'I can.' Amina grinned again, her pride shining through.

'I'd have been lost without your support, Amina. Thank you again for dinner.'

'No problem. What time will you be home tomorrow?' Amina started heading back out, taking her oven gloves with her. The door to her flat was open and cartoons could be heard blaring from the television, her sons holding a screaming match.

'My last appointment is at three so I'll be back around four thirty. I'll be over to hang out with the boys at five.' Faith edged the door shut, laughing when Amina offered her a salute and disappeared.

She looked around her flat, suddenly feeling very sentimental. Was she going to have to leave it behind? It had been a sanctuary for her and Bea after they'd graduated, and they'd made it feel like a real home through Bea's excellent decor skills. She didn't want to say goodbye, but she didn't know how often she'd be back in London throughout the race season.

Each IEC season was different, with the locations varying depending on individual agreements between the circuit owners and the championship organizers. This season's calendar had been released a few months ago, and it began in Spa, Belgium. Spa was always her favourite to watch. It was a beautiful circuit surrounded by the Ardennes Forest. It was usually in April or May.

Six weeks or so later, it was time for Le Mans. That was arguably the biggest race in motorsport history, where drivers raced for an entire twenty-four hours, with two or three drivers per car to allow for breaks. Then there was her home race at Silverstone in August, Fuji in October and Shanghai in November. Fast-forward through winter to Sebring in the United States the following March; plus, this season they were doubling up with a second round at Spa and Le Mans.

That meant the season lasted just over a year, but Faith knew from following the drivers and existing social media personnel that they were almost always on the go. With work events, team trips, factory visits, testing, fundraisers and holidays, nobody seemed to have much of a permanent base. She loved that. She wanted in on it. Perhaps she could even go as far as saying that her desire to travel stemmed from her love of motorsport. She wanted to walk into work every day and hear the Ferraris out on the track, to travel with like-minded people and attend events that were a perk of the job rather than the job itself.

Maybe she'd keep her flat until she'd established her role in the organization and knew if she was staying on. She had plenty of savings from brand deals, and she'd be saving money on accommodation thanks to the organization covering it, so continuing to pay rent here in London wasn't *that* big a deal. She was extremely lucky to have made a life for herself which meant she didn't have to suffer financially, but she had known what it was like to go without at uni, and had watched her mum struggle to pay the bills growing up. It pained her to throw money at an empty flat, but it was her safety net.

As she dug in to her shakshuka, she made a list of questions for Gabriel Lopez. Right now, her mind was running wild. The IEC had hundreds of drivers spread across four classes, with about forty cars from various manufacturers. Drivers from all over the world raced and fans travelled to different countries to be part of the atmosphere. Faith had never been to a race. She was always stuck watching the live streams rather than managing to go trackside. She'd been so focused on university and then building her career that she had never got a chance to go. She let her mind wander, imagining the tarmac of the pit lane beneath her feet and the wind in her hair, the roar of the engines coming from the track and the smell of burning rubber. The busy streets of London were a far cry from a racetrack, but finally the only thing between her and the biggest goal of her life was a flight to Belgium.

# 2

A spring morning in England meant stepping out into the most irritating kind of rain: drizzle. London didn't offer the beautiful scent of the damp earth or the sea air that Cornwall could provide, and when Faith was running through the streets to the nearest Tube station, she thanked her choice of footwear. Stiletto heels and puddles were never a good combination, so she'd opted for a trusty pair of trainers and shoved her heels in her bag. One of these days, she might consider wearing her beloved wellington boots in the big city.

Faith darted down the steps to Bond Street, by some miracle avoiding her blonde wavy locks going wild with frizz, which would be a terrible look for her meeting. She hadn't worn a raincoat, praying the drizzle would pass quickly as suggested by her weather app. She had become more fashion-conscious as her social media presence grew and it meant that her clothing choices were not always practical.

She was relieved that wouldn't be a problem at the racetrack. Everyone wore team merchandise or general IEC-branded clothing, depending on their role or what they were doing on a particular day. All Faith needed to pack was a decent pair of trainers and a couple of pairs of jeans, and her work wardrobe was sorted. No more blazers, heels that made her feet ache or blouses that creased as soon as she dared to move.

Thankfully with no delays on the Jubilee line, Faith made it to Canary Wharf only seven minutes behind schedule. She'd been working with these clients for a few weeks now and was unsurprised by the lack of a representative in the lobby. It was supposed to be standard protocol to send someone down to get her, but here she was storming past security alone. Again.

'Good morning, Miss Jensen. You can go straight up.'

'Thanks, Mark. Have a good day!'

The building's security guard was the only positive thing about coming here. Sometimes she thought about actually befriending him out of sympathy for the arrogance he had to encounter on a day-to-day basis. At least Faith was usually in her mostly friendly bubble of influencers and racing fans.

She braced herself before entering the boardroom. Only two men acknowledged her: her favourites. The only two who ever paid attention to what she was saying and took notes. Half the time she wondered why they'd even hired her. Faith didn't often find herself wishing for a client meeting to be over, but a boardroom full of middle-aged men making jabs at her work was enough to leave her staring at the clock in agony.

After the meeting, she hurriedly made her way to the lifts. She was desperate to hunt down some food and get some work done before her three o'clock meeting, but as the metal doors slid closed, her phone rang.

'Is this Faith? It's Gabriel Lopez speaking. Is now a good time?' That familiar thick French accent came through the phone and she almost melted. She could get used to hearing voices like that.

'Hi, yes, this is Faith. Now is good!'

'Ah! Miss Jensen. Now listen, I am in London and one of my meetings has just been cancelled so I was aiming to get back to France today for my daughter's birthday. That means I won't be here on Monday as previously discussed. I don't suppose you have time to meet me and discuss the role now? If not, we could have a video meeting but I'm not really a fan of these Zoomies things. Can never get the camera on. Coffee and cake is more my style.'

'Of course! Where were you thinking?'

'I'm stood in front of a wonderful little cafe in Borough Market as we speak.'

'I can be there in thirty minutes. I've just finished with a client in Canary Wharf.'

When Faith opened the door to the coffee shop she scanned the tables for Gabriel. He was hard to miss – a man in his late forties and a crisp navy suit, so familiar to her after years of watching the sport.

He looked exceedingly well put together, and she was glad she was wearing a trouser suit today. She'd usually stick to casual wear when visiting clients at home, but office-based meetings were a whole different ball game. He had salt-and-pepper hair, and the only other way she could describe it was 'tousled'. He was handsome but not her type. Thank God. She could see herself having a hard time not getting distracted by some of the younger drivers. *Professionalism, Faith.*

His brow was furrowed as he typed furiously on his laptop, but when he looked up a smile lit his face and he waved Faith over. She began heading towards his little corner table and he stood up, almost knocking his chair over.

'You must be Faith!' He kissed her on both cheeks and gestured for her to sit down. She could smell his cologne. A definite rich-older-guy smell, but not at all offensive.

'I am. It's a pleasure to meet you, Mr Lopez.'

'Oh, please, enough of the formalities. It's far too exhausting to keep up. What can I get you to drink?'

'I'll just have a black coffee, please.' She smiled at him as she made herself comfortable.

'Ha! I like it, no fuss. I'll be right back!'

Faith felt at ease in his presence. He was warm and enthusiastic, and something told her they'd be in stitches in no time regardless of how professional she tried to be. He wanted human, though, right? That was the whole point of the job he was employing her to do. Gabriel came back with two coffees and sat across from her, grinning like the Cheshire cat.

'I got us a slice of chocolate cake each too. I couldn't resist. If you don't want yours, I will happily eat it. My wife doesn't usually let me have it. She says I must be as fit and healthy as possible with all this travel taking a toll on me.'

'Well, I hate to be the bearer of bad news, but I think you'll only be having the one slice today. It's my guilty pleasure too.'

'I'm sure I'll survive,' he chuckled. 'So now you're here, let's get down to business. Thank you for meeting me and discussing this role. We're shaking things up this season, because our social media content has become a bit stagnant. I'll be the first to admit that; we're too focused on the formal logistical side of things. Fans don't just want statistics; they want personality, fun. They want to see the drivers participating in the latest video trends, for example. We need to really focus on short-form content, but I also want to allow the world to see our drivers on a more personal level.' He leaned forward slightly and lowered his voice, as if they were exchanging government secrets. In his defence, the motorsport industry was very high profile. 'In this role it would be up to you to work with your designated team and figure out their boundaries. See what you can come up with to get fans more engaged.'

Faith paused in her frantic note-taking in case she forgot something later on.

'Personal? Like their lives away from the track too?'

'Yes! See, you're already getting it. The social media crew we have right now don't delve deep enough and our engagement ratings are much lower than we need them to be. I want the fans to see them as real people, not just these drivers who sit behind the wheel, sign autographs, do interviews and stand around chatting to their engineers.'

'So you want less formal, less structured content?'

'Exactly. While we need the actual racing content, the garage interviews, press conferences et cetera, that's all covered by the wider media at races and the TV networks. From a more dedicated social media role, we need to show that our team and our drivers are people beneath the livery. To form deeper fan connections.' Gabriel shovelled a piece of chocolate cake into his mouth with childlike enthusiasm.

'Almost in the style of a vlog?' Faith was already imagining behind-the-scenes highlight reels, personal video diaries and a-day-in-the-life videos.

'Just like that. They go out to eat; they explore the cities they race in. The camaraderie on the grid is truly magnificent, but the media coverage just doesn't show it to its full extent.'

Faith mulled it all over. This sounded like it could be her dream job, and Gabriel made it sound so easy. Capturing the more personal stuff meant the drivers needed to trust her and open up to her when she had a camera pointed at them. She couldn't do that if they weren't willing, and a lot of them had zero social media presence. There would be a lot of building from the ground up; it wouldn't be an overnight success.

'Why me? I've never even been to a race.'

'You live and breathe motorsport, Faith. I've been observing your social media interactions for a long time, listening to your podcasts. I've seen it. You know a *lot*. That background and knowledge, on top of your business and entrepreneurial mindset, your client testimonials and brand work show that you're the right person for the job. I've already got someone volunteering to take you under their wing.'

'How many people would I be working with exactly?'

'Right now, we have a general team who cover the entire pit lane. What we want is to have two social media staff assigned to each individual racing team. The problem is, we have a *lot* of interns and not many experienced staff, but we don't want to lose the interns. It's important for us to develop them with the aim of employing them in our social teams full-time.'

'OK, so who's going to oversee what the interns are doing?'

'You. Well, not just you. There's Lucie Carolan too. As I

mentioned in our phone call, I want you both on the same team, one of our top teams, and also responsible for the overall management of content across the whole organization. We want your ideas, your feedback and your planning to kick things up a notch.

'Plus, bonus for everyone, you can use your existing audience to bring us some extra attention.' Gabriel winked.

'I'm going to be relying on Lucie's help initially, though. A quick-start guide to the IEC would be great. I've seen TV coverage and obviously I know plenty, but I also know it's different once you're there and you're actually in it.'

'Absolutely! Lucie will happily adopt you into the family. She's been with us for years, so she is a fountain of knowledge and all the drivers love her. The two of you can cross-pollinate your experience and learn from each other.' Gabriel's vision and enthusiasm were catching.

'We need you. Say yes and come to Belgium for the first race of the season next month; it's the perfect place to kickstart a new job, a fresh start. I'll introduce you to the team and the interns, then you can cover the practice sessions before you're thrown in at the deep end.'

A week in Spa? In the heart of the Ardennes Forest? She was in heaven already and she hadn't even booked her plane ticket.

'This all sounds fantastic, but I do have a concern. What if I don't gel with the team I'm assigned to? This is going to be incredibly important for getting pure unfiltered content for social channels. They need to feel relaxed and at ease with me. Obviously I'll do everything I can, but have you told the drivers about all these changes?'

'You will gel with them, I promise. That's another reason

we were drawn to you. When I told them I was coming to track you down, they were over the moon.'

'Well, I'm glad to hear that. It makes me feel a lot better about coming in as an outsider.'

'I will follow up with the job description and contract, with all the salary info and legalities. If you have any questions, you can drop me an email and I will get someone at the organization to contact you. I would like to add that we are also open to negotiations, because we are committed to investing in you. We'll do whatever it takes to get you on board.'

With all the important stuff out of the way and Faith's ego boosted, they ordered another cup of coffee each and Gabriel tried out the carrot cake. Faith couldn't help but start to view him as a father figure. Maybe it was his authority, but he had that paternal air about him. She liked it and she was excited to work with him and learn more about how the IEC worked.

'You'll have to share a hotel room, I'm afraid. Lucie begged me to expand the budget for this season so you two can have a suite. She said that with the workload the pair of you will have, the need to have a space to hold content planning meetings and edit in peace and quiet will be important, especially when the drivers are being divas. Otherwise you'll be in hospitality and you'll have them bugging you.' Gabriel slurped his drink and Faith chuckled softly.

'I like her already.'

'You two will be as thick as thieves, especially on your days off. You and Lucie will always be on the same floor as your team; it just makes things easier. We try to keep everyone together. You'll also have our head photographer, Beatrix, on your floor at all times.'

Faith's heart dropped slightly at the mention of Bea. 'How much will we be working with her?'

'She and her team will be providing a lot of the stills content, primarily for more official account purposes and the media. You'll, of course, be using your own more candid pictures and images, but there might be occasions where you'll want to use their work. I'm leaving it up to you and Lucie to decide what works best.'

Faith wasn't so sure she liked that idea, particularly the part where Bea would be in a room near hers in every hotel. Figuring out where their friendship stood was one thing, but doing so while simultaneously adjusting to a new job and a whole new lifestyle was going to make it ten times harder.

'Are there any big personalities I should be aware of? Anyone who might make my job more difficult?'

'Well, in terms of being open, we may have one driver who's a tough one to crack. It takes him a while to warm up to people, so it's not personal.' Gabriel bit his lip, looking uncomfortable.

'Is there going to be a problem there? I just want to know what I'm getting myself into and what I can do beforehand to make this transition easier on the drivers. It will be a lot to get them to open up if they're uncomfortable from the start.'

'He knows what you need from him and he's promised to step up. It might just take a little extra effort, some more quality time before he feels he can trust you. Lucie was scared out of her mind when she first met him, then the team went out for drinks and, next thing I know, they're best friends. Simple.'

'I can do drinks.' Faith smiled and took another bite of cake. She couldn't wait to find some cute little bakeries on her travels. From the looks of her social media accounts, Bea seemed to avoid such places and opt for fine dining these days, but you couldn't beat a good old Danish pastry and a park bench with a view.

'He is an onion.'

'I'm sorry? An onion?'

'He has layers.' Gabriel grinned proudly at his analysis and Faith realized he was still talking about the closed-off driver, not Danish pastries.

'I'll keep that in mind. Which team is it?' She knew the teams like the back of her hand. If Gabriel told her she could only have this job if she listed every driver of every team for the last five years, including reserve drivers and which number car they were in, she'd nail it.

'You'll be head of social media for Revolution Racing. Jasper, the team principal, wanted to be here, but duty called and he had to fly to Monaco.'

Faith did all she could to not choke on her cake crumbs. No pressure, Gabriel was giving her the most successful team in the history of the whole championship. He was out of his mind.

She managed to squeak out a response. 'OK.'

'OK?'

'Yep. That's great.'

'I'm guessing you know who our potential problem driver is?'

'Julien Moretz. Thirty-two years old from Belgium.

He's won the championship five times with Revolution Racing and has never finished an IEC race lower than third position.'

'That's the one.'

'I think it's safe to say I have my work cut out for me.'

# 3

Having never stepped foot in an airport before, Faith's stress levels were high. Almost as high as the Boeing 747 she had disembarked from not even ten minutes ago. It was the first time since moving to London that she wished she could drive. A ferry crossing alone? Easy. No security officials staring her down as she fumbled to place her belongings in the awkwardly sized plastic tray. No kids kicking the back of her seat and screaming at the top of their lungs. All that stress for an hour in the air was ridiculous.

If she'd thought boarding the plane and getting off again was stressful, baggage claim was hell on earth. The luggage carousel was a blur of black suitcases and Faith cursed herself for not getting a brightly coloured one. She might try to get one before going to her next destination. Wherever that ended up being.

The woman stood next to her yanked two cases off and set them on the ground, as if they weighed next to nothing. Faith was so busy gawking at her in awe that she nearly missed her red luggage tag.

She felt her whole body relax. That was one less thing to worry about. Next up, find Lucie Carolan. According to her vague airport knowledge, she should be around here somewhere, holding a sign with Faith's name on. Faith squinted as she looked through the doors to where there were dozens of people all holding signs and banners. Another scene of chaos. Brilliant.

Faith pushed through a swarm of equally stressed passengers and out through the automatic doors. Almost immediately she spotted a petite brunette waving manically at her. A sign with Faith's name on it was flailing around above her head.

'Faith Jensen? Hi! I'm Lucie Carolan, great to meet you.' She smiled warmly at her.

'Hi, Lucie. Thanks so much for coming to my rescue. It's a little overwhelming in here. Gabriel said that you volunteered?'

'I did. Us girls have got to stick together. I didn't have a me when I was you. And it was a lot to fend for myself. Does that make sense? Oh! Let me take your case for you! Follow me – I'm illegally parked.' She talked at a million miles per hour, but all the excitement was hyping Faith up too, the woes of the plane forgotten.

'Sorry if my case is heavy! I didn't really know what to pack or how much.'

'Don't be silly – it's not heavy at all. You'll never have to wheel your own case again with our team around. The guys practically fight to help me when we're on the road. I'm all for equality, but you won't catch me complaining.'

They walked to the car and Faith's jaw dropped. Her new work colleague had only gone and shown up in a bloody Porsche.

'Yours?' Faith practically sputtered.

'I wish. I borrowed it. I could hardly welcome you to the world of motorsport in a Citroën, could I?' Lucie wedged the suitcase in the back seat, standing up victoriously when she was done. 'There we go – it's sandwiched in but it fits!'

Faith lowered herself into the car in a way that suggested if she moved too fast, it would vanish beneath her. Was this her life now? What was next, caviar? She laughed aloud. That probably wasn't far off, all things considered.

'Where are you from then, Lucie?' Faith asked. She could hear the American accent, but she was no expert on the United States.

'Good old California. Los Angeles to be exact. I honestly can't remember the last time I was in the US for anything other than Sebring, mind you. Oh, and my mom is Italian and moved back there a few years ago so you might hear an accent when I'm drunk.' Lucie started the engine and Faith felt goosebumps on her skin as she took it all in.

'You travel a lot then, I'm guessing?'

'All the time. Once you start, you can't really stop. I didn't even have the travel bug until I got this job.'

'I've had the travel bug for years, but not gone anywhere yet. I can't wait to explore the countries we're racing in and actually see the world with my own eyes.'

'So this is quite literally your dream job, huh? I'm a big fan of *Across the Line*. I've got my fair share of merchandise; the pastel pink baseball cap is my favourite.' Lucie hit the horn as someone cut in front of her. 'You absolute fucking idiot!'

Faith couldn't help but blink at her, like a deer caught in headlights. Sweet and innocent little Lucie was a feisty one. They'd get along just fine if she kept that up.

'Really?! I'll admit Gabriel's call took me by complete surprise.'

'Gabriel has been keeping tabs on you. You were kind of hard to miss with the whole viral-podcast thing you've got going on. I think it was when Casey Winters guest-starred that the grid started really taking notice.'

'I'm pretty nervous. Is it a bad move to confess that to a co-worker?' Faith blushed. She was letting her profession-alism slide momentarily, but there was something about Lucie that felt safe and secure. She reminded her of Amina.

'Of course not! I was in your position once, and I had literally zero social media experience. Barely even used my own accounts. After a few races on the catering team, I managed to get an intern position purely because of my passion for the sport and I worked my way up. That was around eight years ago. We need you, Faith. Something and someone new.'

Faith finally allowed herself to settle into the cool leather seats and released a breath, feeling more confident. 'I think I'm worried about the team not being super recep-tive. They have no reason to trust me straight off the bat, and yet that's exactly what we're asking them to do.'

Lucie shook her head. 'You don't need to worry about that at all, I swear. We're a family. A very big, very bois-terous family.'

'A family, huh?'

'Yup! We eat together. Live together. Travel together. That's what families do, right?'

Murmuring in agreement, Faith turned to look out of the window.

How would she know? She had no first-hand experience of what families did. Growing up, she spent her evenings and weekends alone. When she reached secondary-school age and was old enough to make dinner for herself, she would cook whatever they had in the cupboard, usually noodles or microwave rice, and she would sit up to the table, do her homework or watch a race and wait for her mum to get home. It was her time to escape the real world, escape that feeling of loneliness that she felt each time she walked through the front door to an empty house. Andrea Jensen had priorities which didn't involve raising her child.

The race circuit was in the most traditional Belgian town Faith could've imagined. Francorchamps definitely didn't belong on one of the tacky postcards her mum was a fan of sending. Postcards Faith shoved in a box under her bed.

Lucie drove them into a car park packed with black SUVs and supercars. Like the cars, the hotel was sleek and modern. Parts of the town had clearly been commercialized for the sake of its clientele, but it was magical nonetheless. They were a stone's throw away from the circuit, so Faith figured that tourists weren't fortunate enough to get a room here when there was a race.

'Welcome to your home for the next week.' Lucie turned to look at her. 'You have your own room this time but that was just in case you didn't like me. If you decide I'm your new best friend, we'll be sharing for the rest of the season. We usually pair up.'

'Important question. Is the breakfast decent?' Faith raised an eyebrow as if there was even the slight chance that a place like this would be slacking on quality.

'Oh, bless your heart. You have *no* idea how lucky we are. Come on, let's go find Gabriel.' She flung the car door open and leaped out like an excited puppy.

The suitcase rattled along the cobblestone path. As they got closer to the entrance, a group of middle-aged men in suits emerged. Faith stepped aside, letting them pass.

'Is the rest of the team here yet?' Faith asked Lucie.

'Yep! Well, as far as I know we're all here. I've seen Mars already this morning, and I'm pretty sure he and Brett travelled together.'

'Mars?'

'Sorry, I mean Marco. I call him Mars sometimes. He hates it. I just like winding him up really. It might as well be part of my job description at this point.' Lucie grinned mischievously as they entered the hotel lobby, which to Faith's surprise was eerily quiet.

There was an almighty clatter from down the corridor and the two of them whipped their heads round. Faith laughed to herself. Of course it was Gabriel knocking into a vase.

'My darlings! Faith, I'm so glad to have you with us. How was your journey? Everything go smoothly?' He came towards them with open arms, kissing them both on the cheek.

'It wasn't too bad for my first-ever flight, thank you.'

'Faith and I will sit down later and plan content. Which reminds me –' Lucie began texting manically as she spoke – 'I should get down to the track and grab some quick-fire interviews while it's quiet. Most of our social media crew don't arrive until tomorrow so it'll save them from having to rush around last minute.'

'We'll leave you to settle in, Faith. Maybe head down later if you feel like it. I suggest hunting someone down in the restaurant and asking if you can tag along with them, so you don't get lost. If I'm done with my meeting by the time you're ready, I may be able to take you myself.' Gabriel placed a hand on her shoulder as he moved past her, and the next thing she knew he was halfway across the lobby. He moved like a whippet.

'I'll get the guys to come and find you and bring you to the garage. You do not want to get in a golf cart with Gabriel, believe me. The man is reckless. Tipped one over a couple of years ago; he still insists he never saw the plant pot, but we all know he was weaving around them at high speed for a laugh.'

'Amazing. Thanks, Lucie.'

'Here's your room key. Top floor, room one hundred and eighteen. See you later!'

Faith had freshened up and swapped her leggings and sweatshirt for black jeans and a basic white T-shirt. Her Nike AF1s were the only pair of appropriate shoes she'd packed, unless she wanted to march around the paddock area in black stilettos. She cringed at the idea.

If there was one good thing her mum had taught her, it was that you should pack a pair of heels and a dress for every trip. How she had discovered that little trick was a mystery. Her mum never left Cornwall, which was hardly the place for such attire.

'Good arvo! You our new stalker then?' A strong Australian accent boomed across the restaurant. Faith looked up from her phone and notes, searching for the source.

'That would be me.' She waved.

A tall, tanned brunette man walked over. He shoved

his sunglasses up on to his head and sat down at her table, helping himself to a fry.

'Brett Anderson.'

'Hi, Brett. I'm Faith.'

'I told you her name wasn't Faye, you doughnut!'

Brett rolled his eyes dramatically, turning to the messy head of curls hovering behind him.

'My apologies, Faith. I'm Marco De Luca.' Marco reached out and shook her hand politely, taking a seat next to his teammate.

'So, *are* you a stalker?' Brett studied her, a cheeky glint in his eye.

'Brett, leave the woman alone.'

'Not a stalker but an admirer.' Faith prayed her cheeks weren't red. She sensed that he wasn't the type to let her live it down.

'We're messing. We know all about you. Lucie said we have to look after you every moment she's not able to be by your side, so here we are.' Marco smiled at her.

'Your knights in shining armour. Although if you're anything like our Luce, you don't need one of those. Right, come on, mate, let's get ourselves some food. We can't be stealing all Faith's fries.'

Marco frowned. '*We* weren't.'

Brett was a real character. She was going to get some damn good content out of him.

She watched in amusement as they placed their order with a waitress and attempted to conceal her laughter as Brett struggled to speak Dutch. He then proceeded to try French. Little did the poor guy know, the waitress spoke perfect English. But kudos to him for not assuming she

28

did. Marco swatted Brett's hand away as he ruffled his curls mid-conversation. The younger driver was significantly shorter and was actually only a couple of inches taller than Faith.

'So is it just you two here?' she asked when they returned.

'Yeah, Julien is driving himself here this afternoon. He only lives twenty minutes away, but he's got to stay at the hotel with the team. It's in our contracts,' Marco replied.

'Lucie gave you the whole spiel about how we're a family unit, yeah?' Brett asked.

'She did.'

'Well, she meant it.' Brett took on a more serious tone. 'Anyone messes with you, any problems, we've got your back.'

'I appreciate that,' Faith responded.

'Some guys might try their luck. We don't have many ladies around, so they get a bit ahead of themselves sometimes. I personally won't fight anyone for you, but Brett will. I'll just have some hard words.' Marco threw his arm round Brett's broad shoulders playfully.

'All right, mate, bloody hell. I'm not the violent type but, yeah, I'll keep people in line if they overstep. Same as I would for Luce. It's Jules you've gotta watch out for.'

'Why have I got to watch out for him?'

Faith's nerves started to bubble again. The more she heard about Julien, the more she worried about the fight she'd have on her hands. Before she'd even started packing, she'd brainstormed her approach for Brett and Marco. She'd spent hours scouring interviews, deep-diving into their social accounts and working out the best tone for them. But Julien was an enigma; he gave nothing away.

'Let's just say he isn't afraid to throw a punch or hurl an insult if someone is disrespecting a woman on the team.'

That wasn't necessarily a bad thing – well, the punching and physical violence part was not so great, but standing up for women? She could appreciate that.

The waitress placed their food on the table in front of them and Faith took the opportunity to show the guys that they hadn't needed to struggle through a language barrier.

'Could I have another glass of water, please?' she asked.

'Of course. Would you like ice with that?'

'Yes, please.'

Faith smiled and looked straight at Brett. His mouth was hanging wide open. Judging by first impressions, it probably wasn't very often that he was lost for words.

'Well, damn. Could've told us before we humiliated ourselves.'

'Where's the fun in that, Anderson? Besides, it's good that you didn't just assume she could speak English. Very admirable of you making an effort.'

'I like you.' Marco laughed. 'What are your plans for content? We know we've all got to be open to your ideas; we've been warned,' Marco said.

'Yeah, like, can I play pranks on people and film it on a GoPro or something? I do it without the cameras anyway. Just thought that might be along the lines of what Gabriel is getting at with the whole personality thing.' Brett shrugged.

'That would be absolutely perfect,' Faith said. 'Each team is getting their own YouTube channel as well as a TikTok account, which will be great for sponsors. Some things are down to team bosses too, but I hear that your boss is a bit hopeless with social media.'

'Jasper is clueless. He was so relieved when he heard you were coming on board. He told us to be nice and welcoming because you're our saviour and must be cherished. You'll meet him later.' Brett took an almighty slurp of his Diet Coke.

'Revolution are one of the best teams on the grid, but there's always more to be done. A strong social media presence is the next step. It will help to open you up to legions more fans and break that barrier between fan and driver, which has been so key in other areas of motorsport.'

'Yeah, we've got to keep up with the times. We seem to have an increasing number of younger fans too,' Marco agreed.

'They travel round the world for races, buy merchandise and hype you up on socials. You need to cater to them.'

'So you're saying that if I'm completely and utterly myself, the fans will flock to us?' Brett raised an eyebrow.

'You two are exactly the kind of drivers that fans love. You have a good bond and take your jobs seriously but still have a laugh.'

'Hear that, Marco? We're perfect.'

'One of us is.'

Faith was optimistic. Her biggest fear had been having to spend so much time earning the drivers' trust that she couldn't produce game-changing content for this first race. She needed to go all out from day one. Prove to the organization, Revolution Racing and her socials team that they could depend on her.

With Brett and Marco already on her side and keen to

get stuck in, she was off to a great start. Two down, one to go. She'd seen interviews with Julien over the years and followed his accounts, and if she was being realistic she needed to prepare for the worst. He came across as blunt, uninterested and, frankly, quite rude. Gabriel had already warned her he was a tough one to crack, but she could only fight her way in if he allowed her to.

'You ready to come down to the track? Jasper wants to meet you and introduce you to the mechanics and engineers.' Marco screwed up his napkin and they stood up abruptly. They certainly didn't take much time out of their busy schedules to relax, that much was clear.

'Of course.' She nodded and grabbed her phone and sunglasses. Her lack of camera had her feeling a little lost, but her phone was in her hand ready for if she saw anything worth capturing. Today was purely about meeting everyone. She couldn't shove a camera in their faces immediately unless there was something unmissable. Save that for the first full day of press and prep.

'Let's go, Jensen.' Brett linked his arm through hers and tugged her gently until she was walking by his side.

Marco trailed behind them in exasperation, but Faith couldn't wipe the smile off her face.

# 4

As Faith walked around the Circuit de Spa-Francorchamps, one of the most famous racetracks in the world, she struggled to believe this could all be real. She had been eagerly snapping away and filming videos, careful not to reveal anything that wasn't supposed to be public yet. She had photos waiting to be edited and videos ready to be turned into montages, and her followers were going wild over the two posts she'd already made. When she'd first checked her phone after arriving at the hotel, her notifications were flooded by people who were stunned she was finally going to a race.

'Is that my Lucie?' Brett's voice echoed through the Revolution Racing garage, startling Faith who had been chatting idly with Marco and his engineer.

Lucie rushed towards the Australian driver and jumped into his arms. Her tiny frame made it look like Brett's six-foot-three self was cuddling a teddy bear.

'I hope you've been behaving yourself the last couple of months, Anderson.' She tapped him on the nose.

'I always do, Luce.' Brett set her down and put his hand on his heart, feigning innocence.

'He hasn't been too bad, to give him credit,' Marco said. 'Although two weeks into our big Australian road trip, I did consider shipping him off to LA so you could take over Brett babysitting duties. Also, he made me skip for part of the walk down the paddock. He's been in one of those moods all week.'

Lucie rolled her eyes. 'Brett! You've got to stop making people do that.'

'Hey, Faith told me stuff like that is great for content!' he said defensively, but a smirk was already working its way on to Lucie's face.

Marco scowled. 'When the cameras are actually *on* you.'

'Got it. Maybe we should get scooters instead?'

'That's –' Lucie started.

'Maybe not such a bad idea,' Faith interjected. 'I'm serious, we could work some content around that. We can discuss it later.'

'Have you met everyone on the team yet?' Lucie asked, turning to her and cutting the boys out of their conversation. They took the hint and wandered over to the car, peering into the cockpit as an engineer explained something.

'I've been introduced to everyone I've crossed paths with, including Jasper, although I'm not sure I'll remember them all.'

'Ha! If you could remember the names and job roles of everyone, then I'd be amazed. I still can't remember that guy's name and he's been here two seasons already.' Lucie pointed at a lanky blond guy with glasses who was checking the tyres.

'I want to say his name is Alan . . . but I could be very wrong.'

'Oh. I thought it was Alec. Who knows! So what do you think about the guys? Reckon we can get some good footage?'

'One hundred per cent. I think Brett might be the key

but Marco sounds like he's really keen too. With Brett by his side I think he'll be a lot more open than if we had him doing lots on his own,' Faith suggested.

'I agree. Are you thinking we could do a series with just the two of them? Something light-hearted, unscripted. Just let them be the complete idiots they are.' Lucie laughed.

'We could have them giving tours of different areas. A track tour, garage tour. Hospitality area, maybe? We could even get them in the merchandise stalls and the fan zones.'

'Where have you been all my life?' Lucie asked, clutching Faith's arm in excitement.

'Sitting in my home office staring at a computer screen or in conference rooms with stuck-up, rich old white men and bratty teenaged-girls?' she offered in response.

'Hate to break it to you but there's plenty of that going on in this industry too. We're just usually lucky enough to avoid them and hang out with the cool kids.' She gestured to where Brett and Marco were analysing statistics with Jasper.

'Let's never tell Brett that he is considered a "cool kid".' She grimaced. He didn't need anyone else to encourage him. The guy was pure chaos but in all the best ways.

The girls watched as Marco came back to join them.

'Hey, Mars. Is Julien *still* not here? He's taking forever.' Lucie was visibly impatient. 'I want to be the one to introduce him to our newest recruit.'

'He called half an hour ago; his car broke down on the driveway as he was trying to leave, but he'll be with us soon.'

'Couldn't he just, like, hop into one of his other many cars?'

'You know how he gets. Doesn't want to bring his

precious vintage classics or his beloved Porsches to the circuit. Security isn't very tight in the car parks.'

'Julien's Lamborghini got keyed a few years ago.' Lucie turned to Faith. 'Since that incident, he's only driven here or to Le Mans in his Range Rover.'

'You should see his car collection,' Marco added. 'It's the stuff of dreams. But I guess living out in the countryside, he has the space for it.'

'You'll probably see it at the end of the week,' Lucie said.

'Will I?'

'I mean, it depends on whether he goes ahead with his annual post-race celebrations. He's notorious around here for going all out, but last year things got a little too out of hand and he vowed to keep it low-key this year.'

'You talking about when we played poker and Gabriel lost fifty thousand euros?' Brett threw his head back in laughter as he joined the trio. 'The dude really tried to blame *us*. We can't help it if beer blinded his judgement.'

'Lucie wasn't in charge of helping to organize that one; that's why there was poker. And a mechanical bull and a bouncy castle in the field.' Marco grinned.

'The what in the what?' Faith couldn't even begin to imagine the scene they were describing. It all sounded far too ridiculous.

'Like I said, things got out of hand. Drivers are like a bunch of overgrown kids after a race, and when we're in a private space like Julien's house, nothing is off limits. But anyway, I offered to plan this one. I'm just waiting for him to confirm, which he should today,' Lucie said.

'She only offered to help him because she fancies him,' Brett remarked, dodging Lucie as she smacked his arm.

36

'I do not!'

'Yes you bloody do!'

'I am *not* interested in him.' She glared Brett down, her cheeks flaming red. Faith knew without a doubt that Julien Moretz was *not* the driver Lucie had eyes for. 'I just get flustered by his distractingly good looks, as anyone in their right mind would.'

'Are you jealous by any chance, Anderson?' Marco challenged his teammate, and Lucie's cheeks got redder.

'What? No, no, I just . . . No . . .' Brett couldn't get his words out, which was clearly a rarity. 'I'm just messing with ya, Luce. You know I don't mean it.'

Lucie was clearly equally embarrassed, but Faith was plotting in her head. There was definitely more to this friendship. Faith would get it out of at least one of them eventually.

'Anyway, shall we go back to the hotel? I don't want to show up to my first team dinner in jeans and trainers.' Faith broke the awkwardness surrounding them.

'Yeah, I want to hear all about your life back in England.' Then Lucie insisted on the two of them walking ahead of Marco and Brett.

As the team walked back to the hotel, Faith felt as though she had known Lucie forever. In a matter of hours they had become what Brett referred to as 'Revolution's Power Couple'.

'I don't suppose you'd want to get ready for the team dinner together? I need outfit advice, and it's not often I get to do things like this,' Lucie asked.

Faith smiled at her. 'I'd love to.'

'Ladies!' They were interrupted by Gabriel zooming towards them in a golf cart, grinning wildly. Faith prayed he wouldn't ask them to hop in, having been warned of his reckless driving. 'Jump in!'

'Gabriel, I swear . . .' Lucie threatened.

'I promise I'll drive slowly!' He raised his hands up in defence, momentarily losing control of the cart. 'And I will keep two hands on the wheel.' He grimaced.

'Fine.' They got in and Faith sat in the front seat. Perhaps not the wisest idea if she wanted to come out alive.

'I just wanted to say I've seen a couple of your posts, Miss Jensen. Of your journey, your arrival, your walk down to the circuit. Even the little hotel-room tour. That's exactly what we want! It's so personal, so genuine.'

'Let's not forget that at the end of the day I am still a huge fan of motorsport. This is so much more than just a job. I want that to be conveyed in the content.'

'Let's get that kind of excitement across on the team accounts. Tell the interns to do the same for their teams, yes? Oh, and tell everyone to throw in all the heart-eye emojis! We love heart-eye emojis!' Gabriel was getting louder and more enthusiastic the more he went on. The cart was rocking slightly with every movement he made. 'They're so cute, are they not? I send them to my wife in every single message.'

'*Every* message?' Lucie asked.

'Every one, Miss Carolan!'

Their conversation was cut off by the roar of an engine coming down the street behind them. A cherry-red Ford Mustang whizzed past and Gabriel brought the golf cart to a screeching halt on the pavement. *Oh.* Julien.

'Oh my *God*. He's actually gone and ditched the Range Rover,' Lucie whispered.

Faith barely heard her. Her attention wasn't on the car that was now parked on the opposite side of the street, but on the golden-blond racing driver emerging from it, his tall frame making him appear somewhat intimidating. She could've sworn he was doing the whole locking-the-car-over-his-shoulder-in-slow-motion thing, but that was just her imagination playing tricks on her. Probably.

The closer he got, the more nervous Faith became. She'd seen him on screen, but the cameras didn't do him justice. As Gabriel shook his hand, she couldn't tear her gaze away from him. This had the potential to be embarrassing, but he hadn't seemed to notice her staring. He was undeniably the most attractive man Faith had ever seen.

'He's finally cut his hair,' Lucie mumbled behind her.

'Yeah . . .' Faith snapped out of it and took a deep breath, hearing Brett and Marco come up to join them. 'Um, should we get out and say hello?'

Lucie pulled herself together immediately, clambering out of the cart and rushing to give Julien a hug. He squeezed her tightly, the familiarity and ease they had with each other obvious. Faith hoped he didn't try to hug her. She wasn't sure she could handle that.

Lucie introduced her as she reached the circle. All eyes were on her, and she'd never felt less confident. 'Jules, this is Faith Jensen, our new social media manager.'

'Hi, Julien. It's nice to meet you.' Sorting herself out in record time, Faith smiled at him brightly and extended her hand. He didn't take it. If she hadn't been so painfully aware of every movement he made and every reaction she was having, Faith wouldn't have let it bother her. But it had bothered her, and her heart was racing.

Julien shoved his hands in his pockets and nodded, avoiding any physical contact with her. But the eye contact was there. It felt like he was staring into her soul. *Could he stop?* Preferably before she hijacked Gabriel's beloved golf cart and drove it all the way to Brussels airport.

Brett broke the tension. 'You coming to the team dinner tonight, mate?'

'I have to unpack,' he said. 'I also need to speak to Gabriel. I'll be at the bar later.'

'OK,' Brett replied, looking between Faith and Julien. He wasn't subtle at all. 'Well, shoot us a text when you're ready then.'

Julien nodded, walking away with Gabriel struggling to keep up with him. Faith noticed people from the hotel rushing to grab his suitcases from his car boot. *Really?* He couldn't have done that himself?

'I'm not the only one who thought that was weird, right?' Marco spoke in a hushed voice.

'Dude's personality was wiped the second Faith came over,' Brett agreed.

'Did I do something wrong?'

'No way.' Lucie placed a reassuring hand on her arm. 'I have no idea what's got into him. He's never so . . . shy? Is "shy" even the right word? I think it's just that he's not keen on this whole increased social media thing. You know how he is: keeps his private life very private.'

'Yeah, he's probably just having an off day, you know?' Marco shrugged. 'His car breaking down will have annoyed him. He really hates bringing the Mustang.'

Faith had a sinking feeling that he was about to make her job hell. He was already rushing to get away from her moments after meeting her, so how was she supposed to convince him to hang around her long enough to get video footage? She knew he was the star the fans would want to know about. Without him she was royally screwed.

'I reckon he was blinded by your beauty, FJ.' Brett winked but it did nothing to make her feel more at ease.

'Brett, who the hell is *FJ*?' Lucie frowned at him, but her features softened in an instant when he held her gaze.

'Maybe the nickname doesn't work. It was worth a shot.'

'He'll come around. Don't stress about it too much.' Brett shuffled his feet awkwardly.

Faith needed this to work. It was everything she'd ever wanted. She didn't want Julien to be the one who ripped it all away from her before she'd even got started. Faith would be damned if she let him have an attitude about having a camera in his face a few times a day. Besides, it was part of his job too. *Tough luck, Moretz.*

'Right, we're going to go and get dressed up for dinner. I want Faith's first team event to feel special. Boys, put on your best suits. We're going all out.' Lucie grabbed Faith's hand and pulled her towards the hotel.

'Meet us at six thirty, Luce!' Brett yelled behind them, but they were already stepping through the door to the lobby.

'Six thirty, my ass.' Lucie snorted. 'Takes them three hours to choose a watch.'

'Red or black?' Faith held up two dresses to Lucie, who was in the bathroom perfecting her winged eyeliner.

'Hold the red one up against you again?' Faith did as requested. 'Black.'

'Excellent, that's what I was leaning towards.'

Her black dress was long-sleeved with a high neckline, ending mid-thigh. It hugged her figure perfectly and made her appreciate her curves. She paired it with black knee-high heeled boots to finish the outfit off.

The style of her dress was just right for the beginning of May, as although the weather was warming up, the summer evenings were still a little chilly and the sleeves would be appreciated. After dinner, they planned on walking into Francorchamps for a couple of beers, much to Lucie's displeasure. She didn't want to walk in her heels, so Brett had promised to carry her at the first sign of discomfort.

'Do I look too much like I'm trying to be a princess?' Lucie emerged from the bathroom in a pale pink ruched satin minidress with puff sleeves. She wore white strappy heels, which told Faith that Brett's offer was definitely going to be taken advantage of.

'You look great, Luce.'

'Thank you. Not looking so bad yourself. Ugh, I never know what to do with my hair.'

'There's not a lot I can do with mine really.' Faith looked in the mirror and tucked her blonde strands behind her ear on one side. Her hair didn't even reach her shoulders, so she tended to just add a few waves and leave it at that. Lucie had been blessed with natural loose curls.

'I think I'm going to leave mine natural for once. We've made the effort with our outfits.' Lucie smiled.

'I can't decide if I should leave the camera here and just use my phone for content.'

'Nope! Gabriel and I agreed it's important that you just settle in tonight. By all means post on your own socials, but don't worry about the team accounts.' Lucie secured her earrings and grabbed her phone, opening the door to let Faith out into the corridor.

'Wait! I need my debit card.' Faith started heading for her own room next door, matt-black room key in her hand.

'No you don't. Our treat. We're welcoming you to the team.'

Walking towards the lift, Faith couldn't help but feel uneasy. The thought of seeing one team member again, who clearly didn't want to see her, was making her stomach churn.

## 5

Faith felt like royalty. Every table was taken, every seat occupied by men of all ages in suits and freshly pressed shirts, and women with diamond earrings that were probably more expensive than the block of flats Faith lived in. The hotel's Michelin-starred restaurant was catering for high-profile clientele, mostly team sponsors and their plus-ones, but it seemed as though most of the grid was also in there. There were dishes on the menu she'd never even heard of, and she'd had to do a sneaky internet search to save her the embarrassment of asking someone what certain words meant. She supposed she could blame the fact that everything was written in French, given that they were in a predominantly French-speaking part of Belgium, but she got the feeling that the team often dined in places like this and it was just her who was used to processed food and microwavable ready meals. The restaurant was nothing like the canteen where the teams ate breakfast.

Revolution Racing's table for the evening consisted of Lucie, Faith, Brett, Marco, Jasper and their engineers, who had departed to get an early night a few minutes ago. Gabriel had been there to help himself to their basket of bread at the start of the evening, then disappeared to speak with another team on the other side of the restaurant.

'So, Faith, do you think this will be a long-term career for you?' Jasper was friendly, but Faith would be lying if

44

she said she wasn't intimidated by him. He was a powerful man with a lot of responsibilities and sponsors to keep happy, and he was trusting her with his team.

'Jasper, mate. She's already had the interview – let her eat,' Brett cut in.

'It's OK! I would hope so, yes. I'm very eager to get started and show you what I'm capable of, and I would hope that we can form a strong working relationship.'

'I have no doubt. My daughters listen to your podcast. I spent their whole childhood trying to encourage them to take an interest in the sport, brought them to races and everything. One episode of *Across the Line* and they were hooked.'

'That's lovely. They're the generation we're trying to target, so it's great to hear a real example of how I've been able to influence them.'

There was an endless stream of rosé wine being poured into Faith and Lucie's glasses, with the promise that tomorrow still wasn't technically their first day on the job. They had two more days until the press tours officially started for the race weekend. This build-up was primarily for drivers and engineers to get settled and work on any kinks with the cars or strategy for the weekend.

Until then, they just had to rally the rest of the social media crew, introduce Faith to the wider team and give them a rundown of what was expected, plus figure out between them what their game plan was for their own team's content. Faith and Lucie had been firing ideas back and forth all day, but they needed to get it written up and have a presentation ready to go.

They were halfway through their second course, and the

salmon dish Faith had been recommended was heavenly. Jasper had left to join Gabriel, and Julien, as he'd said, was a no-show. Whether he would actually join them at the bar in Francorchamps was yet to be seen. She was on edge from the possibility that he could waltz in at any given moment and disturb the peace, but she was trying her best to focus on the conversation. After all, the entire team had questions for her.

'So –' Brett put his fork down and took a sip of his drink – 'have you had the pleasure of meeting the IEC's head photographer?'

'Actually I've known her since we were eighteen.'

'You know Bea Miller?' Marco's eyes widened.

'We were flatmates at uni. Then we had our own place and worked together until she joined you guys.' Faith suddenly stopped. For some reason she wasn't entirely comfortable with everyone finding out she was friends with Bea before she'd come face to face with her again. It had been too long and there was too much left unsaid that they needed to work through first.

'My heart goes out to you, truly,' Lucie muttered, trying to hide her disgust.

'OK, what is *that* about?' Faith gestured to her grimace.

'Luce and Bea are always at odds. They haven't ended up in a screaming match yet, but you could cut the tension with a knife when they're in the same vicinity.' Brett placed a hand on Lucie's knee to get her to relax.

'Yeah, well, I'm not sure if we're on good terms or not any more. Our friendship was becoming strained, but we'll see.'

Faith did a quick scan of the restaurant. No sign of long

dark hair anywhere. Besides, if she had been in there, she'd have come running for a grand reunion, sure to make a scene.

'I don't know about you guys, but I'm skipping dessert in favour of the beers I'm going to devour,' Lucie declared.

Faith nodded. 'I'm with you on that one.' The amount of bread they'd consumed, followed by appetizers and the main course, had been more than enough. She was grateful that she'd lined her stomach accordingly, because they'd already consumed a lot of wine. She couldn't afford to be careless with alcohol, despite how much fun she was having.

Brett waved at Gabriel, who flagged down a waitress and pointed at their table. Just like that, their bill was covered. Faith didn't even want to think about how much it had cost, but to most of the people in here it would be considered pennies.

As they departed the restaurant and subsequently the hotel, the effect of the wine made itself known. Nothing drastic, just a slight buzz. The beer would be their downfall.

'Are we waiting for Jules?' Lucie asked.

'Nah, he'll meet us there. He's got a few calls to make.' Brett crouched so Lucie could climb on to his back.

She wrapped her arms round his neck to avoid falling off.

'Luce! I'd like to be able to breathe.' He pretended to choke until she loosened her grip.

'I would like to point out that I am walking perfectly fine, completely unaided.' Faith gestured at her own heels and was met with a scowl from Lucie.

When they turned the corner at the end of the road,

the bars and restaurants of Francorchamps were revealed. There were only a few to choose from, but they looked warm and welcoming.

'Is anywhere actually open?' she asked, having expected the town to be busier with people visiting for the race weekend. Maybe it was too early in the week.

'Yep!' Brett set Lucie down on the pavement and held her arm while she steadied herself. 'Most of the teams will either stay at the hotel or head into Spa for somewhere classier.'

'We're not classy,' Marco said, holding open the door to the first bar they got to. It was tiny but the ambience was perfect. Dim lights, a few locals and lots of mismatched chairs and tables. She didn't care about all the fuss and the extravagance that she might get elsewhere; she felt comfortable here.

'Speak for yourselves, I am a very classy girl. We just like the homey feel that you get here. Beer, not champagne.' Lucie flung her bag on to a table and hopped on to a bar stool which wobbled as a result of its uneven wooden legs. *So* classy.

Before Faith managed to sit down herself, Marco appeared at her side with a beer for each of them. She took a sip and raised an eyebrow. She wasn't usually keen, but she liked it.

Marco seemed excited by her reaction. 'It's a traditional Belgian beer, local to Spa. This is the stuff they serve at the track, at the top of Eau Rouge.'

'Another reason we brought you here instead of taking you to the casino. Got to let you experience the true culture of this place, from more of a fan perspective,' Lucie said.

They settled into a conversation about the history of the circuit and Faith didn't have the heart to tell Brett and Marco that she knew all this already.

Marco told her about the Italian restaurant on the corner which had an old Formula One car under the glass floor. When you passed through the restaurant, you walked right over it. It was where a lot of the teams went for dinner after qualifying and mixed socially with the fans who had been lucky enough to get a table.

Brett told her all about the hotel where the track had been designed on a napkin, right down the road from the circuit. It hadn't had enough money poured into it in recent years, so it had been allowed to fall apart. It closed a few years ago, which devastated some of the more local drivers. Julien included.

'So have ya left a significant other back in rainy old England then, Jensen?' Brett asked.

'I haven't,' she replied, not particularly wanting to go into any more detail. She was never sure if she should be embarrassed about never having had a serious relationship at her age.

'God, I wish I had time for dating. It's all work, work, work. Never gone further than a third date before I have to leave the country,' Lucie chimed in, and, just like that, the shame was gone.

'Me neither. When Bea was in the UK, I went on a lot of dates but then when she left I was just trying to sort my businesses out and stay afloat. I didn't have time for anything else.'

'Come on, girls! Loosen up a bit!' Brett's comment had Lucie glaring at him again.

'Number one –' Lucie's tone was mildly threatening – 'you haven't had a serious relationship since what's-her-name fucked off four years ago.'

'Sienna,' he corrected.

'Irrelevant. Number two, I don't want to settle down. Ever. Especially in this industry.' She frowned so intensely, Faith was certain she'd be left with permanent lines.

'Bullshit. If I got down on one knee right now, we'd sail off into the sunset. Don't even deny it, Carolan.' He was joking, but he was looking right into Lucie's eyes. Maybe he *wasn't* joking.

'Pipe down, Anderson. Not even you could hold me down.'

'Yeah, we'll see. Lucie Anderson has a nice ring to it.'

Marco interrupted the lovers' tiff. 'In all seriousness, it's hard to meet anyone normal when you're in this line of work. Everyone seems to have an ulterior motive, so most of us drivers are in it for a good time not a long time.'

'Does Julien still get any action after his latest fling ended?' Lucie took a swig of beer. It was definitely going to her head.

'Who knows with that bloke. Maybe that's why he's so tense today – hasn't got any recently,' Marco replied.

'Where the hell is he for crying out loud? We've already been here an hour. It'll be time for bed soon,' Lucie said.

'Text him. See where he is,' Marco suggested. 'He might've headed into Spa for drinks instead; maybe to the casino. Francorchamps isn't to everyone's tastes. You know how the Talos boys are.'

'No, remember last night? I sent a message in the group chat and told you all that you had to be here for either all or part of the evening to welcome Faith. Team orders from Jasper,' Lucie reminded him.

Faith felt honoured that they'd all gone out of their way for her. Except Julien.

'Aw, you guys! Let's add Faith to the group chat!' Brett yelled enthusiastically, patting her on the shoulder with force. He was like a dog who had forgotten how big and strong he was and desperately wanted to be close to his humans.

'Who's in this group chat exactly?'

'Us three, Jules and our engineers.'

'You might be shocked to see that Julien has a personality over text. I know your first impression of him was . . . uncomfortable, but we promise he's not like that all the time,' Lucie assured her.

'I think I'll take your word for it for now. Give him some time to warm up to having me around.' She bit the inside of her cheek, her thoughts all over the place.

Faith's phone came to life in the middle of the table with a notification that told her she'd been added to *Revolution Royals*. She swiped across the screen and was greeted with very unflattering selfies of all three drivers from this morning.

'Don't feel obligated to send one of those. You won't catch me with a camera at that angle, that's for sure,' Lucie said, but Faith laughed. She wasn't sure what she'd been expecting from this conversation thread, but it hadn't been that.

'What's with the name?' she asked.

'That was my idea!' Brett needed a volume button. 'Get it? We're a multi-championship-winning team, so we're extra special. Like royals.'

'You're divas is what you are.'

'Excuse me, Lucie. You're part of the same group chat.'

Marco grinned. 'Someone's got to keep us in line.'

'Well, aren't you lucky? Now you've got two of us.' Faith raised her drink to Lucie, who clinked her bottle against it.

Their phones buzzed again in response to Brett's firing line of questions aimed at Julien's whereabouts. He wasn't coming. He claimed to be going to bed with a headache and that he'd see them down at the garage in the morning. From the way Lucie and Brett looked at each other and then at her, she could only assume that it was her presence that was keeping him away from their beloved tradition of drinks in the local town. What could she have possibly done to annoy him this much *already*?

Her one glimmer of hope, albeit a shit one, was his follow-up text two minutes later. *Welcome to the team, Faith.* Two minutes seemed like a long time to come up with such a mediocre welcome, almost as if he'd considered it carefully and still somehow thought it would do the trick. No emojis, no sign of genuine enthusiasm at all. Just a full stop.

They made it back to the hotel shortly before midnight, and despite Brett and Marco's best attempts at keeping everyone's spirits up, the evening had taken a strange turn. Faith felt nauseous, and not just from the alcohol consumption. None of them had mentioned Julien again, to the point where Faith was scared to ask questions about, really, *anything*, out of fear that his name would come up.

Faith thought she'd settled in easily today, and she could see herself forming a makeshift family with this team. But the two interactions she'd had with Julien were enough to have her questioning whether she'd be able to get a rapport in place to properly use him on socials and as part of her media plan. She needed him to like her. The rest of the team shouldn't be walking on eggshells. If he didn't get over whatever his issue was, there was going to be a bigger problem and the team was going to fall apart.

Tomorrow would be the day that Faith was going to win over Julien Moretz.

# 6

Julien was a bundle of nerves the next morning and he was eager to escape the hotel before he came across Faith in an empty corridor. Or Lucie for that matter. He didn't want to be berated for missing last night. He knew he'd messed up; he should've just sucked it up and made an effort like he would for anyone else.

Exiting his room and sneaking into the hallway, he didn't have time to bolt when he heard her door open. He turned and faced her, and the dread he felt was mirrored on her face. That damn face. It truly was the source of his inner turmoil. He never thought he'd see a face like it again. He'd felt immediately drawn to her and he knew he was in for a season of absolute hell, because he needed to stay far away from her. He was here to work, and he didn't intend on mixing business with pleasure . . . again. He'd made that mistake a few too many times.

He hadn't meant to make her feel so awkward yesterday. He had reacted on instinct and now he needed to fix it.

'Morning. You heading down for breakfast?' He attempted to smile but he was certain it came off as more of a grimace.

'Yes, are you?' she replied, her tone painfully polite.

'Yeah. Look, I'm really sorry about last night and yesterday in general. My head was all over the place after my car broke down and that manifested as me wanting to be alone.

It wasn't about you.' He cleared his throat and waited for her reply. It was only a half-lie.

She tucked her hair behind her ear and shrugged. He hoped all was forgiven, but he couldn't tell. Why were women so damn hard to read all the time?

'Yeah, you were kind of a dick. But, hey, let's just take it one day at a time.' She smiled warmly this time. A genuine smile, not one she was putting on to keep the peace. Her dimples were cute, but he couldn't let himself get distracted by them if he was going to salvage this.

He felt better, but now he was desperate for Lucie to come out of her room and save him, to give him a buffer. This was their first real conversation and he was already at risk of being in too deep and fucking up his anti-women policy for the season. It was those eyes. When he'd met her yesterday he'd felt as though he was staring into her soul. Maybe he was. It was like something within her was crying out to him and he was fighting everything within him not to grab hold of it. He knew what sexual tension was, and that wasn't all this was. It was a different feeling that he didn't want to even attempt to figure out right now. He had too much on his plate.

Julien was trying not to admire her figure from behind, but he couldn't help it. She walked with confidence. Typically women were nervous around him. It was never the other way around. This was only the second time he'd ever felt this way in a woman's presence and he hated it.

Picking up his pace, it didn't take long before he was a few steps ahead of her. He made a beeline for the stairs and Faith followed him without hesitation. *The lift is right there.* Just his luck. Six flights of conversation. Being a professional athlete, he couldn't exactly pretend to be too out of breath to talk. It was tempting, though. He was so busy mentally cursing the situation that he didn't have time to think of an excuse to double back and leg it back to his room. Sunglasses? On his head. Phone? In his hand. Room key? In his wallet. Wallet? Very much visible in his back pocket.

'Got to get my steps up!' she commented, falling into place beside him.

Her hand brushed against his. Immediately he jolted at the touch; he tried to make it look natural but the tingle her graze had left was still going strong. Suddenly hyper aware of himself, he noticed he was sweating profusely before they'd even descended one floor. Did the stairwells in this hotel have air-con?

'Me too. Need to keep my weight down for race week,' he mumbled. He wasn't sure she'd heard him. Seasick might be the best way to describe how he was feeling.

Faith almost knocked into someone running down past them on the fourth floor and jumped. She laughed, further unsettling him. He should take that guy's lead and start running too. Hell, maybe he should start doing morning runs to the circuit to avoid her.

'Didn't see him at all. Is that a blindspot?' she asked.

He turned round and she looked down at him from a few steps up. He noted that she was significantly shorter than his six-foot three height. Dainty. But she looked like she could pack a punch when necessary.

'You should know, shouldn't you? You drive, right?'

'I never passed my test. Hadn't even left my home county until I moved to London.'

Julien was intrigued. He had spent hours last night scrolling through her social media, and he had just assumed that with her love of cars and racing that she drove. Maybe his other first impressions of her were slightly off too.

He had this thing about influencers. Influencers and motorsports did not go together. People like Faith were the kind of people who were just here for the fame, and he wanted no part of it. He saw people with more than fifty thousand followers and immediately labelled them as gold-diggers and fame-hunters. He couldn't help it; he'd just had too many negative experiences.

Faith's personal account was full of selfies and outfit photos, a stark contrast to her social media for *Across the Line*. But even with that kind of content maybe he was barking up the wrong tree. It wasn't like his own social media was much better; it was just incredibly sparse. She was warm, friendly. So far she hadn't tried to get in his pants or make him spend all his money on her. If anything, she had avoided him as much as he had avoided her. But she still had time to prove his theory right.

They were near the entrance to the circuit now, having met up with the others after breakfast and deciding to walk down. She and Julien had helped themselves to more than their fair share of pancakes, fresh fruit and croissants at the breakfast buffet. Bad idea. She was so full, she felt like she might explode if she wasn't careful. Julien was slightly further ahead now with Marco and Lucie, and Brett was talking Faith's ear off.

'So are you and Moretz the best of pals yet?' he asked.

'We didn't talk much at breakfast. I don't know what

to say to him if I'm being totally honest. He seems very closed off.'

'Yeah, that's pretty standard for Jules, unfortunately. It's the drinks thing that's getting to me. He never skips drinks on the first night. Ever. Especially at his home race.'

'Am I that bad?' His apology had initially put her mind at ease, but then the lack of a proper conversation as they demolished the buffet had stressed her out all over again.

'Nah.' Brett flung his arm over her shoulder. 'He'll warm up soon. Promise.'

He gave her a little squeeze and tugged her through the gates. She'd been so busy thinking about Julien's salty attitude that she hadn't even registered the fact she had just stepped foot into one of the most famous race circuits in the world for the second day in a row. In a *Revolution Racing* T-shirt with an IEC lanyard hanging round her neck and her own ID badge.

'You look like a kid on Christmas morning,' Lucie commented when they got to the garage.

The drivers headed straight for their engineers, who had already been there for hours with the mechanics. Jasper waved and went back to his conversation. The environment was lively and everywhere Faith looked she saw something that caught her attention. Whether it was the boys practising a driver change or the screen of stats, she was mesmerized.

'Do you ever get used to all the excitement?' she asked Lucie.

'Never. You wait till they unleash the spectators on us. It's a whole other world.'

'Ladies?' Gabriel burst into the garage in a sing-song

voice, clapping his hands together when he saw the two of them sitting off to one side, observing the mechanics hard at work.

'Morning, Gabriel. What can we do for you?' Lucie asked.

'I just came to see how you're doing and checking in on our new friend,' he said, smiling at Faith. He sat down in the empty chair next to them and promptly kicked over the full cup of steaming hot coffee at his feet.

Faith couldn't quite fathom how this man who was so sweet ran an international racing championship. But behind his joy, bumbling nature and general charm, he was clearly an incredibly intelligent and beloved man. Not many people would be capable of running this organization.

The rest of the social media crew were beginning to arrive at the hotel and Lucie had already had texts asking when they were going to meet Faith. It felt strange being in charge of a group of people she'd never met in a job she was new at, but with Lucie by her side she felt confident that it would all go smoothly.

'We're having a meeting this afternoon. We've booked out one of the press rooms for ourselves. Lucie and I are mapping everything out over lunch,' Faith informed him.

'We're not having photographers at this one. We want our crew to have a more hands-on approach with the content. We'll still use the professional images for promotional purposes, but the day-to-day content will be captured by us. Faith has got all sorts up her sleeve for video content, especially for Revolution.'

'I'm putting all my trust in you two. I don't have much idea about Twitter and Instagram, but I do know it's integral to our business thriving. That Tickytock nonsense is beyond me, though. You're far younger and more culturally up to date than me!'

Between them they'd already determined that Lucie would hold the more formal interviews as she had more experience of being at the races, while Faith would take the casual, friendly approach that a fan would want to experience for themselves. After all, as Gabriel had told her, she had been hired partially due to her fan status.

'We'll email you our ideas and plans for the weekend for each team by twelve thirty, so you can tell us if there's anything you don't like.' Faith smiled at him.

Gabriel climbed out of the folding chair, which was a bit of a struggle since it was so low down, and saluted them before scurrying out of the garage again. As he passed the Revolution car, it started up and he jumped out of his skin, causing a few smirks among the mechanics.

While Lucie disappeared to replace the coffee that Gabriel had knocked over, Faith observed Julien in silence. He was getting into his racing suit and leaning in to talk to his engineer. Faith didn't particularly care for a man in uniform . . . until now. His white long-sleeved top clung to his biceps, so even when the suit wasn't done up to his neck she was still enjoying the view. The suit itself was black with white and red detailing, and there was something about the way he zipped it up and ran his hand through his thick mane of hair that sent her heart rate soaring. *It's not the suit, Faith. It's just the man.*

Lucie wandered back into the main part of the garage, coffee in hand. She stopped by the car and said something to Julien, standing on her tiptoes to talk directly into his ear. He responded by placing his hand on the small of her back and leaning down to hear her better. Then he smiled. It was the second time Faith had seen him smile at anyone or anything. She felt a twinge of something, although she wasn't sure it was jealousy.

There was nothing between Julien and Lucie, right? The rumours were nothing more than rumours. Lucie and Brett had more chemistry than Faith had ever seen. No way. She would know if they were involved. Lucie would've warned her off him for that reason, not because he had layers. Screw the layers. She was getting more frustrated by the second and she hadn't even tried to approach him yet.

When Lucie caught her staring, she said a swift good-bye to the driver and headed over. She had one eyebrow raised. 'I know what you're thinking, and you're wrong. I've known him since I was eighteen; he's just a friend. He's fair game.'

'Fair game? No, no, no. I'm not going there. Not a chance. I am here to be a consummate professional, not to date the drivers.' Faith was flustered and felt her cheeks flaming.

Lucie winked, seeing right through her. 'But you're curious.'

'I just think he's attractive. I can't help but stare. I'm human.'

'Whatever you say, Jensen. Right, I'm going to take a walk down the pit lane and scout out any new season drama. You coming with me?'

It was at that moment that Julien tore away in the car, the roar of the engine startling her. Her eyes lit up as she watched him disappear down the pit lane and out on to the track. It sounded so different when you were actually there rather than watching a live stream on a laptop with speakers that crackled.

'Sorry. Yes, I'm coming!' she yelled above the noise. The other garages were coming to life now, each team wanting to squeeze in as much track time as possible before the first qualifying session.

'You look so happy to be here. We made the right choice bringing you on board.' Lucie beamed.

The pit lane adventure had been eventful. Faith had now met the majority of the social media team and been introduced by Lucie as their big scary boss. One girl had looked genuinely fearful, and Faith had never been so quick to reassure someone that she wasn't going to rip anyone's head off. Some of the younger staff had begun listing off their own ideas, particularly for trending short-form content, and she had attempted to take a mental note of them. Everyone seemed to be on the same page.

What she hadn't expected was for a lot of the drivers to know her name or recognize her face. Faith was popular on social media and her podcast had made waves, but not to the extent that everyone who was someone knew her. When Lorenzo Garcia and Max Edwards had waved across the garage and shouted their greetings, she'd almost fainted.

Lucie had taken her for lunch in the hospitality tent, where they'd sat with a couple of the mechanics, who soon scarpered when the girls started content planning. The mechanics were lucky; they pretty much always had helmets on so their faces weren't going to be visible in photos and videos. Personally Faith was relieved she'd remembered to pack her make-up for the sake of the vlogs. She didn't like filters any more. They made her feel like a fraud.

Back in the garage after lunch, Faith was taking photos of the team hard at work. Julien was in a better mood and was allowing her to get up close with her camera. He had achieved good results in free practice this morning, which was a big weight off his shoulders, and he had participated in a group selfie with Marco and Brett with minimal grumpiness. It had helped that it had been Marco's idea and not Faith's, but she wasn't knocking it.

He had even returned her phone to her personally and asked her to whiten his teeth slightly before posting it as he was in talks with a teeth-whitening company regarding sponsorship and brand deals. She couldn't quite believe her ears. Was he really taking social media seriously? Perhaps it was his publicist's influence. Even so, if he kept this level of professionalism up and put some effort into their personal relationship, then she wouldn't have to fight him.

'Oh my God!'

The peace and quiet everyone had been enjoying was interrupted by an almighty shriek at the back of the garage. Every person in there rolled their eyes and pretended not to notice the gorgeous woman who had walked into their workspace.

Faith turned round with a horrible feeling in the pit of her stomach.

There she was: eyes sparkling, skin glowing, teeth . . . almost blinding. Maybe she had helped Julien get that sponsorship he'd mentioned.

'Hi, Bea!' She quickly plastered on a fake smile and was

almost suffocated by Bea's perfume. *Christ, that was a bit much.* Her friend gave the kind of hugs that to someone a few inches shorter than her were — how do you say it politely . . . ? — smothering. She for one did not appreciate having hair in her mouth either.

'Oh, darling, I am so happy to see you in my stomping ground! I knew when I gave Gabriel your number it would lead to this. How have you *been*?' She seemed sickly sweet.

'I've been g—' Faith began.

She soon shut up when Bea hit her arm in excitement like she was swatting a bumblebee. That was Faith's part of their conversation over. Duly noted.

'Have you met Julien properly? Did you know he and I are super close? Julien! Come over here! We have so much to talk about. I have so many stories to tell you about our weekend trip to Monaco the other month.'

Julien, who had been innocently sitting in his chair eating an apple, promptly stood up and shook his head. He looked genuinely fearful for a second and Faith couldn't blame him.

'He's had a busy —' Faith started again.

'Julien! Come on, come and give me a hug. I haven't seen you in forever!' Just as quickly as Bea had shut Faith up, Julien was gone with Bea chasing after him in her heels. *Heels.* Of course she was wearing those in this environment.

Marco had been observing their reunion and came to Faith's rescue. See, Marco was like a puppy in all the best ways. He was loyal, soft and sweet. He was a people-pleaser. Man's best friend. Bea, on the other hand, was yappy and desperate for attention. Labrador vs chihuahua.

'What just happened?'

'Julien isn't very tolerant of Bea these days. None of us are. It's a little exhausting trying to keep up with her and her demands. We go out for drinks and she's constantly requesting shots and asking whose round it is. Never hers, might I add. At dinner there's always something wrong with her food and she always has to be glued to a driver at any given point in the day. Doesn't matter if it's Jules, me, Brett, Lorenzo. Anyone. As long as they're a driver and she can post selfies.'

'I was really hoping to see a little bit of the old her.' Faith couldn't hide the disappointment.

'We don't know that side of her, but maybe you can bring it out of her. Might do her some favours. And save our sanity, especially poor Julien's.' He shrugged.

'Maybe . . .'

'That's what we mean when we say it's hard to find someone normal to date as a racing driver, by the way. Our world is filled with people exactly like her.' Marco grimaced. 'It is what it is.' He gave a sad half-smile and left Faith alone with her thoughts.

She wondered what was going on in Julien's trailer right now. Did she even want to know?

It wasn't just the drastic change in Bea's behaviour that Faith didn't understand. That made total sense to her; she'd come to accept it over time. People grew apart, and people were easily influenced by a lot of things – lifestyle changes being one of them. That was OK. The question playing on her mind was what in the world was Julien Moretz doing spending the weekend in Monaco with Beatrix Miller?

# 7

Faith had just settled down at the table for dinner with the other drivers, when Julien sat down with an irritated sigh. Conveniently, the final seat available was next to Faith, almost as if it had been orchestrated so he had no choice but to engage in non-work-related conversation with her. His jaw was tightly clenched but he showed no other signs of emotion. He was scarily good at concealing things.

'What happened?' Lucie asked him and promptly plonked her glass of champagne in front of him. OK, maybe he wasn't so good at concealing things. However, despite how much he might have wanted to take the edge off, he pushed it back towards her with a shake of the head.

'Bea happened.' He looked at Faith and she saw a flicker of regret in his eyes.

'She got her claws into you again then?' Lucie raised an eyebrow disapprovingly.

'Well, you saw her storm out of the trailer earlier this afternoon, right?'

'We couldn't miss it,' Faith replied. If the conversation didn't have such a serious tone, she'd have laughed at the memory.

The girls had been heading to their social media meeting with Brett and Marco in tow when they'd spotted her. The doors to the trailers were generally kept open until the day fans were allowed into the circuit, but Revolution's had been closed. Bea had slammed it open with so much force it flew all the way back and banged against the side of the trailer, and then stomped down the steps. Yes, stomped. The metal had rattled.

'That was the result of me telling her I didn't want anything to do with her. So obviously when I came back to the hotel to shower, I was expecting my room to be empty. Do not ask me how she got in there, but there she was. Sitting on my bed, feigning total innocence.' He frowned. Faith desperately fought the urge to pull a face.

'Jules, please tell me you didn't sleep with her again . . .' Brett pleaded, and Faith could have sworn Julien flinched, his cheeks turning red.

'I told her no. I really pushed back, but Bea is good at saying all the right things at the right time. She made me feel like, for a second, she cared about me. So yeah. I did.'

'Julien! Bloody hell.' Lucie put her head in her hands. At any other moment, Faith would've teased her for the Australian accent, but she didn't have it in her right now. This shouldn't be bothering her as much as it was.

'It was the last time!' Julien said defensively.

'Mate, you say that every time,' Brett hit back. 'I bet every driver she's ever been entangled with says that every time.'

'I mean it, and I'll be telling her that.' He held Faith's gaze, like he was speaking directly to her.

'Be careful how you approach that one; she could easily turn on you. She's already done it to Lorenzo,' Marco added.

Faith tried hard not to roll her eyes. Of course Bea was working her way through the drivers to see if one stuck.

'I just keep going back to her because she knows I have no interest in being tied down and nor does she. It's been refreshing for us to both know that it was always going to be casual. At least that's how it was when we first started this. It would appear that she wants more now.'

'She said she doesn't want to be tied down? Bea *lives* for the whole straight-out-of-a-movie romance thing.' Faith frowned, wondering if her friend had actually changed her mind or if she was just trying and failing to fit in. Judging by the way Lucie's jaw dropped, she had added something of value to this whole Julien and Bea saga.

But Julien didn't want to settle down? That should be Faith's cue to kill the butterflies that had been residing in her stomach from the moment he'd stepped out of his Mustang. Instead, it sent them wild. She couldn't focus on much else.

'I'm sorry, Faith.' Julien reached across the table and squeezed her hand. That was *weird*. And nice. Comforting. She pretended not to notice the way her heart threatened to leap out of her chest. 'I know she's your friend. I don't mean to speak so badly of her. She's just . . . a lot.'

'Just because we played such a big role in each other's lives, it doesn't mean I don't recognize her flaws. We all have them. It's OK.' She smiled reassuringly at him, trying to pull herself together.

'Brett told me you guys aren't close any more. I have to say, I can't imagine you being friends with someone like her. You're not quite what I expected,' he said.

'Well, you can imagine my surprise when I found out she's the one who gave Gabriel my number. It came out of nowhere, truly.'

'Are you sure about that? I thought it was Casey Winters. He still had it from when he was on your podcast. He told me last week,' Lucie commented.

'Why would . . . ? She said she did.' Surely Bea hadn't lied about that.

'Faith, she's never mentioned you. Even in multiple meetings about hiring someone for your role, she didn't bring your name up once. Gabriel had been doing his own research.' Julien was speaking softly.

'So she's full of shit,' Faith said.

'Yeah. You get all the credit here. Not her.'

'What he's saying is you're a bad bitch. And Beatrix Miller is just . . . a bitch,' Lucie quipped, getting a laugh out of everyone.

'Yeah, you're a . . . you know. What Lucie said.' Julien blushed and hastily reached for his phone. The light coming from the screen concealed the redness in his cheeks before anyone else caught it, but she couldn't help the minuscule smirk. Perhaps Julien *did* have a sense of humour.

As much as she would like Julien to distract her from the disappointment she felt, Faith couldn't believe Bea, her supposed friend, was keeping up with the manipulation to such an extent and thinking nobody would figure it out. Any hopes she'd had for reconciliation had been dropped now; she didn't want anything to do with her going forward. The past was in the past. If Bea dared to post photos of them together, she would have hell to pay. Life wasn't a game. A seven-year friendship was not supposed to be a game to get into the spotlight.

Faith swiftly changed topics. 'Does anyone want to split an appetiser with me? I really want bruschetta but I can't handle it all on my own. The portion sizes in this place are crazy.'

'Me! Julien, switch seats.' Lucie stood up and waved him across to her seat with a menu. He did as told, albeit reluctantly.

As much as she loved Lucie, and it made perfect sense for them to sit next to one another, she missed the newfound closeness she'd been sharing with Julien. She'd been looking forward to some one-on-one conversations over dinner but now he was sat closer to his teammates and anything said between them would become a whole-table conversation.

'Faith?' Julien called over.

She blinked at him. 'Sorry, what?'

'I just asked where your family is from.'

'Oh. R-right, sorry,' she stammered. 'I was born and raised in a little town in Cornwall, England. My mum is from there and my dad was from Australia but settled in Cornwall after uni.'

His eyes widened. 'No way, Cornwall? Isn't that a major surfing hotspot in the UK?'

'Yeah, it is! I used to surf whenever I could, even before school some days. I lived right by Praa Sands, one of the best beaches for surfing on the south coast.'

'I love it. I got into it right around the time I started my career with the IEC, and I find time for it whenever I can. The feeling I get from surfing is very similar to the feeling I get when I'm behind the wheel.'

'I'm assuming you don't do this surfing in Belgium, right?'

'No, no. Just when I'm travelling. Are you close with your family?'

Faith hated discussing her family. She knew she didn't have the kind of upbringing a lot of people did, and she could never be sure how others would respond. It always made her feel vulnerable to judgemental thoughts and words from people.

'No, I'm not. I never knew my dad. I don't know where he is, if I'm honest, or even what his full name is. Mum is . . . we're no longer on speaking terms.' She looked down at her hands and waited for him to take the hint.

'Enough said.' He smiled.

'What about you?' She knew the answer. Things like that were public information for most drivers and a quick internet search could reveal a lot. Not that she'd stalked him . . . It was hard *not* to know these things when you had such a deep interest in the sport. She just wanted him to open up.

'Mother is from Liège in Belgium. Father is from Rust, Germany. I grew up between the two after their divorce and decided to settle here in Belgium in my early twenties.'

'You're never even in the damn country, dude. Always off gallivanting around the world, even on breaks. Where *do* you go?' Marco asked.

'He goes to Monaco for a three-day sexscapade with Beatrix Miller apparently,' Brett snorted, earning him a forceful shove in the ribs from his teammate.

Faith wished they would stop bringing her up and that Bea didn't fit into this new world she was in. This job was supposed to be her dream. She'd known Bea would be part of it somehow, but couldn't she just be in the background? Not attached to the people she was forming both working and social relationships with? Every big step she took in her life was connected to Bea and she wanted, for once, to have one thing that was just hers.

Faith needed sleep. She had been told about every wild post-race celebration they'd had over the years in infinite detail. Lucie was immensely proud of the time she'd dive-bombed into a pool in Dubai and surfaced to a round of applause and a champagne toast in her honour. She hadn't revealed the fact that she had later smacked her head on a rock under the pool's waterfall and had to seek medical attention, but Marco made sure to remind everyone.

Julien had become increasingly at ease talking to Faith, which was a slight surprise. Where was the blunt arrogant man she'd met? Maybe her charm offensive was working? He had swapped seats with Lucie again when she'd got up to go to the bathroom and leaned over the table so he could be heard over Brett's obnoxiously loud laughter. She guessed he must be letting his hair grow out as a section of it kept falling over his eyes, no matter how often he re-positioned it. She found herself staring on more than one occasion and he'd caught her each and every time, but she didn't shy away once.

'I'm heading up to bed. Anyone else?' Lucie stretched her arms above her head. It was getting on for nine o'clock and the restaurant was slowly getting emptier.

'Get me into those fancy cotton sheets ASAP. I need to lie horizontally,' Faith agreed.

The bed sheets were the best thing about her hotel room and she wanted to make the most of them before returning to her cheap ones back home. Plus, tomorrow was press day, which meant an exceedingly early start. She didn't dare take the sleeping tablets she'd been prescribed for fear of messing up her early-morning plan.

'I'll walk up with you.' Julien stood and waited for Faith to leave the table ahead of him.

Lucie was giving Brett a goodnight hug while Julien and Marco exchanged an eye roll. They might be tired of the flirting with no follow-through, but Faith was not. She was loving it. She wasn't loving having to physically drag a protesting Lucie towards the lobby, however.

The lift was packed with stray team principals going up to their various floors, which meant that Julien and Faith were shoved into the corner by the buttons. Every time someone needed to get out, Lucie would move towards Faith who would then take a step closer to Julien. If that was even possible.

When they reached their floor, he let the girls out ahead of him and placed his hand on Faith's back. She almost yelped in surprise. This casual intimacy was very out of the blue. The hand squeeze at dinner had been mixed with an apology, but this new gesture was a little too normalized and she wasn't sure how it was making her feel.

'Faith, can we take a few minutes to discuss the logistics of tomorrow?' Lucie asked. 'Then we can send out an email to the interns first thing and save the hassle of them hunting us down with a million questions.'

'And that's my cue to leave. Night, girls.' Julien swiped his key against his door.

Faith followed Lucie, dragging her feet.

While they waited for the hotel's Wi-Fi to connect to Lucie's laptop, Faith took the opportunity to write a list of video ideas she wanted to discuss with Jasper in the morning. It was one thing getting the drivers to agree, but he was the team principal and had to give every single content idea the green light. She didn't want to overstep boundaries on her first full day on the job.

'I miss sex,' Lucie stated, jolting Faith from her task. Now was not the time to be having this conversation. Faith was shattered and her mind was on Julien.

'When is the last time you actually *tried* to meet someone, Luce?'

'I have a rule.' Lucie looked appalled that she would make such an insane suggestion.

'And what rule is that?'

'While I'm travelling for work, there will be no shagging. I love that word. *Shagging*. I looked up loads of British phrases to use so that you feel more at home.' She beamed. She was so proud of herself that Faith couldn't tell her how alien it sounded coming from someone with an American accent.

'Oh, is *that* why you use Australian phrases and accents half the time? So Brett also feels more *at home*?' Faith raised her eyebrow and was soon smacked over the head with a pillow.

'Screw you! I don't even realize I'm doing that. I can't help it.'

'It's OK, Luce. His accent is strong, I get it.' She smirked.

'I swear, if you tell him . . .' Lucie blushed furiously and brushed her hair out of her face, setting the pillow back in its place on the bed.

'Your secret is safe with me, I promise. I'm not sure how much of a secret it is, though.'

'I appreciate it. And as a thank you, I promise I won't tease you about your gigantic crush on Jules.'

'Oh, would you look at that! Our work here is done.'
Faith jumped up and bolted across the room.

'Goodnight, Jensen,' Lucie called.

'Night, Carolan.'


Julien entered his room to find Bea still there. She was sitting in bed in his spare robe, with chocolates and cookies from room service. She paused the TV when she saw him.

'I told you to leave earlier. What the hell are you doing in here? It's been hours; this isn't your room.' He tossed his wallet on to the bedside table and sighed. 'Get the fuck out, Bea.'

'I didn't think you meant it, Jules. You've never kicked me out before. Ever.' She pouted. It wasn't cute.

'Things change. Out.' He started unbuttoning his shirt, which was an action she would no doubt try to twist to work in her favour. He wasn't having it.

'Not until you give me a reason.' She crossed her arms, trying to draw attention to her chest.

'Bea, for God's sake!' he exploded. 'I do not want you in here. I do not want *you*. Go ahead and sleep with some other driver to get all the benefits of this life, but that guy isn't me any more. No more trips to Monaco, or Ibiza, or Barbados. No sex, no borrowing my cars. No designer brands or social media facades. Nothing. We're not a couple, Bea. This was only ever meant to be fun.' He threw her clothes at her. Clothes he'd paid for actually. He was well within his rights to keep hold of them out of spite.

'You've been acting so weird since Monaco, but you've outdone yourself this week. Fuck you. I don't need you. I can do ten times better than you, Julien.' She flung the duvet back and took the robe off. Standing there in her lingerie, she paused for a second.

'That isn't having the effect you think it is,' he scoffed. Any sane person would be long gone by now, but here she was. Although any sane person in his position would cave and let her stay. She was a real piece of work, but he couldn't deny that her body was incredible.

'You need your head checked.' She walked out and slammed the door behind her, the walls shaking. He was stunned. She had gone out there, into the corridor of a fully booked hotel, in black lacy underwear.

As he was settling into bed a few minutes later and sweeping Bea's chocolate wrappers on to the floor, he was muttering curse words under his breath. He wanted a simple life, which was hard to achieve in his position, but he seemed to manage in every department except women. This race season appeared to be presenting him with a brand-new selection of choices to make.

His phone buzzed with a notification. It was Faith, telling him she hoped he was OK. She'd heard the yelling and the slam of the door, probably felt it too, and was concerned. It made him feel things he didn't want to feel. He texted back that he was just dealing with the fallout from stupidly getting mixed up with Beatrix Miller and locked his phone.

Faith wasn't at all how he had expected her to be. She was so similar to Lucie, whom he considered one of his best friends and, hands down, one of the most genuine women on the planet, that it was starting to scare him. It meant he couldn't find a way to hate her. And there was the fact that only one other face had drawn him in the way hers had. A face that haunted him more than Faith ever could. Why had the universe thrown him such a sensational curveball? He didn't do romance. After Bea, he wasn't going to do casual. So what was he supposed to do with Faith Jensen?

# 8

Faith woke up expecting her hotel room to be illuminated in a golden glow. She'd left the blackout blind up last night so she could wake up with the sun this morning, but she'd beaten the sunrise and woken up too early. She lay there in a state of pure bliss for a few minutes, soaking up the cloud-like softness of the pillows, before she reached for her phone.

If she got out of bed now, she could head down to the track early and get some shots of the sunrise. She doubted any of the food vendors would be open by the time she got there, but she had a granola bar from the hotel's vending machine in her bag.

She struggled her way into a pair of blue mom jeans and a basic white tee, shoving her feet into her trainers. She wished she was wearing a team shirt so she felt a little more put together, but the organization had only provided her with two and those needed to be saved for qualifying and race day.

Eyeing the mascara on the bathroom counter, she decided it was necessary. She had been blessed with long lashes but rarely went without it. That, a hydrating lip balm and a dab of concealer, and she was good to go. She grabbed her camera, leather backpack and laptop and made her exit, trapping her bag strap in the door in the process. 'Fucking hell.'

'Good morning, I think.' Julien was coming out of his room, pulling on his black leather jacket. 'Let me help.' He pulled her bag strap free as she put the key card back in the door to release it.

'Thank you. Headed to the track already?'

'Yeah, I like to go for a walk around the track most mornings. Helps clear my head of the chaos and get me in the zone.'

'Oh, that's what I was planning on doing. Figured I could shoot some content.' She was shy now, worried she was intruding on his personal time. It was a big track, but it would be very strange if they walked in different directions and met up in the middle.

'I don't mind you tagging along. If you're nice, I might let you include me in a few of the photos.'

They took off down the corridor side by side. They mutually opted for the stairs again but on this occasion Julien wasn't mumbling his responses at her. However, the man walked *fast*. Faith did her best to keep up but Julien was a professional athlete who worked out every single day. The only time you'd see Faith break out into a run was when she was trying to catch the Tube. By the time she was out of the hotel, Julien was making a break for the golf cart that was sitting out front. He gestured for her to get in, a mischievous glint in his eye. She had been planning on walking down, but this was definitely the more fun option.

'Were we allowed to take this?' she asked. They were hurtling down the road at max speed. If she was fearing for her life at the hands of a racing driver, she didn't want to think about how she'd feel with Gabriel behind the wheel.

'We're just borrowing it. It belongs to the hotel, so as long as we return it later we'll be fine.' He grinned at her, and Faith couldn't help but smile too. He was loving this. Who would've thought hijacking a golf cart would be such a thrilling concept?

'OK, but are we supposed to be driving it on the road?' she said, panicking. They hadn't taken the private road behind the hotel because the gravel wasn't golf cart friendly.

'Do you know what? I have absolutely no idea,' he replied.

Faith reached into her bag and dug around. She pulled out the granola bar, tearing the wrapper and holding it out to Julien.

'Want some?' she asked. He leaned his head forward and took a bite while she was still holding it, his own hands still on the wheel. At least he took golf cart safety semi-seriously, unlike their boss.

'Thanks,' he replied, mouth half full. 'I'll get us breakfast when we get to the garage since we're going to miss the hotel buffet. We can eat while we work.'

He pulled up outside the gate to the pit lane, flashing his badge at security who let them through. The track was eerily quiet, and Faith wondered how many people got to experience it like this. Fans were only allowed in when there were tens of thousands of other visitors, and, according to Lucie, most people who worked for the organization took advantage of every extra minute of sleep they could get because their days were stressful and they worked into the night. Faith had always been an early riser because of her love for surfing. Her body was used to waking with the sunrise and making the most of every day, and she often started work in her home office before the rest of London had even headed to the Tube.

'You ready for a trek?' Julien looked at her, and then up ahead.

'You want me to walk up Raidillon?' She eyed the steepest part of the track, which was connected to Eau Rouge. It was iconic. Hell yes, she was ready to walk it.

'Think your little legs can make it?' he teased.

'Moretz, please. I live in London and I refuse to pay for taxis ever. I've got this.'

She was eating her own words by the time they reached the top, and she wished the beer tent was open so she could neck ice-cold bottles of water. The cars always made it look so easy with the way they shot up there, but Faith hadn't been prepared. Julien, of course, had walked up with ease. His constant turning round to tease her and video her struggling did not help her situation, but she'd keep her mouth shut as long as he was having a good time.

They had made it to the top at the perfect time, right as the sun was rising over the circuit and basking everything in a soft orange glow. The trees of the Ardennes were often shrouded in mist and drizzle, but this morning they were visible for miles. In her twenty-six years she had never seen something so breathtaking. In Faith's world, the beaches of Cornwall simply didn't compare to a racetrack that was over a hundred years old and had such a rich history. This felt like home. Thousands of drivers had raced here, shaped their careers here. Some had even died here. The soles of her feet were on the same track that she'd dreamed of visiting since she first discovered the world of motorsport. If she didn't feel herself tearing up or the cool morning air on her skin, creating goosebumps, then she might have had to pinch herself to believe that this was real. That she was actually here.

'Beautiful, isn't it?' Julien interrupted her thoughts as they sat down on the tarmac. Their arms touched, both of them secretly trying to get some warmth from one another. 'Even now, it still takes my breath away.' He gave her a small smile.

'I understand why you chose to live so close.'

'There are some beautiful places in the world and I'm very lucky to have been to most places on my list, but Spa is special. It feels like home, like when I come back here I'm in touch with who I was before the success.'

'Makes you feel more normal?'

'Yeah. Let's face it, my life is far from normal. I mean, I don't have cameras in my face every time I leave the house, but my online presence is monitored heavily. Fans don't like that I keep part of myself hidden. I see them in my comments, theorizing about why I haven't posted in a while. Why I'm not seen much outside of the race week-ends like the other drivers who can be quite forward-facing. Maybe I'm just not glued to my phone, you know? Maybe I'm just living my life in real time.'

'I get that. I try to have detoxes, despite it being my job. Last summer I took two weeks off and spent the whole time being a tourist in my own city. Didn't post a thing.' She said it as she took another video to post as soon as they had a stronger internet connection. Apparently the steepest part of the circuit was anti-technology.

'You were a tourist in London?' Julien scrunched his nose up in disgust.

'You don't like London?'

'I think London is hell on earth. I need to be surrounded by nature.'

'Well . . . Hyde Park has trees. Grass. Flowers . . . I'm not convincing you, am I?' She looked over at his face, which hadn't moved from severely 'unimpressed'.

'No.' He laughed. 'I like forests, beaches, open spaces. I don't even like going to the supermarket; there's too many people, too much happening. I have enough of that at work.'

'I do miss Cornwall for that reason if I'm being honest. Nobody rushes; it's just calm and peaceful. Even tourist season isn't as bad as London on a normal day.'

'What made you leave all that behind? Couldn't you have gone to university there, or at least somewhere similar? Like Devon or Dorset?'

'It was all about the opportunity. Cornwall doesn't have a lot to offer except beaches, and I wanted a totally different change of scenery. A fresh start. London seemed like the most out-there option for a small-town girl like me, and it made the most sense career-wise. I suppose I wanted to see what the bright lights of the capital were all about.'

'Understandable. And, hey, you never have to worry about getting sand everywhere.'

'I miss the feeling of sand being blown into my eyes and temporarily blinding me.'

Julien laughed. For the second time today. At something she had said. It was a tiny victory, but it felt huge considering that a couple of days ago he couldn't stand to be near her or even shake her hand.

'Do you want to go on an adventure?' he asked, staring ahead.

'What, now?' She checked the time. It was already seven.

'Yep. We have time. Come on.' He stood up and held his hand out, pulling her up.

Each driver had an interview with a French media network first thing. Julien's slot started at eight thirty, and Faith was supposed to be at the interview with him. Whatever this adventure was, he'd better be good at time management.

As they walked back through the paddock, where the volume of people had significantly increased, everyone stared, and she meant *everyone*. A few fans and VIPS were starting to gain access from today, so of course they had their eyes peeled for any driver sightings. So the staring might have been because of Julien being, well, Julien, but there were mutterings and eyebrow raises at the mysterious woman by his side. Not in team uniform. She thanked God she had her sunglasses on.

'You two are up bright and early!' Jasper called out from the garage.

'Morning, Jasper. You don't need us for another hour, do you?' Julien asked.

'No, enjoy your freedom. Also, Faith, while I've got you, there needs to be more focus on Julien initially because he's been so MIA online over the break. So we want you to film some vlog footage with Jules. OK?' He looked at them both for confirmation, but Julien shifted uncomfortably.

'I'll film the whole day today,' Faith assured him. 'Might as well milk the entire weekend for content.'

'Amazing! Fans don't usually get to see what goes on today in detail,' Jasper agreed.

'In that case, let's go, Jensen.' Julien waved to his engineer, who was observing stats in the garage, and lightly tugged on Faith's arm to lead her back down the paddock.

The concept of taking time out of such a busy day to go and get food together was wild to her. He was in a weird mood this morning, way too relaxed in comparison to the Julien she'd met so far. Had ditching Bea been enough to spark such a drastic change? She doubted it. He had gone from avoiding her like the plague, to asking about her life back home and taking her for breakfast. It was odd.

'Where's good to eat around here?' she asked.

'I have a surprise. It means going to the fan zone, so I'm hoping the place I'm thinking of is already set up for the weekend.' He let go of her arm but picked up the pace.

The area they'd come to had a few merchandise stores but it was mostly food trucks. As soon as she spotted the waffle and crepes truck, she knew what they were here for.

'Please tell me my guess is right,' she said, her mouth watering.

'You couldn't come to Belgium and not have waffles, could you? We don't really eat them for breakfast – they're more of a dessert – but I'll make an exception. We also have different types, like the Brussels waffle and the Liège waffle. This truck does the Brussels one; it's bigger, more rectangular and sprinkled with icing sugar.'

'While it's lovely to learn about the history of the Belgian waffle, I'm *really* hungry. Which toppings do you recommend?' She turned to look at him but he'd already started heading over to place his order with the lady behind the counter.

'Why don't we get one strawberries and cream and one Nutella, and share?' he suggested. She agreed and recalled the gigantic tubs of Nutella she'd seen at the airport. She'd have to treat herself to one of those one day.

'You're not paying for mine!' She tried to swipe her card on the machine, but he batted her hand out of the way.

'*Dank je*,' he said to the woman serving him, a smug look on his face having beaten Faith to it.

The woman laughed and went about constructing their orders.

She scowled. 'Julien.'

'Faith.'

'I can pay my way.'

'You could, but I brought you here as my guest. So stop moaning. They're ready.' He reached out for the paper trays and handed her one along with plastic cutlery.

'Thank you,' she said, her scowl gone when she caught sight of the melted chocolate and fresh fruit piled on top of her waffle.

They sat down at a picnic table in front of the food truck and Julien immediately stretched his legs out so they were on either side of her. She pretended not to notice and recorded a few shots of the food, where they were and of Julien. He didn't clock the fact the camera was on him, which worked to her advantage. The more candid, the better.

Halfway through an unexpected conversation about Julien's love of dogs, they were approached by some younger fans who had been patiently waiting a few tables away for him to finish eating. He happily interrupted their breakfast to take some photos. Faith didn't film the exchange out of respect for the girls' privacy, but she noted how enthusiastic he was towards them. The youngest girl, who was around seven, was as quiet as a mouse. Julien crouched down to speak directly to her and signed her ticket. Then their dad shook his hand and the group departed.

'We should head back,' he said.

'Oh, sure. OK,' Faith replied. Time was getting away from them, and she still had a lot of content to shoot, which she was excited about. But she couldn't deny that she was disappointed to be going back so soon. Julien was starting to open up to her, albeit in small doses. However, she would take it considering she'd only known him for two days. Less than two days, in actual fact. It was still progress.

The Revolution Racing garage was buzzing with activity. Their first, second and third rounds of press duties were done and the fourth had been rescheduled, which was allowing the drivers time to practise. Faith had busied herself with capturing video content for the team's channel, and Julien had gone out of his way to be on camera. At one point he'd taken hold of it and gone to film himself and Marco telling the viewers what Brett was doing in the car. Faith was impressed, and she wasn't the only one. Lucie had raised an eyebrow of approval and Jasper had told the girls they were doing a great job.

Three of the social media crew members for other teams had come in to share their own progress with Faith, and it was all running smoothly. There was Esme, who worked for Eden Racing and evidently loved the colour yellow, which was her team's colour. She had a yellow bandana in her hair, yellow nail varnish and white and yellow trainers. It was a little too bright for Faith's personal taste, but Esme stood out for her enthusiasm too.

Then there were Levi and Ben, who were in charge of socials for Havelin Racing. They were throwing ideas at Faith at an overwhelming speed, but she encouraged them all. Gabriel wanted creative content and that's exactly what he was going to get. Except for the video which involved Havelin's drivers going bungee jumping. She didn't think the team principals or sponsors would be particularly happy with that idea.

Faith and Lucie had asked everyone to really focus on using colour filters on photos and videos so the feeds were cohesive. It was up to each duo whether they went for bright pops of colour and crisp contrasts or warm and neutral tones. Revolution opted to bring out the red of their team's livery and uniform. Faith was relieved that they only had to make slight tweaks and not play around with tints and filters too much, since she and Lucie had a bigger workload than everyone else. Of course she paid special attention to whitening Julien's teeth, as requested.

The positive feedback pouring in from fans so far had been uplifting. The girls kept notifications off so their phones didn't freeze from the constant pop-ups, but they kept checking in and replying where they could – engagement was key.

On Faith's own account, her followers were as excited as she was about her new adventure. They were loving the change of scenery from the boring grey tones of London, and they loved Lucie. They started following the team account and asking questions, and she was doing her best to keep up. The only disappointment was the amount of comments regarding a reunion with Bea. She didn't tell them that wouldn't be happening.

Julien had just come back from a five-minute break in the drivers' trailer and was climbing into his racing suit again. Why couldn't he have done that before he came into the garage and saved her from drooling?

Lucie nudged her in the ribs with her elbow. 'Close your trap.'

'What?'

'You're gawking at him like he's performing in *Magic Mike XXL*.'

'I am not!' she protested.

It was no use. Lucie could see right through her. She just hoped everyone else was oblivious. She would never live it down if Brett called her out on it and teased her.

'I can relate. Most of us can. I'm surprised Esme even came in earlier. Julien passed her a plate at the buffet in Singapore last season and I thought she was going to cry. Ben had a similar reaction when he handed him a beer once too.'

'Faith!' Marco called across the garage.

'What's up?'

'Pass me the camera! I want to film my view of the cockpit, give a little tour,' he said. She walked over to the car and passed it to him. He struggled to press the record button with his gloves on, so she came to his rescue.

'You're all set,' she said.

'Can you put an overlay on it? Have it say "De Luca Cam" at the top of the screen?' He grinned at her, and Brett and Julien laughed behind them. Poor guy. In his defence, it was a good idea.

'Your wish is my command. Guys? You want the same?' She turned to the others.

'Oh, go on then,' Brett replied.

Glad that she'd got them to agree to it, she headed back to Lucie who was now sat in a folding chair with her phone plugged into a portable charger.

'They really are like overgrown kids, aren't they?' Faith laughed. She felt more like a babysitter half the time, and that would no doubt become truer as time went on.

'It's still early days, you've seen nothing yet. I truly don't know how I've survived in this job for so long.' Lucie shook her head in exasperation, but she couldn't hide her smile. She adored those boys more than anyone, and Faith was starting to see why.

Brett and Marco had taken Faith under their wing the moment they'd met her. She felt safe within this team, and that was enough for her to know that taking this job was the best decision she'd made since leaving her hometown. It might even top it.

Faith scrolled through her camera roll on a mission to find a photo for her personal account. She didn't want that account to be all about the work side of things, that wouldn't be appealing to the majority of her followers. Her own content needed to focus on her new friendships and the places this new life took her to. The foods she tried, the cultures she learned about and the memories she was creating. She found a few photos of Julien proudly taking a bite of a strawberry at breakfast this morning and whacked a filter on them. *Perfect*.

'Why are you smiling like that?' Lucie gave her a weird look.

'Can't a girl just smile?' she replied.

'She can.' Lucie nodded and pulled Faith close to her

side, squeezing her tight. She was not used to this kind of affection and it made her eyes water with emotion.

'All right, Mrs Moretz?' Brett strolled over with a huge smirk on his face. The girls frowned up at him.

'What are you talking about?' Lucie asked.

'The photo Faith just posted,' Brett said.

'Of Julien eating the strawberry?' Faith asked.

'Yeah. You two are adorable, aren't ya? Looks like you were on a cute little breakfast date. Fans will love it,' he teased.

'It wasn't – Oh God, what have I done?' She put her hand over her mouth, utterly mortified. Was Brett just trying to wind her up or were people genuinely going to think it was a date? People would use their common sense, right? She barely knew him. The rest of the world would know that, surely?

'Don't stress! It's OK. Post one of you and Marco later, balance it out. Any comments that pop up will all seem irrelevant.' Lucie spoke with an air of confidence but her facial expression begged to differ.

'Why do you look like that?' Faith pushed.

'Julien might freak out . . .' Brett said.

'That's the last thing I want! I can't delete it, can I? That will look even worse. Should I edit the caption with a disclaimer?'

'Faith, leave it. It's fine. It's just a photo, and as you fill your feed up with content it will take the attention away from solo driver photos. I post them all the time; it's just that this whole thing is new to your followers. And Julien is the first driver you've posted a solo photo of, so it's going to stand out to begin with.' Lucie held her hand out to her and she took it, traipsing after her.

'Where are we going?' Faith asked.

'I'm taking you to get food, and you're going to take a photo of me, post it on your personal account, and caption it "lunch date".'

Brett patted her on the back in a show of solidarity as the girls departed the garage. Faith took some deep breaths when they passed Julien and searched his face for any sign of anger towards her. Instead, she got a show-stopping smile. If his own best friend thought he was going to panic, then there was no way he had seen the post yet.

# 9

Crowds were the only downside to the race weekend that Faith had discovered so far. They had finally made it to qualifying day and Faith was proudly wearing her Revolution Racing shirt and rain jacket. She'd got an early night after Marco's final interview yesterday, opting for room service with Lucie so they could squeeze out one more round of video edits. She had been asleep by ten o'clock, although the nerves had threatened to keep her awake. She had waited for an angry text from Julien or a knock on the door, but they didn't come. Maybe he just didn't care about the photo.

The week so far had passed by in a blur of meetings and content creation, and today was the first day of autograph sessions and pit walks. Tomorrow, on race day, there would be an autograph session combined with a pit walk at eight o'clock in the morning, but today was just a pit walk where fans could get a look at the cars while the drivers hid. It meant that for now Faith could just stand back and capture content for the team accounts from a distance.

It was one o'clock now, and she was frantically trying to get back from her lunch trip to the hospitality tent. All she'd had time for was a sandwich but with the way she was having to fight through people, she could've done with something more substantial.

A group of middle-aged men noticed the IEC lanyard

round her neck and yelled at the people around them to let her through. She was more than halfway down the pit lane now and she could see the sign above the garage with Julien's, Marco's and Brett's names and photos, but she wasn't tall enough to work out exactly how many fans she had to battle her way past.

When she reached the back of the crowd for Revolution's garage, someone tugged on Faith's arm. It was Bea, camera in hand.

'Hey! How are you doing?' Bea asked.

'I'm great, thanks for asking.' Faith hoped she could hear the sarcasm dripping from her tone. This was the last situation she wanted to be in.

'I'm so glad. You might want to be careful, though,' Bea said.

If Faith could have slapped that smirk off her face, she would have. However, she was not into physical violence. She would continue to take the moral high ground. 'With what?' She smiled, feigning politeness.

'What you post about Jules. He's a closed book.' Bea whispered loud enough for Faith to hear over the noise, as if she was revealing some big secret that only she knew.

'I'm aware. Now if you don't mind, I've got a job to do.'

Faith marched through the gathering of fans head on, desperate to get out of that conversation. As if she didn't already know how Julien was. It was her job to know. Just as she knew Brett was the one who carried the group with his humour, and Marco was the sweet and knowledge-able one.

After what seemed like a lifetime, she reached the front of the crowd and was able to shuffle down the side of the barriers. Lucie was laughing at her as she attempted to squeeze behind their security guard.

'Oops! Sorry, Faith! Come on through.' Eduardo let her past and the big scary facade that came with the sunglasses and muscles diminished when he realized it was her.

'Why did you go that way, you wombat!' Brett yelled out as she got through, earning laughs from the group he was talking to.

'Yeah, why did you? Why not go through the paddock like any sane human being?' Lucie questioned.

'I wanted to get a feel for the atmosphere with it being my first time here! I'm regretting it now. I'm pretty sure I broke a rib,' she said, placing a hand on her side.

'The crowds will be twice as horrendous tomorrow. Poor Eduardo is gonna have his work cut out for him keeping everyone back. Definitely don't go the same way.'

'I've seen it on social media. I'll be staying safely on this side of the autograph table, thank you very much,' she replied.

She used to sit at her kitchen counter and watch the live videos of the autograph sessions, and her heart would ache because she wanted to be part of it so badly. She always had hope that she would attend a race, but never in a million years would she have predicted being in the position she was in now.

Faith snapped a few photos and videos of the fans admiring the cars, then scheduled some posts. Brett being there had been a stroke of luck, since the drivers weren't usually in the garage at the time of the standard pit walks unless they were in the middle of something. It was their one chance to take a break, hence the decision to stick to one autograph session per race weekend. Having got enough content, she walked through the garage and out to the drivers' trailer. She wanted to talk to Brett about getting a VIP pass for race day for the fans he'd been speaking to just now. She knocked on the door and entered, but Julien was the only one in there. He was on the sofa, zoned out.

'You OK?' she asked, hovering in the doorway.

'I don't know, you tell me,' he snapped.

'Excuse me?' She knew exactly what was coming but she still wasn't prepared for his wrath.

'You want to take a photo of this moment? Me sitting here on the sofa. Nobody else around. Which emoji are you going to put in the caption? A heart, flowers?' He sat up, staring her down. So he *was* mad. She had been naive for thinking anything different. Faith shrank back in fear and it was only then that his expression softened a little.

'I only put a strawberry . . .' she whispered.

'Faith, it looked like a special intimate moment just between the two of us. I have people in my life outside of this industry who are going to see that and demand answers from me.' He placed his head in his hands and she kept a firm grip on the door handle.

'I know how it looks, but it *was* just the two of us. I'd have posted whoever I was with; it's my job. I'm sorry, Julien. I know you're not used to this, but you just happened to be the first solo male I uploaded a photo of. It seems like a big deal now but in less than twenty-four hours you'll blend in with Marco, Brett, your engineers and the mechanics.' She was fighting to keep him calm but she knew he was going to shut down again.

'No more photos or videos of just you and me, OK?

*Especially* not on your personal social media accounts,' he snapped.

'No, not OK. Julien, it is part of my job. Yes, I posted it on my personal account, but can't you understand how it all ties in? Gabriel specifically hired me because of my passion for the sport. I'm supposed to bring in more fans from my *own* following. I have to document everything, the race preparation and the races and everything in between. There will be moments where, yes, it is just you and me hanging out whether it's socially or otherwise. I am simply doing what I was hired to do. You don't get to be an exception.' She could feel her own anger brewing.

How could he possibly expect to pull this off, especially when the IEC were drastically changing their approach to content? Gabriel and the execs wanted multiple vlog-style videos for each race, and for Faith, Lucie and the rest of the crew to get up close and personal with their respective teams. If Julien was going to have a seat next season, he had to step it up. The sponsors were watching them closer than ever.

'Get out.' He was refusing to look at her and her temper was getting the best of her. She couldn't fathom why he was being so obnoxious.

Yanking the door to the trailer open with force and slamming it behind her, just as Bea had done two days before, Faith jumped when she ran into Brett at the bottom of the steps. Her eyes were so blurry with tears she couldn't even see two feet in front of her.

'Hey! What's going on?' He put his hands out to stop her and wrapped his arms round her.

'Sorry, I know this is really unprofessional. I'm just so

frustrated.' Faith took a few deep breaths and tried to gather her thoughts. She didn't want to say too much to the wrong person, but Brett felt like someone she could trust.

'Julien?' he asked.

'No. Well, yes but it's all my own fault. I messed up posting that photo so early on in our working relationship. I'm aware that he's a very private guy, and I didn't even think to ask his permission to post it. I should've been more considerate, and now he's shutting me out.'

'Give him time, Faith. With each race week that passes he'll open up more and more.'

'What makes you so sure?' Regardless of their sunrise track walk and breakfast adventure, they were close to slipping back into hostile territory.

'He has way more going on behind the scenes than anyone realizes. I know that's frustrating to hear with no context, but just trust me – he's not a bad guy,' he said.

That was the thing, she did trust Brett. Lucie too. The question was, how long would it be until she saw the same Julien Moretz everyone else did?

Julien had singlehandedly managed to potentially ruin Faith's Spa race experience and knock her confidence, and it was killing him. He didn't know what had come over him this week. One minute he was keeping his emotions in check and going about his day perfectly fine, the next he was taking it all out on her.

The truth was, Faith had done absolutely nothing wrong. It was all on him. If he didn't want that kind of content being broadcast to the world, he shouldn't have taken her for breakfast. Now he was going to have to pull a similar move to gain her trust again. It was a vicious cycle – however, he had no choice but to repeat it for the sake of the team.

It was different with Lucie. Everyone knew the deal with them, from fans and followers to family. Lucie was just Lucie. But Faith? Nobody here or in his life outside of work knew her yet, and nor did he. He wanted to get to know her and he wanted to let her in, but it was more complicated than she could ever understand. She had a hold on him that she was blissfully unaware of. Every time he saw her, all sense of rationality was gone.

Unless Julien's perception of human emotion was wildly off-kilter, Faith was upset. He couldn't blame her given the way he'd exploded. When she turned to watch him walk in, her eyes were slightly puffy. She looked away quickly but it was too late.

Bea flounced into the garage in the red-bottomed heels he had got her for her birthday last year, and he cursed. This was so far from what Faith needed right now. Bea was cold and calculating, but something told Julien that Faith would look beyond it all because of their history. He watched as Bea headed straight for Faith and started babbling utter nonsense about the post-race party and what she was going to wear. If only he could uninvite her; that would send a clear message to the paddock – her behaviour was no longer welcome.

'Dude, focus. You can fix that problem some other time.' Brett clicked his fingers in front of his face, bringing him back to the task at hand. He was clutching his beloved new custom helmet, his knuckles white.

'Someone needs to say something. Faith's too good for her, Brett,' he said.

'Jules, getting in the middle of whatever their friendship is at the moment is not the way to go. If we want to support Faith, we have to let her make her own decisions. You know Bea will manipulate the situation if you involve yourself, and it won't end well for you or Faith.'

Brett was right, but that didn't stop Julien clenching his jaw until it ached.

He spent the next few minutes trying his absolute hardest to listen to what Brett was saying about the best approach he'd discovered to turn one, but his head wasn't in the game. They had good competition out there today and Julien couldn't have Faith in his head the whole time he was in the car. He'd had his own bad experiences with Bea and seen her wreak havoc on various other drivers on the grid, but they weren't afraid to stand up for themselves. Faith didn't seem like she would hurt a fly, so she probably wasn't going to defend herself against her friend. He didn't like to label her as naive, but she was definitely too kind-hearted for Bea's drama. He knew from overhearing snippets of conversations between Faith and Lucie that their friendship was vulnerable, and Bea was the type to take advantage of that. What for? That remained to be seen. He needed to get a word in with Bea before she could start playing games.

Out of the corner of his eye a camera flash went off and startled him. He whipped his head round and saw Bea with her hefty DSLR aimed right at him. Enough was enough.

'Can we talk?' he snapped.

'Anything for you, Jules,' Bea replied.

Julien's vision was zeroed in on Faith. There was something about her that told him he needed to protect her, but he had yet to work out if that stopped at removing

Bea from her life. He kept a firm grip on her freshly fake-tanned arm as they came to a stop at the back of the garage. He didn't care who overheard them, as long as Faith wasn't within earshot.

'Stay the hell away from her,' he said.

She laughed. 'Why would I do that?'

'I know you better than you think I do, Bea. She has people on this team who already care about her a million times more than you claim to, so you can come after me if you want but I am telling you now that she is not a pawn in your childish little games.'

'Screw you, Julien,' Bea hissed.

He felt her yank her arm out of his grip before she stormed off into the paddock, and grimaced. He hadn't meant to keep hold of her while he spoke, and was very aware that it could come back to bite him when she played her next card. Whatever, it was done. He still needed to apologize to Faith, but that was a bigger conversation and it wasn't one he particularly wanted to have with all these distractions around them.

Julien began walking back in to join the others, but he bumped into Jasper. 'Sorry, Jasper. Didn't see you there,' he said.

'You look troubled, Moretz. Everything OK?' Jasper asked that question at every race, but this time he had a look on his face like he knew there was something else on his driver's mind. Julien typically kept his personal life entirely separate from his work life, but the gorgeous blonde girl a few feet away was making it an impossible task.

'Just struggling a little more than normal with adjusting,' Julien said.

'Ah, you can go home again soon. Only a few more days!' Jasper was beaming but he couldn't quite match his enthusiasm.

Julien wanted to be at home more than anything, he always did, but he wouldn't be able to settle there either until he got his head straight, and he couldn't get his head straight if he kept pushing his emotions down.

Faith felt a rush of adrenaline as Julien was preparing for the qualifying session. He was a nervous wreck but the team were so busy analysing statistics and working on the car that they weren't paying him much attention. He had barely uttered a word since his conversation with Bea, and as much as she wanted to ask him about it, she didn't know if she'd like the answer. She wanted an apology from him, but Brett's reassurance of his good nature made her believe there were bigger things going on that were none of her business. She had to continue trying to work on their friendship and give him the benefit of the doubt. It would either work or it wouldn't. Either way, Julien was no longer the only one of them with walls up.

He was sat on his own at the back of the garage, visibly trying to calm himself down. She wasn't the best person to approach him in this state, considering he was angry with her, but it was worth a shot. Swallowing the lump in her throat, she sat down next to him. He glanced at her with his eyebrows raised in surprise. She had half a mind to jump right back up and scurry away to safety again but one of them needed to get over their tiff and Faith got the impression that he was even more stubborn than she was.

'Can I do anything to help? Are there any rituals you do before you get in the car, or maybe I can get you a bottle of water?' she asked. She was shaking ever so slightly, so she sat on her hands.

'No, I'm OK . . .' He insisted on holding her gaze again, his expression unreadable but anything but blank.

Faith broke their eye contact and stood up reluctantly, clearly not getting anything out of him. At least he hadn't been blunt. 'I'll leave you to it then,' she said, offering him a weak smile.

'Faith –' he spoke as she took a step away from him– 'I wanted to wait and talk to you alone, but it could be hours yet and I feel awful. I'm sorry about before. I just really value my privacy, and I don't like the fans discussing my personal life online and speculating. I've never been open, and it's hard taking the steps the organization are asking me to take. I respect that you're doing your job, and it's my responsibility to work with you, not against you. So maybe just warn me next time you're about to post, but I don't want you to feel like you're walking on eggshells.' He still didn't smile at her, but it felt like a genuine apology.

'Thanks, Julien.'

Five minutes later, the television cameras were outside their garage and Julien was patiently waiting in the car for the team to give him the go-ahead. He was given the signal, and Faith eagerly watched him drive down the pit lane on the TV screens. With Revolution being such a prestigious team, the cameras tracked the car round a large portion of the circuit. All eyes were on him. The entire team's trust was in him to get a good time and put them at the front of the grid for tomorrow's race. She couldn't begin to imagine the pressure he was under every time he stepped in the car for qualifying.

Marco and Brett were gathered round the screens with Jasper, who looked more relaxed than one might expect for a team principal. But he had been doing this job for a long time, and Faith imagined he must do a lot of focus rituals.

Julien was currently making the fastest time, and she and Lucie were capturing footage of everyone's reactions. He was smashing it. Marco gave Faith his headphones so she could hear the team radio, which only made the whole experience more real. This was the kind of access most motorsport enthusiasts would never get to experience and she was embracing every small moment.

When he returned with the pole position secured, the team were in high spirits. He high-fived and hugged anyone he came into contact with, the girls filming it all. Faith wasn't expecting a similar exchange, but Julien stopped right in front of her and took his helmet off, grinning widely at her. She lowered her arm so her camera was no longer aimed at him.

'That one was for you, Jensen. Welcome to the team.'

## 10

Faith had been sitting in the restaurant with her laptop, staring at the spread of fresh fruit, cereals and pastries, for a ridiculous amount of time. She felt too nauseous to eat anything, but she knew she'd regret it in two hours' time. It was five o'clock in the morning, but a few people were already in there. Even Bea, who was sat in the far corner alone, reading what looked to be a romance novel. It was so much like the old Bea that Faith had fought the urge to join her.

Faith was the first member of the team up and ready. The red on her team shirt matched her nail polish and her hair was beach-waved to perfection. She had done a full face of make-up today, highlight and all, since she'd had time to kill. There was no need to be down here yet, but she had decided to take advantage of the gap in her schedule and create a checklist for filming later and ensure the schedules across the other teams were all looking strong. The reports from the social managers across the pit lane had been positive after qualifying, with engagement already up across channels. But now her mind kept drifting to every little thing that could possibly go wrong.

Today was race day, which meant she had to bring her A game. She wanted to prove she was the right hiring choice and that her plans were going to increase their following from day one.

Julien joined her at ten past five, walking into the restaurant all bleary-eyed and dopey. She laughed at him and he responded with a disapproving scowl.

'What on earth are you doing awake?'

'I couldn't sleep.' She shrugged, not wanting to confess that she'd actually only slept for three hours because the nerves had kept her up. He didn't respond but sat down opposite her. As he yawned and stretched his legs out under the table, they brushed against hers. There was minimal contact, but enough that her eyes immediately darted to his. He didn't move.

They sat in silence for another twenty minutes until members of the team slowly trickled in, helping themselves to food. Once it was all in front of her, Faith realized how hungry she was. Julien was texting furiously. He'd hardly spoken to Marco or Brett other than muttering a 'hello', so she placed a muffin in front of him. He swiped it as though he was afraid it might disappear and took a bite, nodding in approval.

'Thanks,' he mumbled, mid-mouthful. While the team chatted among themselves, he didn't look up once. He was still glued to his phone, oblivious to the world around him.

Faith was uploading yesterday's vlog to the channel and working on the content schedule, but her mind was focused on the feeling of Julien's leg on hers. She wondered if he would reposition if she moved, so she didn't dare so much as flinch. She wished her brain would normalize physical contact with him the way it did with the other drivers, but so far every slight touch sent her pulse racing.

Her saviour came in the form of Lucie, who rushed into the restaurant at five forty-five and started dishing out hugs to the whole table. She came up behind Julien and wrapped her arms round his shoulders, kissing him playfully on the cheek. Faith was thankful when he sat up straight and his leg was no longer resting against hers, but a green-eyed monster was lurking. She couldn't tear her eyes away. Lucie noticed and swiftly skirted round to Faith's side of the table to sit by her. She passed her a huge bottle of water which, frankly, was big enough to knock someone out.

'You're gonna need that today,' she said.

'Thanks, Luce.' Faith smiled appreciatively. She had been warned that they wouldn't get much chance for a break because from the moment they got to the circuit, it was *go, go, go*.

They needed to stay glued to the drivers, and they would no doubt be sending other people on errands for them. She wasn't feeling great about needing to be so close to Julien at all times, given how snappy he could get when he was in the zone. Even sweet and pure little Marco had sworn at his engineer yesterday.

When most of their food had been cleared from the table, the team started getting up.

'Guys, we'll meet you down there. We're going to walk,' Lucie told the team. They said their goodbyes in the car park and the drivers and their engineers got in golf carts. At least these ones weren't being hijacked and illegally driven.

Faith sighed. 'I'm so tired.'

'Me too,' Lucie said. 'The boys are lucky, during race day they can nap any time they're not in the car. We don't have the same advantage,' she said.

'I'm sure I'll survive; the adrenaline will keep me awake.'

'I'm assuming Jules is still hosting everyone tonight for

post-race celebrations, he hasn't said otherwise. So prepare yourself.'

'Really? By the time the race finishes and everyone leaves the circuit, won't it be really late?' Faith asked. The race wouldn't be over until six and then everyone needed to get ready. Was his house even set up?

'Julien's parties don't start until eleven. We'll have loads of time! We can fit in a quick power nap too,' Lucie replied.

'Eleven?!' She would have sat this one out if it wasn't for the fact it was her first post-race party.

'We always go out for dinner first, but I might skip it to prioritize getting myself ready. You and I could do that and just grab something when we get to his place?'

'Sure. God, I feel so old.' Faith groaned.

Lucie patted her on the back. 'You'll get used to it, sunshine!'

The girls walked into absolute mayhem. Their social media crew were rushing around creating content, drivers were zipping into the paddock on mopeds and narrowly avoiding the crowds, and camera crews were darting back and forth with heavy equipment. Faith dodged Jasper marching into the garage on a mission and stood blinking like a deer caught in headlights.

'Sorry, running late!' Jasper yelled.

'On that note, I'm going to grab that man a coffee and get started on posting. I think Gabriel has a surprise for you; he should be here soon!' Lucie said.

'Faith!' Right on cue, Gabriel came running over. He looked like he'd just done a marathon, and Faith was incapable of concealing her amusement as he put his hands on his knees and panted like a dog.

'Good morning, Gabriel. What can I do for you?' she asked.

'Jasper and I have arranged something. It's waiting for you in the trailer.' He gestured outside and then he was gone.

She climbed the steps and pulled the door open slowly, peering round. It was empty. She stepped in further and closed the door behind her, the blinds rattling against the window. Hanging up directly in front of her was a racing suit with a note attached.

*We wanted you to feel like a real part of the team, so you and Lucie both have a suit each for race day – Team RR x*

Faith tried not to let the tears fall. This was the final piece of the puzzle in making her first race the perfect experience. This job was hers and she wouldn't let it fall from her grip without a fight.

She locked the door and stripped down to her underwear, a black lace ensemble that although hidden gave her a confidence boost. Matching underwear was one thing that always made her feel put together. T-shirt bras were a thing of the past in Faith's world.

There was a cough behind her.

Faith swung round and saw a half-naked man emerging from the bathroom. Julien. In a white towel. Rock-hard abs on full display, water droplets falling from his blond hair. There might as well have been steam coming from behind him like that iconic scene with Mark Sloan in *Grey's Anatomy*. She blushed and reached for her T-shirt in an effort to cover herself up.

'I'm so sorry. I didn't think anyone else was in here,' she said.

'It's fine,' he replied. He edged closer to her and she tried to control her breathing, hoping he couldn't hear her calming technique. This man's body was ridiculous; Faith had every right to be stunned into silence. Why on earth had he never done a magazine shoot with this physique? She knew for a fact Brett had done one a couple of years ago. Not that she would admit to having seen it.

'I'll get out of your hair.' The words fell out of her mouth in a rush and she stumbled over them.

'I said it's fine.' Julien's voice came out hoarse and it sent shivers up her spine.

'What are you doing?' She breathed out, his hand already reaching for a strand of her hair. As he played with it, she couldn't take her eyes off him. But he wasn't looking her in the eye. His gaze was fixed on her necklace. A gold choker with tiny diamonds in it, an old gift from Bea.

'I wish I knew. You're nothing like I thought you were, Jensen.' He looked right at her then, his pained expression catching her off guard. Had he been feeling the spark too? And what did he mean? What had he thought of her before?

His touch found the curve of her waist before he trailed his hand up her back, freezing for a split second when she inhaled sharply. Alarm bells were sounding in her head, but she'd be lying if she said she wanted him to stop.

His entire body was against hers. There was nowhere for her to go. He pushed his hips into her, only the thin material of his towel and her lace underwear separating them. She could feel all of him and the desire pooled between her legs as he rested his forehead against hers, one hand at the nape of her neck.

Faith almost let out a whimper when he reached forward again, but then he reached past her into the wardrobe and pulled out his own race suit.

The interruption brought her back to reality. This trailer was far too small. She was feeling claustrophobic. And *hot*. Did the windows open? Faith wrapped her arms round herself. It didn't do much considering she was wearing a *thong* and his dick had just been pressed right up against her. That was it, granny underwear was essential in the future. High-waisted and all.

Looking very calm and controlled, Julien turned round while Faith jumped into the suit. It was a snug fit, but it was comfortable. Plus, she felt ten times cooler than she probably looked. She did a subtle check over her shoulder and saw that Julien was fully dressed too but had his back turned. She thanked the heavens that she hadn't witnessed him whip off his towel, or something else might have been occurring in this metal box.

'I'm decent. You can look,' she mumbled.

'Sorry about that. I completely forgot they were sending you in here. It's usually just the guys who come in. Does your suit fit OK? It looks good.' Was he not going to address what had just happened?

'I'll make sure I knock in future. I wouldn't want to traumatize Marco,' she said. That got a smirk out of him and he walked past her and took a seat on the sofa.

'You can stay in here if you want, we've got about an hour until the autograph session.' He patted the spot next to him and leaned back, putting his feet on the coffee table.

Faith hesitated for a moment, unsure of whether to leave, but she desperately wanted a moment away from the chaos back in the garage. Especially after what had just occurred. She climbed over his lower legs and sat on his right, copying his position. What she really wanted to do was sit totally upright and not move a muscle, but it was better to play down how uneasy she felt around him. She couldn't stop replaying the image of his bare chest in her mind. He had light tan lines where his T-shirt sleeves would've ended, and she tried to focus on that memory rather than his perfectly sculpted abs. She suddenly felt very conscious of her body.

She was slim but she had curves, and she usually embraced them and was proud of them, but over the years she had compared herself to Bea, and considering he'd been sleeping with her, it wasn't doing much for her confidence. Julien may have had his hands on her but he hadn't looked Faith up and down the way she had to him, or maybe he had and she had been so mesmerized by her own view that she hadn't noticed. She wished she didn't care. She also wished she couldn't feel him studying her.

'What are you staring at?'

'You have freckles,' he stated. 'They're pretty.'

'I didn't take you for a freckles kinda guy.'

'I'm not. But I like them on you.'

'What else do you like?' she challenged.

'I like the way you only have one dimple, and you only have to give a hint of a smile for it to appear. I liked the way that during our sunrise track walk, the light hit your eyes in just the right spot and they transitioned into a completely different shade of blue. They reminded me perfectly of the ocean in the Maldives. You know what I don't like?'

'What?'

'That you underestimate how beautiful you are.'

'How can you tell?'

'It was written all over your face just now, Faith.'

'Oh.'

She leaned closer, giving him the signal he'd been waiting for. They were so close she could hear the way his own breath was shaking, but despite a quick glance, his lips never touched hers.

'Are you OK?' Faith put a hand on his chest and pulled back.

'I just think, maybe we should think about the consequences,' he mumbled, and then he was on his feet and walking across the trailer. Was that it? He was just going to leave?

But then he was back with a bottle of water, which he handed to her in silence.

'Are *we* OK?' She looked at him quizzically.

'You've driven me insane in a very short space of time.'

'Oh. Well, what can I say? I'm a powerful woman.'

'Ha.' He didn't laugh. 'Believe me, you have no idea.'

'We've got ten minutes, need to get back. Here, you'll need these. People always forget to turn their flash off, bunch of idiots.' He threw his gold-rimmed sunglasses to her and she caught them effortlessly. They'd lost track of time chatting, trying to forget what might have happened between them.

He knew from experience that the trailer became very dark behind the tinted lens, so Julien reached out for her arm and led her through the gap between the sofa and the table, towards the door. He pretended not to notice the goosebumps that appeared all over her body.

Talking to Faith so easily, away from the madness outside the garage, had provided Julien with an odd feeling of inner peace, like all was right in the world, and yet it had also unsettled him tremendously. It had kicked his emotions up a notch. He felt a connection to her and he couldn't shut it off, but what he had almost done to her in that trailer was unfair when he couldn't give her anything emotionally.

Julien hadn't felt this torn about anything or anyone in his thirty-two years. It was no wonder he had nearly allowed such an intimate moment to happen. He needed to get a grip and let her do her job too. If fans wanted to suggest there was chemistry there, then fine. They wouldn't exactly be wrong.

'Those suit you.' He gestured at his sunglasses. She was relieved that things weren't weird between them. If that had been the case, she might've gone back to London and vowed to join a convent because she was thinking with the wrong part of her body.

'Maybe you should consider donating them.' She grinned up at him.

'Um, I think not. They're my favourite pair.'

'How many pairs do you have?'

'I do not want to continue this conversation.'

'Is it more than five?'

Julien didn't speak but he shrugged.

'More than ten?'

He smirked.

'More than twenty?'

'How old am I?' He stopped when they got to the garage.

'Thirty-two . . .' She trailed off. 'Oh my *God*, Julien!' As she stood there, dumbfounded, he backed away, innocently shrugging and laughing at her shocked expression. 'That is ludicrous! I hope you know that deserves therapy!'

The security guy gave the first fan the go-ahead to walk up to their table: a little girl no older than seven. She was an absolute sweetheart and the drivers took an immediate liking to her. They let her get a few selfies, and her dad thanked them and collected a couple of signed cards and posters. The next fan was a middle-aged British guy carrying a gigantic backpack with a flag sticking out of the top. He'd poke someone's eye out if he wasn't careful. He shook all their hands proudly and wished them luck.

Marco passed autograph cards to Julien, who signed them and passed them down to Brett. They followed their usual system and answered questions from the journalists who made their way down the pit lane. The crowds seemed never-ending as the minutes ticked by.

The fans were growing more and more impatient, and it didn't take long for people at the back of the so-called 'queue' to start aggressively shoving into people. Fans near the front were getting knocked into the table and trying their hardest to stay upright, and everyone was yelling at each other. It was usually the grown men who behaved like complete animals, and this time it was no different. The drivers were treated like zoo animals and the fans behaved like chimpanzees.

Faith and Lucie were stood off to one side getting photos and videos of the chaos when a man was unintentionally rammed into them. Lucie managed to dodge him, which meant Faith took all the impact in her small frame.

'Hey!' Julien stood up angrily, almost knocking his chair over, and yelled in the general direction of the shoving. 'Everyone move back!'

Eduardo was already in front of the girls, trying to calm people down as he called in reinforcements. Brett and Marco were desperately trying to keep the autographs flowing but with Julien not participating, some fans were getting left out. Julien gestured for the fans at the front to wait a second.

He took a few steps towards Faith and led her back to safety, checking her over. She was shaking a little, but she seemed OK.

'Are you all right, Faith?' Lucie rushed towards her, taking over so Julien could go back to his seat. He hovered by his chair, not wanting to sit down until she confirmed she was OK.

'I'm OK. You can carry on, Jules.' She smiled softly and relief washed over him.

He was definitely overreacting, but he could've sworn he could hear his own heart beating. The crowd was calmer following his explosion of anger.

'Hi, excuse me?' The last fan reached the table and the rest of the queue dispersed. Their time was up. The girl stood in front of them looked pretty young, and she was very softly spoken.

'Hi! What's your name?' Marco asked her.

'Sofia,' she replied.

'Hi, Sofia. Would you like a photo?' Julien reached out for the phone she was holding. When she nodded, the drivers got up from the table, walked to the other side and gathered round her.

'Hang on!' Faith ran over. 'Let me take it.'

They threw their arms round her and smiled while Faith carried out a full-blown photoshoot. She must have hit that shutter button thirty times. Girls always did that and it drove him up the wall. He was a 'click the button once and if it looks shit just don't post it' kinda guy.

'Thank you so much!' Sofia gushed. 'Um, Faith? Could I get a photo with you too? I'm a big fan,' she said.

Julien couldn't help but smile to himself.

'Of course! Here, let's take a cute selfie.'

'I can't believe you work in motorsport after all this time. I've been following you on social media for, like, four years and got into racing because of you,' Sofia said.

'I can't believe it either, to be quite honest. That's so lovely to hear, though. We could do with more female fans.'

'You inspired me to take a gap year.'

'That's amazing! What are you doing with your year off? Any big plans?' Faith was just as excited as Sofia was.

'I'm actually travelling Europe at the moment, and I've managed to get tickets to every race of the season,' Sofia replied.

'*Every* race? Even in Asia?' Faith's jaw dropped.

'Yep! I'm meeting friends at some of them.'

'Well, I'd love to hang out when I have time! I might be able to get you some merchandise or VIP passes or something.' Faith was still chatting away as staff started removing the tables and chairs from the pit lane.

Julien was being dragged back into the garage by Brett for a water break, but he couldn't stop observing the scene in front of him. He had been so wrong in his first impression of Faith. He had thought Faith just sat around and posted photos all day, but he was *very* far off. That girl had been working her ass off since she got here. Every time he looked her way, she was filming something, chasing down interns in the paddock, furiously typing on her phone or hiding in the corner with her laptop, getting work done in the quiet moments. On top of that, she genuinely cared about people. She cared about making a difference and making strangers feel like they had a friend in her. He wanted in on that. He wanted to share the parts of himself that he kept hidden, and he didn't just want to share them with the world; he wanted to share them with Faith. But it could never be as sweet and simple as he was idealizing in his head. Some things had to stay buried deep.

# I I

The whole team was gathered round the screens in the garage, but while they were fixated on the almost non-existent gap between the two cars, Faith was focusing on the shift that had occurred between her and Julien in the trailer.

This was far more than sexual tension. He'd sat there and complimented her on things that most people didn't notice. Or at least things that nobody had mentioned before. This felt like something much bigger. But work was the priority, and, besides, it was only yesterday that they'd been screaming at each other in that same trailer *about* work. They had a long way to go before they could risk mixing business with pleasure, which she'd always promised herself she never would. Faith refocused her attention on the race and bit her lip as Julien momentarily locked up, afraid that there would be a big crash. She'd seen them on television before and she really didn't want to witness one today. It was inevitable in this sport, though. It was just part of the risk the drivers took each time they got behind the wheel.

The car came into the pits and Julien hauled himself out of the cockpit, switching places with Brett. He came into the garage looking utterly euphoric, knowing that his work was done and that he couldn't possibly have done a better job. Talos's third driver was new this season and probably wouldn't be able to overtake a seasoned driver like Brett.

Once he was out of shot of the TV cameras, he lifted his helmet off and gratefully took a bottle of water from his engineer, gulping it down. He was a hot, sweaty mess and Faith couldn't tear her eyes away from the strands of blond hair plastered to his forehead.

'Good work,' she said, smiling at him.

'Thanks, Jensen.' He nudged her arm. His good mood was contagious but she was painfully aware that this happy-go-lucky version of Julien probably wasn't here to stay.

Brett tore past the chequered flag in first position, winning the six hours of Spa. The atmosphere in the garage was like nothing Faith had ever experienced before, but it was Julien who stunned her into silence. He threw his arms round her, spun her round and planted a kiss on her cheek. It took her a few seconds to register what he was doing, and then she was back on her own two feet as they swayed side to side. Lucie and Marco joined in, Marco ruffling Faith's hair and yelling in her ear. Faith had never received so many hugs in such a short time span.

Julien put his arm round her again, but faint horror set in when Faith noticed who was stood at the entrance to the garage. Bea was taking photos of them, which meant she had *definitely* caught the moment Julien had kissed her cheek. If she posted them anywhere, he would flip out again. She gently pushed him away, but he and Marco were already on their way out to Brett.

Gabriel congratulated the team, shaking hands with a very relieved-looking Jasper, and headed towards them, his lanyard swinging wildly as he ran. 'Girls!'

'Gabriel!' Lucie shouted back above the buzz of excitement.

'Come to the podium! You can get great content up there.'

'You want us *on* the podium?' Faith asked. Social media staff didn't get to do that. Only drivers and whoever was handing out trophies. It was televised across the globe.

'We want the fans to feel like they're actually here, remember? And you can't do that from down here.' He hurried them along.

It was all happening so fast. Gabriel shoved them out on to the platform and Talos's and Havelin's drivers walked out followed by Julien, Marco and Brett. They were met with rounds of applause and the girls had their cameras out, filming both the crowd below and the drivers receiving their trophies.

Julien smiled at Faith, and with her camera pointed at him she pleaded with the universe to keep him on this high. She didn't want to go back to walking on eggshells around him whenever she needed to do her job.

Narrowly dodging being sprayed with champagne, Faith and Lucie were called over to join the guys. Brett passed them his bottle and took hold of Faith's camera to film them both taking a sip. It was absolutely vile but all part of the experience. Media crews dispersed along with everyone else, giving them a chance to congratulate the other teams on the podium properly.

Faith had never realized how close the teams were despite the on-track rivalry, and she was now looking forward to tonight's after-party. She was, however, counting on being able to stay glued to Lucie's side. There was something about losing control around a massive group of men she hardly knew that made her nervous. She was determined not to embarrass or endanger herself, but she also didn't want to be so reserved and 'tame' that anyone thought she was putting a downer on things. Girls had to stick together but Bea was the only other woman going as far as she was aware. There wasn't enough space to have every single person from the organization at these parties, so it was pretty much just the drivers and the three of them. Even the engineers and mechanics still had work to do post-race. Open-invite events were held once a year at whichever luxurious resort the organization could get exclusive access to.

'How do you feel?' Lucie asked, clutching Faith's wrist in excitement.

'Bewildered,' she replied.

'That's the first time I've ever gone up there! Wow. The rest of our social crew are gonna be devastated, bless them. Maybe we should ask Gabriel if that can be a regular thing. If a team wins, their social media people get to go up.'

Faith laughed. 'Slight problem there, Luce. Revolution always wins.'

'Ha! You're right. Screw 'em.' She shrugged.

'I can't believe you just did that, you jammy devils!' Esme from Eden Racing called out to them as they got near the garage.

'Neither can we,' Lucie responded.

'Listen, I just wanted to say thank you to you both for giving the rest of us so much creative freedom this week. We're loving it.'

'Of course! But really it's Faith here you should be thanking.'

Faith smiled proudly. 'It's an honour.'

'Anyway, congrats on your first win of the season!' Esme smiled and left to follow her team.

It suddenly hit Faith that she now had time to fill between now and Le Mans, which was in six weeks' time. She had no plans except her podcast. It was a totally new concept, and she felt suddenly lonely at the prospect of returning to her empty flat.

'There they are. The two luckiest ladies in the world, getting to go up there. Not every gal gets the full Brett Anderson experience, you know.' Brett smirked playfully as he flung his arms round their shoulders.

'No, but most get at least half.' Lucie offered him a sarcastic smile.

'You can have the other half if you want it, Carolan,' he replied.

Faith shrugged herself out of his grip, not wanting to be physically attached to them while they flirted.

'I know, and that is precisely why I don't.'

'I don't know why you keep lying to yourself, Luce. You can admit it, nobody will judge. I come with a great feedback rating.'

'You're disgusting.' She rolled her eyes.

Faith caught Julien's eye and they laughed. As the group started to walk through the paddock, Julien held back so Faith wasn't walking alone, handing her the same gold-rimmed sunglasses she'd returned to him earlier.

'The sun is getting pretty low – thought you might want them,' he said.

'Thanks,' Faith replied. Even with the rush of adrenaline gone, he was still treating her like they were friends. She could work with that.

Julien was soaked from head to toe in champagne and he felt grim as they drove back to the hotel. He was driving a cart with Faith in the front and Marco, Brett and Lucie in the back. There were only four seats, so Lucie was sat on Brett's lap. Marco had offered Faith his seat up front so she didn't have to put up with any lovey-dovey nonsense, and Julien was debating turning a corner very abruptly so the pair of them would be thrown out. That would put a stop to it.

'Are you two coming to dinner tonight?' Julien directed the question to Faith and Lucie. 'We're just going to shower and freshen up then head into Francorchamps to the Italian restaurant.'

'What the hell are we doing about the party?' Lucie questioned. 'I tried to catch you earlier but you were too busy. Everyone on the grid is just assuming it's still happening.'

'I didn't really think about it this year. I figured everyone could just stop and get beer on the way; there's a Carrefour near mine.'

'Jules, you can't host a party with zero preparation. You need cups, music, food, alcohol, valuables put a–' Lucie rambled.

'I'll skip dinner and go home first then.' He sighed, irritated. He had only had a couple of days at home before race week began, which wasn't enough time to prepare. He would much rather let someone else take responsibility for this.

'No, you won't. Faith and I will go back to yours and organize everything; we can get takeout,' Lucie suggested.

'There'll be plenty of dinners to take Faith to over the rest of the season.'

Julien would be lying if he said he was totally comfortable with that idea. There were things in the house that might raise questions, and although Lucie knew the answers, he really needed her to do him a solid and brush them off. Or, better yet, hide everything. Preferably while Faith waited outside on the driveway.

'All right. You can take my credit card and my keys.' He kept one hand on the wheel of the golf cart and handed both to Faith.

'Your credit card?' she asked.

'Don't look so surprised. You're not planning on buying a giraffe or anything outrageous, are you?' He raised an eyebrow.

'No, but honestly now you've said that I might. Perhaps a zebra.'

He laughed. 'See that gold key?' He pointed at it. 'That's my house key. Take that off. The other ones are my car keys and I need those to get back. Do not let Lucie keep hold of that house key; she'll lose it for the third year in a row.'

'I will not!' Lucie protested behind them.

'Noted.' Faith nodded as her friend scoffed.

'You girls can sleep in my room tonight, OK? I'm not having you getting a cab back to the hotel on your own. I'll sleep on the sofa and the boys can share the guest bedroom. Brett, Luce, no funny business,' Julien warned, smirking when Brett flipped him off.

'With that horrendous image in my head, I might take the other sofa.' Marco shuddered and earned himself a punch in the arm from Lucie.

Arriving back at the hotel, Julien parked the cart next to his beloved Mustang. He needed to get a word in with Lucie about Faith being in the house. When she told them she was going up to her hotel room, he almost collapsed with relief.

'You are OK with this, aren't you?' Lucie asked once Faith was out of earshot.

'I think so. If she sees anything and starts asking about it, just make something up on the spot, OK? Doesn't matter what it is; if she mentions anything to me later on, I'll go along with it. I think I still have things hidden from when some of the guys came over a few months back . . . I hope.'

'I've got it, just focus on celebrating. Do you want me to pick Ford up from the neighbours?'

Ford was Julien's dog and any time Julien was out of town, the family at the farm down the road took care of him. He'd got him as a puppy seven years ago, a husky. He loved people, and when Julien had parties he was the centre of attention.

'If you have time, that would be great. You girls can shower at mine too. Might be more relaxing than a hotel shower. You know where to find the guest towels, right?' he asked.

'Yes.'

'And how to work the shower?'

'Yes.'

'Actually the shower in the guest bathroom doesn't get very warm, so use mine. I need to get someone out, but haven't had time yet. I have wine in the cellar so help yourselves but don't let other guests drink it all. It's from my personal collection and I don't want it all wasted.'

'Julien.'

'Oh, don't worry about putting the dishwasher on. I'll just do it in the morning. I've moved the cutlery to the second drawer on the left by the way, and if you could give Ford a treat so he doesn't feel left out, that would be amazing.'

'Julien?'

'Yeah?' He frowned and looked at Lucie.

'Quit stressing. I've got this. You've known me for years now. You know I do. You've put us in charge, so go to dinner and let us get everything sorted. Hush.'

'OK.' He exhaled and nodded.

He knew he was taking a risk by letting Faith into his home. She was never meant to be anything more than a co-worker, but Julien had been forced to push that idea aside the second he saw her; the moment she spoke to him he knew he was in trouble. It was too late now. The things he'd been trying not to face would have to be dealt with, whether tonight or in the months to come.

The team dinner set the tone for the rest of the night, and Julien was loosening up a considerable amount. He had yet to touch a drop of alcohol since he was driving, but he felt a buzz. The restaurant was bursting with as many people as the manager could cram in, which had resulted in extra tables being brought out of storage and put in the marquee on the side of the building.

There were front bumpers of old racing cars hanging from the ceiling and memorabilia plastered all over the walls, which gave it the feel of a teenager's bedroom, but this place was home. Everyone came here every year after the race, and the staff ran around like headless chickens trying to get everyone's next round of shots to them before they could even ask. They lived for it.

Julien had received a flurry of texts from Lucie who had been in the supermarket getting enough alcohol for more than a hundred drivers and support team members. She would ask if she should get one brand of beer or another, then if he took longer than ten seconds to respond she would text again to tell him she had got both. He could only imagine how heavy the shopping cart was, and he would bet all his money on Faith being the one stuck pushing it.

'So, guys,' Jasper began, 'how are we liking Faith?' He sat back and crossed his arms, studying them all.

'Love her,' one of the mechanics replied.

'Yeah, second that,' another agreed.

'Moretz?' Jasper looked him dead in the eye and Julien nearly choked on his steak.

'Yeah, she's great. A real asset to the team,' he said, hoping it came across much smoother than it had sounded in his head.

If he was being honest, Faith failing to deliver and Gabriel and Jasper sending her back to England and terminating her contract would solve all his problems. He'd never have to see her again. On second thoughts, she would still be all over social media and in Julien's head. So she might as well stick around for a while.

They were just finishing their main course when Lucie texted again and informed him that they had arrived. She had started setting up while Faith was in the shower, then Faith was going to lay out snacks while Lucie got ready. They were begging for a two-hour window to get it all done, which meant Julien was tasked with dragging dessert out for at *least* an hour. He would say it was an impossible task but with Brett and Gabriel talking so much it wasn't an issue. The impossible thing would be getting them to shut up long enough to guide them out of the restaurant.

'Oh my gosh, hi! Congratulations on the win, my darlings.' Bea waltzed in wearing a hot-pink satin dress and heels. A week ago, Julien would've thought she was an absolute knockout, but that was before Faith. Now he was blind to it.

'Hello, Beatrix!' Gabriel stood up to give her a hug and a kiss on each cheek. He was the only one who was good at pretending she was well liked.

The problem with Bea was that she was so good at her job, and when it counted she was professional and good with people. That was how so many got sucked in. Too many drivers hadn't seen the ugly side of her, but the guys in the bigger teams had.

'Can I steal your seat, Bretty?' she asked Brett, placing a hand on his shoulder gently. He threw Julien a look. They were sitting next to each other, which meant she was painfully desperate to ignore Julien's boundaries.

'I don't know who Bretty is, but, nah I'm gonna stay here. You can sit over there, though. In the empty seat.' He pointed across the table at the chair next to Marco's engineer.

She sulked as she sat down opposite them and crossed her arms, refusing to look at them. She couldn't look more childish if she tried. When Gabriel brought up Faith's latest video, Bea asked the waiter for a glass of champagne at an obnoxiously loud volume. She drowned out any talk of her friend and Gabriel stopped mid-sentence and tensed his jaw. This was going to get very awkward very fast if someone didn't start asking her questions about herself.

'So, Bea, you coming to Julien's tonight?' Marco asked, earning discreet glares from the entire table. Her presence was inevitable, but they'd all been hoping she would have other last-minute plans. What a ridiculous thought – Beatrix Miller always went wherever the drivers went.

'Of course. It's the party of the year; I wouldn't miss it for the world,' she gushed.

'What, Julien's parties are better than the ones the organization throws? That *I* plan?' Gabriel feigned hurt.

'You know I didn't mean it like that! Speaking of, where are you taking us this year, Gabriel?' she asked.

He winked. 'Ah, that's a secret. You'll find out right before we go.'

On the table Julien's phone buzzed and he caught Bea trying to catch a peek of whose name popped up. She raised an eyebrow.

It was Faith, asking him where the remote for his fancy lighting system was. He told her to check in his bedroom drawer and cringed. He was sure there were some Polaroids sitting in there. Perhaps he'd moved them. They were usually carried through the house with him when he was stuck in a downward spiral, but wherever they were, if Faith found them she was probably going to freak out.

Time ticked by at a painfully slow pace as they ate dessert. He hadn't received any further texts, which meant either Faith was interrogating Lucie about Julien's personal life or they were going about their evening and getting all dressed up. Something told him that they wouldn't be spending hours smothering their faces in make-up, unlike Bea. He was all for make-up and he thought contouring was an art form, but it was a little much at times. Faith adopted the natural look and he loved it. If she ever fully covered those freckles of hers, he'd be devastated.

'Is the coast clear yet? I want a beer.' Marco sighed. He'd cut Bea off mid-sentence and she was pouting again. Nobody wanted to hear about the date she'd been on with Garcia last month. Even Garcia probably didn't want to hear about it.

'They asked for two hours, so —' Julien checked his watch. 'I'd say it's safe to start driving back now.' For the love of God, could someone in this restaurant stand up and claim Bea as a passenger.

'After you.' Brett let him out.

'Cheers. You driving with Mars? I've got luggage on my front seat, suitcases in the back and helmets in the boot.' Julien listed off all the excuses he could think of to keep her out of his car. It worked; she didn't follow them out.

'Good save, mate. We racing?' The Aussie driver grinned mischievously.

'Follow the speed limits in built-up areas; other than that, we're racing,' Julien replied.

This was a piece of cake since he lived in the middle of nowhere. He could count on one hand the number of times he'd passed another car on the first half of his journey here. Once they got past a certain point, the road belonged to them.

'You're on.'

# 12

Faith perched on the edge of Julien's bed, afraid to crease the perfectly ironed duvet. Had he done that before he'd left for the hotel or had a cleaner come in while he was away? She felt like a bull in a china shop in here. The place barely looked lived in. The walls were all white, not a mark on them. No grease marks from fingerprints, no mud splatters from his gigantic dog running in from the back garden, no chips of paint missing in the skirting boards as a result of being too vigorous with the vacuum. She thought back to her flat in London and the lines of crayon from letting her neighbour's little boys run riot on babysitting nights and the huge dents in the carpet that had been left behind when she'd rearranged the furniture after Bea moved out.

Julien's home felt lonely and isolated, and it didn't help that his closest neighbours were a five-minute drive away. When Faith and Lucie had gone to pick up his dog from them, she had not been expecting a massive husky to come bounding right into the front seat of the car. Lucie had made the mistake of leaving the driver's side door open and hadn't had a chance to encourage him on to the back seat. He had taken an immediate liking to Faith, licking her nose enthusiastically and hauling his dinosaur-sized body half on to her lap and half in the footwell of Lucie's tiny rental car.

The alcohol was piled up and securely wedged on the

back seat. Crates of beer, vodka and high-end gin clinked into one another and between that, Ford panting and Lucie blasting Ariana Grande on the radio, Faith had been itching to get out.

Her wishes had been granted when they'd pulled up outside Julien's. It was dark now but the outside lights were on, illuminating everything in a warm glow. It looked magical. It was an old farmhouse but it had been modernized with large windows and a concreted driveway. There were trees surrounding the property and the land seemed to go on forever.

The inside was open-plan and absolutely flawless in design. There were large white oak beams above them, and wide archways connected the kitchen, dining and living area to the main entry hall. The staircase led to a mezzanine which held a bedroom, bathroom and guest bedroom. He had nailed it on the textures, with wooden floors, cream rugs and tan leather sofas and leafy green plants in ceramic pots. The coffee table appeared to be a slab of oak tree placed in the middle of the living space.

The kitchen was Faith's favourite part, though, and was one of the many areas that made the space great for entertaining. There was a spacious centre island, which the girls had covered with bottles of drink. It was lined with black metal industrial-style bar stools, and Faith knew she'd be sitting on one of those with a headache tomorrow.

Ford had barrelled up the stairs by her side and led her into Julien's room. The master bedroom had high ceilings and a fireplace, with French doors leading to a private balcony. She had been tempted to open them but was terrified she'd set off an alarm and the police would show up before they could work out how to switch it off. The balcony over-looked the swimming pool and the built-in hot tub. The house had been designed to provide Julien with a pictur-esque view of the adjacent woods beyond the fields and she could imagine him with horses.

'You seem kinda nervous, Jensen,' Lucie called through from the bathroom where she'd just got out of the shower and was doing her make-up.

'I am a bit. I just don't really drink other than the odd glass of wine. I guess I just worry that because addiction runs in my family, I'll end up going down the same path.' It was so much easier to talk to Lucie about this with a wall between them.

'Let yourself have fun tonight, but in the grand scheme of things don't worry! I've got you covered. And, hey, if you decide you want to be sober buddies tonight, we can totally do that. I don't mind at all, and we don't have to make a big deal about it.'

'Thanks, Luce.'

'Did you bring a swimsuit?' Lucie emerged from the en suite wrapped in her towel, hair dripping wet. Ford tugged at the end of her towel, begging for fuss.

'I didn't,' she replied.

'Neither did I. We'll leave the *Baywatch* remake to Bea.'

'Christ, I forgot she was coming.' Faith threw herself back on the bed, forgetting about how crisp the sheets were. Now they were going to have huge paw-sized dents in them, because Ford had jumped up and was chasing his tail.

Lucie laughed. 'If you stick with me, chances are she won't come anywhere near you.'

'If I know Bea as well as I think I do, she'll be wherever Jules is.' Faith could hear the bitterness in her own voice and she didn't like it.

'And I think Julien will be wherever you are.'

'Yeah, right.'

'You two are idiots.'

'What do you mean?' Faith sat up and brushed against Ford's side. He settled next to her and nudged her with his snout.

Lucie shrugged. 'I'm just saying, there's something there. Tension always reaches a climax at parties, and this is a party in his own home, so he'll be feeling waaaay more comfortable.'

Faith smoothed down her hair and patted Ford's head, getting up to join Lucie at the mirror. She wanted so desperately to confess to Lucie that they'd almost kissed, but she was still gauging how much she could trust her. After all, Lucie had no reason to be loyal to Faith yet.

'How about this? I'll make a move on Julien when you make a move on Brett,' she said, deadpan.

'What?!' Lucie stared at her in the reflection. 'Not happening.'

'Well, then.' Faith shrugged, hating that she was concealing the truth.

They connected Faith's phone to Julien's speaker system and selected a playlist while they got ready. It had a good mix of artists but they were counting on Brett having something more suitable. A party full of male racing drivers probably didn't want to listen to Doja Cat.

'Hello?' a deep voice called out. The music was so loud they hadn't heard any cars pull up, and if it wasn't for the echoes in the entryway the girls probably wouldn't have heard them arrive. Ford bolted out of the room to reunite with his owner.

They left the bedroom to lean over the railings and say their hellos. Faith could've sworn Julien inhaled sharply. She shouldn't be leaning over the way she was in this dress; she was exposed. A female voice singing about various body parts was not helping her feel any less indecent. Maybe it was the glass of wine she'd already devoured, but she didn't feel an urge to stand up straight.

'Everything's all laid out in the kitchen, hot tub is on, and look out the back!' Lucie pointed excitedly and they peered through the window overlooking the terrace.

'Ah, you went in the barn!' Julien called out.

'Sorry, we didn't know if we were supposed to, but Luce said the fairy lights must be in there and we couldn't resist,' Faith admitted.

'It looks great. Thanks, girls.'

They had gone out looking for the pool inflatables and had found a flamingo, a doughnut, a swan and a watermelon. The pool was big enough for all of them, so they blew them all up and threw them in. They'd got the rickety old ladder out and strung the fairy lights up, screaming when Lucie had lost her footing and almost gone into the pool fully clothed. That was *before* they'd started on the wine from the cellar.

'I'm ready when I've curled my hair, so you can go on down if you want. I'll be fifteen minutes tops. Pour me another one?' Lucie asked, passing her wine glass to Faith.

'All right, see you in a minute.'

Faith was carrying two glasses and an empty bottle

down, which meant she didn't have a spare hand to grip on to the banister. It would have been wise to put her heels on once she reached the last step, but when Julien appeared at the bottom, she was glad she had made a grand entrance.

'Let me take those.' He held his hand out and took everything effortlessly, offering her his arm too. 'You look incredible, Faith.'

She stopped walking. 'Thank you.' Her body tingled with anticipation from the heat in his eyes, and she became hyper aware of his hot breath on her neck. How could he turn her on so much just with words?

They were reminded of their company when Brett cheered at the sight of his favourite beer in the fridge. 'This place looks amazing.'

Julien was cool, calm and collected, leaving Faith to wonder what this might mean for them. 'Well, we had a lot to work with. You have a beautiful home, and an even more beautiful dog. I may have to steal him,' she said as Ford circled them, tail wagging.

'He likes you,' Julien commented.

'Yeah, I was getting that impression. The only time he's left me alone for even a minute is to come and see you.'

'He didn't follow you into the bathroom, did he?' Julien cast a weary glance at her.

'He did. Sat there good as gold the whole time I was in the shower, though. Only ducked his head under the water once.' Faith reached down to stroke Ford's fur, realizing too late that she was on display again. Julien averted his eyes quickly when she stood back up, swallowing nervously.

'I've been trying to get him to stop that. Drives me

fucking insane and it's inappropriate when I have guests.' Julien scratched behind the husky's ears fondly.

'Girls love dogs, though, Jules. If you introduce him to someone who doesn't love him even half as much as you do, she's not the one,' Marco chimed in and Julien looked uncomfortable.

Faith concealed a smirk. There was one girl she could think of who hated dogs, and she had been swiftly booted out of his personal life a few days ago.

'How was your first European supermarket trip?' Brett asked, helping himself from the bowl on the counter. How was he *still* eating?

'You know what, I think I'm actually getting the hang of foreign languages! We know the most French between us so we tried that, and the staff seemed to understand us.'

'Ah, the beauty of being in a country where one half speaks French and the other Dutch,' Julien laughed, and smacked Brett's hand away as he went for yet another handful of tortilla chips.

'I'm gonna go to the bathroom,' Brett said.

'You know where it is, right?'

'Yes, Julien. I have been here many times.' Brett rolled his eyes dramatically and wandered off in the direction of the stairs.

'Shall we remind him there's a bathroom down here?' Julien smirked.

'I think we all know why he's chosen to go upstairs.' Marco raised an eyebrow.

'Yep, and he'll head straight for the en suite instead of the guest bathroom,' Faith replied.

They stood in the kitchen laughing, the boys enjoying

their first sips of beer. Lucie had insisted that nothing would happen with her and Brett, but their friends weren't stupid. That meant that there was more pressure on Faith to act on her feelings for Julien. He was practically a stranger, and from what she could gather he wasn't a relationship kind of man. But despite the rational part of her brain deciding to take it slow, as she watched him, she wondered what it might be like to wake up here every morning and stand in this same spot drinking coffee from the Nespresso machine in the corner.

The party was in full swing now, music was blaring and drinks were flowing. Faith and Lucie were side by side, wine in hand, gratefully accepting compliments on their semi-matching dresses. Lucie wore a pale purple satin minidress and Faith had chosen a black one. They both had clear strappy heels on and had their hair in waves, except Lucie's reached her waist and Faith's was above her shoulders. The only thing they had intentionally matched was gold eye make-up.

When Lucie had finished getting ready, she'd sent a reluctant Brett downstairs with strict instructions to send Faith back up for photos. They had gone out on the balcony, and Brett and Marco had stood down below hyping them up. Julien stood quietly to one side, sipping his beer and pretending he wasn't looking. But she kept catching his gaze. Every so often, his attention would drift up to Faith. Faith hadn't felt this confident in years. Next to Lucie, she felt like an equal. That wasn't to say that her friend wasn't absolutely stunning, because she was, but she didn't have an ego the size of Jupiter like Bea was so often guilty of.

'I have arrived!' Gabriel strolled through the patio doors with a crate of beers and everyone cheered. He was grinning so widely that anyone would think this was a party in his honour.

'What took you so long?' Marco teased, looking like he already knew the answer.

'I drove Bea here with Jasper and a couple of others,' he said sourly. 'She had to run back to the hotel to change her dress.'

With that, Bea walked out in a black dress, identical to the one Faith was wearing. The group looked back and forth at them, stunned into silence. The thing was, Bea knew that Faith only owned a few dresses and that this one was her go-to for big events. They had gone shopping together and bought one each. Faith had a distinct memory of how she'd squeezed into hers, and her best friend managed to fit into one two sizes smaller and hadn't shut up about it for ages. Of course she would wear it tonight; this was her territory and she wanted to make sure Faith didn't get too comfortable. Faith was growing tired of feeling like she was still in school.

Jasper joined them, looking far more relaxed than he ever did at the track. The pressure was off, at least until they got back to the factory and started preparing for Le Mans. 'I think we should raise a toast.'

'I agree. Here's to the success of Revolution Racing, Marco, Brett and Julien, and of course to Lucie and Faith. Our sport wouldn't be the same without you all,' Gabriel said.

They raised their drinks and clinked them, smiles all round as more drivers arrived and greeted them. Bea firmly planted herself next to Brett, who was trying to edge closer to Lucie at every given opportunity.

Six shots of tequila in, and Faith was feeling the effects. She'd lost count of how many people were stood in the circle she was in. Everyone seemed to have gathered where the host was, and Faith was stood right next to him. Another driver shuffled into the circle and Faith moved aside, falling over her own feet and right into Julien. He put his arm out to steady her and she instinctively leaned into him. He didn't stop her; in fact, he kept his arm round her. The dynamics were shifting and she wasn't sure it was a good idea given the alcohol clouding her judgement. She was the kind of drunk who made regrettable decisions. She vowed to move on to water now.

'Uh, guys?' Lucie said. 'Have you two checked social media?'

'Us?' Faith asked with a frown. She went to her notifications.

Silence fell over them and her ears tuned out the rap music in the background. She broke away from Julien and showed him her screen. Right there on Bea's account was a perfectly filtered photo of Faith and Julien embracing with his lips against her cheek, with thousands of likes pouring in from adoring fans, gushing over their blossoming romance. Faith knew without a doubt that there was not going to be anything blossoming after this. Julien looked furious, and Faith's anger was bubbling under the surface too.

'For fuck's sake, Bea,' she muttered.

'I've got to take this.' Julien's phone lit up with a call and he tried to turn it away from her view but he was too late – she'd seen it. *Jasmine* in big white letters.

Whoever she was, Faith was under the impression that a totally innocent moment between friends was about to cause hell for Julien.

She had no idea where Julien had disappeared to but thought it best that she left him to it. This clearly wasn't her business, and in his mind she had probably done enough. Grabbing a glass of water from the refrigerator, ice cubes and all, her quiet moment of reflection was interrupted by the clatter of heels on the wooden floor. Bea helped herself to whisky from the drinks cabinet like she owned the place, even though everyone had been told it was off limits.

'Hey, can we talk? Not just about the photo, about us. I have a lot to say,' Bea said, pouring some into a glass. Just enough to take the edge off.

They headed up the stairs and Faith led the way into Julien's bedroom, settling on the king-size mattress. It wasn't until Bea sat next to her that it hit her. Bea had probably been here before, in this room. They would have had sex in this bed, and she really didn't want to think about that. Now or ever.

'Faith, I really didn't mean for that photo to get posted. I hit the wrong one by mistake, and then once it was up I kind of just figured it wouldn't be a big deal.' Bea was practically whimpering.

'But you have to go through so many different steps before you hit upload.' Faith studied her face for any sign of a lie.

There was a loud scoff from the doorway. They looked up to see Julien stood there, beer in hand. He must have followed them up. 'Did you really think we were gonna fall

142

for that, Bea?' Julien snapped. 'You wrote a caption to go with it. That was no accident and you know it.'

'I was meant to save it in my drafts, I swear!' Bea stood up in protest. 'I was in such a rush and you know how Instagram gets, Faith. It's temperamental and it's super easy to click the wrong button and then, whoosh, it's out there.' She looked from Faith to Julien with tears in her eyes.

'Why would you *ever* post that, though? You knew how people would respond.' Faith's voice was barely a whisper.

'Faith, I promise you I didn't mean to do it. I'll take it down right now.' She was giving her friend all her attention, turning her back on Julien.

Faith wanted to believe her and trust her, but she'd been told so many things in the past week that she didn't understand who Beatrix Miller was any more.

'Stop lying to everyone, Bea. You might think it's all a bit of fun but these are people's lives you're messing with. You need to learn to fix the damage you cause.' Julien stepped into the room and subtly gestured for her to go.

'Once again, I'm sorry.' She bit her lip and looked at Faith, then brushed past Julien and left. So much for their big friendship talk.

Swallowing the lump in her throat and taking a sip of water, Faith stared down at her hands and refused to make eye contact. He sat down next to her and rested his elbows on his knees.

'Jules?' she mumbled.

'Mmm?' he mumbled back.

'I'm sorry I seem to be causing so many problems for you.'

'What?' From the corner of her eye she saw his head turn.

'I'm –'

'No, no –' he interrupted. 'You have nothing to apologize for, absolutely nothing. If anyone should be sorry, it's me. I've treated you like crap since you got here and taken my frustration out on you. You deserve better than that, and I'm going to do better. Seriously, no more games from me.'

She didn't know how to respond so she just stared down at the cream rug under their feet.

'I'm gonna go for a walk,' he said.

'Are you sure that's wise? It's pitch black out there.' She looked through the balcony doors to the fields beyond the courtyard. There was nothing but darkness.

'I won't leave the property and the outdoor lights are bright enough for me to see by. I just really need to get out of here, away from the chaos, and clear my head for a minute.'

They stood up and made their way out of the room together, walking down the staircase and back into the party. People were in the kitchen getting drinks and Faith squeezed Julien's arm reassuringly as he departed, sneaking out via the side door. She spotted Lucie leaning against the breakfast bar and made a beeline for her, grateful for a friendly face.

'Everything OK?'

'I'm worried about Julien; he's taken himself off for a walk.'

'He does that a lot – don't stress about it. He'll come and join us again when he's ready.' She poured Faith another glass from their secret stash of white wine.

Although he had distanced himself again, she wasn't

144

so positive that he was distancing himself from *her*. If it had been about her, he wouldn't have sat down next to her and had that conversation. Would he? It was still progress, however you looked at it. As long as this didn't go against her and he didn't push her away for the billionth time. Faith wanted to know what he was thinking, how he was feeling, but they weren't there yet. With each day that passed, each issue that arose, maybe they never would be.

# 13

Julien was sat at the bottom of a field on an old tree trunk. He'd cut some of these trees down last year and it had left him with the perfect space to sit and watch Ford run around in the grass. Now it was nearly midnight on a Sunday in early May and he was watching his friends having the time of their lives, wishing he could just get his head straight and be part of it. He had started out the night relaxed, and although Faith had been on his mind it didn't feel like a burden for once. He had reached a point where he could just accept his feelings for what they were. Then the photo thing had happened and knocked him for six.

Jasmine calling him had reminded him of how much was at stake here; it wasn't just about him. It was about the people in his life who were entirely separate from the world of motorsport, and it was also about Faith. He couldn't drag her into his mess. She was oblivious to it all and had somehow not seen the Polaroids in his bedside drawer.

'You OK?' Lucie was walking through the grass towards him, holding on to her heels and a bottle of wine. She held it out to him and sat on the edge of the tree trunk.

'Could be better,' he admitted.

'That's why I brought this.' She gestured to the bottle in her hand.

She snuggled into him, providing them both with some warmth in the light breeze. Lucie had undoubtedly become one of Julien's closest friends and confidantes over the last few years, and she always knew what to say. He could rely on her to tell him whether he was overreacting to something, and he really needed that tonight.

'I can't look at her without falling apart, Lucie. It's eating me alive.' He sighed.

'Faith?' she asked.

'Yep.' He nodded. 'Everything is weighing on me; there's too much pressure on my shoulders. If it was as simple as acting on my feelings, I would. You know how complicated things are for me, why I don't do long-term. I'm at a complete loss with her. Every conversation we have, the more I want her.' He was gripping the bottle so hard his knuckles were white. Julien hated dealing with his emotions, and he'd been working on it for fourteen years without an awful lot of progress.

'I think you should just lay it all out on the table, but I'm not in your shoes and I never have been, so . . . I don't know, Jules. Maybe you should focus on keeping your distance.'

'I don't think I can.' He exhaled deeply and Lucie sat upright. 'I need to, though.'

'Do you? *Why* do you need to?' Lucie looked at him and he could see her frustration clearly for the first time. She was as fed up with Julien as he was with this whole moral dilemma. 'She's nothing like Bea or any of the other women you've been involved with. You can trust her.'

'I know.' He frowned. 'It would be a lot of easier if she was one of them, though, then I could write her off, but I tried telling myself she was no different and she keeps proving me wrong.'

'I'm just saying, Jules. You've only ever dated women who use you, and all this no-relationship rule has done for you is put your walls up even further than they were all those years ago.' Lucie rose from their makeshift bench and put her hands on her hips, looking back at the party.

'I really like her,' he mumbled.

'Oh, really? I thought we were having this conversation just because she has pretty eyes.' She pretended to be shocked.

'I'm a grown man with a crush.' He laughed pitifully. It was embarrassing to admit it out loud.

'We both know this is more than a crush.'

'Am I just going insane? Should I call my psychologist? It's been less than a week. What if it's just because she's got bright blue eyes and cute freckles?'

She raised an eyebrow. 'This doesn't happen to you, ever. It's been too long since you let someone in. I think it's time.'

'Maybe you're right.' He threw his head back and looked at the moon. On the other side of the world, where part of his heart belonged, the moon hadn't even risen yet.

'I'm going to go back now. You coming?' she asked.

'I'll be there in five.' He'd like to stay out here longer but it was reaching the time when everyone was about to be off their faces and things started getting wild. He couldn't miss out on that.

'One last pearl of wisdom for ya.' She shivered in the breeze and wrapped her arms round herself. 'You can't live two separate lives forever. At some point they've got to link up. Otherwise they'll come crashing together without you being able to control it.'

She promptly took the wine bottle back from him and

waved as she stalked off across the field. He hated it when Lucie Carolan gave him advice because she never steered him wrong.

Faith had a way about her that made Julien feel alive again, and Lucie was right; it was about more than the way she looked. It wasn't just her eyes that reminded him of his past – it was all of her. Her fiery temper when he was being an arrogant piece of work, how she called him out on his shit, the way she treated everyone as an equal. If he could dig deeper and find out what made her *Faith*, what made her similarities to his past less scary, maybe he could let her in.

Since Lucie had rejoined the party, she had already managed to encourage Faith to help her set up a game of beer pong outside. Faith hadn't played beer pong before, but Brett had taken it upon himself to explain it to her in thorough detail at a very high volume. He was loud without the help of beer, but he was on another level tonight.

Julien returned soon after and she felt a lot more at ease. He came over to stand with them but purposefully avoided standing too close to her. Once again, she didn't know how to act. Were they OK? He caught her eye and raised his drink to her. That didn't help.

On a mission for food and a get-out clause, Faith went into the house and hunted down the leftovers from hers and Lucie's takeout. She hopped up on to a bar stool and tucked in, attempting to be graceful but failing to keep her arms steady as a result of the alcohol coursing through her veins. She felt fuzzy.

'Enjoying that?' A voice she didn't recognize came from behind her. She spun round, fork in hand, and saw Lorenzo Garcia.

'Yep,' she mumbled through a mouthful of food. Not flattering in the slightest, but with any luck he would look past that.

'May I?' He gestured to her food.

Lorenzo was around five foot nine and his dark hair fell in front of his eyes. She hadn't heard him speak much English, and got the impression he wasn't fluent. Before she'd flown out here and met him, every time he spoke his native Italian it sent shivers down her spine. Then Julien had happened and the effect had worn off.

His aftershave was strong. As strong as Bea's perfume. Perhaps they had read the same advice on how much they should use to attract members of their preferred sex, but as Lorenzo got closer, Faith resisted the urge to let him know he needed to tone it down.

'Congratulations on coming second,' she said.

'Thank you. I must admit I am a sore loser.'

'Maybe you'll get 'em next time. Not that I'm suggesting I'd like to see that, obviously.'

'Hmm. Do you know what I'd like to see?' Lorenzo's eyes glistened and she didn't like his tone in the slightest.

'No, what?'

'You, me, skinny dipping.'

She choked. 'What?'

'Come on, Jensen! It'll be fun, give everyone a show.' He ran his thumb along her jaw and she tensed up. This was getting very uncomfortable very fast.

'I'm going to pass,' she said.

'Don't be boring, Faith. Loosen up.' He tucked a strand of hair behind her ear.

There were always rumours swirling that some drivers on the grid took advantage of their power, and Faith should have predicted that Lorenzo would be guilty of that. He was one of the few who was very active on social media, constantly flaunting his lavish lifestyle. He favoured wild parties and beautiful bikini-clad women hanging off his arm.

She gritted her teeth. 'I'm not interested.'

'We can go hand in hand if you like?'

'Get out.' A deep voice boomed behind them. Faith looked over Lorenzo's shoulder. Brett was there with a face like thunder, Lucie by his side and Julien coming up behind him.

'All right, all right. I'm going, no drama.' Lorenzo held his hands up in defence and brushed past both men roughly.

'What was that about?' Julien asked.

'Garcia being his usual charming self,' Brett replied, tracking his movement.

'Faith?' Julien's expression changed from confusion to concern.

'I'm fine. Thought he was one of the good guys; guess I was wrong.' She tried to laugh it off but she felt nauseous.

'Do you want to go upstairs for a bit? I can take you.' Lucie asked, coming over to stand near her and placing a reassuring hand on her arm. She was unsteady on her feet.

'Yeah. I think I need to lie down.'

'Luce, I think you need looking after too. You're a little bit tipsy. I'll take Faith up, get her some water,' Julien said. 'If you're all right with that?' he asked.

Faith nodded, maybe a little too enthusiastically. Lucie gently kissed the side of her head and wandered back over to Brett, who took her hand and led her back out to the pool area.

She sighed heavily while Julien got her a drink, and watched the ice cubes drop into the liquid with a splash. She could sense there was anger brewing under the surface but he kept his cool and spoke softly.

Placing his hand on the small of her back, he let her lead the way up the stairs and kept hold of her glass. So this was what he was like when he cared? She was a fan. Faith walked into his bedroom and he hesitated in the doorway.

'You can come in, Jules,' she said.

'Should I sit down?' He gestured to the bed, a red flush creeping up his neck.

'Oh my God, have you gone shy on me?' Faith teased. She had seen Julien lost for words numerous times – he wasn't much of a talker – but this? He looked like he wanted to bolt.

'No . . . I just don't want to overstep,' he mumbled.

'Is it considered overstepping if I specifically ask you to stay?' Faith stumbled over the word 'specifically' but continued, oblivious. 'I just want to lie down until I feel less tipsy. I don't really want to stare at the ceiling and get lost in my own thoughts,' she said.

They lay back on the bed and sank into the heavenly memory foam mattress. She didn't think she could get much better than her first brand-new mattress back in her London flat, but she was wrong. Is this what people with money did? Spend it all on finding their perfect mattress and bedding combination?

Julien's shirt rode up to reveal his abs and Faith's mouth watered. 'Jules?' she whispered.

'Yeah?' He didn't whisper back, just spoke in that low, seductive tone of his. He wasn't even trying to be seductive, but the wine was going straight between her legs.

'Do you fuck women in this house?'

'Never.'

That was all Faith had needed to know. She was well aware of Julien's reputation for casual flings.

'Will you fuck me now?' She draped her leg across his waist and sat up, straddling him on the bed. It was difficult in this dress, and the hem ended up rising and revealing her underwear. She'd opted for blue lace this time, and no bra.

'Faith. Don't do this to me,' he groaned, and put his hands on her hips.

'What am I doing to you, Julien?' she asked innocently, grinding against him slowly, the alcohol taking control. He let out a low growl and flipped her over so she was underneath him.

'Making me insanely hard. But as much as I want to, I can't fuck you yet. You're way drunker than me, and you've just had a run-in with Garcia. When I take you, I want us both to be stone-cold sober so we can remember every single second. It will be worth the wait, believe me.'

'It had bloody better be.' She sighed and he laughed, moving off her. 'So . . .' she said.

'So?'

'Does that mean you *are* going to sleep with me one day?'

'One day. Just not today. We're going to be super sensible about this.'

'Sensible is boring.'

'But necessary. Now will you behave yourself? I'm trying to focus.'

'Focus on what?'

'My big important question.'

'I'm all ears.' Faith readjusted her position and waited for him to speak.

'What's your favourite dog breed?'

'What?' She couldn't do anything to stop the snort that came out of her nose.

'Answer the question, Jensen. A person's favourite dog breed can reveal a lot about them.' He laughed. 'I think that giant monster of a dog out there tells you what mine is.'

'Mine's probably a husky too. I've never had a dog, though. Never had a pet actually.'

'Not even a hamster?'

'Would've died with Mum taking care of it.'

'Is there a reason you're not close with her?' He turned to lie on his side and face her.

The fact that he'd remembered her telling him this surprised her and she wasn't sure what to do with it. People rarely paid much attention when she spoke about little things like that, although it was probably because she was always so quick to change the subject.

'Mum didn't have her life together while I was growing up, so I sort of raised myself. Took care of my own food, got to and from school, cleaned. She took it to heart when I got out of there,' Faith bit her lip, unsure if she should've unleashed all that on him.

'Now I see why you're so quick to forgive Bea. You're used to being on your own, and she was the first person who made you feel like you belonged. Right?' he asked.

Faith gazed at him absent-mindedly for a moment and didn't respond. He might despise Bea, but he understood her perspective. 'Yeah.'

'Well, I think you should hash it out. Sit her down and tell her how you feel and where you stand on your friendship. She needs someone like you to sort her out.'

'You think so?'

'I do, and I never follow my own advice so it would be really great if someone else did.'

She laughed and rolled on to her side, face to face with him. His eyes were even easier to get lost in this close. They were the kind of icy blue that made people stop talking mid-sentence and they made Faith feel self-conscious about her own. When the light hit hers they were beautiful, like Julien had told her during that moment in the trailer, but nobody had ever got lost in them. Except him. The soft lighting gave him an ethereal glow and his blond hair brushed past his eyes ever so slightly. She resisted the urge to sweep a strand aside. His hand was resting on the duvet, in the empty space between their bodies. She wondered what it might be like to intertwine her fingers with his, to feel the lightest touch of his fingers on her skin.

Faith felt her eyes flutter closed. She didn't want to sleep, she just wanted to block out the light. Today had been exhausting and it was nearly two in the morning, but this was an event she couldn't miss. She'd be back out there with Lucie and the guys once she'd sobered up a little, and she'd be good as new.

She felt Julien exhale next to her and the mattress shifted with his movement. *Please don't leave*, she thought. She didn't have the energy to call out and stop him. Except Julien didn't go anywhere, and the next thing she knew he was playing with her hair. It was soothing. The only person who had ever played with her hair was Bea, and this didn't feel even remotely like that.

'I wish you hated me,' Julien murmured.

She froze but didn't open her eyes. If she opened them it would be game over and he'd stop talking. He needed to say it.

'I'm so scared to get close to you. I'm not good at this. I've done it once and it ended in heartbreak. I'm used to being alone but I don't want to be this way forever. My instinct is telling me to let you in, but I come with a lot of baggage. Some of it you could never understand. I don't want you to *have* to understand.'

He stopped talking and the room was eerily silent. She listened to the sound of him breathing. What baggage could Julien have that made this so difficult for him? Faith could handle baggage. She had plenty of her own.

'I wish I could stay away from you, but I don't think I have it in me to keep pushing you away. I know you're not going to do it yourself, because that's not who you are. I don't know what the right thing is here. I think . . . next time we have a moment we should embrace it. But I'm scared.'

Faith was struggling not to ruin his heartfelt speech with the revelation that she wasn't asleep. Her heart was beating so fast, he must be able to hear it. Somehow, despite his own fears, Julien had managed to make all her own disappear.

She was feeling brave. Not brave enough to say anything right now, but brave enough to do as he had said.

Embrace the moment. Faith and Julien were the kind of people who didn't let themselves enjoy anything or anyone too much, and she for one was tired of it. She wanted to feel something, to let genuine connections into her life. Julien deserved the same.

# 14

Faith felt like she'd been taken for a lap around the race circuit at full speed with no helmet. Her head was excruciatingly painful, and Julien's Egyptian cotton sheets were doing nothing except making her too hot. She kicked them off and a disgruntled Lucie stirred beside her. Thank goodness it was only Luce.

Last night had taken a turn once Faith had surfaced from her fake nap, and she had found herself recreating a musical number from *Mamma Mia!* on a balcony with Lucie and Bea. Yes, Bea. They had put the drama aside with the help of more wine, which Julien had eventually hidden from them. The girls had, of course, switched to gin in protest. Which did not seem like it had been a good idea at this moment in time.

Crawling out of bed, Faith hunted down some mouthwash and a hairbrush, attempting to feel human again before she faced the team downstairs. She looked at the mass of dark hair against the white sheets and debated waking Lucie up, but thought better of it. Hungover Lucie was not someone she wanted to experience before she had food and painkillers in her system.

The smell of bacon wafted up the stairs as she made her way down into the unknown territory of a post-party apocalypse. She could hear voices, which meant the boys were up and they were going to drag her to hell over the girls' antics.

'Morning, sunshine!' Brett yelled with sheer enthusiasm as she entered the kitchen.

Faith squinted in the direct sunlight coming from the floor-to-ceiling windows. Hadn't Julien considered black-out blinds?

Brett grinned. 'Smashing outfit, Jensen.'

She looked down and realized she had skipped the vital step of looking in the mirror. Nevertheless here she was, stood in the middle of Julien's kitchen in boxers and a T-shirt that drowned her. Who those items belonged to remained a mystery.

'Thanks,' she said wryly. 'God, why did I drink so much? I feel horrendous. I never let myself take it that far.'

'To be fair, it's hard not to at Moretz's parties. Told you they're wild.'

'Hey, it's not like you ran naked through the fields,' Julien said, referencing Casey Winters' behaviour in the early hours of the morning. 'You're fine, Faith. Nobody took any notice of you; they were all too drunk themselves.'

'Yeah, I guess.'

'You want something to eat?' Julien got up from his spot at the breakfast bar next to Marco, who was resting his head against the cool white marble surface, and took charge of the frying pan that Brett had abandoned on the stove.

'Have you got mushrooms? I fancy mushrooms on toast,' she said. That was her comfort food when she was feeling under the weather. Plenty of grease equalled a perfect hangover cure.

'You're in luck.' He pulled two cartons of chestnut mushrooms out of the fridge. 'Anderson? De Luca?' he asked, receiving an enthusiastic nod from Brett, whose appetite was unmatched, and a grunt from Marco.

'You'll be pleased to know we have footage of you and the girls performing that ABBA song. I was gonna post it, but Gabriel told me to play nice.' Brett grinned.

'You'd better be on your best behaviour, Anderson,' Lucie's voice croaked from the doorway, and she scowled in the harsh sunlight. Brett passed her his sunglasses.

'You guys looked great! So glad we found the feather boas in the garage; they really completed the look,' Julien said, laughing, popping the bread in the toaster and chopping the mushrooms.

Faith smacked him lightly on the arm. 'Keep quiet and stick to frying those mushrooms.'

She vaguely remembered how the idea had come about. Julien and the girls had been rummaging in the garage for the air pump for one of the pool inflatables when they had discovered a box partially hidden under a blanket. Faith had spotted a neon-pink feather sticking out of the top and lunged for it, revealing a mass of feather boas in various colours. Nobody had questioned why he had such items sitting in his garage. Instead, all three girls had looked at each other, eyes wide with the realization of what they absolutely must do.

They had pounded up the stairs, high heels flung in the general direction of the front doormat, and run straight on to Julien's balcony. It was as though everyone by the pool had worked out what was going on from their giggles and squeals, because a crowd had already gathered and Brett was waiting for his instructions of which song to play.

Faith cringed at the thought of her bosses witnessing

such unprofessional behaviour, but then she remembered her friends' stories of previous parties and thought that last night had probably been relatively tame in comparison.

As Lucie hopped up on to the counter next to Brett and dangled her legs in the air, a horrific memory popped up. Had Faith kissed someone last night? Her brain was foggy, but she was sure it had happened out by the pool.

'You look like you've seen a ghost,' Lucie said.

'Did I kiss someone?' Faith asked, looking at Julien to gauge his reaction. There was a splutter of laughter, which meant if she was right then it wasn't him.

'Oh! Yeah, that was me! We won a game of beer pong and celebrated. Sorry, I think I might've initiated it.' Lucie grimaced.

'No, it's OK! I'm just glad it was only you.'

'*Only* me?' She feigned hurt.

'Could've been worse.' Marco came to life all of a sudden. 'You could've kissed Gabriel.'

Faith couldn't resist letting out a snort, a common occurrence now that she was comfortable around them, which triggered Julien to do the exact same thing. Judging by the looks on their friends' faces, that wasn't normal for him.

She sidled up next to him and peered over the frying pan. The oil hissed and spat at her, making her hand sting.

'You good?' Julien looked down at her and she smiled up at him, crinkling her nose when he smiled back.

He looked cute this morning. His hair was ruffled and he wore a creased white T-shirt that clung to his biceps. He must own a lot of white tops because aside from one black one and his racing suit, that was all she'd seen him in this week.

'Are they cooked yet?' she asked him.

'Try one.' Julien reached into the cutlery drawer for a fork and stabbed a piece of mushroom, holding it out to her.

'Mm-hmm, they're good to go,' she replied and turned round to grab a plate for the toast.

Marco, Brett and Lucie were all gawking at them like they were from another planet.

Julien scowled. 'What?'

'Nothing mate, nothing at all,' Brett said.

Except Faith knew what it was, because inside her head she was having the same reaction. Julien and Faith were flirting. Very mildly, but you couldn't call it anything else. Not when they'd gone from zero to one hundred overnight.

Jasper had kindly sent them a car to pick them up from Julien's shortly after lunch, giving them time to recover and freshen up. They needed to get back to the hotel and get their suitcases, and then it would be time to drive to the airport and go their separate ways across the globe. Lucie was going back to LA, Marco to Italy, Brett to Australia and Julien to who knows where. Faith assumed he'd be staying at home in Malmedy, but he had a flight booked later that night. She didn't question him.

They had received a text from Gabriel stating that he wanted a quick meeting with Revolution Racing at the hotel's bar, including the mechanics and engineers. They had groaned at the thought of being in the general vicinity of alcohol so soon, but it was a necessity apparently. Gabriel told them it would be informal and last less than five minutes, which was just as well because none of them were in a state to absorb important information. They weren't even convinced poor Marco had the ability to board his flight in time.

At the hotel Faith was saying a sad goodbye to her hotel room. She hoped she would be returning next year, but if not then she would just have to miss it forever and get used to her flat's terrible water pressure again. She dragged her suitcase out into the corridor with an almighty struggle, hauling it over the threshold and promptly bashing it into Julien's.

'Sorry!' she cried out.

He laughed. 'It's cool – these corridors are narrow, huh?'

Neither of them addressed the fact that the only reason they had collided was because she had got her case caught on the door strip and yanked it free with so much force that she'd hauled it into the air.

'We are taking the lift, yes?' Faith raised an eyebrow. Julien had a bag not a case, which made taking the stairs easier for him than her.

'We are. Here, give me that.' He took the handle from her and dragged her case behind him as he headed to the other end of their floor. 'Jesus, what have you got in here?'

'I'd never left the UK, so I had no idea what the weather was going to be like! The internet is a confusing place,' she replied.

Stood in a small metal box eight floors up, Faith realized that this was the first time they'd been alone since last night in his room. As the doors shut in front of them, she didn't dare confess to hearing every word he'd said while her eyes had been closed. Silence fell over them once again, and she could feel the tension.

'Fuck this.' Julien threw his bag down, slamming his

fist into the panel next to the lift door. The lift came to a sudden stop and he backed her into the corner. 'We've been depriving ourselves all week. I don't want to do it any more. I'm tired of fighting it.'

'Aren't there cameras?'

'The staff in this hotel have seen much worse than this, Faith,' he murmured, his head resting against hers. He looked like he was still contemplating his next move.

'We don't have to,' she whispered as his mouth hovered above hers. They both knew where this was going; it was inevitable. As he pulled back to gaze down at her, it was like Julien was all Faith could see. All she wanted to see. She didn't want to think about consequences or boundaries or all the reasons they shouldn't.

'Yes, we do.' And, with that, he closed the gap and the second his lips came crashing down on hers that invisible line they had drawn was erased.

His hands were in her hair, tugging her closer. He pulled on her bottom lip, causing her to moan, and she melted into him, the wall of the lift supporting her. It was stone cold against her back, but the discomfort faded the more he teased her.

Faith had never been kissed like this. Never felt this kind of passion for another person. This was like they were on another planet and the outside world couldn't get to them. Like they weren't themselves. They were untouchable.

Julien's hands were roaming her body, following every curve and caressing every inch. He was appreciating her in a way that made her feel special. In a way that made her feel seen. No, she wasn't comparable to the women he'd been with before, but if her freckles and her eyes made her so hard to resist that day in the trailer, she could only imagine the way his body would respond to hers.

He gripped her thigh, hiking her leg up round his waist as her sundress rode up and revealed her tanned skin. Her own hands wrapped round his shoulders, one hand finding the back of his neck and pulling him in even closer.

When his hips pushed into her, she became painfully aware that things were at risk of escalating beyond either of their control. Faith needed him in a way that she hadn't needed anyone, ever. She hadn't been with many people, but the ones she had couldn't even come close. Except it wasn't her body that was reacting to him so strongly; it was her heart. Now that she had him in her grasp she didn't want to let go.

'Faith.' Julien moaned into her, causing a wave of pleasure. 'Faith.' In the next breath, his hands were on her face and he was pushing her away. He rested his forehead against hers, struggling to steady his breathing.

'Are you OK?' She ran her hand through his hair, both of them in a daze. Just like that, reality shattered the moment.

'Shit! We can't do this. I'm sorry, Faith. I want to, you have no idea how much I want you and I know you do too, but this isn't the time or place.' He had one hand round her waist, drawing circles over the cotton of her dress. She shivered and he stopped. 'We have a meeting to get to, and we have flights to catch.'

Faith felt tears threatening to form and detached herself from him, shrinking back out of embarrassment. 'I'm sorry.'

'Why are you sorry? We just need to use our heads. Because the next time I kiss you, I don't want to have to stop.' He slammed the button for the ground floor, sending the lift into action.

All of the obstacles were still there and they weren't going away. It was up to Faith and Julien to be adults and figure out how they were going to go about this. They needed to set boundaries of their own, determine what each of them wanted out of this. Faith knew she was at risk of getting hurt. They both were. But maybe it was worth the risk.

He reached out his arm and squeezed her hand in his, giving her a knowing look. If that kiss had done anything, it had confirmed that they weren't crazy. There was a spark. She and Julien could never be just friends. Just co-workers. There was always going to be something more, whether it was explored or not.

'Ah! There you are. Our guest of honour.' Jasper was waiting outside the lift for them and ushered them out excitedly. Could he tell? Would *everyone* be able to tell? She'd smoothed her hair down but she feared her face or their body language would give them away.

'Who's the guest of honour? Me or Jules?' she asked.

'It's you,' Julien whispered beside her.

'Yes, come on! Everyone's waiting in the bar.'

Faith checked the time. Nope, she wasn't late. She was more than ten minutes early, so why was the rest of the team already here? Julien abandoned their bags in the lobby and gestured for her to follow them with a grin on his face.

They walked into the bar and Gabriel leaped out of his seat and clapped his hands together. Julien rushed to sit down with the boys, and Faith saw Lucie sat up front looking smug.

'We would like to officially welcome you to the IEC and Revolution Racing as our full-time social media manager. You've gone above and beyond this week and as a result we've gained thirty thousand followers across all platforms, which to be honest has blown our minds, and you've passed your probationary period with flying colours. We would be over the moon to have you as a permanent part of the team,' Gabriel gushed.

Faith truly felt like she deserved this. She had grown up alone, clinging to the belief that there was more out there for her. For twenty-six years she had waited to know what it felt like to have a family, to have a shot at seeing the world she'd grown up learning about, and to turn it all into a job she loved. One out-of-the-blue phone call had given her everything.

'You're definitely stuck with me.' She smiled at Gabriel and then looked over at the team, the people who had swiftly become firm friends. Brett led a round of applause and Lucie rushed to wrap her up in a warm hug. These were her people.

The team trekked out of the hotel in a blur of suitcases and were piling into the cars provided for them. A long line of SUVs was parked on the side of the road, chauffeurs patiently waiting. It was a bit like trying to organize a school trip, right down to people shouting excitedly to their friends who were stood too far away. Brett and his engineer were guilty of that.

'Are we going in the same car?' Lucie asked Faith and the guys.

'I'm actually heading off with Joel and Will. We're all on

the same flight,' Marco replied. With his giant rucksack he really did look like he was on a school trip and not a successful race car driver.

'Take care, Mars,' Lucie said, and the curly-haired Italian driver went round the group, giving everyone a hug goodbye.

Faith waved as he disappeared. 'Bye, Marco!'

Julien took it upon himself to slot everyone's luggage into the back of the car and excuse the chauffeur from his duties. If he had it his way, Julien would be driving too. Perhaps Faith had been wrong for judging him when he let the staff get his bags when he'd first arrived here. She had been wrong about a lot of things with him.

The girls squashed up next to each other in the back seat and tuned out the guys' conversation about football. The car departed the hotel and as they drove through Francorchamps Faith was already feeling nostalgic. She wished she'd had more time to explore and vowed to travel here on her own terms soon. She wanted to visit the casino in Spa, take the lift up the hillside to the wellness spa, go to the village of Coo and see the waterfalls.

The problem was, she didn't want to do it alone. She didn't want to do anything alone now. She hoped the friends she made here were the kind of friends she could experience life with, and she was worried that they would lose touch over the next six weeks and she would come back and feel like a stranger. Starting afresh every time.

At Brussels airport, everyone hopped out and Julien took charge of their luggage again. It was great not having to struggle, but Faith felt like she should have trained in preparation for her arrival back in London. Getting it here in the first place had been hard enough and now she had more in there, like hats and T-shirts and model cars for her neighbour's kids.

'I'm really gonna miss you, Luce,' she said sadly. They were walking from the drop-off zone, towards the terminal.

'Wait!' Lucie stopped abruptly and dropped her bag on to the pavement in front of them. Julien and Brett, who had been walking closely behind, bumped into her.

'Bloody hell, Luce!' Brett cried out.

'Call me crazy, but what if I came back to London with you?' Lucie asked.

'Yes! Please come. You can take Bea's old room.' Faith didn't even hesitate. She might as well kick things off with some spontaneity.

'OK, I need to change my flight. Do you think they'll have any seats left?' Lucie was getting more and more animated as the reality of their adventure set in.

'I'm glad you two are gonna stay attached at the hip but I've gotta love you and leave you. There's a plane to Sydney calling my name.' Brett sighed.

The Aussie giant gave them all bear hugs and lingered on Lucie. Not wanting to intrude on their moment, and that was exactly what it was even if they denied it, Faith stepped away and turned to face Julien.

'You all right?' she asked, noticing that he seemed deflated. It could be the adrenaline of the weekend leaving his system, but he'd been upbeat until now.

'I'll be honest, no. I don't like goodbyes.' He shuffled his feet awkwardly. He was adorably shy all of a sudden.

'Me neither. But it's not goodbye forever. I'll see you in six weeks and at every race after that. You're stuck with me.' She looked down at their shoes. Her tiny little white trainers versus his big leather boots.

'Come here,' he mumbled and pulled her towards him. This was the first time they had shared a hug without the excuse of Revolution getting a podium, and she wished she could stand here at the side of the road forever.

'I'm glad you're talking to me now.'

'I'm glad I got over myself,' he replied.

Faith wished they had more time to get to know each other now that they were on good terms, now there was something brewing. She wanted to ask him where they stood. Would they exchange texts? Share phone calls and update each other on what they were doing with their time off? Or was this hug the last encounter they would have until they met in France?

She feared that applying even slight pressure would send him running back to the old Julien and undo all their progress. Unfortunately that fear also meant she wouldn't have the courage to contact him first unless it was regarding work. She still had to bug him for photo and video content in his downtime.

'We should get moving if we're going to get my ticket sorted in time,' Lucie called over.

Julien cleared his throat and she stepped backwards. His hands returned to the comfort of his jean pockets and a cloud of tension drifted over them.

'That's my cue,' Faith said.

'I guess it is,' Julien replied, his expression unreadable behind his sunglasses.

She picked up her bags and smiled, giving Lucie the signal that she was ready.

'Hey, Faith?' Julien said.

'Yeah?' She turned and looked at him.

'When we see each other again, I'd like to take you for a drive. Would you be up for it?'

She could see Lucie practically bursting at the seams a few feet away, and she was trying not to have the same reaction.

'I'd love that.' Faith smiled at him, feeling heat rising in her cheeks and her mind raced with thoughts of where this could lead. She tried to squash the thought of her and Julien alone, and just how dangerous that could be for them both.

Lucie hurried them along. 'You guys are cute and all, but we have places to be and exciting things to organize.'

'Good luck with this one in London, Jensen. She's an absolute terror when she's impatient,' Julien said, laughing.

'Bye, Jules. See you soon,' Lucie yelled out behind them as they walked away and she gripped on to Faith's arm excitedly.

Faith swatted her friend's hand away and shushed her. 'Play it cool, Luce. I can feel his eyes on us.'

'Oh yeah, I bet his eyes are on *us*. They're on your *ass*.' She let out a slightly manic laugh. 'Also, *what*? Play it cool? Faith Jensen, you have a date with that man.'

'I do not!' she protested.

'I've known him for years and he's never taken me for a drive anywhere other than a supermarket. There is nothing romantic about buying bread. This is a date.'

'It's definitely not a date. I will be sitting in the passenger seat very innocently.'

'Yeah, until he puts his hand on your thigh just a little

too high up to be considered friendly. Good luck with the innocence then.'

Faith tutted, her face turning scarlet. 'Lucie! For heaven's sake.'

'The only girl capable of remaining innocent in a car with Moretz is me, and that is because I'm immune to his charm.'

'Oh, right, so it's got absolutely nothing to do with you fancying his Australian teammate instead?'

'I do not!' Her face faltered. 'I'll shut up.'

Faith stood to one side while Lucie changed her flight, and observed the sea of irritable passengers. People were arguing, kids were screaming, and young couples were crying as they wished each other farewell. Faith, however, was in a state of bliss. The invitation Julien had extended to her, date or not, was the cherry on top of an already perfect week.

With Lucie's plane ticket to London secured and adrenaline coursing through them, the countdown to Le Mans began before they'd even got back to the UK.

# 15

The coffee shop Faith had once frequented with Bea was a lot quieter than she'd seen it before. She silently thanked the universe that they were the only customers in there at ten o'clock on a sunny Wednesday morning, because Lucie was gushing over literally everything her eyes landed on. Other than fly-in visits to Silverstone, Lucie had never explored the UK, so now she got to be both tourist and inhabitant while she stayed with Faith. Her excitement never ended.

If it wasn't the cherry blossoms lining the street outside, or the miniature dachshund passing by the window, it was the teacups they were given by the handsome posh British waiter with great dress sense. That was Lucie's description of him anyway. To Faith, he was just a plain old Brit.

They had been here for less than twenty-four hours and already done a walking tour of Faith's neighbourhood, had dinner with Amina next door and tried three brands of tea. Yorkshire Tea was Lucie's favourite apparently. It was tiring, but Faith wasn't about to kill Lucie's vibe for the sake of sleep. She was used to a busy schedule; she just needed to get used to one with travelling on top.

'Did you know most of our social media staff are fresh out of university or sometimes high school if we've spotted them online? We scoop them up straight out of education and train them on the job,' Lucie remarked. 'The younger you are, the more up to date with trends you're likely to be, but, hey, that's not always true. Besides, we have the wisdom to go with it too.'

'Luce, you're really not helping me feel less old. "Wisdom" is a word you use for old men called Cyril who have been through wars and lost the loves of their lives twice over. Do I look like an old man?' Faith raised an eyebrow.

'No, but you are starting to sound just as bitter. Oooh, we need a night out! Know any good clubs around here?' Lucie bounced in her seat. This was going to call for a trip to Oxford Street for new outfits, she could see it now.

'You're in luck. Bea and I were frequent visitors when she lived here.'

'Do you think we'll make any new British friends in the clubs? Hey, maybe we could get some of the British drivers out! There's a few Londoners, I think.'

Faith laughed. 'You're really not used to your own company, are you?'

'Nope.' Lucie shook her head. 'I grew up one of six, big Italian family, and I'm always travelling with someone else. Usually Brett, but I've replaced him with you this time. Alone time is just not a thing in my life any more, and I've fully embraced that.'

'Sounds like heaven to me. Even after this first week I can't imagine sitting in my flat alone any more. No amount of reality TV is a match for the company you guys provide.'

'Yeah, you're absolutely stuck now. I go where you go, like a puppy. Oh my God, like that one outside!' Lucie pointed behind her to a tiny English bulldog waddling along the pavement.

Faith laughed fondly, grateful that she no longer felt quite so lost and isolated in a big bustling city. Seeing London from a tourist's perspective again almost made her want to keep the lease on her flat, but plans for upcoming trips were being made in the group chat after just one day apart and she couldn't let the opportunities slide. A few days in Nashville to visit country bars and the Grand Ole Opry sounded very appealing.

They had come home to a postcard from Faith's mum and as she filled Lucie in on the drama, of how her mum would send these postcards under the facade of travelling, Faith felt a pang of sympathy for Andrea. The resentment she had felt not even two weeks ago had been replaced by this alien concept of wishing she could pluck her mum out of her dingy caravan in Cornwall and take her around the world with her.

'I've got to say, I'm impressed at the little empire you've built for yourself,' Lucie mumbled through her cake. 'Elegant' was not a word that suited her, which was becoming increasingly obvious the more time they spent together.

'Thank you. I'm actually quite impressed myself, looking back. I didn't think it would lead me *exactly* where I wanted to be. I just figured it would get me somewhere equally as good.'

'And yet here we are.' Lucie smiled.

Faith grimaced. 'Running on minimal sleep.'

'It might kill you initially, but it's worth it.'

'I'll power through.' Faith took a sip of tea.

'I can't even express how happy I am that Gabriel hired you. I was pretty much the only woman when I started, then other women came in as engineers and even drivers, but they were either more junior or senior to me and I felt like I had to maintain being professional rather than being friends. Of course, eventually Bea came along but we were vastly different so we never bonded. I mean, you and I are different, but Bea is – how do I say it politely? – from another planet.'

'I don't know precisely when she was abducted, but I'm sorry I didn't do more to stop it.'

'That girl scared me off dating in the industry. It's not just how complicated things can get; it's also the fact that I always felt like I was competing with her. You can't deny she's a goddess and heads turn for her, and I am by no means saying that I'm not confident within myself, but it's the snarky attitude that comes with it. My cheeks don't ever even flush until Bea sticks her nose in directly in front of someone I'm attempting to flirt with.'

'Why do you think I'm still single? Any time a guy even got close to me, regardless of whether she was acting as my wing woman or not, the attention was diverted to her.' Faith thought back to all the men who had been mid-conversation with her and then asked if the 'brunette with the gold hoops' was single.

'At least we have glowing personalities to go with our looks. Plus, you've already pulled Julien Moretz and it's only week one.'

Faith frowned. 'I have not pull–'

'Shut up! Embrace it. Embrace *him*. Oh, wait, you already did that at the airport.'

'You're a pain in the ass, Carolan. I told you: I want to be professional.' She hated this little lie, but she also wanted to keep Julien to herself for the moment. She didn't know what it could be, and she didn't want people to know that she'd broken her number-one rule – don't date where you work.

'You don't say "arse"?'

'Just because I'm British doesn't mean I'm posh. We don't all speak like the king.'

'Well, no, but you are quite well spoken. Anyway, back to Bea, you should know the history with her and Jules.'

'You mean why he hates her so much? Please, enlighten me. He literally curls his lip up in disgust when he sees her.' Faith grimaced once again at the thought of Julien and Bea ever having been entangled. What if she slept with him and then found out he'd never stopped sleeping with Bea? It was just another obstacle, another reason they shouldn't go there.

'And then when he sees you he goes all soft and gooey . . .'

Lucie's teasing was greeted with a napkin being thrown across the table.

'You're skating on thin ice.'

'I promise I'll be quiet for the rest of this trip. However, once we get to France, my silence will be lifted. *So* Julien and Bea never really openly flirted or made it obvious; it was all kept under wraps until she opened her mouth at a party.'

'I bet he loved that.'

'It gets better. She started telling everyone that they were dating, and he pulled her aside in front of everyone and told her she knew that wasn't the situation, as he had made clear a number of times. She flipped her *shit*.'

'This was a couple of months ago, wasn't it? Right after their Monaco trip.'

'Yeah, and notice how he isn't in any of the photos? He'd sue her ass, that's why. Besides, that trip was a work trip with, like, six other people. I know they've been away together before, but there's always been someone else tagging along. He has also bought her things, but Jules is just that kind of guy. He doesn't spend much money on himself, so he spends it on other people.'

'You said she flipped out. What did she do?'

'She tried her damn hardest to paint Julien as this toxic, condescending bad guy and worked her usual magic to turn everyone against him. It semi-worked on a few people, but it didn't last because she kept losing track of her lies.'

'I should've known she'd turn out like this. When I first came to London, she was so good to me. Then our social media presence started to grow and before long she was constantly begging to post selfies; she'd tweet about all these fun things we were doing, which we actually *didn't* do, and she stopped caring about the emotional aspects of our friendship. She was chasing followers and chasing fame.'

'From what you've said, it seems like she got lost somewhere along the way. Maybe you could give her a little nudge,' Lucie suggested.

Faith stared into space for a few moments, trying to figure out exactly how she felt about it all. It might be an almighty strong tug to get Bea back down to earth, but it could be worth it – she could get her friend back.

Julien had arrived at his destination in the middle of a torrential downpour. He could see the rain pelting the ground from his spot at the baggage claim and regretted his decision to show up here in a T-shirt and leather jacket. At least hungover Julien had failed to muster the energy to put product in his hair. The luggage belt was taking its sweet time and he was getting impatient. Sometimes everything in his life felt like a race. Getting in and out of airports was up there with one of the more stressful ones, but it was part of the job. Except this occasion wasn't.

Locating his rental car was one hell of an experience. The lady at the desk recognized him and welcomed him warmly. Not because of his profession, because he was sure she was totally oblivious, but because he came here multiple times a year and had built up a rapport with staff at various establishments across the island. He had opted for the usual: a red jeep. The aim was to blend in and feel like he belonged, which should be easy considering everything that was waiting for him here, and yet he still felt like an alien who had landed here by mistake each time.

The steering wheel of the jeep was the only thing that felt both familiar *and* comfortable, a combination he wasn't used to these days. The car was old and it meant he had to sacrifice Bluetooth, so when he got an incoming call he had to scramble to answer his phone and put it on speaker on the seat next to him. It might fly off if he was lucky. He hated answering calls when he was here.

'Hello?' he yelled towards the passenger side.

'Julien!' Gabriel's voice boomed and almost frightened the life out of him. In retrospect, it was just as well he hadn't been able to connect to the car's audio system.

'Hi, Gabriel. What can I do for you?'

'Where are you off to? You're very muffled.'

'I'm away.' Julien sighed. Quite frankly it was nobody's business where he was in his free time, but Gabriel was one of the few people who knew all there was to know about Julien's life. But he had to; he was part of how Julien managed to keep everything secret.

'Oh, of course you are! You're not in the middle of anything, are you? I just called to update you on Faith's position in the team and what it means for you.'

'No, I'm alone.' Julien sighed. This traffic was infuriating.

'Now, I know we've had this conversation a few times but now you're in the States . . . I just want to reassure you again that what you get up to in your downtime is not going to be made public.' Gabriel's voice had thankfully lowered a few octaves.

'Thank you, Gabriel. I appreciate that.'

They said their goodbyes after Gabriel promised to leave him alone for the course of his trip unless there was an emergency, and Julien was left in a suddenly claustrophobic environment. He stopped at a set of traffic lights and it felt like everything was closing in on him.

Winding the window down and letting the rain spit on to his arm and the black plastic of the jeep's driver side door, he looked to his left. There was a blonde woman in her mid-twenties sitting in the passenger seat of the car next to his. She looked over at him and smiled, and he returned it half-heartedly. He was trying desperately to see something familiar in her eyes, but he was met with nothing.

He had done this with every woman he had passed at the airport, but he knew, just as he had the very first time he had come face to face with her, that Faith Jensen had a light in her eyes that made him feel alive again. He wished she didn't. He wished nobody did, because it terrified him. He never imagined he would feel this kind of connection to someone again and until he had met Faith outside the hotel in Belgium, he hadn't actually *wanted* to. He still wasn't convinced he wanted to, but it was too late.

One thing Julien was certain of was that he couldn't have his mind on Faith today. Every year on this date he let his past consume him. This day didn't belong to her; it didn't belong to anyone or anything except a past he couldn't bring back.

# 16

Packing was near impossible when they didn't know where they were going after Le Mans. All they had been told was that they would be leaving Europe and they needed swimwear. That didn't cut it for Faith, Lucie *or* Bea, and the three of them had banded together to ask everyone they could think of. It hadn't taken long to determine that Brett had an inkling based on something he'd overheard in the hospitality tent, but he wouldn't budge purely because he loved seeing Faith and Lucie get so wound up on FaceTime.

Lucie's excessive amount of Oxford Street purchases and tacky tourist finds had fallen victim to a temper tantrum as she threw herself across her suitcase in a desperate attempt to close it. It would be safe to say that they were one angry screech away from panic buying another case each and begging someone in the organization to contact the airline and up the team's luggage allowance. Brett was having a similar issue with his outrageous collection of trainers, although the girls weren't sure why he needed to take six different pairs of Nikes.

'Zip it! Go, go, go!' Lucie yelled and Faith went running on cue, yanking the metal zip while her friend's petite frame crushed the contents.

'Success! Mine next, please.' Faith gestured to the living room where her trusty new raspberry-red suitcase was waiting.

'How have you managed to keep everything so neatly folded?' Lucie scrunched her nose up at the perfectly organized clothes.

Faith shrugged. 'I made a spreadsheet with everything I needed, and I keep photos of all my possible outfit combinations in an album on my phone. I used to do it for content shoots.'

'That is absolutely genius.'

'I thought so too. The heels were the only thing I struggled to get in, so they're sort of shoved in the corners.' Her nonchalance received a bitter glare from Lucie, who had put her own heels in Faith's carry-on as a last resort.

'You've got the team rain jacket?' she asked.

'It's underneath everything.' Faith lifted up a pile of jeans to show her. She had been warned that although it was currently quite warm in France, it had been known to rain heavily in previous years. The weather in Le Mans was wildly unpredictable.

After they had wheeled their cases out into the hallway and planned their airport outfits, which matched despite Faith's protests, they fell on to the sofa. Faith was going to miss this sofa. It was green velvet and it had been hers and Bea's pride and joy – they'd saved up for ages. Wherever she settled, if she ever did, a replica was essential. Her mum had one just like it in the caravan in Cornwall and it had provided Faith with a lot of comfort when she was growing up, as she dived deep into fictional worlds or watched reruns of old American sitcoms. A green-velvet sofa was a subtle way of paying homage to the inner child she was still nurturing.

The girls had decided that after these next two work

trips they were going to explore the British coastline, which meant going back to Cornwall and trying to replace the negative attachments to her home county.

Whether she took the opportunity to visit her mum or not was a decision she didn't think she could make until she was minutes away from the patch of grassland where Andrea resided. They had started out in an actual caravan park, but moved when Old Al had offered up a section of his farm for a cheaper fee. Faith still wasn't sure why Andrea had put all her money on a heap of plastic rather than a slightly bigger, better-insulated heap of bricks. In fact, she could've rented or purchased quite a nice house; she had a decent job in a care home – she was just a mess in every other aspect of her life. But still, the caravan was home.

Faith's mum thought that she could only be classed as successful if she had a ring on her finger. That resulted in a string of failed relationships and engagements because nobody was quite right, or they tried to help Andrea kick her alcohol dependency, which, if you asked her, was not a problem in the slightest. Faith would champion the men who were trying to help her, join them in encouraging her mum to seek help, and in return her mum would get angry, send them packing and take it out on Faith. Eventually Faith had to accept that the only person who could help Andrea was Andrea herself.

Thinking about it all now that she was removed from the situation, Faith came to the conclusion that perhaps all the self-sabotage was a simple case of her mum punishing herself for letting Faith's dad go. From what she'd heard growing up, the man was the full package. She wished she knew where he was. *Who* he was.

'Do you have any crumpets? I've always wanted to try them; they look really weird.' Lucie piped up halfway through an episode of *The Bold Type*, looking at her with curious eyes.

'You need to calm down with your stereotypes, Luce. I don't, but I promise we'll get some when we're next in England,' Faith replied.

'Suits me just fine. Hey, what are you thinking for Le Mans content?'

'I'm thinking a team trip to the funfair in the fan zone is in order. We can really milk that for content, film for all platforms. Maybe we should take a film camera too!' Faith jumped up and went into Bea's old room, returning a few seconds later with the one she had left on her desk when she'd moved away.

'Oh, wow! The team are going to *die* over this! We can get properly established on TikTok too; do a little montage.' Lucie was buzzing.

'Great idea. I just need to check with Bea that we can go ahead and use this. I'll buy it off her if necessary.' Faith took the camera over to her suitcase, already dreading the drama involved with getting it through security.

'I hope you can handle the waltzers, though, because I can't. I always outdo myself on the snacks and regret it. You can take my place.' Lucie grimaced as if she was recalling a memory.

'As long as you do the rides that involve heights. They're really not my forte.' Faith thought back to the trip she had taken to Alton Towers with Bea and felt nauseous.

'It's a done deal.'

They settled back into their feminist binge session, PJs

on and popcorn in a bowl between them. This had become their almost daily ritual over the last month and life felt strikingly normal in contrast to what they were heading into tomorrow morning.

Julien hadn't been active on social media for the entire month they'd been apart, and the contact they'd had with him had been minimal. He had texted Faith a couple of times outside of the group chat to check in with her, but other than that it was just the odd emoji in response to someone's message in *Revolution Royals*.

Lucie insisted this was standard behaviour for him, but Faith still wished they'd had a more in-depth conversation to put her mind at ease about where they stood when they were reunited. Did he still want to take her on a drive, were they still friends, was he ever going to touch her again, or was he going to keep her at arm's length and make her job hell? It was making her head hurt, and her heart.

Her phone buzzed with a text to the group from Marco, asking if they were all packed and had solved their crisis. Lucie replied with a 'No thanks to you' and got devil emojis in response. Faith had caught her on solo video calls with Brett numerous times, but vowed not to mention them because she didn't want to be teased about Julien for the billionth time.

'I'm going to ask if anyone is staying in the hotel between test day and race weekend or if they're all staying in their rooms in the hospitality area. The drivers share rooms behind the garages and that's where they nap in the twenty-four-hour race period, but you and I will either have to go back to the hotel in shifts or sleep in the chairs in the garage. This is nothing like the six hours of Spa, believe me. We'll all need the extra sleep,' Lucie explained.

'I'm not trekking back to the hotel, thank you very much. The chairs will do for me,' Faith responded as she got up and went to the kitchen to make them another cup of tea.

Her phone lit up with a series of messages from the team. All three drivers were opting to make the most of the comfortable hotel beds until they were forced to give them up for the race, which meant team breakfasts would remain.

'Luce! Did you see Julien's message? He's getting an overnight flight and he's scheduled to land in Paris at midday; he wants to know if anyone wants to grab lunch in the city before we make the drive to Le Mans?' Faith called through to the bathroom where Lucie had disappeared to do an intense skincare routine.

'We land at eleven, right? We might as well wait around for him. By the time we're through baggage claim, he shouldn't be too much longer.'

Faith typed out Lucie's exact words and hit send. Why was the concept of a sophisticated lunch in Paris with her co-workers so daunting? It could be worse – she could be alone with him. She just prayed nature didn't provide Julien with a light breeze to drift through his hair, or a ray of sun across his face to highlight those baby blues. With any luck he would have his sunglasses on, hair gelled firmly into place. *Please, Jules, for the sake of my sanity.*

Faith wrestled the key into her flat door at six thirty the following morning, scowling heavily. This was supposed to be a wholesome moment where she said goodbye to the flat and to Amina for a couple of months, and she and Lucie sailed off into the sunset together. Many sunsets actually. In the beautiful landscapes of Europe.

Instead, Lucie was in a foul mood after getting no sleep and the coffee machine breaking, and Faith's rusty old key just did not want to turn in the lock. Amina and her sons had emerged from across the hall to two very stressed women who were anything but happy and upbeat.

'Oh, don't worry about that, sweetheart. I'll call the landlord. You haven't left any valuables, have you?' Amina asked.

Faith shook her head. Any tech she wasn't taking with her, such as her record player and speakers, she had given to Amina's sons. All that was left in the flat was furniture, which she was keeping so she could come back in between trips. Her savings account was crying out for her to break her lease early, but she didn't like not having a safety net. She had six more months to figure out if she wanted to keep the flat for another year.

'Thank you for everything, Amina. I don't think Bea and I would've survived our first few months here without you, and I definitely wouldn't have survived the last year on my own.' Faith pulled her in for a hug. She had promised to stay in touch and the kids had followed all the team social accounts so they could see everything she was up to, but it still pained them all to know that their weekly pizza nights and Sunday-morning market trips would cease to exist.

'If only you knew what you've done for us, the impact you've had on Caleb and Rhys. It feels like one of my own is flying the nest, but I am immensely proud of you.' Amina spoke softly, which only resulted in sniffles and tears.

'Will you and Lucie come and visit?' Rhys looked up at her, and it broke Faith's heart.

'Dude, come on. We're best friends now; you can't get

rid of us.' Lucie ruffled his hair and captured him and his brother in her arms.

They squealed but Caleb fought his way out of the embrace. He hated affection unless he was feeling under the weather, and would much rather show love by wrestling people to the ground MMA style. These boys were a huge part of Faith's suddenly ever-growing world, and she hadn't recognized it until it was time to say goodbye, but she had been blessed with some form of a family all along, even after Bea was gone.

They were interrupted by a notification that their driver was here to take them to Heathrow. Faith caught Lucie's eye mid-sob and signalled that it was time to go. She had become so attached to the twins, and Faith guessed she was missing her own siblings.

'Our Uber is here,' Faith said.

Amina smiled warmly at them. 'OK. We'll say goodbye up here.'

The streets of London passed by in a blur of red buses and black cabs. It was the middle of June and the British heat had yet to make an appearance. Usually Faith would be complaining and begging nature to work its magic, but as she sat in the back of the cab with her passport in her hand, she couldn't care less.

## 17

'Get that wine down you.' Lucie pushed the glass of wine towards her, finding the whole ordeal rather amusing. The landing in Paris was a bumpy one and it had left Faith feeling rattled, both literally and emotionally. She had barely spoken from the moment the plane had hit the tarmac until right now, sitting in a bar in the city with Lucie. She was just grateful to be back on land with this dark red liquid in her right hand.

Julien was due to get here twenty-five minutes ago, but there was still no sign of him. Faith was starting to think he might have bailed just like he did with her first team dinner in Spa, but she kept reminding herself of the traffic they had fought through to get into the city. It was a miracle they'd even got a seat in this bar. Paris was so much like London, except it felt ten times more magical. Even the light drizzle didn't matter.

'So do you think this is a permanent thing for you? This job, travelling?' Lucie asked.

'There's nothing keeping me in London, so I guess I'll just go wherever life takes me.' Faith shrugged, feeling very peculiar about not having a structured plan once this race season was over.

They chatted between themselves and sipped their wine, which was very overpriced. Faith was accustomed to a bottle of Echo Falls on a Friday night, but Lucie was determined to give her the best of everything. She lived well within her means and she wasn't a huge shopper, but Faith had to admit that a trip to the fashion district of Paris was tempting for the experience alone.

Julien breezed in an hour late, looking as immaculately dressed as ever. He took his sunglasses off and blinked a few times as his eyes adjusted to the dim lighting, scanning the room. He grinned when he saw them sat in the corner with their luggage and weaved effortlessly through the crowds of rich French businessmen. Even with the leather jacket, he could easily pass as one of them. It was all in the way he carried himself. He could go from Bad Boy to Sugar Daddy in seconds, as Lucie had pointed out when their eyes landed on him.

'Hello, stranger.' Lucie smiled and stood up to hug him, stealing him a chair from the adjacent table. Faith cringed inwardly, likening their behaviour to Brits in their local pub rather than classy, civilized young women in a sophisticated Parisian bar.

Faith hadn't risen from her seat for a hug, worried that it would send Julien into a blind panic. She froze when he leaned down to place a kiss on both of her cheeks, something he hadn't done for their friend. He pulled back with a twinkle in his eye and settled down next to her, his leg brushing against hers. This was going to her head more than the wine was.

Julien signalled for a waiter and ordered himself a non-alcoholic beer, since he was in charge of driving. He asked if the girls wanted another glass each to which they shook their heads. They were only drinking it so Faith could say she had experienced a bottle of expensive red in one of the most romantic cities in the world. Although she had to admit she hadn't actually remembered Paris's reputation as the city of lovers until her favourite driver had arrived.

'How was London?' he asked. The question was aimed at both of them, but Lucie was bursting at the seams to tell him everything from a tourist's perspective.

They let her babble on for fifteen minutes as she hyped up Faith's home turf and tour guide abilities. More than anything, though, Lucie applauded the way Faith had made London feel like it belonged to Lucie, like she had been there just as long. She recalled their night out with two drivers from the Hudson Sport team, trips to museums, galleries and cafes, dinner with the neighbours. London was Lucie's second home now apparently, but Faith wasn't sure she wanted to rush back. There was so much more to explore.

'She basically gave up her apartment, you know?' Lucie gestured to Faith who was caught off guard. She had zoned out in the middle of Lucie listing all the types of tea she had tried. Poor Julien was doing his best to feign interest.

'Oh? You're not going back to the UK?' He raised an eyebrow.

'Well, I still have it for six months but, no, not for a while,' Faith replied. 'I sold everything in it except the basics, and Lucie and I are going wherever we feel like going in the moment. Gallivanting, as Luce keeps saying.'

'Maybe I'll have to join you for a few trips here and there, when I don't have other commitments. We usually do a couple of team trips, don't we, Luce?'

'We do,' Lucie agreed, smiling at Julien.

Not once since he sat down had Julien mentioned what

he had been doing with his time off. So not only was he keeping it quiet online, but he wasn't discussing it with the girls. Did Lucie know? That was a horrible thought.

It seemed like they were back to playing their strange little games again, never giving away any details and never getting too close but acting as if they were friends. It was just like when they were barely speaking but had celebrated the race win together, or when Faith had pretended not to hear his heartfelt confession in his bedroom and the next morning they had stood cooking breakfast together like it was just a normal thing they did.

Lucie excused herself when the conversation was dying out and left Faith, who had been relying on her friend to keep any awkward silences at bay, to fend for herself.

Julien shuffled in his seat and she could've sworn she heard every sip and gulp of his alcohol-free beer. She had to speak up at some point.

'Back to this, huh?' she asked, biting her lip. Was this weird vibe between them going to last the whole trip?

Julien looked at her longingly, like he was desperate to say something. 'This is just how it has to be for now,' he said. No sign of a mutter or a mumble, just bullshit. What was that even supposed to mean? It was the 'for now' part that baffled her the most. How long did she have to wait? How long until he started treating her the way he treated everyone else? It didn't have to be this hard.

'What about that drive?' she asked.

'After the race. I promise.' The way he looked at her sent a thousand volts jolting through Faith. It was as though he wanted to rip her clothes off right here in the middle of this restaurant.

'Oops, excuse me, sir! *Pardon!*'

They heard Lucie returning from the bathroom and Faith swiftly changed the topic.

'I'm taking you to the funfair and you're going to have fun. I can't post content if you're looking miserable all the time,' she teased and got a cheeky grin out of him.

'You're buying me candyfloss.'

'Obviously.'

A very small insane part of her wondered what he would do if she grabbed his face and kissed him right now, but she feared he might have a heart attack and be out of the race. She wasn't often confident in people's feelings towards her, but her intuition told her that he wouldn't pull away from her if she tried. Still, she wasn't going to cross boundaries. His walls were up for a reason, and she needed to respect that. Who ended up making a move first was giving her a bit of a thrill.

Two hours later, they had Brett with them and were on the road to Le Mans. His Australian accent boomed so loudly from the back seat that there was no need to turn the music down, although Lucie might end up deaf by the end of the journey. Faith was sat in the front with Julien who had lightened up again now that he was behind the wheel.

The drive was due to take just over two hours, but that was without the crazy levels of traffic coming out of the city. By the time they had escaped it, Brett had drifted off to sleep with Lucie's head resting on his shoulder. All that talking had worn him out.

Julien was concentrating hard on humming the ACDC track that was playing, and Faith was concentrating equally hard on his arms as he gripped the steering wheel. She let her mind wander back to their half-naked encounter in the boys' trailer. It seemed like forever ago now, and if she was going to stick to her plan of not pouncing on him, then she was going to have to avoid being in confined spaces with him.

'So what did you think of Paris?' Julien's voice scared the life out of her, and he laughed when she jumped. It was his fault she'd been distracted. He had no right to find it funny.

'I liked it. I just wish I'd had more time here. It's so different to Cornwall, but not so different from London,' she said.

'Tell me more about Cornwall.'

'Well, aside from the beaches, it hasn't got a lot going for it. I grew up in a very rural part: barely had an internet connection or phone service, very little public transport.'

'Sounds like the part of Belgium I was raised in. We're still catching up with modern times, so much so that my mother doesn't even own a smartphone. You should convince Lucie to come back out to Paris in the week before qualifying gets under way. You have plenty of time since we've come out so early,' he suggested.

'I might do that. I'd like to see the sights.' She didn't want Paris to just be a place to land; she wanted to experience what the city had to offer. She envied every post that Bea put up of her time there, and was keen to find all the cute cafes and bakeries and climb the steps to the Sacré-Coeur.

'You should go to Italy between Le Mans and Silverstone too. I know you two said you were touring the English coast after the IEC trip, but even a weekend getaway to Rome would be worth it.' He spoke of it fondly.

'Why don't you join us? We can convince Brett and Marco too while we're at it. Italy can be our first non-work trip,' she said.

'Ah, I have somewhere to be after the big mystery holiday. I can't stick around.' He looked nervous. Screw the mystery holiday, the biggest mystery here was where Julien was spending his time when he wasn't with the team. A secret girlfriend was on the cards, but Faith didn't think he was capable of that level of deception so she shook the insecurity from her mind. She was all for leading a private life, but for him to not even tell his best friends where he was going? Something wasn't adding up or someone was lying.

'No worries.' She gave a half-hearted smile.

'We'll definitely plan something soon, though. We could go to Thailand maybe? I haven't been before.' Julien kept eyeing her cautiously and it made her want to scream. She wasn't made of china; she could handle whatever it was he was clearly dying to blurt out.

The hotel was beautiful. It wasn't modern like the one they'd stayed in for Spa, nor was it right by the circuit. It was in the heart of the town and full of motorsport history. The girls were sharing a twin room and Julien was in the room next to them again. He was complaining that they'd keep him up with their gossiping and giggling when they stayed up late to edit content and plan their meetings and schedules, but he admitted it was better than hearing Marco's snoring coming through from the other side.

A lot of the smaller teams hadn't arrived yet, resulting in a shorter wait for the lift, which Faith had been told was usually chock-a-block and had a queue of ten-plus people. She and Julien had glanced at each other when Brett and Lucie were moaning about it, and agreed they would make their stairwell sprints a tradition. But no golf cart speeding this time. They didn't want to be arrested by the French police.

The sun was out and the temperature was heating up rapidly, so Faith and Julien were taking full advantage of the hotel's air-conditioning system and holding their impromptu work-related meeting in the lobby. There weren't many people around but they were very conscious of the way their voices carried and echoed throughout the building, so Julien was leaning on the wall next to Faith. He lowered his head so he could speak quietly but it meant their faces were inches apart. She was struggling to stay on task.

They were discussing the idea of Julien taking over the team's Instagram story tomorrow. He wouldn't have any actual work to document; it was just whatever he and the boys chose to do with their day off. The drivers had come out to relax for a few days before race preparation began. She was showing him how to access filters and helping him save his favourites. In normal circumstances everything would be pre-filmed and edited on standalone apps before posting, but that seemed like too much pressure for a post-and-go kind of guy.

'Jules, you don't have to do this. We can ask Marco to do it instead,' she said.

'Hell no, I'm doing it. You were right back in Belgium, I've got to do my part in this whole online thing. I can film my coffee art in the morning.' He *almost* sounded excited.

Every once in a while he would post a short video of himself making a coffee with patterns in the foam, a skill he had perfected over the last few months. His morning coffees were his pride and joy, and Faith's marketing brain was thinking about how if he kept that content up, he could collaborate with a coffee brand, whether it be purely promotional or they allowed him to create his own signature blend. He could even start up his own brand. *Baby steps.*

'You know, if you wanted to get into the whole social media thing a little more on your own, just when you're at home doing your own thing, Ford would be a great asset. People love dogs, and he's a husky. Lots of personality there.'

'He'd be the star of my account, wouldn't he?'

She nodded. 'Absolutely.'

'I think you've hit the nail on the head there, Jensen.' He smiled down at her, his hair falling in front of his eyes again. She thought he'd have cut it after Belgium and go back to his perfectly styled short trimmed look from last season, but thankfully for her and not so thankfully for her heart rate, he had kept it longer.

'If you ever need any help, shoot me a message,' she said.

'What, I can't ask you in person?' He raised an eyebrow.

'Not if you're on the other side of the world.'

'I didn't think of that part.'

If they didn't get it together soon, if one of them didn't take the plunge, they might never do it. They owed it to themselves, right? To see if whatever this was could be something, or if the sparks they'd felt during that kiss had been a one-off.

'Hello, everyone!' a shrill voice called out and they both rolled their eyes in unison. Bea strutted in wearing those damn stiletto heels again, click-clacking her way across the lobby. Lorenzo Garcia was traipsing behind her, despite previously claiming he wanted nothing to do with her. No wonder Bea didn't change.

'He'd better stay away from you.'

'He won't come over now you're here.' Faith grabbed Julien's arm and led him away, down the corridor to the stairwell. It was better that they skipped the lifts and minimized the risk of Bea and Lorenzo catching up with them.

'If he makes you uncomfortable, you tell me.'

'I will. Don't worry.'

'I've known him a very long time, my whole career actually, but I don't trust him with you. After that little performance at my place, he'll be lucky if he gets an invite next year.' Julien was literally stomping up the stairs and Faith had to stop a few steps behind just to laugh.

'Calm down, Jules. No harm was done.'

'Calm down?' Julien whipped round to face her, looking exasperated. 'Men like him should be held accountable for their actions. It's not OK. In an industry with as much toxic masculinity as ours, we should all be more mindful.'

'Noted. I appreciate it,' she replied.

'You and Luce should start your own movement for women in motorsport,' he suggested.

'Those exist, don't they? Is there any point?'

'They exist for aspiring female drivers. Just an idea, but you have a lot of women on your media team and you would gain so much traction with your following. As much as I hate to suggest it, get Bea on board, get her to sort her priorities out a bit. The three of you would be a force to be reckoned with. Just think about it for next season, once you're all settled in.'

Faith stood on the stairs for a few moments, feeling dumbfounded. He had a point. This was the perfect way to bring Bea back in line with her morals, and it would give Lucie a huge career boost, plus their current crew. Then there were all the girls who had grown up just like Faith, who had never thought she would get here. Motorsport shouldn't be all about men. Female drivers existed within this organization, and yet the guys still got all the focus. The women of the paddock had the power to shift some of the attention on to them, and it was about time they took hold of it.

# 18

The team were at the track taking a first look at the Le Mans specific set up and establishing what was on the menu in the hospitality tent. According to Brett, that was one of the most important parts of the week and he had requested some changes which he had to double-check had been done. Lucie said she wasn't sure exactly what he was going to do if they hadn't since it was too late and he wasn't the type to kick off, but he was adamant. Marco reckoned he just wanted an excuse to sneak into the kitchen and help himself to some food even though they were scouting out the food trucks later that evening.

Faith walked into the garage alone and was met with a warm welcome from everyone who didn't have their head buried in an engine or chassis. She didn't feel the same nerves she'd felt the first couple of times she'd come in here, and instead felt like she was playing a significant role in the team's development off the track. Their social media presence tied in with all the work they did on the actual car and out on track. It all brought attention and of course sponsors.

Lorenzo walked past the front of Revolution's garage on his way to Talos, which was unfortunately right next door. Julien had texted her earlier to forewarn her, but she was sure he was more bothered than she was. The way he had behaved towards her at Julien's party happened to women all the time and while that didn't make it OK, it did mean she was sort of desensitized to the situation. He waved at her but she ignored it.

'Trust me, he won't be a problem,' Julien muttered under his breath as he came to a stop behind her. That statement concerned her and made her think he'd had a threatening word.

The drivers were taking advantage of the gap in their schedule to practise driver changes. Faith captured some footage and sat down in the far corner, gratefully accepting a cup of coffee from Lucie regardless of the fact she had put three sugars too many in it.

Gabriel bounded in like the greatest thing in the world was happening, with a girl no older than fifteen following behind him with significantly less energy. She looked shattered.

'Faith! Do you have a second? I have someone I'd like you to meet. This is my daughter, Alessia. She's a *huge* fan.'

'Of the team?' Faith asked.

'No, darling, of you!' He clapped his hands together enthusiastically.

'Dad, you're embarrassing me. Hi, Faith, it's nice to meet you.' Alessia shook her hand. She had pink hair and was wearing all black, with winged liner and a nose ring. Something told Faith that Gabriel had his hands full with her, although she was sure the same applied the other way around too.

'It's lovely to meet you too, Alessia. Are you here the whole week?'

'I am. It's the only race I go to. Dad says the race is such a historic event that there's no way I should miss it. I will give him credit – it's exciting.' She smiled and Faith noticed that her green eyes crinkled the exact same way Gabriel's did and she had his dimples. She definitely hadn't been switched at birth.

'Well, you've been here more times than me!'

'Can I hang out with you for an hour? My dad has a meeting with one of the team principals so I have to keep myself entertained. I don't want to go for another walk.' She sighed.

Faith nodded, grateful for the company. Lucie was off overseeing the work of a few of their new interns, hired specifically for this race, and the boys were preoccupied with the car. Having minimal content to capture today and taking a much-needed break from emails, charts and spreadsheets, she was impatiently waiting for their food truck adventure to roll around. She was really hoping for dirty fries, but pizza was also tempting. Or she could just have countless doughnuts, but that wouldn't fill her up quite the same, and food would be what fuelled her through the late nights and early mornings.

It was nearing sunset when Julien appeared. She was drifting off in a camping chair with no sign of Lucie yet. Alessia had left a while ago to eat dinner with Gabriel, which had left Faith bored out of her mind if she was being honest. There was only so much excitement involved in watching the drivers hop in and out of the car as it sat stationary in a quiet garage.

'Fancy that trip to the funfair?' he asked.

'Yes, but can we do food afterwards? I'm not sure it's wise to eat before going on a waltzer. The ride operators can be brutal.'

'Of course.' He laughed. 'It should be quiet because most of the teams are heading back into Le Mans for dinner now. There might be a few fans floating around, though, so I can't promise we won't have to stop for a few photos and autographs.'

Julien gestured for Brett and Marco to follow them and they set off to find Lucie in the paddock. She was lounging around in another team's hospitality tent with a group of media and photography interns, enjoying an iced coffee. Brett strolled in like he owned the place and whispered in her ear.

'Let's go!' She came bounding out and linked her arm through Faith's, hurrying everyone along. If Brett wanted to do his usual skip through the paddock like he had on her first day, now would be an appropriate time. They were like a group of kids who had just been let off the coach on a school trip to Disneyland.

The funfair was ten times better than the rundown ones they had back home. The skies were a soft candyfloss pink with streaks of orange and the lights from the rides, and the music playing over the speakers and the red-and-white-striped stalls and marquees had Faith feeling like she'd walked into a movie. She might even try to win a giant stuffed shark toy on the hook-a-duck.

The team made a beeline for the waltzers, where the ride attendant looked like he could do some serious damage. Faith eyed Lucie, who already looked like she might faint.

'I'm sitting this one out.' She stopped walking and crossed her arms. 'Look at that guy; he's plotting to kill us all.'

'Death by spinning funfair ride is a good way to go,'

Brett said teasingly, flinging an arm round her shoulders in hopes of swaying her decision.

'Sure we can't convince you?' Marco asked.

'Absolutely not. I'll film it from back here – we don't want Faith's expensive camera flying through the air.' Lucie took the camera from her and exchanged it for a GoPro, which Faith immediately handed to Julien.

'Jules, you're in charge. I'm a small human, I need to hold on with both hands. Please try to avoid crushing me,' she warned the guys as they all climbed into their seats.

The ride operator started it up with just the four of them on the ride. That was the downside to coming here so early in the week; all the attention was on *their* ride experience and meant that it was likely to be more intense than usual. The ride began moving around, gradually getting faster until it was time for the first almighty spin.

Faith gripped the metal bar and braced herself for impact but it wasn't long before Marco, being quite light himself, came sailing across the seat towards her. His weight plus Brett's resulted in Faith being squashed up against Julien's muscular frame.

Julien threw his head back, unable to control his laughter, and put his arm round her so that their bodies would move together with the next spin. Marco scuttled back to his left, towards Brett who was laughing so hard he looked like he might actually cry.

As the ride slowed down, Faith tried to look for Lucie with blurred vision but could not for the life of her work out where she was stood. The ride operator looked immensely proud of himself as they stumbled off the platform in a fit of giggles, falling into each other. Brett tripped down the steps and knocked into Faith, who promptly fell into Julien and sent the two of them tumbling on to the grass. They sprawled out, legs intertwined and arms stretched out.

'Uh, guys, where's Mars?' Brett asked.

They scanned the area and spotted him at the back of a marquee, dry-heaving into a wheelie bin. Faith and Julien leaped up from the ground and ran to him but he batted them away.

'I'm fine. It's been a while since I went to a funfair,' he mumbled. A racing driver, who sped around a track at over two hundred miles per hour, couldn't handle a funfair ride. Faith tried to hide her smirk until she noticed nobody else was bothering to hide theirs.

'Hey, guys!' Lucie ran to catch up with Faith and Julien on their way over to the dodgems.

'What's up?' Faith turned her head to face her, and her hair blew in front of her eyes in the light breeze. She had her hands full with cameras and phones, so Julien reached out and brushed it away from her face. A few strands caught on her eyelashes and he tentatively removed them. Faith did her best not to look at him with heart eyes.

'I got some great shots of you two collapsed on the grass; is it OK if I post them? It's perfect behind-the-scenes footage.' She looked to Julien for confirmation, already knowing that Faith couldn't care less.

'Go for it.' Julien smiled. He was still giddy from the waltzer, but he was looking down at Faith like she was the only person there.

'Wait, really?' she asked.

'Really.' He nodded.

She snapped out of her trance when the others joined

them, Marco looking much brighter than he had a couple of minutes ago. Lucie edited photos while she walked, applying filters and making a few adjustments. The colours of the funfair were rich and vibrant, and the red tied in perfectly with the colour of the team's uniform and livery. Even Faith was wearing a red denim jacket to fit the theme, which had been unintentional but might have to become a regular thing.

Faith refused to go on the Ferris wheel. Julien offered to stay with her, but Marco told him there was no way he was going up on his own. It was only the first day, but this week was becoming more unpredictable than she had been prepared for. Perhaps it was just Julien's adrenaline influencing him or the pure magic of being at Le Mans, but Faith's intuition told her it was far more than that. This was him letting go of his fears and embracing the little moments between them. Just as he had promised in the soft light of his bedroom all those weeks ago.

Julien couldn't take his eyes off Faith as she walked ahead of him back to the paddock. They were going back to the hotel after stuffing their faces with burgers and fries. He'd had avocado with his burger so he didn't feel so guilty for eating so unhealthily, but that hadn't stopped him taking a bite of Faith's doughnut. How was he supposed to resist something so soft and warm and doughy? It was heavenly.

He also couldn't resist spending ninety euros on winning a stuffed shark for her after she had tried her best to do it herself. He walked away angrily insisting that hook-a-duck was rigged, but nonetheless couldn't wipe the smile off his face when she gratefully took it from him and asked for a name suggestion. They settled on Mustang, taking inspiration from the name Julien had given his dog: Ford.

He was in a complete world of his own when Lucie interrupted with her burning questions. She wanted to know if he'd had a change of heart about Faith, following on from their conversation at his party. Little did she know he had. He wasn't fully ready yet, but he was working on it. Going with the flow. Rather than having walls up, he had fences. Wooden ones that could be knocked down with a little less force.

'I don't want to take a giant leap until I know I have the capacity to let her in all the way.'

'What are you classing as a giant leap?'

'A kiss,' he said, pretending like that hadn't already happened. It hadn't happened the way he wanted it to. He wanted their next one to be special, to mean more, for Faith to come away from it knowing how he felt about her.

'*Oh*. Yeah, if the sparks are flying before you make that sort of physical contact, then one kiss and you'll both be head over heels.'

He let out a little grunt in agreement and watched as Brett wrestled Mustang the shark from Faith's arms and attacked Marco with it. Julien felt a pang of jealousy, even though he knew Brett could sense their connection from a mile off and would never betray him. The hard truth was, Julien already *was* head over heels for her.

'Maybe this week isn't the time for it. I think I need to have an honest, open conversation with her first. I said a few things in Belgium when she was asleep, but there was so much I didn't say even when she couldn't hear me. It's like I don't want to admit certain things to myself, let alone Faith.' Julien sighed.

'You're allowed to feel things, Jules. It doesn't make you a terrible person; it makes you human. There are worse people you could be drawn to.' Lucie tucked herself under his arm.

'You know it's not just me I've got to worry about,' he said, hugging her appreciatively. He would give her similar advice about Brett, but that connection had been building for years. It would take a lot more effort to make those two budge.

'Everyone just wants you to be happy. It's about time,' she said.

Julien bit the inside of his cheek. Lucie was right, he deserved to be happy, but it might end up being at other people's expense and he didn't want to hurt anyone. All he knew was that he was getting close to making a decision. There were some things Faith deserved to know.

As they got nearer to the team's garage, Jasper caught his attention. He looked nervous and Julien had a sinking feeling.

'Can I have a word, Moretz?' he asked.

'Sure.' Julien led him to one side, out of earshot of the team who were already halfway down the paddock by the time Jasper worked up the courage to start speaking.

'It's about the trip next week. I was actually fighting to move the location, but the executives wanted it to be at this specific resort because they're offering a huge discount, exclusive access to the entire place and no fear of noise complaints or trespassers,' he said, his confidence knocked down a peg or two.

'Let me guess, this resort is on an island.'

'Yes . . .'

'An island you knew I wasn't happy to go to for work events.' Julien clenched his fist because he didn't want to take it out on his boss. He had already said he'd fought to get it moved, and the other execs had no idea what his problem was with this specific island. Gabriel did, but that was one guy versus at least five others.

'Oahu.' He nodded. 'I'm sorry, Moretz. I tried.'

'It's OK, Jasper. Honestly.' Jasper apologized again and said his goodbyes.

The thing was, nothing about going to Hawaii was OK. Julien had just come from there, and he had promised certain people there that he would visit every single time. They would be able to see that the organization was there from social media and he couldn't sneak away for the day without being asked where he was going, because where would he possibly have to be on an *island* in the middle of a work event?

He drove back to the hotel solo and left the others to fend for themselves. He couldn't be in anyone's company tonight; he had too many demons to fight. He could just not go, but that would lead to more questions. Plus, it would be breaking a work commitment, which he had only done once in all his years of racing.

He had to suck it up this time. It was all on him if he was honest with himself. While he was so busy trying to protect people, he had ended up alienating himself and leading two separate lives. Lucie was right; he couldn't do it forever.

He crashed on to his bed and kicked his shoes off. Digging his phone out of his pocket, he looked through Faith's Instagram. A significant amount of posts were similar to those he saw on his own profile or Brett's, Lucie's or

Marco's. There was even a photo of her and Lucie posing with Ford at the party.

Their lives were aligning very quickly; the only difference was Julien always had somewhere to be but now Faith could go wherever the wind took her. As he scrolled through years' worth of photos, he read every caption in her voice and he could feel the warmth of her personality through her written words just the same as he could in person. Julien realized once he hit the three-year mark that she was the same now, as he knew her, as she had been when she'd first started her career. Fame and success hadn't tainted her, and she didn't get involved in gossip or drama. Even when it came to Bea she was reserved.

He could be honest with Faith; he knew he could. She wouldn't share his secrets with the world. There didn't seem to be a bad bone in her body. There was no manipulation, no little white lies or want for anything other than genuine friendship. He had been terrified that she would be just like every other woman who threw themselves at him, that she wanted a lifestyle, wanted to flaunt him and use him. But she hadn't done that.

He got up and looked out of the window, wondering if they were back yet. Their car pulled up a few moments later and he watched her get out, Mustang in tow. She clung to that shark for dear life and it confirmed everything he needed to know. He sighed and sat back down as she disappeared from view.

He could do it. He could take the leap and everything would be OK, but there was always the tiny chance that it wouldn't be. The chance that she would get hurt even if nobody else did. He *could* do it, but he wouldn't.

# 19

This morning's team breakfast was taking place at a cafe opposite the hotel and was a couple of hours later than usual. The lie-in had been needed. The girls had stayed up until three a.m. working on the funfair content; the footage was beautifully shot, and they were excited to share it with the fans.

Bea had given them permission to use the camera she'd left behind, which had given them photos that looked like they were from another decade, and Lucie had made sure to capture some for their own personal keepsakes. The world wasn't ready to see the way Julien looked into Faith's eyes as they shared a cardboard tray of chilli-topped fries. Faith hadn't been quite ready for that either.

'Please come with us. You guys aren't even supposed to be here yet; you just came early for the hell of it. There's a whole city waiting for us, and Faith hasn't been before.' Lucie was begging all three drivers to join them for an action-packed day in Paris with an overnight stay.

'Fine! But when you go shopping, I'm going to magically disappear into the Rolex store,' Brett huffed.

'Well, one of you has to come shopping with us. Luce and I don't speak any French, remember? Mars and Jules are both fluent,' Faith chimed in to back her friend up, but in reality it was mostly because the girls planned on buying so much they were going to need another suitcase between them, plus three extra sets of hands to get everything back to the hotel.

'I don't know if I'm going to come . . .' Julien was hesitant as he sipped his coffee and Faith's heart dropped. She didn't want him to miss out on things just because he wasn't fully comfortable around her. He had nothing in his schedule, and yesterday he had been enthusiastically telling them about the boat trip down the River Seine. How could they have such a fun time last night and now they were back to this?

'Come on, Jules.' Faith nudged his knee gently. 'What else are you going to do? Sit alone in the hotel bar?' She smiled at him and he held her gaze for a moment, not saying a word.

'OK.'

Lucie wandered over with a map when they got off the Metro. They had driven into the city but abandoned the car at their last-minute hotel so they could have a more authentic tourist experience, much to the displeasure of Brett, who hated being squashed up against strangers in the summer heat.

'There's a place just over there where we can rent bikes.' She pointed to a row of bicycles and gestured for everyone to follow.

Faith picked up a helmet and tucked her sunglasses into the neckline of her T-shirt. Brett had beaten them all to it and hopped on to his bike, already causing havoc and narrowly avoiding people on the pavement.

'Can someone help me? I can't get it to fit quite right.' Faith frowned at her helmet, not quite managing to make the correct adjustments.

Julien took pity on her and sorted it out. 'Safety first,' he said, patting her on the head with just enough force to earn him a scowl.

Faith and Julien barely had time to get on their bikes before everyone was pedalling off the pavement and on to the road, giving Faith the fright of her life as people began hitting their horns. She swore they did it on purpose, but then again it was such a frequent occurrence in Paris that maybe they actually had something to complain about. Like the Fiat that barely avoided smashing into the car in front of them.

They took a break on the steps of the Musée d'Orsay after a speedy tour of the museum, narrated by Marco, and indulged in Nutella-coated crêpes from a nearby kiosk. The sun was beating down on them and a jazz band was busking. The girls got up and danced, placing a few euros each in the saxophone player's case.

When they finally sat down, they were worn out and in dire need of a drink of water. Before they could say a word, Julien handed them a bottle each from the kiosk they'd got their desserts from. They took them gratefully and leaned back on the steps, soaking up the sunshine while letting the breeze hit them.

A huge gust of wind would be lovely right about now, but they would just have to wait patiently for the air conditioning of Louis Vuitton. Or in Lucie's case, not so patiently. She had been pleading with the group to make their way to the Champs-Élysées since they left the museum but everyone else was desperate for food and rest. They had abandoned their bikes already, realizing it was probably safer and less stressful to catch the Metro or just walk.

'Did you guys know Bea lives in Paris?' Faith asked, wondering where her apartment was.

'Who doesn't?' Julien muttered. 'Sorry, I'm being bitter.'

'It's all right. We're going to be having a long overdue conversation. I can't let her carry on like this.'

But Julien didn't look convinced. Nobody did except Lucie, who had heard the stories of their university days and was encouraging a reconciliation. Their ABBA performance at Julien's party had provided a stepping stone to friendship and they'd slowly been getting to know each other via text since.

'Where have you two got on your travel bucket list then?' Marco asked.

'Croatia, Iceland, Greece, Dubai, Nashville, Vegas, Switzerland, South Africa. The list goes on and on,' Lucie said.

The good thing about this job was that they were on such a strict schedule that wasn't likely to change a lot year in, year out, and it meant they could plan long-term. The only things they needed to make time for were events for sponsors and teams, but even those were such big events they'd have a few months' notice.

'I was telling Faith we should all go to Thailand together, maybe at the end of the season so we have a few weeks to explore Indonesia at the same time,' Julien added.

'Yes! I've always wanted to go back there,' Lucie eagerly agreed.

Faith wanted to suggest a trip to Melbourne too. She wondered if her dad had gone back when he'd left Cornwall. Although she didn't know a lot about him, she knew he had the travel bug, and Faith liked to think it was where she got it from.

Marco laughed. 'How are you two going to get by speaking minimal foreign languages?'

'We will very politely request that you three come on as many trips as you possibly can. Mars and Brett, there are zero excuses for you. You two travel all the time, and, Brett, you're usually with me anyway.' Lucie was insistent that they make some team traditions and give Faith a tour of all the places she hadn't yet visited, Revolution Racing style, which she was certain equalled chaos, judging by the trouble they caused in a standard working week.

There was a buzz among the group as they talked about where they would go and when, but it didn't take a psychologist to work out that Julien was significantly more reserved each time specific dates were brought up. Faith watched him for a moment and sighed inwardly when she saw his smile falter yet again at the mention of Christmas in Norway.

'What's wrong?' she asked.

'Hmm?' He tore his attention from the others.

'You've gone very quiet all of a sudden. Just checking everything's all right.'

'Uh, I'm just not sure how much I'll be able to travel with you all this season. I have other commitments. I need to work out a balance.' He was trying so hard to play it off like it wasn't a big issue, but his face suggested otherwise.

'I'm sure we can figure something out.' She smiled warmly at him and he seemed to relax a little. Not much, but enough so that he didn't look so downtrodden and miserable.

'I'll make Thailand happen for sure. Consider that one a promise because there's no way you're going without me

and showing me photos of everything I missed out on.'
He laughed softly when her eyes lit up. Thailand was the
one she was most excited for.

'Sounds like a deal.'

As they started preparing to leave the steps of the museum,
Julien got a call. He grinned at the name on the screen and
leaped up, taking it and moving away from the group.

As Faith watched him talk animatedly, she feared that
he was still viewing her as someone who was only trying
to get close to take advantage of him and the kind of life
he could offer. She didn't know how to prove to him that
she wasn't anything like the other women he had dated, to
prove that she wanted him and not his money.

It wasn't until they were sitting around feeling like they'd
just eaten enough for the entire race organization that
they wished they still had access to those rental bikes. The
trouble with Europe was the endless availability of pasta
dishes. Despite their location and their love for embracing
the culture of wherever they were, French cuisine wasn't
enough to tempt the group away from their favourite kind
of carbs. They had *almost* opted for seafood tonight, but
Marco was trialling a vegan diet and they didn't think it
was fair to expect him to eat an entire meal of side dishes
and nothing else. The girls insisted the Italian across the
street was a good alternative, and Marco managed to enjoy
a giant vegan-cheese pizza.

They hadn't steered the boys wrong, clearly. Brett was
currently collapsed in his chair, head thrown back as he
exclaimed that he was more stuffed than a turkey. Lucie
tutted and scolded him, telling him that he made the classy

establishment look shabby. Faith didn't dare admit that she still felt out of place in environments like this.

Lucie thrived on getting all dolled up so she looked like she belonged, but Faith was still a joggers and trainers, sunglasses-shoved-on-top-of-her-head kind of girl.

'Shall we go, guys?' Lucie prodded Brett's arm out of fear that he was going to drift off to sleep and his mouth would drop open in the middle of the restaurant.

According to Lucie's digital map, which she had now favoured above the huge paper one they had started out with, they were only a ten-minute walk from the Eiffel Tower where they were heading next. They were following on from there to the River Seine for a boat tour to end their Parisian adventure.

'I'm exhausted, guys. I don't know if I can survive all those steps,' Faith complained before they'd even taken a left turn at the end of the street. This was the problem with cities; everything seemed so close until it was time to walk.

'Come on.' Julien stopped walking and gestured for her to walk towards him. She had no idea what he was hinting at, and she stood there dumbfounded. The others had kept walking and left them a few feet away from the front of the restaurant among streams of tourists.

'What?' She blinked at him.

'Get on my back, muppet.' He rolled his eyes but she giggled at the fact he had adopted her British vocabulary. It sounded so alien with his accent.

'Are you sure? It's a long walk.' She admired his muscles and decided he could definitely handle her weight, even if only for half the journey. The soles of her feet needed this.

'I've trained for this moment.' Julien bent his knees,

bracing for impact as she jumped on to his back. If Faith still went to music festivals, he would be the perfect companion with those shoulders and all that height he had going for him.

'Onward,' she teased.

Julien carried her all the way to the ticket booth at the base of the Eiffel Tower, not stopping once. When everyone noticed they were lagging behind, they turned and Lucie's camera was immediately zooming in on them. Julien posed dramatically, like they were on a catwalk.

'Those are going to be on social media, aren't they?' Julien muttered.

'Lucie! Don't post those!' Faith called out, to which Lucie gave her a thumbs up and Julien said a quiet 'thank you'. She didn't want to push Julien too much, nor did she want the fans getting too carried away. At what point would the mass of posts of Faith and Julien seem suspicious?

Faith was doing her very best not only not to fall but also to compose herself, because though Julien was facing away from her and wouldn't catch her expression, their friends and that camera lens most definitely would. She was very aware that she looked like she was fighting some serious hormones.

Her arms were wrapped round his neck but it was his hands on her thighs that were the biggest distraction. It didn't help that he was absent-mindedly humming, which she could feel as she clung on to him. It was driving her crazy to the point that she almost begged him to put her on the ground.

'Stop humming. *Please*. I can feel every vibration.'

'Oh, sorry. Is it annoying you?' he asked.

'No, it just . . . Never mind. Just stop it.'

'Oh my God,' he laughed. 'It's turning you on, isn't it?' The amusement in his tone made her blush. In fact, her whole body was flushed with warmth.

'No comment.'

'As much as that makes me want to continue, I will behave myself for your comfort.'

The glass floor at the top of the tower was far scarier than Faith had imagined it would be. She had thought the excitement of being in Paris would detract from the fact that she felt like it was going to smash and they were all going to fall to their deaths, but she stood to one side, hands shaking and nausea rising through her body.

Everyone went and lay down, taking selfies and commenting on how small the world looked from up here. Faith refused to get close enough to agree with them, and insisted that she was fine where she was.

'Get your arse over here!' Brett yelled from the floor, surrounded by the shopping bags he and Marco had been lumbered with.

Julien took her hand. 'Do you trust me?'

'Jules . . .' She tried to resist but he was already leading her over to Brett like a lamb to slaughter.

'On the count of three, we're going to sit,' he said, stopping when they were stood next to Brett. She felt like an absolute wimp.

Admittedly Julien started lowering his body to the floor before she did and ended up yanking her down with him, but, regardless, she let her body relax and followed his actions until she was lying between him and Brett. It took a few reassuring squeezes of the hand from the pair of them before she was ready to look down, but when she did she was blown away. The people below looked like teeny-tiny ants. A mere twenty minutes ago that had been them.

Julien turned to face her, looking equally mesmerized. Suddenly the view underneath them wasn't quite as interesting as the view in front of her and he had a glint in his eye that was making her body tingle all over. Faith felt her cheeks turning pink and turned to look at Brett, Marco and Lucie, only to find that all three of them had disappeared. She couldn't handle another moment of staring into Julien's eyes.

'Can we go to the gift shop?' she pleaded.

'Yeah, I want to buy a magnet,' he said.

She couldn't recall seeing magnets on either the indoor or outdoor fridge at his house. He was a minimalist when it came to decor and she would've assumed that he found magnets as tacky as she found postcards, which left her with the question of who the magnet was for. She was being dramatic; she knew she was. It was a magnet. A lot of people liked magnets. If there was a woman in his life she was sure he would step up his game and at least buy her a T-shirt.

They found their friends gathered round a shelf of teddy bears with *I Heart Paris* shirts on, gushing over how cute they were and insisting that the team needed a cute new mascot. The bears were too generic but it had sent them running wild with ideas and they were throwing different animals into the mix.

Lucie and Marco were favouring a zebra, but Brett was insisting it wasn't cool enough and they needed a shark.

Faith's shark from the funfair, to be specific, despite Mustang being gigantic. She still wasn't sure how she was going to transport him and was succumbing to the idea of holding him on her lap for every flight in the future. She didn't like the idea of depositing him at her flat and him being all alone.

When they left the shop in time for the sunset, the crowds had almost doubled. There wasn't a lot of space at the edge so they got separated, and Faith and Julien found themselves alone and gripping on to each other as impatient tourists shoved past on the hunt for the perfect photo opportunity.

Eventually they managed to find a gap, but Julien was left with no choice but to stand directly behind Faith, body flush against hers. He put his arms on either side of her and held on to the barrier in front of them so nobody could knock into her, and his muscular frame meant that he was solid as a rock. He was not about to risk a repeat of the autograph session at Spa when she had been sent flying. Her ribs were very much safe under Julien's protection.

'Do you ever wish you weren't you?'

'All the time,' he mumbled into her hair, and she leaned her head back so it was resting on his chest. If not for the picturesque view of the city, she would close her eyes and soak in the feeling.

'I know how lucky I am, and I don't take a single day for granted, but sometimes I wish I was just a normal guy. This job has made my life complicated in ways I can't even begin to explain, and sometimes I wonder what my life would look like if I hadn't chosen this path.'

'If you weren't you,' she said quietly, 'would you trust me?'

'Faith, I do trust you. I just haven't felt like this for a very long time, and it's scaring me half to death. If we're going to do this, I need to approach with caution and make sure it's real.'

'OK.' Faith didn't know if she completely understood.

He was making their whole connection feel very heavy on her shoulders but the kiss he placed on the top of her head filled her with comfort. She came to her usual conclusion: *time will tell*.

# 20

It was the morning of race day and the entire grid were run off their feet. Julien hadn't seen Faith unless they were filming for the team's channel or they were in the garage at the same time. He didn't go for lunch with her and Lucie because he'd had a meeting with his engineer, he'd skipped dinner at the hotel in favour of a quick visit to team hospitality in between phone calls, and he had spent breaks in the trailer or in his room at the back of the garage, taking all the peace and quiet he could get in order to stay focused. He missed being around her, but only in the rare moments he sat down long enough to shove some food down his throat.

He loved race day. He thrived off pressure. But Le Mans was incredibly busy, on a completely different level to any other race on the calendar. There were more interviews, more statistics and strategies, more media crews and press, more fans and VIPs who stopped the drivers for a chat before they could advance more than three feet through the paddock. Julien was almost grateful Faith was barely around to distract him. They limited their staring and intense eye contact to when they were actively working together.

It was when he and Marco were getting changed into their race uniform that he got a call from his mum. He had turned the volume down, but his teammate had still heard every word: every single moment of him denying that there was anything between him and Faith, and his mum on the other end of the phone squealing about how perfect she was. He hurriedly said his goodbyes and hung up, turning to find Marco grinning at him.

'I thought you two had a great time in Paris? You looked like you were hitting it off,' Marco said, T-shirt stuck halfway over his head.

'It was perfect,' Julien stated bluntly. Grabbing his own top from the trailer's tiny wardrobe, he pulled it on angrily.

Marco frowned. 'So . . . what's the issue? Why are you crushing your mum's dreams?'

Julien sighed. 'We're going to Hawaii next week.'

'I don't understand why you don't just lay it all out there with her, let her make a decision for herself. You keep doing what you think is best for everyone, but have you actually asked anyone other than yourself?' Mars looked so sweet and innocent stood in the doorway.

'This is more than just wanting to go on a couple of dates and see where things go, De Luca. I think it's pretty safe to say I'm in this for the long haul.'

Marco exhaled. 'Oh, dude, you're so screwed.'

He was right: Julien was in deep trouble. He couldn't plant another kiss on that girl without it shifting their whole world, because the sparks would develop into full-blown fireworks.

Faith had dragged Bea out of the paddock to find the iced coffee truck half an hour ago so they could have a friendly chat away from everyone. She was saving the serious friendship-development stuff for when the race was over and they were jetting off on their big holiday.

'How have you been finding the job?' Bea asked.

'A breeze. It genuinely doesn't feel like work because I love it so much. The creative freedom I've been given has been such a relief.'

'That's exactly how I felt. Turns out we're pretty bloody talented, Jensen. Who would've thought?' Bea nudged her elbow. 'Have the rest of the grid been as welcoming as Revolution?'

'Surprisingly yes. We've tried to let the rest of the social media crew have quite a lot of free rein but my emails have been bombarded with questions and ideas. Lucie and I can't walk the length of four garages without someone tracking us down to show us something.'

'I suppose I have it easy because I can be sneaky with my camera, but you need to get up all close and personal. Rather you than me! Have you *seen* Jesse McAlpine first thing in the morning? He's terrifying.'

'Bit like you then.' Faith laughed.

'Hey, I'm not that bad!'

'Beatrix Miller, don't lie to yourself. You once swore at me and told me I was a horrible person because I dared to knock on your door and tell you that you'd slept through four alarms.'

'That was in uni and I'd been out the night before!'

'Uh-huh.'

'I miss those days.' Bea looked down at the ground.

'I do too. We should have a night out in London again. For old times' sake.'

'Really?'

Faith shrugged. 'Yeah. Don't get me wrong, I know we've drifted in the past few years and we still have a lot to talk about – there are things we properly need to discuss in time – but I don't want to lose you, Bea.'

'I don't want to lose you either.' Bea threw her arm round Faith's shoulder. 'Hey! We could go to that bar that's like a prison. You know the one where they give you an orange jumpsuit and you have to surrender your phone?' Bea grinned, and for a moment Faith saw a glimpse of the old her again. If Bea wanted to go somewhere she couldn't post about, that meant she actually wanted to hang out with her friend. It was a small step, but it filled Faith with hope that they could salvage their friendship.

As they walked through the paddock, iced coffees in their hands, Faith caught Julien watching them with caution. He was overprotective, but he had every right to be. Bea had hurt her with her insincerity, and she'd royally pissed him off too, but Bea had also been hanging out with the wrong people since she'd got into the motorsport industry. She needed to be reminded of her roots and be surrounded with the *right* people.

'Faith!' A reporter rushed towards them, recorder waving in the air. Faith vaguely recognized her from the drivers' press conference, and she remembered her being very invasive.

'Hello?' Faith blinked at her. Reporters usually only wanted to speak to drivers and team principals.

'I just wanted to get a word about this new approach to social media. Fans are noticing some big changes, and I hear that's all down to you.'

'Oh! Well, Lucie has had a big input in everything we're doing, but the organization are really trying to give fans of the sport more insight than they get in other championships. Social media is constantly evolving, and it's important that we change with the times.'

'Would I be right in thinking you're here as a fan? To get closer to the drivers?' the reporter asked, and Faith didn't like the way her tone was laced with insinuation.

'You would be very wrong actually,' Bea interjected. 'Faith is one of very few people qualified to do the job she's doing, and in years to come people are going to thank her for the positive impact she's had on our sport. Her passion and commitment is unmatched, and it has nothing to do with "getting closer to the drivers". Feel free to quote me on that, Lauren.' Bea tugged her along, leaving the flustered reporter behind them.

Faith caught Julien's bewildered gaze and shrugged, still processing what had just happened. 'Thanks, Bea.'

'She's such a nosy cow, that woman. She is utterly obsessed with Casey Winters, by the way. I'm surprised he hasn't had her kicked out of the paddock. She publicly went after his girlfriend last season. It was a total mess; Charlotte stopped coming to races all together. I wasn't about to have her taking shots at you too. Just because you're a woman and you have links to the motorsport industry. I mean, honestly, she should know better.'

'I'll be sure to avoid her in future. Right, I'd better go. I've got captions to write.' Faith decided to give Bea a hug goodbye, and it was returned with a proper squeeze. Like that hug was important to them both.

'OK. Faith? We *will* talk properly. Next week,' Bea promised.

*

Julien had been acting strange for the last couple of days but so had the other boys, which was making her uncomfortable. Lucie told her to put it down to the stress of the race; after all it was the biggest race of the year and the pressure was on a level that nobody else could possibly fathom, but Faith suspected that some of his behaviour was because of her. Again. Now that she knew he was scared of the way he felt about her, she wondered if he let his emotions get the better of him when he was supposed to be in the zone. The team psychologist was good, but the drivers were still human.

She was counting on next week's trip to change things between them for the better, with all the stress of Le Mans over and done with and the next six weeks of relaxing to look forward to. For five of those weeks he could stay away from her in terms of physical distance and sort his head out. She didn't need to sort hers out; she knew what she wanted. A chance. No more of this hot-and-cold nonsense.

Faith stepped out of the garage to stand in the sun for a second, hoping the short burst of vitamin D would calm her nerves and give her a boost to push her through the next couple of hours until their next scheduled coffee run. Catching her off guard, Lorenzo Garcia ran down the side of the Revolution trailer and approached her, hands up in defence.

'Can we talk?' he asked. To give him credit, he looked terrified of her. As he should.

'Sure.'

'I'm sorry for my behaviour at Moretz's party last month. I honestly didn't mean to make you uncomfortable. I just got a little overconfident. I should've backed off as soon as you hinted that you weren't into it.' Lorenzo held eye contact with her. Most people who apologized stared at the ground out of shame.

'Thank you for your apology. I appreciate it. For what it's worth, my opinion of you hasn't changed drastically,' she said, a small smile on her face.

'Thanks for not setting the guys on me.'

'Oh, they tried. Jules especially,' Faith warned.

'Speaking of Jules ... He's pretty great, you know. We've all seen the way you two interact, and I just thought I should say he deserves a good woman like you.'

'Hmm.' She wished him good luck in the race and went back into the garage.

If Julien Moretz was anything less than a genuine kind man who cared deeply about his friends, this would be an easy fix. If he had remained as arrogant as she first thought, she could put him out of her head and insist that she was better off without him, and more importantly she could find better, but Faith had tried to date before. She'd had summer romances in Cornwall with guys who had travelled there from various parts of the world, been wined and dined by businessmen and gone to museums and gigs with artist types in London, but nothing could match the way she felt around Julien. Letting go wasn't an option. It would be easier to give things a shot and deal with any heartbreak later. The *what if* was eating her alive.

Busying themselves with posting and responding to comments, Faith and Lucie stayed out of everyone's way once the race had begun. The first few laps were stressful and all eyes were on the TV screens, but once Julien had set the pace and put a decent gap between Revolution and Talos, the garage settled down a little. Faith had no idea how the mechanics and engineers stayed so focused for such a long period of time, because for them the race extended far beyond the twenty-four hours. She was struggling to keep her eyes open an hour in.

Once again they were having to focus the social media content on Brett and Marco because every time the camera came out Julien magically disappeared in a puff of smoke. Thankfully he had been cooperating for the majority of the week, so he had been a huge feature of the funfair posts and the Paris footage, which were a hit with the fans, Gabriel and Jasper.

Faith really didn't want the Brett/Marco to Julien ratio to be obvious to the point where people would comment on it and Gabriel start asking questions, so the girls were hoping that after Julien's nap he would be a lot more willing to shoot some video content with Faith. That included her tagging along to hospitality with him and getting a personal room tour.

Faith perched herself in a chair to the side of the garage and took everything in, waiting for her own followers to flood the comments on her personal feed. She had a perfect view of the team's stats and could clearly hear Jasper and the engineers discussing strategy, which she had a growing interest in now that she was actually here in the midst of it all. Marco's engineer, Mattia, had taken it upon himself to educate her. Her heart still leaped every time the cars passed the pit lane, or when someone got close to overtaking in another class. It was a feeling she didn't think she would ever get tired of, and even from outside the car she could understand why drivers risked their lives out on the track. Everything about it was addictive. The adrenaline racing through her bloodstream was a feeling like no other.

As Julien re-entered the garage and swapped with Marco so the Italian driver could carry out his first stint, Faith felt a wave of anxiety. He sat down next to her without a word, and she didn't dare open her mouth out of fear she would embarrass herself and say something stupid like she'd missed him. He had been so in his head that they'd barely interacted.

The two of them were called over by Jasper to look at the stats, freeing them from the awkward silence filled only by the squeak of the camping chairs they'd been sitting in and the occasional roar of an engine. Marco had just set a record for the fastest lap but Talos's rookie driver, Lucas Fitzpatrick, was catching up rapidly. The tension should have been building, but these drivers were abnormally zen. That was what made them the best of the best. You could throw anything at them and they took it in their stride, pushing themselves to the absolute limit and refusing to crack under pressure.

'Bloody hell, I've got a lot to live up to out there, haven't I?' Brett said.

'Not at all, Anderson. Just a lap record *and* my record from two years ago,' Julien teased. She liked it when the boys let themselves get cocky and Jasper encouraged it based on the sentiment that some healthy competition never hurt anyone.

Faith sighed and pressed her hand against her temple, willing her headache to go away. Perhaps she had overdone it on the coffee. It was barely seven o'clock in the evening and they had a long way to go, but she didn't know how she could stay awake without the aid of caffeine. A walk in the fresh air with a light evening breeze might have to suffice, but first she needed to hunt down a jacket.

'You're cold,' Julien commented, pointing out the goose-bumps on her arm.

'Only a little, I'm fine.'

'Go get my hoodie; it's on my bed.'

'Jules –' she tried to argue.

'Go,' he instructed, giving her a gentle shove when she didn't move.

She started heading towards the back of the garage where there was a corridor consisting of the drivers' rooms and Jasper's office. Faith wasn't sure why the boys didn't just share one room since they were never all in it at the same time, or why they didn't use the sofa bed in the trailer for such a short sleep, but she guessed that was what happened when you were a valued world-class athlete. You were given special treatment. She cast a sorrowful look at the camping chairs she and Lucie would be sleeping in.

The hoodie was waiting for her exactly where he said it would be, looking very warm and inviting. Significantly more so than its owner. The bed was practically crying out for her to crawl into it and steal a quick twenty minutes of peace and quiet, but with things between her and Julien as sensitive as they were she didn't dare. He'd be in here any moment for his nap and she highly doubted he was up for a spooning session.

She yanked the hoodie over her head and inhaled the smell of his cologne, wrapping her arms round herself. It was too big for her but it would do for a walk to the food trucks at the opposite end of the paddock. She had promised Lucie she would get them a pizza to share and she was desperate for some chips and mayo. The girls were starving and the constant adrenaline running through them was making them burn off food a lot faster. On her way out, Faith turned and knocked into Julien.

'Sorry!' she squeaked out.

'My bad, I thought you'd have heard me coming. Forgot how loud it is around here,' he replied. 'That really drowns you, doesn't it?'

'Fits fine. I like oversized.'

'The team uniform was one thing, but this . . . I like seeing you in my clothes.' He glanced down at her bare legs, his gaze lingering a few seconds too long.

'Are you being sentimental right now, Julien Moretz?' Faith raised an eyebrow.

'Um . . . yes? Is it weird?' His confidence faltered.

'No, just unexpected. You've been a little bit distant the last couple of days.'

'You're right. Sorry, you deserve better than that.' He cleared his throat.

'Hey, I get it. Doesn't mean I'm *happy* about it, but it's been chaos around here.'

'It would be nice to finally have some time to ourselves . . .' He tucked a strand of her hair behind her ear, scowling softly when it caught on her earring.

Faith frowned up at him. 'I wish. We're constantly surrounded by hundreds of people. When are we ever supposed to have time just the two of us?'

'Right now?' He nodded at the empty, enclosed space behind them. 'The silent treatment stops, whether I'm focused or not. I'll cheer up. You can even let me loose with the camera completely by myself. I promise. I just need to get out of my head.'

'And I need to get *into* your head.'

'You already are, Jensen.' His lips hovered above hers. Not wanting the moment to be shattered by reality, she reached up and traced his jaw, edging closer to meet him halfway. It took mere seconds for him to register that she was giving him the permission he was seeking, and then he was kissing her. A kiss filled with all the frustration that had built up over the last couple of months. His arms snaked round her waist, pulling her into him as she melted into his touch. But then her common sense, for a split second, managed to override the butterflies.

Faith pulled away reluctantly. 'Julien.'

'Do you want me to stop?'

'No. I just want you to shut the door before a mechanic walks past.'

He smirked and walked her backwards, the door slamming shut behind them. The walls rattled. If nobody suspected them before, they might now. But Faith didn't care. She was tired of dancing around this, wondering when it was going to happen.

Faith lifted the hoodie over her head. She was wearing a Revolution shirt under it and Julien took a second to admire her in his team colours, but hesitation was written all over his face. The switch hadn't quite been flipped, but he wasn't going in all guns blazing like he had been a second ago.

'Do *you* want to stop?' she asked, afraid of the answer.

'No, but do we really want to take this where we know

it's going? Do we really want our first time together to be on a camp bed at the back of the garage? We could be caught.'

'Jules, in the grand scheme of things, does that really matter? We could be caught sneaking into your hotel room too. This option is as good as any.'

'I could take you away somewhere,' he suggested.

'Like you did with Bea? No thanks.' She scrunched her nose up.

'It wouldn't be like it was with Bea.'

'Still, the location isn't a factor for me. I want this, Julien. And if you want it half as much as I do, I'm giving you the green light.'

With that, Julien wrapped her up in his arms again and the two of them kept walking towards the bed, bodies melded together.

'I don't think I've ever been more attracted to you.'

'Really? Not even when I had a bright blue feather boa wrapped round my shoulders and I was singing ABBA on your balcony?'

'I take it back. I wish I could watch that a thousand times over. All you needed was the shiny flared jumpsuit, and I'd have taken you right then and there.'

She grinned at him and sat back, watching him undress. She would have done it herself, but she wanted to enjoy the show. And a show she got. Julien was stood in front of her with his dick in his hand, stroking his already-hard length as he held her gaze.

'You're in control; we'll go at your pace,' he murmured.

Faith moved towards him, licking his tip and tasting his pre-cum. She usually avoided giving head. She found it boring and tiresome, but it was different with Julien. She wanted to please him. For his own pleasure and for hers. She ran her tongue up and down his length a few times, then closed her mouth around him fully.

'Fuck me, that feels so good,' he moaned, and he placed his hands in her hair, gently guiding her movements. She looked up right as his eyes rolled to the back of his head. Faith had him right where she wanted him. In this moment, in a tiny room at the back of the garage, he was hers.

Before he could get too carried away, Julien stepped backwards with a dark look in his eye. Faith stood up to meet him, holding his gaze and removing her bra. She had worn red especially for him today, never imagining it would actually pay off.

Julien turned them around and sat on the edge of the bed, grabbing her hips and lowering Faith on to his lap, placing soft kisses all over her collarbone. His hands travelled up her back but she stopped him before he got to his destination, aware they didn't have much time until someone found them.

She guided his hand between her legs, her attention on the pulsating feeling. She shivered as he made contact, pressing his palm against her while he kissed her neck. She began to move her hips, matching his pace and moaning. As she threw her head back in pleasure, he moved faster, somehow knowing exactly what would send her over the edge. But Julien didn't let her get that far.

'Not yet,' he breathed out. Removing his hand, he moved them until he was lying down with her still on top of him. There wasn't time for foreplay right now. He had to be behind the wheel soon. 'You have no idea what you do to me.'

'I didn't take you as the type of driver to do this. You're so serious.'

'What, you thought I was immune to hormones? I am insanely sexually frustrated because of you. Look at you, Faith. You're unreal.'

Faith lowered herself on to him, catching him off guard. She ran her hands across his bare chest as she rode him, moving faster the more he moaned. She widened her eyes at him in a playful manner and he quickly shut up. They would definitely be caught if he kept going at that volume. Focused on being quieter, he took over and thrust his hips up into her, and she knew she wouldn't last much longer. He pulled her closer and his teeth grazed the sensitive skin of her neck. She whimpered, his hands roaming every inch of her body.

'Are you OK, sweetheart?'

'Yeah.' She slowed to an agonizing pace, lifting herself off him almost completely before sinking back down again. Repeating this a few times, she watched his jaw clench and she knew he was close. Faith gasped when she felt Julien's hand on her clit, moving his fingers in circular motions. He was *way* too good at this. 'Fuck, Jules . . .' Faith whispered.

Julien closed his eyes as she sped up again, bouncing up and down on his cock. Unable to hold it in any longer, Faith's body began to twitch. She felt the release as he buried himself deep inside her and they came together. She swore she could see stars as he held her close to him, panting in her ear while she shook against him. Sitting up to enjoy the view and allow him to admire his own, she couldn't help but laugh as he lay there with a sleepy smile on his face.

'So worth the risk of being caught,' he breathed out, smiling.

# 21

Faith awoke in her camping chair at six o'clock the next morning with Julien's jacket draped over her like a blanket. She scrunched her nose up and squinted, the bright lights of the garage a little too intense so early in the day. She had only slept for three hours while Lucie took over filming, but she felt strangely well rested thanks to her and Julien's antics.

She was desperate to talk to him and establish what this meant for them, if anything, but mid-race wasn't the time. He had offered her smirks and smiles across the garage ever since they'd emerged from his room, like they had a secret. Which they did. She didn't know if he would tell Marco and Brett, but she was keeping her lips firmly sealed. She didn't want to be the talk of the grid for anything other than her stellar work.

Although she and Julien had physically explored their connection, they hadn't done so emotionally. They'd gone from swearing blind they couldn't cross a line, to crossing it in a way Faith was, honestly, a little mad about. She wasn't mad at Julien, just at herself. She had vowed to think with her head and not with the other body parts that were crying out to her, but Julien was like a magnet. She hadn't had a hope in hell.

Her legs were hanging over the side of the empty chair next to her and she was still in Julien's jumper with the hood up, probably looking very much like she was nursing a hangover. She hoped and prayed Lucie hadn't seen the state of her, or worse that the television cameras hadn't panned over to the side of the garage while she'd been passed out. The TV crew loved catching people out, whether people were asleep, exercising, eating or just goofing around. Faith, in all her professionalism, or rather current lack thereof, did not want to be victim to such entertainment.

It took a few minutes for her to be able to open her eyes fully and sit upright, just in time for Lucie to deliver a cup of black coffee and a croissant.

Lucie collapsed into her chair in a heap. 'How did you sleep?'

'As well as I could. Wish I'd taken Jules up on his offer to use his room,' Faith said. He had tried very hard to encourage her to shut herself away in there when she'd complained of a headache a few hours ago, but she had refused. Partly because she felt weird about stepping foot in that tiny room knowing what she and Julien had done in there, but mostly because the night-time portion of the race was known to be full of action and she wanted to be right there in case anything happened. Earplugs had done the trick.

'I drifted off for an hour or so. Brett woke me up ten minutes ago to tell me that Talos's rear bumper flew off after a collision, Fitzpatrick was behind the wheel. He's fine, he's already back out there, but the good news for us is that it gives Mars an advantage.' Lucie looked smug, which might be considered a little dark and morbid, but Talos falling behind took a huge amount of pressure off the team for the time being.

'When are we doing the next driver change?'

'Ten laps. Brett is in the car next, then Jules is taking us over the finish.'

Julien heard his name mentioned and turned his head to see what was going on. Upon seeing that Faith was awake, he wandered over while he peeled an orange. The hospitality team had showed up early with the fruit platters then. She should probably help herself to some of that and stop shovelling down the pastries. Her body would thank her for it.

'Morning, ladies. Glad you're up early; the sun is rising and the sky is all pink and orange and pretty. Would look great on the feed.' Julien held the orange segments out to them.

'How's the race going?' she asked. 'We haven't had a lot of chance to talk overnight.'

He had been begging her to let him have the camera since he'd returned from his nap, but she had spent most of the night filming with the mechanics in between pit stops, or with Marco or Brett who were battling for the spotlight. Then she'd had to walk through the paddock with Lucie and check in with the interns. Now it was time for the one-on-one Julien content.

'Yeah, it's going great so far, but you know Le Mans; things can change in the blink of an eye. The team are communicating well, though, so there's that.' He smiled.

'I spoke to Paolo earlier and he said that we're expecting some rain. Surely they'll want you out in that instead of Brett?' Lucie questioned.

Julien had a reputation for getting great results on a wet track, but he couldn't cover the rain *and* the finish. It would be breaking the rules regarding how much time a driver could be in the car without a break.

'That's not expected until the final hour of the race now so we should be all right. We'll keep Brett out if the weather gets bad and then I'll give us one final push when we change over. It isn't looking like Talos will catch up, but you know Lorenzo; he'll give it everything he's got.'

'I hope it definitely does rain then, because Garcia is shit in the wet. So is Fitzy actually, so they've got no hope at catching us if that's the case,' Lucie stated. 'Right, I'm going to go and grab some of that fruit before the mechanics get to it. I don't like oil and dirt on my watermelon.' She scurried off and left Julien and Faith alone, both of them stealing glances at each other as if the other wouldn't notice.

'We need to film together. We're running out of time in the schedule,' Faith said.

'Sure.' His calm, relaxed mood faltered. 'Just give me a moment. I have a video call to make. I'll come and find you when I'm done.'

Faith stared at him as he walked away. What kind of video call needed to be made at this time of the morning in a locked trailer? The work she needed to get done was time sensitive. She had to shoot content with Brett when he was out of the car, and she needed time to edit some of last night's content and get it posted before Julien went back out.

He couldn't just film on his own terms in the middle of an actual race. But still, at least he was willing to do it at all.

The day passed by in a blur of excitement and it was soon mid-afternoon. The race was coming to an end. When it had started raining four minutes after Julien had got in the car, the energy in the garage had been electric.

Every pair of eyes was glued to a screen and although Brett and Marco were trying to maintain professionalism, every time the camera crew disappeared again they were back to behaving like overgrown kids. Even Jasper was jumping up and down whenever another car in their class made an error.

Nobody had been involved in a serious accident yet, but a few cars were out of the race. Unfortunately for them Talos were still in with a shot at winning. Lorenzo Garcia was holding his own out there, which frankly was surprising to everyone.

Talos were known to crumble under pressure in the wet; plus, Julien usually had the upper hand in his rivalry with Lorenzo. The boys suspected that his personal issues with the Italian driver following the Spa after-party were giving Julien an edge. He was angry and Lorenzo was a little scared of him, and off-track drama often came to a head on track even for the most experienced drivers. Faith was secretly taking some of the credit.

Lucie was in the pit lane with one of Talos's mechanics, much to Brett's annoyance. He kept his eyes off them and on the TV screen. Faith was certain he'd perk up soon because if the race kept going the way it was, there would be a monumental cause for celebration.

With less than three minutes to go, Lucie darted back into the garage to join the rest of the team. There was too much of a gap for Lorenzo to close it – plus, his steering had locked for a fraction of a second. This was it; they were going to win.

'Ready?' Lucie grinned at Faith like she knew something her new co-worker did not. This wasn't going to be as tame as the race celebration in Belgium and, in all honesty, she was almost scared. Brett was very tall and very strong and could crush her like a bug if she wasn't careful.

She had forgotten that the winning teams tended to run out to the pit wall and climb up, leaning over the barriers to cheer as the cars crossed the finish, so before she had time to process what was happening, Lucie was grabbing her hand and yanking her out of the garage with everyone else. The pit lane was full of other teams doing the same thing. It was nothing short of a miracle that the girls were managing to keep hold of their cameras.

Julien crossed the line and the team took it to another level. Between the cheering, whistling, applauding and the roar of engines, the volume levels were deafening. Faith loved it. She must have hugged every single person who was associated with Revolution, plus at least half of Talos and every other team who had earned a place on the podium, whether she knew them or not. The energy was euphoric.

They rushed to find Julien and the car when he came back around to the pits. The wait for him to detach himself and get out was painfully slow but when he did, he removed his helmet to reveal the most radiant smile Faith had ever seen written across his face. He embraced his teammates with tears in his eyes as if he couldn't believe that they had done it yet again.

Faith wondered if the feelings of joy were ever diminished by the repetitive wins. These boys had been racing together for five years now and that was just as part of Revolution. They had known each other a very long time, worked together across different teams and championships and been childhood rivals. It was a bond that was totally unique to their sport, and one that nobody except the other drivers could ever comprehend.

Faith was still recording when Julien spotted her stood off to one side and having already received a hug from Lucie, he flung his arms round her and squeezed her tight. Faith held on for dear life, soaking up every second.

'Congrats, Moretz.' Her voice was muffled by his shoulder, their height difference coming into play. It didn't help that he had his arms round the upper part of her back and not the middle or lower, so she had a mouthful of racing suit.

'Thanks, Jensen.' He kissed the side of her head and lingered just a fraction too long, not noticing the TV camera immediately to their left. When he let her go, Faith nudged him and gestured at the camera. They had approximately point two seconds until that was all over social media. Revolution's PR team were going to have a field day with this.

It didn't matter that he did that to Lucie all the time, because Faith was new here. Fans knew he hadn't had the time to build up that level of connection with Faith, and it must mean there was more to their relationship. They would be right, but that wasn't going to make Julien feel any better when he started getting interrogated.

After a champagne-filled podium celebration and even more shouting and cheering, mostly from Brett, the team were heading back into the garage at a much more peaceful volume.

They had been warned that the media team would want

to catch up with them for post-race interviews, which was standard, and it was live. The live part terrified Faith. She could see the crew coming towards them now and Julien had his arm resting on her shoulders as they walked. The garage was close enough that she could dart in ahead of everyone, but it would look more suspicious if she tried to hide away.

'Julien! Can we get a word?' The interviewer jumped in front of them to block their path and a camera was shoved in their faces.

'Of course.' Julien smiled widely, his arm still in the same position. This was getting dangerous. He should have taken the opportunity to move it and let Faith run away.

'Oh good, we're the first to interview the grid's newest couple!' the interviewer exclaimed. The poor woman looked so innocent, Faith prayed Julien kept his cool. He tensed but that was all. No correction, no topic change. Faith was frozen to the spot.

'Faith, what's it like to be working in an industry you've loved for so long?' she asked. For a second, Faith forgot that she was kind of like a celebrity in her own right but when she realized, she wished she'd had media training at some point in her life.

'It's an absolute dream. I really couldn't ask for a better job or a more welcoming group of people. The fan feed-back has been incredible too. I just love being able to give them what I always wanted as a fan myself,' she replied, feeling Julien squeeze her shoulder reassuringly. She was handling her first TV interview well, but she couldn't help but feel that it had been tainted by the journalist's assumption.

'So, Julien, it must be pretty fantastic to be celebrating another win here at Le Mans?'

'It's always an honour to take home a trophy. The team works really hard. I couldn't do it without Anderson and De Luca. Revolution is a team and we all need each other to win.' He waved at a group of drivers as they passed.

The camera crew left to find Jasper and the other drivers after a few more questions about Julien's thoughts on the car, but frustration had been bubbling away at Faith the whole time. She calmly removed herself from his grip and located Lucie. Steam must have been coming from her ears because her friend immediately took her arm, abandoned her conversation with a mechanic, and led her to the boys' trailer.

Lucie grimaced. 'I witnessed the whole thing.'

'I mean, honestly, what the *hell* was that all about?' Faith was exasperated.

'Sweetheart, I hate to say it, but it really does look like you're dating to the outside world. After that photo Bea put up of you two hugging, rumours have been swirling. And there was the one of your little breakfast date. I deleted comments on some of the posts so you wouldn't notice but the rumours are there, and people can see the chemistry. It's our own fault really. We should've controlled the content better.' Lucie sat down next to her on the sofa and looked like she might throw up.

'OK, we could have cut some clips, but people would still have seen the chemistry,' Faith said. 'It's there and it's natural; if we took all of it out, Julien would barely exist in half the videos. It would be a race-week vlog with only two of the drivers. He's the one who just stood there on camera and pretended we were a couple instead of saying "Hey, we're not actually dating – we're just great friends!".' How hard was that?'

Lucie sighed. 'You have a point. God, this is so messed up. He's going to lose it.'

Right on cue, Julien flung the door open, his face dropping when he saw the two of them.

Lucie stood up and gathered the cameras, offering a weary smile and shuffling out of the door. Faith waited for it to close before she let rip.

'You –' she started.

He cut her off. 'Don't say a word.'

'Excuse me?' Faith gawked at him in disbelief. She was going to say exactly what she needed to say, because she wasn't about to have the blame put on her.

'Your stupid little social media posts have led everyone to think that we're together and now I'm in a huge mess,' he said.

'My "stupid little social media posts" which are part of my job, you mean? You know I get paid for those, right? I was hired by *your* bosses to boost *your* career and *your* sponsorships. Don't stand there acting so entitled when you know you wouldn't have half the things you have if it weren't for people like me and Lucie. You're part of a team, Julien.'

'All you've done is complicate my life, Faith. You live in a bubble. You snap a few photos and make them all pretty and colourful and fail to see that there is so much more to life than fucking filters and flying around the world sipping cocktails. You're just another stuck-up influencer, like I thought in the first place. Try spending one day as an actual adult with real responsibilities.' Julien was seething.

'You have no idea how hard I worked and what pushed me to get there. I'm here because I earned my position, just as you did. Lucie and I sit up for hours editing photos and videos and strategizing how we can make you guys look more approachable and less big and famous and scary, but it's kinda hard to do that when you're so arrogant that you think the world revolves around you and shielding your private life. A life you won't breathe a word about because you think I can't keep my mouth shut or I won't understand. Maybe I won't understand because we haven't walked the same path, but mine left me with baggage too.' Faith's vision was blurred with tears but she wasn't done.

'I forgot about –' he mumbled.

'My past? My feelings? You seem to have pushed all that aside and done what was right for you without stopping to think for a second how this hot-and-cold behaviour might affect me. You have *sex* with me, which by the way we once agreed could never happen, and then hours later you're screaming at me for something that is out of my control? You could have denied it right then and there!'

Julien stared at her with sad eyes and her anger subsided enough for her to feel some sympathy towards him, some forgiveness. 'I thought I was protecting you.'

'All you did, all you do, is hurt me. Pull me in and then let me go. I want you to feel like you can trust me, because you can. It doesn't matter if nothing comes of this connection we have, but I'd at least like to know your reasons for not pursuing it further than sex, so I'm not left feeling like it's something I did.'

'I do trust you, Faith.' His tone was soft.

'Then stop wrapping me up in cotton wool and just

open up to me. I care about you, Jules. A lot. It's why I've been putting up with your crap for weeks now. Otherwise, I would have walked away and kept this strictly professional. Let me be part of your world instead of shutting me out and wishing I would go away, because I'm not going anywhere. You're stuck with me, the same way Lucie is and the same way you're stuck with Brett and Marco. We're a team, and as the boys told me when I first arrived in Spa, we're a family. I'm not going to betray you.'

Faith didn't give him a chance to say anything else, it was her turn to give him the cold shoulder. She needed space to think, to get away from him. If he was going to tell her whatever it was he'd been hiding, whatever had his walls so far up, then a trailer at the back of his racing team's garage wasn't the time and place. She left him sitting alone while she tried to rationalize what in the world could be such a big deal to him that he hid it from almost everyone he knew.

# 22

Each team had been sent to their garages with a glass of champagne each, and strictly instructed not to leave until Gabriel had been to speak to them. He was going to be announcing the destination of the annual trip, but although they were all excited, they were also itching to get back to the hotel so they could pack their bags. They were leaving at seven o'clock the next morning for their flights, which meant no drinks or bar crawls tonight.

Faith and Lucie had already decided to ditch dinner at the hotel and order room service while they got some work done. They didn't want to be working on their first day of the trip, and it didn't matter to them if they had to catch a flight with three hours of sleep.

'Congratulations, team!' Gabriel came to visit them first with his daughter in tow. Alessia did not look amused in the slightest, and, given her age, it would be safe to assume that she was not invited to wherever they were going.

'Gabriel, come on! We have suitcases to pack,' Lucie complained.

'Lucie, I am about to make your year. Tomorrow . . . we're heading to Hawaii!' Gabriel cheered, before leaving to head to the next garage.

There was chatter among the mechanics and engineers but Faith noticed that Julien had ducked out. He hadn't said a word to her since their argument, even though by the end of it they had stopped screaming and there had been a sliver of hope for their relationship.

Glancing at her friends, she realized that none of them looked excited. Lucie actually looked worried. Faith had a sinking feeling that Julien wasn't going to be joining them on this trip, and she couldn't help but think that it was her fault.

Did she even deserve to go? She had worked a mere two races, and Julien had just won arguably the biggest race of any motorsport championship in existence. There was a possibility that she was taking this away from him just because he didn't like people thinking they were dating. She shouldn't be going with them if that was the case.

'You excited then, Jensen?' Brett asked with forced enthusiasm.

'Yeah . . . but seems like I'm one of few,' she said.

Brett shrugged nonchalantly. 'Nah, Hawaii is just not really where Jules wants to be.'

She sighed and gathered up her things, ready to go back to the hotel for a long night of packing and editing. She couldn't hype herself up for this trip, with all the work they still had to get done and the Julien drama weighing on her mind. If he could just get out one sentence, one hint at what was happening in his world, she was sure it would lead to him revealing everything.

'Girlies!' Bea stopped them before they could get even a quarter of the way down the paddock.

'Hey, Bea!' Lucie called back. At least *they* were being civil.

'Oh my goodness, I've heard all about your big interview with Julien! I can't believe you two are actually a thing! I'm so happy for you, Faith, really.'

'Thank you, Bea. That means the world.' Faith pulled out her best acting skills and smiled with a glint in her eye that she was sure Lucie would call her out on. If Julien could play this game, so could she. The lie no longer belonged solely to him; it belonged to *them*.

'Well, I am over the moon for you. I shall see you ladies in Hawaii!' She floated away, oblivious to the chaos she had just been involved in creating.

Lucie whipped round to face her. 'Faith!'

'Well aware of what I've just done,' she said.

'You're doing exactly what you're mad at Julien for.' Lucie flung her arms out in despair.

'I just wanted to go along with it and see how genuine she was,' Faith said defensively.

'You'd better hope and pray she doesn't go and run her mouth to Jules, otherwise you two are going to have yet another fight and God knows whatever your relationship is can't survive that.' Lucie tutted and shooed her down the paddock like she was scolding a child.

'I think the champagne is getting to me.' Faith stuck her bottom lip out in hopes that she would look all sweet and innocent and Lucie would stop shouting, even if she deserved it.

'Are you going to admit it yet?' Lucie questioned.

'Admit what?'

'You have feelings for Julien.'

'You said that like it's a known fact.'

'Oh, don't worry. The team is clueless. But I see the way you look at each other, Faith. You like him. More than you ever planned to.'

'Well, shit. You caught me.'

'Of course I did. Because I know you both. I think in some ways, I already know you better than I know Jules. Do you want to talk about it?'

'No.' Faith pouted. But she did. More than anything. She just couldn't betray Julien's trust, because this was his secret as much as it was hers.

'I think the sexual tension is getting to you,' Lucie stated, trying to make light of the situation.

Little did she know Julien had already seen to that.

'Yeah, well, nothing will be done about that for a long time,' Faith lied. 'Julien and I will be old and crippled by the time he pulls it together and makes a move, and he won't be able to lean far enough forward out of his armchair to kiss me. He might even die of a heart attack from all the excitement.'

'I reckon he's already got a few grey hairs hiding in that blond mane. He doesn't have enough fun in life.'

'You mean to tell me that Julien Moretz has spent the last ten years shagging models and gallivanting around Europe, but he doesn't have enough fun?' Faith raised an eyebrow.

'I knew you used those words! So British. I love it.' Lucie grinned and walked down the paddock repeating the word 'shagging' to herself. She was in such a world of her own that she didn't notice Julien exiting the hospitality area and joining up with Marco and Brett, who were pretty far behind them but not far enough for Faith's rising anger levels.

'Luce,' Faith snapped, 'walk faster.'

She turned round, confused. 'Why?'

Faith scowled. 'Keep me far away from my fake boy-friend, please. I'm very tempted to rip his head clean off and that won't be good for the team. We need him.' If she wasn't careful she'd be needing to ask Bea for Botox recommendations.

'Let's get you back to the hotel. Room-service sushi will fix you.'

It was too early to be awake for Faith's liking, and the decision to work through most of the night was met with heavy regret from her and Lucie. They had managed to get an hour of sleep, and when they joined the rest of the team downstairs, with their messy buns and oversized T-shirts, all the drivers were way too boisterous to deal with. The girls stood to one side, itching to get their suitcases bundled into the car and get on the road to the airport so they could squeeze in a nap.

The team had been split into two cars with Elliot from Havelin Racing joining Lucie, Julien and Faith. He didn't know it but his sole purpose on this two-and-a-half-hour journey was to dissolve the tension between the grid's newest non-couple, and keep Julien distracted enough to be able to engage in a normal civilized conversation with Faith. He had been a gentleman and carried her case out of the hotel, but she hadn't spoken more than one sentence to him in the ten minutes they'd been stood outside together. It was uncomfortable to say the least.

A fleet of Range Rovers picked everyone up just past seven o'clock. All the team lorries were leaving the circuit this morning too. Eyes were already on them given that they were in a relatively small town full of racing fans who had yet to head home, and taking all these vehicles to the motorway at once was bound to draw attention.

Elliot was Faith's saving grace. They had barely plugged their seat belts in before he started chatting about growing up on his parents' vineyard in France. He was British but had moved to Bordeaux when he was six and married his childhood sweetheart when he was eighteen.

She was called Valentina and it was sweet to listen to him describe the moment he knew he was going to marry her. Julien still looked like he'd rather be anywhere else, but at least he was actually using his vocal chords now.

'I've been to Cornwall a few times for family holidays over the years. It was one of the first places in the UK I took Valentina to, St Ives. She wasn't a fan of the pasties.' He laughed.

'I mean, you can't come to Cornwall and not try one. It's what we're famous for,' she said. Pasties were also not her favourite, and she hadn't eaten one since she moved to London.

When she took Lucie to the coast in a couple of weeks she might have to indulge just for old times' sake. Devon and Dorset also called for a traditional cream tea, which she knew would have her friend rambling on about British stereotypes again.

'Are your parents from Cornwall?' he asked.

'Mum is. Dad is from somewhere in Australia; he left when I was a few months old.' Faith almost wished she hadn't revealed that to a stranger.

Elliot smiled. 'Bet your mum is super proud of everything you've achieved. Probably made her feel like she did the right thing staying here instead of chasing after your dad.'

Faith saw her mum in a different light for a moment. He

was right: Faith's success probably made everything her mum had been through seem worth it to her.

Andrea hadn't always been able to give Faith everything she needed, but that wasn't necessarily her fault. She had unfortunate taste in men and had been swindled out of her savings on two separate occasions, barely managing to keep a roof over their heads and put food on the table. Faith had split her wages from her part-time job so she had enough to help her mum out and some to put aside for when she moved to London. She had to give her mum credit; she had never discouraged Faith from following her dreams despite being bitter about being left behind.

Faith had felt the same when Bea had left for Europe. She wondered how her best friend could just go and live a life without her while Faith yearned for more for herself too. It was selfish. Faith knew that now. But that bitterness, the 'why not me?' attitude was exactly what Faith's mum had expressed from the moment Faith had told her she was moving.

In Andrea's eyes, her daughter was everything she couldn't be because she'd never had the courage to hit the reset button on her life. She'd let a series of bad relationships send her so far off course that it had damaged not only the way she saw herself, but their mother–daughter relationship too. Her mum was too trusting. She had too much hope that the next guy would be different, that this would be the one who saved her and gave her and her kid the picture-perfect life. It wasn't a bad thing to want that; she was human. But it was no good for her mental health to go into every relationship with her walls down.

She would meet a new guy, sort out her drinking, claim

that she was OK, and Faith believed her. Every time. Because she was her mum and Faith was too young to understand the complexities of addiction. Then, as she got older, Andrea's rough or creepy boyfriends would lay their hands on Faith, and that was when her mum had fought for *her*. And yet, when the latest boyfriend left and Andrea and Faith were all alone again, the drinking would get bad again and Faith, somehow, was left to pick up the pieces. That, Faith suspected, was why her mum had never come after her. It was a chapter that needed to be closed in order for Faith to move on.

London and her introduction to Bea had given her everything she had imagined and more. She found it difficult to enjoy the opportunities she was given for the first couple of years because she felt that it could be taken away at any given moment, and it took Bea dragging her to events and parties to open her up to the world and actually experience life. She had to keep reminding herself that Bea would never let her get wrapped up with the wrong guy, she didn't have a problem with alcohol and never touched drugs, even though the city was full of them. She wasn't going to be a carbon copy of her mum or the men in her life.

Faith hadn't had any experience prior to moving to London, and despite living through the chaos of her mum's relationships she wasn't good at recognizing red flags. Bea was her saviour. She taught her all there was to know about how to actually enjoy dating, the kind of men to avoid, and about refusing to settle for less than you deserve. It was probably why neither of them had been in a long-term relationship, but at least they hadn't had their hearts broken beyond the point where a glass of wine and a gossip couldn't fix their problems.

'I never realized how you grew up . . .'

Julien's voice brought Faith back to the present moment. She stared at the back of his head from the seat behind him and her eyes widened. She had said all of that out loud.

Faith let out an awkward laugh and shrank back in her seat. 'Sorry, I didn't mean to offload all of that. Haven't had my morning coffee yet, I guess it's getting to me.'

'Don't apologize. And what's said in this car stays in this car, right?' Julien reached back to place his hand on Faith's knee. Faith tensed but didn't shy away from his touch.

'Absolutely. We're always here if you need us. I know I'm not part of Revolution Racing – technically I'm a rival – but you can consider me part of the racing family,' Elliot said.

Lucie rested a head on her shoulder, knowing her friend enough by now to understand that more sweet sentiments wouldn't do anything except keep them all stuck in a weird limbo where nobody knew what else to say.

Elliot swiftly moved the conversation on to cars, leaving Faith to quietly think about what she'd just shared with everyone.

# 23

The entirety of first class had been booked out by the organization. Julien and Faith had been seated next to each other, causing Julien to ask Gabriel when the flights had been booked, wondering if they were together because of their now viral couple's interview.

Much to their horror, Gabriel had politely informed him that his assistant had arranged it a month ago because she had seen how close the two of them had become and thought it would be appreciated. Faith thought that everyone should have been in alphabetical order according to surnames.

Faith surfaced from her nap mid-flight with one headphone in but before she could search for the missing one, she overheard Julien whispering to Brett across the aisle. She couldn't make it out word for word, but the general gist was that he was going to have to be careful to keep everything under wraps and that if he was absent for a while, Brett knew where he'd be.

He didn't want anyone else to know until he'd spoken to Faith, but he didn't know how he should tell her. Brett suggested just telling her at dinner, but Julien felt that a beach walk would suit the situation better. There was not one hint at what the big secret was, but when Faith finally put her other headphone in she did it with a smile on her face, safe in the knowledge that Julien was finally letting his walls down.

Over twenty-four hours after leaving Paris, having briefly stopped at LAX, they were pulling up outside the hotel in Hawaii. They had the *entire* resort to themselves and nobody dared to think about how much it had cost, but money was no object to most of the execs and CEOs. The drivers were usually a little more reserved with their money, but for Faith and Lucie and the rest of the media personnel this was the kind of trip they could never fund themselves. Most of them could afford to splurge on a shopping trip here and there, but when it came to food, travel and daily life, they had to be conscious about what they were spending.

There were palm trees everywhere, brightly coloured flowers blooming all around them, and the weather was blissful. They were offered sunset-coloured cocktails as soon as they walked in and their suitcases were quickly whisked away by staff.

They were gathered in a circle to receive room keys. With people already wandering around and admiring the views and paying zero attention, treating them like school kids was necessary.

Lucie and Faith learned that they were unsurprisingly sharing a room, much to their delight, and that the entire Revolution team was on their floor. They doubted they would be getting much sleep since the week would consist mostly of pool parties and late nights, and there was no need to keep the noise down for the sake of other guests at the resort.

'Moretz, we have a room for you.' Gabriel side-stepped towards them and whispered loud enough for only the team to hear him. 'You're not obligated to stick around, but it's there if you want it. Steph will give you the key in a moment.'

Julien smiled gratefully and glanced over at Faith, accidentally catching her eye. 'I'll be present for the whole trip.'

Why wouldn't he stick around? Brett had said that Julien didn't want to be in Hawaii, but where else would he be if he wasn't with them at the hotel? This whole secret thing was becoming weirder more than anything else.

The girls' room was beautiful. It was light and airy, with lots of white linen and light-wood furnishings. There were fresh flowers on the dresser with a welcome note tucked into them and the doors to the balcony had been left open with the curtain blowing gently in the breeze.

There was a view of the pool area and the sea beyond it, and yet again palm trees as far as the eye could see. Their suitcases were waiting for them at the end of the bed, a king-size which they had no problem with sharing, and Lucie nearly tripped over them as she ran out to peer her head round to the neighbouring balcony.

'Oh, Christ, it's you two,' Brett teased from their left, and they were soon joined by Julien on their right. Marco was to the right of Julien, so they could all talk in one long line.

It really was feeling more and more like a school trip, albeit a very expensive and alcohol-fuelled one. Faith was used to caving and abseiling on Cornish beaches, not diving in the deep blue waters of the islands of Hawaii. It was quite the contrast.

'I'm surprised they didn't put Faith and Jules in the same room with all the rumours flying around,' Lucie commented.

'You mean the rumours that Jules basically confirmed on live TV?'

'Anderson, shut up,' Marco scolded Brett, who smirked but shut his mouth. It was more likely Lucie's glare that did it.

'I'm gonna take a quick drive, but I'll see you all at dinner tonight. Enjoy the pool.' Julien gave them a friendly smile, coming across as scarily calm given the joke that was just made.

Faith wondered what could possibly be better than an afternoon by the pool in a private resort, but nonetheless she was relieved.


The sky was getting darker and the twinkling lights created a perfect atmosphere for their evening meal. There was a live band playing Elvis songs – an experience that would feel horrifically cheesy if they were at a pub in England. Everything just felt magical and Faith was in heaven.

Food and drinks were flowing and the servers were doing an outstanding job at staying on top of it all no matter how many drivers had gone full diva mode and were demanding adjustments and extras. Lucie and Brett were in their own little bubble, ignoring the rest of the table, which left Faith, Marco and Julien to chat among themselves.

Julien had returned an hour before dinner and popped into the girls' room to ask for fashion advice and help Faith get her necklace on, a delicate gold chain with an aquamarine pendant that Bea had given her a few years ago. Two hours later and she could still feel the warmth of his fingertips on her bare skin.

On the next table Bea was up to no good. Faith knew

when she was interested in someone and right now she might as well be literally fluttering her false eyelashes in the face of Ricardo de la Rosa, the top driver for Odesza.

Men were always drawn to Bea's natural sex appeal, so when she put in some effort she really meant it. Ricardo was handsome. Tattoos covered his body and he had a mane of jet-black hair that constantly fell over his grey eyes. He hadn't shaved for a number of days and wore a patterned shirt with the top few buttons undone. His whole demeanour suggested that he was the most laid-back man on the planet. He was the polar opposite of the dark-haired woman beside him. Especially in her black-lace bodysuit, white tailored trousers and matching blazer. Her heels made her almost the same height as him. Ricardo was so far from her type yet Bea was blushing so hard she needn't have bothered to fake it with make-up. Faith hadn't seen her friend this nervous around a guy, ever. Ricardo was staring into her eyes as she spoke, as if he was hypno-tized by her.

'Bea,' Faith called over.

'Yes?' She turned and abruptly cut off her conversation with the Odesza driver, who simply smiled and went back to his bruschetta.

'Can we have a chat?'

'Of course!' Bea excused herself and waited for Faith to join her so they could head over to the sun loungers where it was quieter.

'I thought it was time we had that talk. We've been getting along OK, and I know you and Lucie are starting to find some common ground, but it's still weird, right?' Faith stared out at the still water.

'It is, and that's all on me. Since seeing you again at Spa, I've been doing a lot of soul searching and I realized I've been losing myself to the whole influencer culture thing. I want to be a better friend, and a better person,' Bea admitted.

They had once had what Faith and Lucie now shared, and it didn't seem right to pretend they hadn't. Nothing about Bea's friendships with the models and influencers who crawled all over the motorsport world was genuine.

'You drifted a little, but you're still in there. I refuse to believe otherwise,' Faith said.

'I was jealous,' Bea said, her face flushed.

'What?! Why?'

'I always felt like you had everything handed to you on a plate, which I know is the furthest thing from the truth. You're just this perfect human being; everyone loves you and fitting in is so effortless for you because of it. The whole world sees in you what I saw the first day we met at uni, and for once I just want someone else to see all of that in *me*.'

'I saw it in you, Bea. I still do. Why do you think I'm having this conversation with you?'

'When I found out you were coming to work with us, I thought I'd get shoved aside. I try so hard to be part of everything, but I guess I try too hard and instead I get clingy with all the wrong guys, who aren't interested in getting to know the real me, and I get on everyone's nerves. All I want is to be included, but when that doesn't happen I just have some stupid dramatic reaction, and now I have a reputation I can't free myself from.'

'You absolutely can free yourself from it. You're halfway

there already. You know everyone at Revolution has been begging me to have this talk with you?' Faith tried to reassure her, squeezing her hand. 'I do have one question, though. Why did you post that photo of Julien and me at Spa, knowing how he would react?'

'Oh, God.' Bea covered her face in embarrassment. 'I was jealous. His affection was one more thing you had that I didn't. I had this urge to cause chaos, and I knew fans would go wild. Lucie behaves the same way with him, but you two have this chemistry that everyone can see except you and Julien.'

'Trust me, we know it's there.' Faith pressed her lips into a thin line.

'I'm sorry, Faith. I want to be the old Bea again, the one who was a lot less worried about what strangers think or the number of likes on a post, the comments from people boosting me. People don't deserve the way I treated them, you especially.'

'Let people see her. I miss her too. And our friends and co-workers will love her just like I do.' Faith was realizing just how insecure her best friend was.

The new version of Beatrix Miller was simply her putting her walls up, and nobody could blame her for that. The social media bubble was toxic and even Faith struggled to stay on the right side of it sometimes. Combine that with the world of motorsport where money talked, and it was a battle that you could very easily lose yourself in.

'I saw the way Julien looked at you the first time I came into the garage to find you. I knew he wasn't into me, but I developed a little crush. Who wouldn't? Not *feelings*, that's a whole different ball game. But I guess the more time we spent together, then the more he pulled away, which made me want him even more. It was like I was seeking his validation. But then you came along and I saw how perfect the two of you were for each other. It isn't just the chemistry you have; it's who you are as people. That's when I realized it wasn't him that I craved; it was the attention he gave me. I got angry when he ended things and I went about things the wrong way. I should've given him a hard shove in your direction.'

Faith sighed. 'I don't know him all that well really. I just know there's something there. And that he's a stubborn son of a bitch.'

'You know his heart. Better than most of us, I think. Which shows just how quickly he's let you in. You have such a good read on people, Faith. Julien is a great guy; he's just closed off. His private life is *very* private and it's hard to accept when you want to know all of him. But that didn't stop you getting close, right? Because your gut feeling is telling you to hold on.' Bea raised an eyebrow, knowing that Faith gave her whole heart to people even when she was scared.

Faith nodded. 'I wanted to keep it professional and move on, but even when we fight and argue and he makes me want to tear my hair out, I still want him. I just don't know how much more time I can give him. I think if he doesn't open up by the end of this trip I'm going to have to let the situation go. He doesn't owe me an explanation of his life, but I owe myself the option to walk away.'

'I vote you confront him and tell him exactly that. If he cares as much as we all think, then he'll recognize what he risks throwing away. Nobody has really forced him to open up before, but something about you clearly gets under his skin. I mean, God, some of the drivers have known him since he was a *child* and even they can't believe how much emotion he's displayed publicly in the short time he's known you. Good or bad. He's like a whole new person, Faith. That's because of you.'

Faith decided in that moment to take her friend's advice, and stood up, pulling Bea with her. Although she knew it would take some time for the trust to properly return to their friendship, she felt positive that this could be the start of a new stage for them and that the past could stay in the past.

# 24

After a dessert spread of profiteroles, cheesecake, fruits and gateaux, everyone was in a food coma. There was hardly anyone sitting down who wasn't collapsed back against their wooden chair, wishing they hadn't indulged quite so much. There had been so much rich, creamy food consumed in the last couple of hours that Lucie, Bea and Esme were even debating going up to their rooms to change into looser-fitting clothes.

Faith didn't want to get up from the table, but she knew they couldn't sit here forever. The staff had a lot of cleaning up to do, and there was a pool and a beach to be enjoyed. There was a campfire down on the sand, plus a firepit and a hot tub by the pool where a live DJ was setting up. Apparently he would be here every night for the next week. That was how committed the organization was to celebrating. Faith had wondered why they chose to hold their annual trips in the middle of a season, but she had learned that the winter break was always insanely busy for the teams and drivers, who spent the entire time prepping for the next season. Plus, Le Mans was such a stressful event, so this trip was always welcomed with open arms. It helped that it was in a long gap between races, and in the middle of summer.

Marco had scooted his chair over to the girls so he could tell them he had gone ahead and organized flights to Italy next week, with plans to drive to the mountains to join Brett's family on their hiking holiday.

Bea had sat down and given a very lengthy and detailed apology to the entire table on what she was calling 'Beatrix Miller's Apology Tour' and Julien had even apologized to *her*, although it was clear he wasn't entirely convinced he needed to.

The effect of the cocktails overpowered their over-indulgence of food and the dancing began. The Revolution team, with Bea as an extra addition, were causing a stir and it wasn't long before everyone was joining in. Clothes and shoes were being tossed to one side and people were taking full advantage of the pool, including Brett, who started a diving competition. You wouldn't believe he was a grown man as he starfished into the water.

'Lucie!' Bea yelled over the music. 'I'm sorry for being a massive bitch! I think you're a lovely human being!'

'Oh, Bea!' Lucie cried out with tears in her eyes. 'Screw the past, life's too short.'

As Faith watched them hug it out and sob in the middle of their makeshift dance floor, she glanced around and found herself face to face with Julien.

He took the opportunity to shuffle closer to her and for a second she felt like Sophie in that scene from *Mamma Mia!*, when everyone was dancing around her during 'Voulez-Vous' and she got dizzier and dizzier. If she didn't get out of here quickly, Faith was going to pass out.

The beach was practically calling out to her, and she had no problem following the overgrown path that led down to the quiet stretch of sand. She settled on a broken tree trunk. She stared out at the horizon, appreciating the pink and purple hues of the sky above. The sea was calm. That was how she felt now that she was away from the pressure of Julien's eyes on her. And his body against hers.

Someone fake-coughed behind her. 'Mind if I sit down for a moment?'

The Dutch accent gave it away and Faith motioned for him to join her without turning round.

'Sorry, just needed some fresh air,' Faith said.

'It was getting a little heated, huh?'

'As always.'

The pair of them sat in silence for a few minutes, just soaking it all in. 'You look just like her.' His voice was barely a whisper. He shuffled awkwardly, too shy to look at her.

'Who?' Faith swallowed the nervous lump in her throat. She felt sick. Unsure if she was ready for this conversation.

'My wife.' Julien chose that moment to pause and gather himself before continuing, leaving Faith's head in a scramble as she waited for more words to come out of his mouth. 'I got married when I was eighteen. I was travelling, met her in Greece and followed her back here to Hawaii. For two years we lived in a tiny little hut on her parents' land. I lost her out there.' He gestured to the water and Faith's heart dropped. 'She drowned. I witnessed the entire thing. I tried to swim out but –' He was getting choked up.

'It's OK, Jules . . .' Faith swallowed nervously. 'What was her name?' She placed her hand over his and he took it.

'Kailani,' he said. He was regaining his composure and he looked relieved that she wasn't freaking out. Faith wasn't really having much of a reaction at all, at least not visibly, but it was a lot for her to take in. 'She was my best friend.

I've never been able to match what we had. Never really tried, because I always felt like she was it for me.'

Faith gave a soft smile. 'I'm glad you got to experience a love like that, even if it was only for a short time. But I guess that love continues for you, right? She's gone, but you're still here with the memories.'

'Mm-hmm. There's more.' A strange noise came from the back of his throat, like he really didn't want to say whatever was coming next. 'I have a daughter, Jasmine. She's almost twelve, but she was barely a year old when Kailani died. I was already racing. I had been for a few years, and I always insisted on keeping that part of my life hidden. Kailani's parents took her in, raised her full-time and let me visit every moment I possibly could. That's where I go when we get a break. I step into my dad role and I spend time with Jasmine, mostly here since her grandparents are native Hawaiians and the island is very important to us, but sometimes at home in Malmedy too. With Ford. I continued with racing because it meant I could financially provide for them all, giving her the opportunities that Kailani would've wanted for her. It just sucks that I'm not with her all the time, raising her myself,' he explained, as if he was afraid Faith might judge his choices.

'So your daughter is the reason you're so cautious when it comes to us?' Faith nodded slowly, finally understanding his behaviour over the last few months, his reluctance to get too close. He was protecting his daughter. Faith realized why Lucie always told her to be careful with him, while also encouraging her not to give up. There was a lot at stake.

'Yes. I also didn't want her in the media. It was important

for my career that I built my brand as a single guy. My management team thought it would bring in more sponsors, and as time has passed and my reputation has grown, it's been more important than ever to conceal the truth. Kailani didn't like social media, and she wouldn't want our daughter to be plastered all over it. It was important for me that Jasmine could grow up as normal as possible. My career is *my* decision. I've only ever told my teammates and my bosses about them. They all had to sign NDAs to ensure the news never got out. I felt guilty asking them for that, but I had to put my family first.'

'I get that. The motorsport industry is intense, and if you don't have to open your loved ones up to certain aspects of it, why would you?'

'Jasmine lives in a very peaceful world out here. She and her grandparents grow a lot of their own food, she goes to a good school, goes hiking on weekends and she can play freely with other kids in the area. I don't want to drag her into my world until she's old enough to understand it. I think that now might be the time to slowly introduce her to it. She's taking a real interest in it all.'

'That makes sense. And, hey, if you need any advice on how to protect her from the media, I'm happy to help. We can find ways to ensure that she's well protected and kept off social channels. I can get further NDAs drawn up and everything.'

'Faith, I'm telling you all of this because I want to move forward with you. To begin with, I couldn't look at you without thinking about my wife. Except for the hair, you look very similar. But over time I've started to recognize all the things that make you different, and you unknowingly forced me to confront a lot of things that I had pushed down for years. I didn't want to commit to anyone because I felt they wouldn't understand or respect my decisions. Can you imagine many supermodels giving up Monaco and private yachts for an eco-friendly lifestyle, an almost-teenager and muddy winter walks with a moulting husky?'

'Sounds like a dream to me,' she said softly.

'Exactly. That's why I knew I had to sort my head out. Because of you. An incredible woman who *already* exists in my world.' Julien held her gaze for the first time since he had told her everything. She saw a light in his eyes that hadn't been there before, and it made all the confusion and pain worth it. Julien was a passionate man. His life wasn't all work, work, work like she had first assumed and wrongly judged him for. He craved the same kind of love and family that she did; the only difference was he already had a family that needed to be nurtured.

'Do you have a photo of either of them?' she asked, tears forming in her eyes.

Julien reached into his pocket and retrieved his leather wallet, opening it up and finding two Polaroids. There was something about him having physical photos rather than digital ones that made Faith's heart melt. It seemed more sentimental, more special. He handed them to her and she took them carefully.

'These were in my bedside drawer at home. I was para-noid you were going to see them.'

Faith laughed softly. 'I don't snoop, Jules.'

Jasmine was beautiful and looked far older than twelve. She had a pink hibiscus flower in her dark hair and wore a white dress as she sipped a smoothie. She had her dad's eyes, a sparkling blue. Julien's wife truly did look like Faith, the only difference being that Faith was blonde, her nose was slimmer and her cheekbones slightly more defined. Even their smiles were nearly identical; she could see why Julien had behaved so strangely when they were first introduced. But he was right: Faith was Faith. She would never be Kailani, nor did she want to be, and Julien didn't want her to be either.

'It feels like everything that's happened since we met makes sense now,' Faith said. 'Every argument, every time you pushed me away, every time you just ignored what we'd got up to behind closed doors. I get it. This is a lot to process for you, and would be for your daughter and the rest of your family too. Jasmine is obviously your pride and joy, and I know I'm not a parent but I understand how important it is for you to do right by her.'

'I tried to stay away from you. I mean, you know that – it's why I kept pushing you away – and I'm sorry. Losing Kailani was the hardest thing I have ever experienced, but I don't want to deprive myself of a second chance at love, and I don't want Jasmine to grow up with a dad who is so afraid of something so human. And I don't want you to sit in hotel rooms every night wondering why I won't let you in. I owe it to everyone involved to at least give us a shot.'

Faith didn't respond as she studied his features, taking in every detail. His jawline was prominent and she was acutely aware that he hadn't shaved for a couple of days. The sun had lightened his hair and brought out his freckles. He was perfect. She wanted to say something, anything, but she didn't want to ruin the moment. Faith didn't care about the hues of the sunset. It was like Julien was all she could see, all she wanted to see. Reaching across, she put her hand on his face. Her body edged closer, and he took note, turning and closing the gap.

His lips were on hers in an instant. Hundreds of seemingly insignificant moments, stolen glances, a light touch here and there, the intimate moments they had shared. They had led Faith and Julien to this one kiss that would ultimately shift their entire world. The sun was setting over the horizon, the waves were breaking gently on to the sand near their feet, the lights and noise of the party were behind them. Nothing could top this.

His hands were roaming her body, following every curve and caressing every inch. His touch was more addictive than ever. She allowed him to deepen the kiss and sank into his arms as if they were melting into one another. All their secrets were out there in the open now, nothing was left unsaid. Except for one thing. Faith was scared. Before she could cut off her thoughts, her hands were on his chest, pushing him away. He rested his forehead against hers and tucked her hair behind her ears, oblivious to the panic rising through her body. She leaned back and ran her hand through his blond hair, both of them in a complete daze but Faith biting her tongue.

'I'm sorry, was that too much?' Julien asked.

'Not at all. I just – I don't know. There's a lot going through my mind right now.'

It wouldn't be fair to make him believe that everything was fine and dandy when she wasn't sure if it was. Now that she had all the information, she needed to be sure that she was ready to give him what he needed from her. This was supposed to be her year to travel the world, to have the time of her life, and Julien had just offered her a whole other path to follow. It was a beautiful, magical path, but for Jasmine's sake, and theirs, she needed to be one hundred per cent certain. Eighty-five per cent wasn't enough in this situation.

As she explained this, she heaved a sigh of relief when he nodded and squeezed her hand. It was her choice. It was a life-changing decision to commit even to the very early stages of dating, since the feelings were absolutely there and there was no turning back without someone getting hurt. Faith had a past of her own that she needed to deal with; plus, she wanted to get to know the real Julien.

'Will you come and meet Jasmine tomorrow? No pressure. We can take Lucie, Marco and Brett too. I just want you to see what she's like, to get to know her a little and see what I'm like in dad mode. I think you'll know instantly if our little bubble isn't right for you, but I'm hoping it might make you feel more at ease about all of this. We can either rule us out completely or give it a little while longer. What do you think?'

Faith leaned her head on Julien's shoulder. 'I think that sounds lovely.'

# 25

A red jeep was driven up to the front of the hotel by the valet, who tossed the keys to Julien. He caught them effortlessly and gestured for everyone to pile in, and although there was only space for four, all five managed to squeeze into what Julien fondly called the Rust Bucket. They learned that he hired this exact same car every time he was out here.

He clearly loved this jeep. He even left his own CDs in it when he gave it back to the rental company since he used it so often. A Bon Jovi album, something by Journey, and one by a band from LA called Saint Motel who Lucie had introduced him to. Faith wondered if he'd ever arrived on the island to discover that the jeep had been given to another customer or if he'd ever had a CD stolen.

The roads gradually got bumpier and a lot less comfortable for the back-seat passengers as they neared their destination. Brett was in the front seat, given that he was far taller than the rest of them. He had taken it upon himself to wind his window all the way down and, as a result, strands of Faith and Lucie's hair were getting tangled together and they couldn't see anything except a mass of brunette and blonde. By the time Julien slowed down to drive along the dirt road to the farm, Lucie had a scowl on her face that threatened to leave permanent lines on her forehead.

The road was long, straight and narrow but it wasn't muddy, just very dusty. Driving at a slow speed was necessary, otherwise they'd have red clouds of dirt surrounding the car. It was lined with plants all the way to the end, and when they turned off they were greeted by a handmade wooden sign that read *The Kalakauas*. It was slightly wonky but it had character. The whole place did.

The exterior of the house was white with a pinky-red coloured roof, and it had a wraparound porch. It was one storey but it was pretty big, definitely big enough to be holed up with a teenager. Although one quick glance of the land surrounding it suggested it was unlikely that Jasmine spent much time inside. There were plants everywhere you looked and a more than generous fruit and vegetable patch.

Jasmine came hurtling out of a red front door and towards her dad as he hopped out of the jeep. Julien scooped her up in an almighty bear hug and spun her round. Jasmine spoke to him in Dutch, which totally threw Faith but made her heart all warm and fuzzy. She'd learned her dad's native language even though Faith had only heard Julien speak it a handful of times. Maybe she could speak Hawaiian too. An older couple in their fifties followed her outside as everyone else got out of the car to say their hellos.

Their faces were full of life and their eyes sparkled as they watched their granddaughter reunite with her dad. They introduced themselves as Koa and Malia, and immediately asked Faith and Lucie if they had ever tried lilikoi, which was otherwise known as passionfruit.

'Lucie!' Jasmine added lots of extra letters on to the end of her name and greeted Lucie like an old friend, though they'd yet to meet in person.

After Jasmine had hugged Brett and nervously said hello to Marco, who high-fived her and told her he liked her braids, it was Faith's turn. Jasmine wasn't the only shy one. Julien noticed his daughter's hesitation and gently nudged her forward so she could see that Faith was smiling warmly at her. That gave her the confidence to step forward and wrap her arms round her dad's mystery friend, and stunned Faith and Julien into silence.

Faith laughed softly and returned the hug. 'Hi.'

'Hey, are you the girl who isn't but definitely should be dating my dad?' she asked with a mischievous grin.

Brett lost it. His laughter broke any tension and Julien gawked at his daughter.

'Where did that come from?' He was stunned.

'Well, you said on the phone that the interview you guys did was a misunderstanding, but Grandma and Grandpa let me see everything that gets posted and I'm not blind, Dad. You like each other.' Jasmine said it so innocently and matter-of-factly that they couldn't help but laugh.

'Why don't you locate the football?' Julien sent her running round to the back of the house and they all followed. Koa engaged them in an animated conversation about racing and Malia hit them with a million different flavour combinations for the smoothies she was about to make.

'How are you feeling?' Lucie lowered her voice once Malia had disappeared inside and left them to it. They sat on the porch while Jasmine instructed her dad, grandpa and honorary uncles on the game she had created.

'It's a lot,' Faith admitted. She was feeling a little out of her depth. She knew that if she and Julien pursued things, it was the real deal. She felt a lot of responsibility to Kailani, a woman she had never met. There was a lot to live up to.

Besides, Jasmine herself had to let Faith into her world. Despite her teasing, she had never met any of Julien's romantic interests before. She had also never had someone playing the role of mum, unless you counted Malia. She might not be ready.

'First of all, do you *want* this?' Lucie gestured at the scene in front of them. A bright pink football went flying towards Brett's head and bounced off the side of the house when he ducked. Julien yelled at his daughter good-naturedly.

She did want this. It was complicated and it wouldn't be easy by any stretch of the imagination, but Faith was falling in love with this man and she wanted everything he had to offer, including his daughter, his dog, his life in Belgium and his regular visits to Hawaii. There was nothing to keep them apart now except for her fears. Julien had battled his. It was her turn.

Faith nodded eagerly. 'I do.'

'In that case, take our upcoming break for yourself. You two need to adjust and get to know each other without secrets, so maybe do regular video calls. Then you can travel with me, maybe visit your mother, and Jasmine has time to get used to the idea of you being around.'

'When did you get so smart, Carolan?'

'I'm the queen of good advice.'

'Here you are, ladies! Passionfruit smoothies, my secret recipe! Not even Koa knows what's in them.' Malia came out carrying yellow frothy liquid in Mason jars with metal straws, and then popped back in and returned with an array of freshly sliced fruits ranging from mangoes and strawberries to bananas and kiwis. It looked beautiful, and she set it down on a wooden table next to them. She was a natural hostess. She called everyone over to help themselves and swatted Brett's hand away when he reached for the chocolate brownies she had also laid out, telling him to wait until he'd eaten the healthy stuff.

Looking at the family sat round the table, Faith hoped that she could give Julien the kind of love he'd thought he would never find again. It was something she had never experienced for herself and thought didn't exist, but Julien made her feel alive in a way she couldn't possibly explain to anyone. You had to feel it to understand. And she did. She understood exactly. Julien was it for her and she was going to fight like hell over the next two months to be the best possible version of herself for him.

'I can't believe you didn't tell me!' Lucie's eyes nearly fell out of her head when Faith pulled her aside back at the hotel pool. 'So *that's* why we went to see Jasmine today? Because you and Jules have been making moves on each other this *entire* time?'

'Well, sort of. We've had a few moments, but nothing really happened until Le Mans.'

'Oh my God, how did I miss that?' Her jaw dropped and if Faith hadn't been so worried about what her co-worker thought of her, she'd have found it comical.

'I was sort of hoping Jules would confess to you, because I didn't want to disrespect his privacy by doing it myself. It's been torture keeping it to myself, Luce.'

'It's been torture for *me* waiting for you two to get your act together! Oh, Faith, I'm so over the moon about this. He told me way back at his party in Malmedy that he felt the spark, and I thought I'd accidentally talked him out of pursuing things.'

'It still took a while – there was a lot of back and forth. We even talked about specifically *not* exploring this. Didn't go very well, clearly.' She cast her eyes down at the bright blue pool water, not wanting to meet Lucie's gaze.

'I don't want to know the full details, but that time in Le Mans, was it everything you expected?' Lucie sipped on her alcohol-free cocktail.

'And more.'

'Ooooh. Save that gossip for someone else, because I don't want to think of Jules in that way, but I'm so happy! Hey, you can share notes with Bea!'

'Lucie!'

'What?'

'Are you sure there's no alcohol in that?' Faith grabbed the drink and took a sip, confirming it was indeed a mocktail. 'You're crazy. And Bea is part of the reason I was so worried about what you'd think.'

'Why?' Lucie looked confused.

'I guess I was a little embarrassed. It's my first year on the job, and here I am sleeping with the top driver. Doesn't exactly scream professional, does it? I know what the grid thinks of the girls the drivers have relationships with. I didn't want to be judged.'

'Jensen, come on. You're only human. Besides, the motorsport world has survived worse scandals than two co-workers admitting they're wildly in love with each other.'

'Whoa, there.' Faith's eyes widened as she processed what her friend had said.

'Well, what else would you call it?'

'Um . . .' Faith was at a loss for words. She still didn't quite know where this would lead or what it was; she just knew she and Julien were being open.

'But seriously, Faith, I'm not upset. I will absolutely be having words with Julien about learning how to be a better gossip and not keeping secrets from his best friend, but we're good.' Lucie leaned across her sun lounger and wrapped Faith in a one-armed hug, her sunset-coloured drink still in the other hand.

'Love you, Luce.'

'Love you too.'

'Do you actually know where you're going?' Faith linked her hand through Julien's as she stepped from one rock to the next. They were hiking near the farm and, despite his confidence, she was growing increasingly concerned that they'd taken a wrong turn.

'Would you hate me if I said no?' He took his eyes off her feet and glanced up at her, innocent as ever. That look could melt even the strongest of women.

'Yes.'

'Shit.'

'You'll have to make it up to me.' Faith hopped off the rocks and back on to solid ground.

'I'll start right now.' Julien got down one knee.

'What are you *doing*?'

'Tying your shoelace, Jensen.'

'Oh, thank goodness for that.'

'I hope you don't react like that when you're actually getting proposed to,' Julien laughed, tying her lace in a bow and standing up.

'Obviously not. Thank you, my knight in shining armour.'

'You're so welcome,' he murmured, stepping closer and wrapping an arm round her waist.

Faith stood on her tiptoes and met him halfway, giving him all the permission he needed to capture her lips with a kiss.

Julien had been respectful of Faith's request for time to process and held back on excessive kissing and touching over the last few days of the trip. They had snuck off whenever they could, trying to establish how to exist as Faith and Julien outside of work. He would place a hand on the small of her back when they walked in and out of the hotel restaurant, tuck her hair behind her ear, kiss her on the cheek to greet her. Small gestures that held so much meaning to them both.

It was just how they had always been, but this time there was no dark cloud above them threatening to ruin their moments of bliss. No pulling back once they realized there was a risk of getting too close.

'So, about those video calls.' They kept walking through the undergrowth. 'I think we should aim for one a week?' Faith had told Julien she wanted to work on getting to know each other properly, and he had eagerly agreed.

'I was kind of hoping for one a day.' He gave her the puppy-dog eyes that his daughter gave him when she wanted something. She would give anything to see his face on her screen every single day, but it wasn't realistic with their schedules and time zones.

'I'm not opposed to it. I just worry if we expect too much from each other, things won't go as smoothly as we're hoping,' she admitted, and Julien pulled them to a stop again.

'On that note, I don't want you to give anything up to be with me. I know you said you love the idea of muddy dog walks and saltwater in your hair, but part of the reason you took this job was so you could travel. So we'll travel together.' Julien looked down at her, gently caressing the side of her face in a daze.

'All three of us?'

'Yeah. I mean, not straight away. It'll just be me for a while, but one day Jasmine will be with us. When she was born, I always envisioned bringing her along for the ride but when we lost Kail, I left her here so she could be with family.'

Faith read his mind. 'But family comes in different forms.'

'Exactly. As long as she's surrounded by people who love her, that's her family. I kind of feel like she and I both missed out on a lot, but Malia and Koa have given her a stability that I never could.'

'You're an amazing man, Julien Moretz. You should be proud of yourself. I'm sure Kailani would be too.' She glanced up at him, worried that her mention of his late wife would offend him somehow, but his lips curved upwards into a soft smile and he did the classic hair tuck, a couple of strands catching in her gold hoop earrings.

'Thank you for being the most understanding woman in the world.'

\*

Faith helped Julien load his luggage into the jeep. It had been a very long week. Every day consisted of swimming, surfing, sunbathing and drinking cocktails, while each morning began with a trip to Malia and Koa's farm to hang out with Jasmine. She was a ray of sunshine and could not be more excited to see them each time. They had enjoyed seeing parts of the island with her that they never would have known existed if they had stayed at the resort, although some other drivers seemed a bit miffed that Faith and Julien kept disappearing.

Julien had confessed to Faith that he felt like he had deeply betrayed the whole community by keeping his daughter hidden and he was worried they might think it was odd. He didn't know if he should make a big deal out of it and sit everyone down in a conference room, or if it was better to just post a photo of them both on social media and let the rumour mill go wild.

Jasmine had put her two cents in and insisted that she wanted a red-curtain reveal at the first race she was allowed to fly out to, but Faith, who was now given the sole responsibility of managing Julien's personal Instagram account, had told her to play it cool. Jasmine had agreed, but only because she was already considering herself extremely lucky that she was actually going to be able to watch her dad out on the track.

Bea had spent her week with Ricardo, enjoying strolls along the beach and cocktails in the sun. He had given her all his time and attention and didn't seem to care that he was neglecting his team. A lot of people had yet to warm up to the new and improved Bea, not trusting that she had changed in such a short space of time. It was just as well

Faith and Lucie saw it, because most people were following their lead.

Bea had gone on a social media strike, claiming that she just wanted to be around the people she loved. Marco had grimaced slightly at the thought of being included in that category, but nonetheless had gone wakeboarding with her and Ricardo and returned to the rest of the group insisting that they had, in fact, all been wrong about her. She was hovering near Julien's car with Lucie and Faith now as he said his goodbyes to the boys.

Julien was staying in Hawaii with Jasmine and would meet them all in England for Silverstone. It was going to feel like the longest break in his career history, or at least that's what he whispered into Faith's hair when it was her turn to say goodbye.

Their friends had gone back into the hotel and left them to it, but Faith could already feel the tears coming. They still had one day left and she didn't know how she was supposed to enjoy it without Julien, and with their future weighing on her mind. They were standing by the fountain in the sunshine, and Julien's arms were wrapped round her.

'I should get going. I promised Jasmine I'd take her out for ice cream with her friends.'

'OK.' Faith nodded and let go reluctantly.

'Come back.' Julien pulled her close again. She lifted her head up and he leaned down to meet her halfway, his lips crashing down on hers. They savoured every second, making it last because they knew it would be a long time before they could do this again. Faith could feel his hands in her hair, tangling it beyond help but she didn't care. She wanted to stay in this moment forever. When they broke apart she frowned, her bottom lip jutting out slightly in protest.

'I'll see you in August,' she whispered.

'Try not to get into too much trouble while you're off travelling the world without me. I don't want to come back to see you in a cast or with a limb missing or something. And don't let Brett convince you to hike the advanced trails – stick to the beginner ones. Or sit it out and sip champagne at the hotel. Take advantage of the Spa facilities,' he said.

'And you try not to strangle your daughter when her typical teen attitude kicks in.'

'I make no promises.'

'Hey, Jules, I've been meaning to ask. What happens to Ford when you're gone?' She thought of his dog, who was often left at his neighbour's farm in Belgium.

'He'll be with my mother in Brussels. I'll take Jasmine back to Belgium for a couple of weeks to see them both during her summer holidays but don't worry, Ford is fine. He loves staying with my mother; she makes a huge fuss of him and he gets two walks a day and plenty of visitors. He's in good hands.' Julien knew that Ford had taken a shine to Faith and vice versa.

'Think I'll miss him more than I'll miss you. He's much better company and he doesn't moan about posing for photos,' she teased.

Julien tutted. 'Get back into the hotel. I'll see you soon. Silverstone will be here before you know it.'

He opened the door to the jeep and climbed in, yanking the sheet of red metal and slamming it shut behind him. It made an almighty creaking sound and they both winced.

As he sat behind the wheel now, Faith felt as though she was watching someone else. A man who was so far removed from the moody, arrogant and closed-off racing driver she'd met in April that she barely recognized him. But it wasn't a bad thing. It just made him human. She jumped when he started his radio and 'Kokomo' by the Beach Boys was blasted on full volume.

Julien threw his head back, laughing wildly in a state of pure bliss. He waved out of the window as he started pulling away from her and she grinned, hearing him sing along at the top of his voice as he drove out of the resort. If Julien opened up this part of himself to the rest of the world, they would see all the things that Faith did. Everything that made it impossible to let him go.

# 26

There were two weeks to go until the race at Silverstone. Faith and Lucie were crammed into a tiny green VW Beetle convertible with suitcases in the back, and the winding roads of Cornwall were throwing them around violently. Lucie wasn't used to the British country roads but that didn't stop her approaching each corner at a far higher speed than Faith would've liked.

She hit the horn on the steering wheel each time, a tip that Faith had given her when they had first picked the car up from the rental company in Devon weeks ago. So far they had only had a few narrow misses, which unfortunately had not slowed her American friend down in the slightest. Lucie claimed she had no fear as she was used to constant angry Los Angeles traffic, but Faith wasn't convinced.

They had been lucky with the weather and hardly had to put the roof up, although they had been caught out during a trip to Lulworth in Dorset. They had been heading back from their trek down to Durdle Door in the most inappropriate footwear they could've chosen when the rain hit. It pelted them at full force and Lucie had screamed that she was sure it was going to physically dent her skin.

She had been such a diva the whole time they'd been on the road that Faith couldn't help but find it hilarious each time she had a minor meltdown. Faith was used to the poorly designed roads, the lack of phone signal, the unexpected torrential downpours and the empty meal deal shelves in the supermarkets, but Lucie had grown accustomed to the luxury that their job offered. They had eaten more egg sandwiches than any human ever should, and didn't want to see another packet of ready salted crisps for as long as they lived. Their daily pub trips were their safe haven and every evening they indulged in a hot meal that rivalled the pasta dishes Amina used to make back in London.

They were a few miles outside Faith's hometown now and she felt nauseous. For once it wasn't just as a result of Lucie's erratic driving although she wished it was. She hadn't told her mum she was coming. Faith's number had changed so many times that she wasn't sure she had it saved any more anyway. She always texted her mum with her new one but never got a reply.

Occasional one-sided postcards were their only form of contact and Faith had only responded a handful of times over the years, never having an awful lot to say. They were showing up with zero warning and frankly it was terrifying not knowing what to expect.

It had been eight years. No real conversation and a lot of resentment from both parties. Turning up like this meant her mother had no time to put on a facade. She wouldn't be able to clean up the vodka bottles or make herself look all fresh and youthful to convince Faith she was doing well. Faith didn't want to be here, but she knew she needed to confront her past. Not just for her own peace of mind, but also so she could heal the wounds her mum had left her with and mentally and emotionally prepare to play a maternal role herself.

'Is this it?' Lucie slowed down, a rarity, and pointed at the rickety wooden sign that introduced Old Al's farm. He had added a cute little painting of a sheep, which made Faith smile. He was a sweet man and had always got excited when Faith asked to hang out with his animals, letting her milk the cows with him before school or take the sheepdogs out into the field. She had watched one too many lambs and calves being born when she was younger, which really hadn't proved useful in the years that followed, but nonetheless she bet Lucie had never experienced anything like that. Faith was definitely a country girl at heart.

'I hope she's not drunk.' Faith swallowed the lump in her throat and gestured for Lucie to park up next to the farmhouse rather than the caravan.

Al was unlikely to be home at two o'clock on a Tuesday afternoon. He still had a shop to run, which they had passed on their way into town, Lucie squealing that it was adorable. Faith couldn't deny that. It was built like a log cabin and there were flowers in planters and hanging baskets, a sign for fresh strawberries placed up on the side of the road. They were already debating stopping in to say hello and pick some up on their way back.

'If I can handle drunk racing drivers, I'm pretty sure I can handle your mom. Don't stress about it.' Lucie squeezed her hand tightly and opened her door, not allowing her friend any time to panic and back out. She was already halfway to Andrea's front door by the time Faith had hopped out in her Doc Marten boots. Lucie had opted for white trainers, which she was trying not to complain about when she stepped in a puddle but Faith could hear the pain in her voice.

The caravan was in good nick, better than when Faith had left it at least. She had only lived here from the ages of thirteen to eighteen, having stayed at the caravan park until then. This caravan was bigger than their original one and had pink, yellow and blue flower stickers on it which were peeling away at the edges. They had actually been Al's choice when he'd offered it to them, thinking that they would make Faith feel at home. He had decorated Faith's room with pastel curtains and bed sheets and a big fluffy rug that covered the thin fading carpet. The local community knew she loved reading, and people would often pop into Al's store with books to pass on to her that their own children had read and didn't want any more. Al came home with a bag full every couple of weeks and she would proudly show her mum, who helped her alphabetize them by author. There would be times when the living room had stacks of them.

'Faith?' Andrea opened the door in her dressing gown, half a face of make-up on and her blonde hair in rollers. She looked good. Not tired and dishevelled like she usually did, and she hadn't aged all that much. She was still relatively wrinkle-free.

Faith swallowed nervously. 'Hi, Mum.'

'Hi! I'm Lucie Carolan. I'm your daughter's friend and co-worker.' Lucie put on her best smile and shook Andrea's hand. Her accent had clearly thrown Faith's mum, judging by the little goldfish-style mouth movements.

'Come in! Gosh, I had no idea you were coming. You didn't send me a postcard to warn me, did you?' She rushed to straighten the cushions on the sofa. 'The postman has been off sick for a few days so everything's delayed.'

'No, I didn't send anything. We're on a road trip around the coast and I just thought it was about time I came back for a visit.' Faith perched on the sofa. The living room was tidy, although there was still a mountain of books on the coffee table. One of Faith's old teddies sat proudly in the armchair she used to read in, holding one of her favourite romance novels. The kitchen was sparkling clean and the few postcards Faith had responded with were attached with magnets of London landmarks.

'I'm so happy you're here. And it's so lovely that you've brought a friend with you. Would either of you like a cup of tea?' She was hovering near the kettle and was clearly itching to give her daughter a hug but thought better of it.

'A tea would be lovely, please.'

'Could I have a coffee instead?' Faith asked.

'Wow, you really are all grown up. Drinking coffee.' Andrea smiled and boiled the water. She leaned on the counter, crossing her arms like she was protecting herself. 'How have you been?'

'Really good. I'm working in the motorsport industry now, doing social media. So there's a lot of travel involved.' Faith took a better look at the collection of things on the fridge and spotted some photos of her mum and a man she didn't recognize stood in front of various landscapes. 'Mum, where were these taken?'

'Oh, these?' She took them down and handed them to the girls. 'Barcelona, New York, Tokyo. That's Mike. We've been dating for a year now. He works in finance.'

'In finance?' Faith's eyebrows shot up.

'Ooooh, he's cute!' Lucie commented.

'Thank you, Lucie.' Andrea laughed. 'He's been very

good to me. Nothing like previous boyfriends. I think you'd really like him, Faith. He'd like to meet you one day but I told him I need to see you first. Don't want to spring him on you. I was going to visit you before the end of the year actually. I was just putting it off because I didn't know if it was a good idea. He's been asking me to move to London with him.'

'So why haven't you?'

'I was hoping you'd get the courage to visit me before I got the courage to visit you. And I thought that if I left here, you might not know where to find me. That if I sent you my new address, the postcard would get lost and you'd never receive it.'

'You've been waiting for me?' Faith's heart softened, even after she'd noticed the beer bottles on the counter.

'Of course I have. I messed up a lot of things, Faith. I know I damaged our relationship with my drinking and my poor decisions. I didn't want to try to force a reconciliation on you.'

'Have you stopped drinking?'

'I have. Those are Mike's beers. I've been sober for two years and I started an online business. Mike got me one of those iPad things, so I've been creating digital prints and it's been going really well so far. It's given me a good focus, and I can do it from anywhere. Mike and I have done a bit of travelling.' Her mum was bursting with pride.

'How did you meet him?' Faith took a closer look at the photos and noted his dark hair and olive complexion. He looked vaguely familiar but she couldn't put her finger on it.

'Do you remember me ever talking about my first-*ever*

boyfriend? Way back in school.' Andrea handed them a mug each and sat down next to them hesitantly. 'Well, that's him. I bumped into him at a service station of all places.'

'Oh, Mum, that's amazing.' She did remember the stories about him, and she knew her mum had always wondered what life would have been like if they'd met later on.

'That was eighteen months ago, but it took me a long time to trust him again and to trust myself. He's been very patient.'

'What was he doing *here*?'

'Faith, have you forgotten where we live?' Her mum laughed. 'It's beautiful. He was just visiting for the weekend, with his dogs.'

'I forget that tourists actually like it. There's nothing here.'

'Only stunning beaches, blue waters and cute little tourist shops,' Lucie interjected.

'Valid point. OK, so he's the full package?'

'Just like I always wanted, yes.'

'And he wants to meet me?' Faith was nervous. If she got a bad feeling from him, it would be like reliving the past. She wanted her mum to be right this time.

'Yes. Like I said, there's no pressure, Faith. It's when you're ready. You and I have a lot to work on first, and he knows that. You're my priority.'

Faith didn't answer for a while. It would do no good to try to fix a relationship with her mum if Andrea was still trying to fix her own messes, but it seemed that she had started taking the necessary steps to sort her life out a while ago.

'Are you OK?' Lucie whispered while Andrea disappeared into her bedroom.

'Yeah, I think so.'

'I have these.' Andrea returned with an envelope full of photographs. 'I've been documenting everything I've been doing the last few years, so when we met again I could prove that I've actually been living my life to the fullest. I haven't just been holed up in here, drowning my sorrows. I want to be someone you can be proud to call your mum.'

'Why didn't you just pick up the phone?' Faith frowned. If her mum had gone to all this effort, why not just call?

'I was scared, Faith. I know I let you down. Every time I hovered over your contact, I just couldn't do it. I'm sorry, truly.'

'Right . . . Well, would you be open to dinner next time I'm in the UK?' Faith still wasn't convinced about the phone issue, but then again she hadn't visited because she was scared of what she would find. Maybe she should let the past remain in the past.

'I'm open to whatever you're willing to give me, sweetheart.'

'OK. Thanks for these.' Faith held up the envelope.

'There are a lot of me and Mike in there. Sorry if that's strange but he's played a big part in helping me get back to the Andrea I was twenty-plus years ago.'

'I might keep one for myself actually. Mike's fit.' Lucie grinned.

Lucie had successfully lightened the mood and got a hearty laugh out of them both, and by some miracle there was no tension in the air. No lingering resentment. Just acceptance.

'Don't let Brett hear you say that,' Faith teased, knowing that he and Lucie had been exchanging flirty texts since their hiking trip. Something had gone down in Italy, and Faith had a feeling it was one of them.

'Oh? Who's Brett?' Andrea asked with a twinkle in her eye. It had been a long time since she had gossiped with Faith and her friends, and it was needed after such a heavy conversation.

'Lucie's man.'

'He's just a friend. My man friend. A male, who happens to be my friend. And co-worker,' Lucie interjected.

'You're dating a racing driver? Or is he an engineer?' Andrea was on the edge of her seat and Lucie looked like she was ready to give up arguing with the pair of them.

'For heaven's sake, you two are a nightmare. He's a racing driver. But actually Faith is the one who has updates on the romance front. Isn't that right, Jensen?' She shot a look at her friend, looking very pleased with herself.

Faith smiled with gritted teeth, mentally cursing her. 'Yes, Lucie. That is right.'

Sitting back into the plush cushions of her mum's old green-velvet sofa, Faith started to tell Andrea everything about Julien. It felt odd to be confiding in her about this, but the way her mum's eyes lit up filled her with a strange sense of nostalgia for her childhood. For the times she would come home from primary school and tell her all about her latest crush and how they'd both stood at the bin to sharpen their pencils together during an English lesson.

This felt right. The whole visit did, and she was glad she had decided to come. Glad that Julien had encouraged her over the phone last week and that Lucie had accompanied her. She was grateful that she had seen the changes to her mum's life for herself. It was just a shame it had taken this long.

Lucie and Faith left Andrea's and found a dodgy roadside pub that looked like it probably served roadkill. To be on the safe side, they opted for a vegetarian dish with a much-needed glass of cheap wine to accompany it. There was a budget hotel next door where they were staying before they drove to Bristol and caught a flight to Cyprus for two weeks in Ayia Napa with Bea.

Faith poked around at her food and stared at the plate. 'I need to talk to you about Jules.'

Lucie frowned. 'You're scaring me. What's he done?'

'Nothing. It's me. I think I have to call things off.'

'What?' Lucie's face dropped.

'He's amazing, and I don't want to do this, but I don't know how to be someone's partner, let alone be a parental figure for Jasmine.'

'That makes sense.'

'You're not going to try to change my mind?' Faith was stunned. Lucie had been the one encouraging her to take her time with Julien and really pushing for her not to give up on him.

'No, I'm not. Your life is a flipping whirlwind at the moment, Faith. You can't be expected to adjust to it all immediately. I personally think that you could do it if you gave it a shot, but if you're not ready, then you're not ready. I also believe, and I think you do too, that Jules is the perfect man for you. Your soulmate even. If that's the case, then you two will figure it out when the timing is right.'

301

'I don't want to hurt him.' Faith chewed her lip, anxiety rising at the mere thought of having to let him down. She didn't want to have that conversation because she knew she was only doing this out of fear, but it was better to leave it all in the dust now than to drag Jasmine into it and shatter her world too.

'He cares about you deeply, Faith. If one of you isn't ready, you shouldn't dive in head first. Look before you leap and all that. I think you're doing the right thing.'

They sat in silence for the rest of their meal, but Faith didn't have much of an appetite any more. She knew the feelings weren't going anywhere, and that their chemistry was stronger than it had been before. The moments they shared would keep happening. But she couldn't let them become anything more complicated.

## 27

After two weeks of trying and failing to decipher Greek and Turkish in Ayia Napa, it was nice to be able to speak and read English again. Bea had booked them an Airbnb rather than an all-inclusive resort, claiming that it would provide them with a more authentic experience, but they had missed the luxury of room service and fresh towels and bedding.

They vowed that next time they had a holiday like that, they would skip the authenticity factor and opt for ease. They had a lot of upcoming trips where they would constantly be hiking and exploring so they needed a healthy balance of relaxing beach holidays in between.

The trip had been successful in bringing the girls together. Each day had brought fresh local seafood and a busy nightlife scene, and Bea hadn't had to fight to get them out past nine o'clock every night. In fact, sometimes it had been the other way around. They had run out of dresses, so they were washing them in the sink, drying them on the balcony and swapping with each other so nobody was rewearing anything.

They had photoshoots in different locations every day, which had resulted in literally hundreds of photos of each of them to edit. Then there were the scenic shots. They spent their days by the pool going through them and deciding what to post and when, and were sure that their followers would soon grow tired of Ayia Napa content.

Bea was saving all hers for when her social media ban was over, and she had refused to let them post photos of her. She instead acted as their 'hype girl', as she called herself.

They wanted this to be an annual thing for them, having fallen in love with the place on day one. It was the perfect girls' trip and they had no intention of letting the boys tag along. As Lucie had informed them in the group chat, if they wanted to come, they could go to a hotel on the opposite side of town and stay out of their way.

Driving from Gatwick to Silverstone was a reality check for them. They had gone from views of boats on the ocean to views of cows in green fields, and instead of smelling seafood all they could smell was fresh manure. Pure bliss. The organization had sent a rental car for them and given them a Range Rover with all the extras, so they were taking full advantage of the cooled seating option. Faith was in the front, gazing at a bright blue cloudless sky. This weather was due to stay for the whole week, but who knew if that would be the case. Right now, though, the air conditioning was a godsend.

The trip had been the final step in Faith and Bea healing their relationship and really proved to Lucie that Faith had been right about her friend being a very different person to the one she had been presenting for the last year and a half. She was still in touch with Ricardo de la Rosa, who had sent a bouquet of flowers to the Airbnb on their second day. They had well and truly hit it off and were sharing a room in Silverstone, which Bea was praying the rest of the grid wouldn't find out. She still had a long way to go in terms of building her reputation back up.

'I want pretzels,' Bea complained from the back seat.

She hadn't been able to find any at the airport or at the Tesco Express Lucie had stopped at forty minutes into the journey.

Lucie rolled her eyes. 'There's a Sainsbury's an hour out of Silverstone. I will get you your pretzels if you promise to drive the rest of the way.' Having Bea in the car was a bit like travelling with a whiny kid who was constantly asking how long they had left to go.

'How am I supposed to eat if I'm driving?'

'I'll feed them to you.'

'Aw, thanks, Luce! That's so sweet.'

In the time it took them to locate pretzels, the guys had beaten them to it and arrived at the hotel near the circuit. Faith was still hoping that the girls would have time to get settled before her big reunion with Julien and was counting on him going down to the track to see the team. At least if they came face to face for the first time in the garage, there wouldn't be a chance for things to be awkward with all the activity around them.

Faith felt sick every time she'd turned down his calls. When she did answer, she tried to change the subject and talk about work. He seemed oblivious, in all honesty, despite what she and Lucie had discussed; and she still wasn't convinced that making him wait even longer was the best thing. The closer they got to Silverstone, the closer she got to realizing she would be making a mistake by ending things.

What if he didn't want to wait and she lost out on her one shot at happiness with him? She would be cursing herself for years to come. She knew that connections like this didn't come around often and part of her felt that she was risking throwing away something, or someone, who was once in a lifetime. She had no idea what to do.

Lucie turned round to Faith. 'Jasper wants us down at the track straight away to get some footage of the new livery.' The car had a limited-edition red and orange ombré livery for the British race, and Jasper wanted that content pushed out today. Tomorrow was free practice and there would be more focus on other teams.

Bea drove them right into the paddock area, still having chocolate-covered pretzels hand-fed to her, and abandoned the car in between two of Revolution Racing's team trailers, right behind the garage. It was the epitome of laziness, but they'd been lounging around on the beach for two weeks and they hadn't quite adjusted to the idea of walking everywhere again. They were still yet to swap their sandals for trainers. Stumbling out of the air-conditioned space and into the muggy, humid air, all three of them groaned in protest. Silverstone's paddock was sunk into the ground, with huge concrete walls at either end, and there wasn't much of a breeze.

'There you are!' Brett emerged from the garage with Marco in tow and scooped Lucie up in his arms. For once she didn't bat him away when he got handsy.

'Nobody touch me; it's far too hot for all this hugging nonsense. Air kisses will have to do.' Bea gave Brett and Marco her classic greeting and shooed them away while she fanned herself with the autograph card Marco had been holding. 'Oooh, I like these!' She looked at the new design and led Mars into the garage, chatting away. He waved over his shoulder at Faith. It wasn't like she hadn't seen him lately.

'My darling Faith!' Brett yelled and picked her up like she was Simba from *The Lion King*. It still baffled her how these drivers were so strong, especially Brett who was near enough superhuman.

She laughed. 'Put me down, Anderson. You're such a pain in the ass.'

'I'm your favourite pain in the ass, though. It's OK, I won't tell Jules.'

Speaking of Julien, she could see the back of his head from here. As she approached him, she couldn't shake the nerves.

'Hey,' she mumbled. He whipped round as soon as he heard her voice and his face lit up.

'Hi.' He smiled and went straight in for a hug, resting his chin on top of her head. She'd missed this. Far more than she realized.

The two of them stood like that until they felt eyes on them, but Faith could have stayed in that position forever. She could feel that he had been working out. His shoulders were broader and his arms were bigger. Even his chest felt different against hers.

When he pulled away she took the opportunity to fully check him out. He was wearing a navy T-shirt which clung tightly to his biceps and abs, and fitted beige trousers. She took a second to admire that view too. Yep, he looked just as good from behind. Not too long ago she'd have been embarrassed if he caught her staring but now she didn't care.

She almost wanted him to notice. It wasn't like she hadn't witnessed him doing the same thing on multiple occasions, especially in Hawaii. It was nice to finally be able to act on their attraction to one another without the risk of Julien storming into his trailer in a dark rage and refusing to speak to her for hours.

After the guys had been out on the track for tests, Faith and Lucie held a meeting. They had put together a folder with plans for the team accounts, plus each driver's personal accounts, which included themes and the type of content they would post on each social media platform. They wanted the drivers to have their own aesthetic, their own brands, but for their content to still be cohesive with the team content.

The attention to detail was something the boys lacked and were begging for help with. They wanted to take their social media presence up a notch, including Julien now that he was going to slowly introduce his daughter to it, and that meant they wanted to stand out from the sea of other racing drivers. Brett wanted bright and bold colours, Marco wanted minimalism with a lot of black and white and empty space, and Julien was copying Faith and opting for neutral and earthy tones. She had created a mood board for him and selected photos of coffee shops and latte art, huskies with the same colouring as Ford, forests and green leafy plants, and sandy beaches and waterfalls. That pretty much summed his life up, whether he was in Europe or Hawaii.

Julien had been posting on his social media a lot more over the last few days, making up for the lack of content being shared while he'd been with Jasmine. He had captured himself on countryside walks with Ford and his mother, his morning coffees, the work he was doing on his property. He had actually listened to everything Faith had told him he needed to be doing when she had first got here. All the things he had insisted he didn't want to do, the things he thought were stupid, he was going to do them for her, because he trusted her.

She grabbed hold of Lucie's arm after the meeting and pulled her to one side. 'I'm making a mistake. With Jules.' She spoke loudly enough that she could be heard over the noise of the cars in the pit lane, but not so loud that the mechanics and engineers in the garage could hear.

'You still want to be with him?'

'Yeah.'

'Hell yeah!' Lucie squealed.

Faith smiled. 'I'm all in. Stroppy teenager and all. I'm going to tell him tonight at dinner.'

'Oh my God, Faith!' Lucie enveloped her in a hug. 'You won't regret it. You've got this.'

Their heart-to-heart was interrupted by the sound of something smashing into the barriers just before the entrance to the pit lane. There were no screens on in the garage. Only five cars were out on track right now, and Faith didn't know who else was driving except for Julien. The look on Jasper's face said it all. Every single person in the garage rushed out to the pit lane and she shoved past them in a hurry to get there first.

She wished she hadn't. Brett was already there, begging her not to come any closer, but she'd seen it. Julien's car ripped apart by the safety barrier.

## 28

He was still in the car, no medics in sight. It felt like everything and everyone was moving in slow motion and Faith couldn't understand why nobody was helping him. The noise was ringing in her ears and she couldn't hear anything else. Brett was facing her, blocking her path.

Faith snapped out of it and the world came back into focus. Marco was talking to Jasper who had a headset on and she guessed he was trying to communicate with Julien, but his expression didn't give anything away.

Jasper beckoned her over and walked back through the garage. 'Come to the medical centre with me.' Faith followed after him like a little lost sheep.

None of this felt real. It shouldn't be real. Julien usually had perfect control. He didn't make mistakes. He definitely didn't spin out and crash the car, near enough ripping it in half. He was a good driver, the best. That was why he was in this sport and in this team. Faith knew it could happen to any one of the drivers at any moment, but she never imagined it would be him or that she would be here to witness it.

She thanked God that it wasn't being broadcast. His daughter didn't need to see this. She wished Brett had let her get a proper look at the car, but he was too tall for her to see past him. She didn't know if Julien had got out or if he'd been talking. Jasper hadn't said a word, and didn't until they were in the golf cart that Gabriel had tracked them down in. He was too calm.

At the medical centre Faith heaved a sigh of relief that no media crews had got down there yet. Although nothing was on television, journalists crawled over this place from the first day teams started arriving to set up. In between trying to calm her breathing and remain composed, Faith had been stressing about Jasmine. She asked Gabriel if he knew how to get hold of her grandparents, so he could warn them if it went public, but after an intense discussion they decided that it might not be reported and they didn't want to scare his family unnecessarily. They reached out to his mum and let her make the decision on Julien's behalf.

Faith couldn't imagine how his loved ones felt every time he raced. She was lucky; she was here. She saw the safety measures in place around the track, the lengths the team went to in order to make the car as safe as it could possibly be. She didn't worry any time one of the three drivers got behind the wheel, but perhaps she should have. Perhaps if she'd braced herself, she wouldn't be sitting here in shock, sick to her stomach.

'He's responsive,' Jasper reassured her and squeezed Faith's shoulder. It didn't help much. 'Responsive' didn't mean he was physically OK. It just meant he was alive.

The medics had reached him in less than thirty seconds; it had just felt like a lifetime to everyone watching. Faith remembered catching sight of the marshals in orange high-vis tabards, but he must have felt so alone in there. She couldn't stand the thought of what might have been going through his head. If anything. Jasper hadn't mentioned if Julien had lost consciousness or not.

The car was a mess and there was no way it would be ready for free practice tomorrow, probably not even for qualifying or the race. It was over for Revolution. That would devastate Julien more than anything, knowing that he had taken that from the team. Faith wished Brett and Marco were here right now. Jasper and Gabriel were too serious, too matter-of-fact. This was work for them. But for the drivers it was personal. It was family.

'We need to get him to the hospital, get him assessed. He's losing consciousness,' the medical director yelled to Jasper.

Faith burst into tears, her lip trembling at the sight of Julien. He was clinging on to his helmet for dear life, looking dishevelled and disorientated, as if he had no idea where he was. The doors slammed shut again, lights flashing and sirens wailing. She tried to tell herself they were just being cautious because of the speed at which he had hit the wall, but the truth was, it could be the worst-case scenario. It felt like her world was crumbling down around her and the only person she wanted to lean on was the person lying on a stretcher.

The hospital waiting room felt like alien territory. Faith had never experienced the misfortune of sitting in a creaking plastic chair, the smell of antiseptic clouding her rationality with every second that passed. It had been four hours and the rest of the team had joined her.

Brett and Marco were frantically checking the media reports and responding to fellow drivers. While Lucie focused on posting content as normal and Bea did coffee and vending machine runs, Faith's attention was zeroed in on every set of blue scrubs that walked up or down the corridor. Nobody had approached them. They might as well be sitting in their hotel rooms refreshing social media until the official team statement was released, a statement they were responsible for sharing. Jasper returned looking stressed to the max, and spotting the girls sat with their legs tucked up under them, huddled together like penguins, all he could offer them was a look of sympathy and understanding.

Marco lurched forward at the sight of a doctor emerging through the double doors. 'Guys.'

The horrible feeling in the pit of Faith's stomach grew. 'Are you family?'

'We are.' Brett spoke in his Australian accent, causing the doctor to raise an eyebrow, but the hospital staff had been briefed.

He continued. 'We've placed Mr Moretz in a private room. We've been running multiple tests and he's been for several scans today. He just needs to stay under observation for his concussion; other than that he has a few broken ribs, but everything has come back clear.'

Everyone visibly relaxed.

'We will monitor him and let him leave when we feel he's ready. Please try not to panic; we're confident he'll be OK. Would you like to go and see him?'

They traipsed after him through the hospital. The further in they got, the more real it became. He was fine. Julien was fine.

Faith thought of all the crashes she'd watched on television and thanked the universe that Julien hadn't become another statistic or another idol who had to give up his career over one tiny mistake, a mistake that could easily have been fatal. Luck had been on his side. Or maybe a guardian angel. Faith wasn't certain she believed in those, but maybe she did after this.

'Moretz, my brother! Good to see you alive and kicking.' Brett grinned at his friend, who was sitting in his hospital bed in a gown looking absolutely over the moon to see them.

'Sorry about that, guys.'

'You scared the shit out of us, dude.' Marco clapped him on the shoulder, perhaps a little too aggressively, but Julien didn't say anything. He welcomed the fuss.

'So no race for us, huh?' His brow creased.

'Don't stress about that. You're far more important. We'll get the car sorted for Fuji,' Jasper said from across the room. He was in the doorway, clearly in business mode and not wanting to impose on them. But he counted as family too.

An awkward silence fell over them as Faith and Julien exchanged eye contact. She had wanted to run to him the second she laid eyes on him but seeing him had stunned her and she was frozen to the spot. She hadn't even smiled. He must be thinking this had scared her off, when all it had actually done was confirm that she truly did want this. She wanted *him*.

'Can I speak to Faith alone for a minute?'

'Behave yourselves.' Brett nodded at them. 'This is a hospital – have some respect.'

Faith took a step closer to Julien, hovering uncomfortably before she sat down on his bed. He took her hand in his, gently rubbing his thumb in circles on her skin. It sent a shiver down her spine. This was a new feeling. She was nervous around him. Usually she was sassy, confident and assertive, but now she couldn't think of anything to say without sounding like a massive idiot. An idiot she would have to be, because he was quiet too. Someone needed to speak.

'I'm so rel–'

Julien cut her off. 'I'm ending this.'

She blinked at him slowly, unable to comprehend the simplicity of those three words. He held her gaze, staring her in the eye as if silently signalling that he wasn't going to back down.

All the progress they'd made came crumbling down as his walls shot back up, leaving her out in the cold.

'Can't we talk this through?' Her voice was shaking and she could still feel the warmth of his hands on hers. His words weren't matching his actions.

'Please don't make this any harder. Just go.'

'Tell me why. I'll leave, but not until you tell me why.'

'I can't be with you, Faith. I can't allow you to stand in the garage at every race and wonder if I'm going to cross the finishing line in one piece. It isn't fair to you, and I can't have that burden sitting on my shoulders. I made a decision a very long time ago, and I knew that I would have to sacrifice a lot of things that most people take for granted.'

'But you *married* Kailani . . .'

'That was before I got to this level of my career. I didn't think I would ever get here when I met her, not even close. Kail still lived in fear back then and it ate me up. I risk my life every time I get in that car, Faith. You know that, and you shouldn't have to risk losing me.'

'Shouldn't that be my choice?'

'You're better off without me.'

Except she wasn't without him. As long as Julien was behind the wheel of a race car and Faith worked for the IEC, she would never be without him. She would have to see him at every race for days at a time. She would see him in the garage, in the hotel, on the TV screens. Hear him on the radio. Sit across from him at breakfast and dinner. Aim a camera at him while he worked. Interview him. Sit in the back of golf carts and SUVs with him.

There was no escaping each other, so why stop this relationship from going where it had inevitably been going? The only thing that would change was that they would have to resist temptation. Pretend that the chemistry wasn't there. That they felt nothing.

So really, nothing was changing at all. It just wasn't moving forward. All that opening up in Hawaii had been a waste of time. But the kiss hadn't been.

The fireworks weren't one-sided and Faith knew he'd spend nights alone reminiscing. Recalling their hands in each other's hair, the softness of her lips against his. Wishing he could taste her again. Julien Moretz was a man who cowered away from anything that was good. He was destined to become the kind of person he said he didn't want to be. He was a fucking *idiot*.

She pulled her hand away and stood up. 'Are you sure this is what you want?'

'Please go.'

He didn't have to ask again. Faith breezed out with her head held high. Lucie and Bea were on her tail, not bothering to ask what had happened. She was sure it was obvious.

Besides, Bea knew better than anyone that this was her way of coping. Act like everything is OK and break down behind closed doors. Faith wouldn't let him embarrass her in front of the whole world.

# 29

The hotel was a hive of activity on race day, but most of Revolution were already on their way back to headquarters. It hurt to be missing out and team spirits were down, but nothing could compare to the emptiness Faith felt without Julien. He was being released from hospital today and he had just pulled into the hotel car park in Gabriel's red Ferrari 458 Spider, their boss in the driver's seat.

Over the past few days Gabriel had seemingly abandoned his daily responsibilities and passed the baton on to his colleagues while he went into full dad mode, doing multiple checks on the girls who had remained holed up in their hotel room trying to salvage and recycle content for social media. Bea had left them to it while she cracked on with her own job, but she'd appear at dinnertime to eat room service with them.

Jasper and Gabriel knew something had happened between their star driver and the team's social media manager, but they didn't pry. As far as they were concerned, Faith and Lucie could leave if they wanted to. Go home and get on with their lives until the next race. They could do what they needed to do from anywhere in the world. But Bea was due to travel with them when the race was over, so they waited.

Lucie hadn't left Faith's side other than to get a bottle of water from the vending machine on their floor. She had got her out of bed at a reasonable time both mornings and into the shower, ordered fresh fruit and orange juice for breakfast, sat next to her in bed all day while they edited, and then they watched noughties romcoms and cried or laughed or yelled, depending on Faith's mood. It was therapeutic, but she was still a wreck.

It wasn't until Faith and Lucie ventured downstairs and Julien walked through the hotel lobby that Faith managed to muster up a bit of strength. Seeing him shuffle across the tiled floor and into the lift without so much as a glance in her direction filled her with an air of determination.

Brett threw his arm round her and squeezed her shoulder. 'He'll come to his senses, Faith. He's as stubborn as hell, you know that first hand.'

He had been less than impressed at Julien's argument for ending things. As he had bluntly said when he'd found out, which Faith wished he would tell his teammate, anyone could die at any given moment. That shouldn't stop you from taking every shot at happiness you get. Though Faith thought Brett should take his own advice on that front.

Lucie patted her knee. 'I agree with Brett. He's battled his feelings for you from day one and he finally opened up to you with his best-kept secret. This isn't permanent.'

It didn't matter if it wasn't permanent. It was almost two months until the October race in Fuji where she would see him again. That was two whole months where she was supposed to be having the time of her life and travelling the world with her friends, and instead she would be thinking about what Julien was doing, how he was, if he missed her, if he had changed his mind. Faith couldn't start questioning their future again. She had to figure something out.

Fans were still losing their minds across all Revolution's social media accounts. Julien had yet to post his own update even though race day had passed and everyone was starting to pack up and head home. He should've shared something with the fans yesterday, telling them he was back on the mend and appreciated their support. But it had been Jasper, Lucie and Faith doing all the talking. Julien was neglecting his fans and avoiding his teammates.

He knew they didn't like the way he'd dumped Faith at the hospital. Well, they didn't like the fact he had dumped her at all and thought his reasons were bullshit, but they argued that he could've gone about it in a more sensitive manner.

Faith hated more than anything that Julien had truly believed he was letting her off the hook. She hadn't even had the chance to tell him she was all in, and if he had just let her get those words out, he would realize that *all in* also covered the whole *you could die on the racetrack but I choose to be with you despite the risk* thing. Love was a choice just as much as it was a feeling. And she had chosen that arrogant, hot-headed, stubborn blond racing driver with his Dutch curse words, his ridiculously beautiful dog and his overly tight T-shirts. She wanted *all* of him.

She had woken up this morning to no missed calls or texts from Julien. Scrolling through her feed, she came across the interview they had participated in. The one where Julien hadn't denied that they were a couple. A move she had lost her shit over. But her eyes weren't drawn to the stunned look on her face or the anger you could see brewing, nor had anyone else's been. All you could take notice of was the love threatening to burst out of Julien when he looked at her, as if they hadn't been at each other's throats on and off for weeks prior.

Crawling out of bed and trying her best not to wake Lucie beside her, Faith slipped her feet into her trainers and left the hotel room. It was seven thirty as she found herself outside Julien's hotel room in an oversized tee and a tiny pair of black cycling shorts.

She knocked and waited, transfixed on the caramel-coloured swirls in the wood. As fascinating as the door was, she wanted to speak to the man behind it. A few moments passed and she knocked again, a little louder this time. Nothing. Sighing and accepting her fate, she made a bee-line for the stairs. At least then she could pretend to be in a rush if anyone saw her. People didn't wait for lifts when they had places to be.

The lobby was predictably busy. Perhaps busier than it had been over the weekend. Faith frowned as she glanced down at her bare legs. You could barely tell she was wearing shorts. A quick scan of the reception desk, the seating areas and the corridor to the breakfast canteen told her that this had been a wasted trip. Julien wasn't here.

'Faith?' Gabriel called out from behind her, surprised when she turned round to face him with dark circles under her eyes and her hair in knots. At least they were recently shampooed knots.

'Hello. I don't suppose you've seen Jules?'

'Ah.' Gabriel grimaced. 'I'm afraid he left last night. He's already on his way home.'

'Home?'

'Yes . . .' He opened his mouth then closed it again, as if he was afraid to say more.

'Oh,' Faith replied, deflated. It would take forever to get to Hawaii, and she didn't know the address of Koa and Malia's place anyway. Plus, she wasn't keen on the idea of trying to win him back with his daughter and his late wife's parents present.

'Faith?' Gabriel stopped her in her tracks.

'Yeah?'

'When I say "home", I mean, Malmedy.'

Faith broke out into a huge grin and thanked him. Malmedy was doable.

She thundered back up the stairs, knocking into a few mechanics on the way. She didn't want to do this alone, which meant getting everyone organized, and the quicker she could convince her friends to join her on her mission, the better.

Within seconds of emerging on the fifth floor, Faith spotted Bea walking down the corridor with her packed suitcase. Looking as glamorous as ever, she turned her nose up at the sight of her. Faith realized then that she couldn't drive herself. She needed time to sort her face out before they got on the ferry.

'Where are you going?' Faith was panting.

'To put my suitcase in . . . Oh my *God*, we're going to yell at Jules, aren't we?' She whipped round, leading the way to Faith and Lucie's room. 'I should've known that downloading our boarding passes last night was premature.'

They had originally planned on a trip to Athens but that was the last thing on their minds now. Who needed historical landmarks when the green fields of Malmedy existed?

'You need to drive. I've seen you in traffic; there's only one woman for the job,' Faith pleaded. She remembered London's rush hour and the way Bea would slam her fist on the horn with no shame, screaming at anyone who dared cut her off.

'I've got you. Lucie!' she yelled before the door had even opened fully and began flinging random objects in the general direction of their suitcases as she waltzed through the room.

'What the hell is going on?' Lucie sat up in bed, bleary-eyed and confused.

She'd better hurry up and change out of those Care Bear pyjamas before Bea zipped her suitcase up and hauled it into the corridor.

'We're going to Julien's farm. Pack your wellies. Wait, do you actually own wellies?' she demanded as another shoe went flying across the room, narrowly missing a lamp.

'What the fuck are "wellies"?' Lucie snapped.

'Those boots that people wear in the – Oh, never mind. You'll have to deal with muddy shoes. It's probably raining in Malmedy; I suggest you wear your team waterproofs.' Bea looked over at Faith like she was telling off a child. 'Faith! *Move!*'

Faith sprang into action and they spent the next twenty minutes cramming their clothes and make-up anywhere they would fit, even borrowing space in Bea's case. Some things could be thrown into the car without a bag since they'd be staying in it for at least the next eight hours. Laptops could be shoved under seats during the ferry crossing, snacks and bottles of water in any available door pockets or storage compartments.

As they hurled their luggage into the car, trying desperately to avoid filling the back seat where Lucie would no doubt be napping with Mustang the shark, they heard shouting from the hotel's entrance.

Brett and Marco ran across the car park with their bags.

'Move that one to the left. No, Luce. Left. Like this.' Brett huffed as he rearranged to make space for their luggage.

Lucie scowled. 'Stop yelling at me! I literally *just* woke up, guys!'

'How did you know we were leaving?'

'I texted them.' Bea grinned proudly.

'Yeah, you thought we'd miss this?' Marco opened the car door and let Lucie in ahead of him. The excitement hadn't hit her yet but it would. On the ferry. Or maybe when they were stood on Julien's doorstep. Either way, she'd catch up.

Shutting herself away and letting herself be heartbroken may have worked, but this was where she needed to be now. Whether she ended up with Julien or not, she knew she would always have this chaotic family around her, ready to pick up the pieces.

## 30

Ferries were more frightening than aeroplanes, Faith had concluded. The crossing was rough, or at least rough enough for the captain to warn them over the loudspeaker before they set sail, and rough enough that she was seriously regretting the cookies and cream Frappuccino she was three quarters of the way through. Thank goodness she hadn't had breakfast this morning.

She was sitting on a bench up on the deck with the hood of her team rain jacket up, her hair tucked into it to keep her neck warm. The weather had changed dramatically over the course of the last couple of days and they were heading into a very wet and windy Europe. Bea might have been half joking when she had asked Lucie about wellington boots, but maybe it wouldn't have been such a crazy idea.

'How are you doing?' With two coffees in her system already, Lucie had perked up significantly since they'd got on the road and she was now very much an active part of their mission.

'I'm OK. Nervous that it will all come out wrong. And that he'll slam the door in my face, but I know what I'm getting myself into.' Faith shrugged her shoulders, the fabric of her waterproof coat rustling.

'He's home safe by the way. I checked up on him and made him promise to keep me updated. I'm pretending that I'm in nurse mode, so he has no choice but to text me about the silly little things, like when he's napping or walking Ford,' Lucie said. It was no use ringing the door bell three hundred times if he wasn't even in the house or he was in dreamland.

Bea plonked herself down between them with her green tea. 'Oooh, Faith! You should've turned up in a nurse costume! He definitely wouldn't be able to resist that.'

'Beatrix Miller, will you behave yourself?' Lucie scolded.

'Should I have dressed up a bit?' Faith looked down at her outfit. She was in a plain white hoodie, black leggings and white trainers. It was basic. Not exactly an outfit that screamed *I'm here to claim my man*.

Bea patted her knee. 'Don't be silly! I was only teasing. You look effortlessly beautiful, as always. Besides, Julien has seen you drunk with make-up all over your face, wrapped in a towel with dripping-wet hair and asleep with your mouth wide open on an aeroplane. Real men don't give half a shit about appearances once they know the person on the inside.'

'My signal is low but I'm waiting for a text – Oh! Here it is. Jules is back from walking the dog and he's going to spend the rest of the day working in the garden. He's doing some intense landscaping apparently.'

'That'll be for the firepit he's putting in. He mentioned it a few weeks ago.' Faith sighed. If this all went according to plan, she could be sat round that firepit with him next summer, Ford at their feet and his daughter toasting marshmallows over the flames. If not, she might not even be there to see it at next year's post-Spa celebrations.

'I can see you stressing again. Stop.' Lucie squeezed her hand.

'Girls, I have to tell you something.' Faith bit her lip. 'Jules and I had sex at Le Mans. At the back of the garage. And our first kiss was at Spa, just before we left.'

'What?!' Lucie choked on her coffee.

'OK, I understand you not telling me because I was still being a bit of a cow, but, *Faith*! That is huge. I don't think he's ever taken a risk like that.' Bea's jaw was almost on the floor.

'I'm sorry! I didn't want to gossip about it because we were so worried about crossing the line, but maybe I should've clued you in.'

'I can't believe I didn't *notice*,' Lucie said.

'Do you think he'll be mad at me for just showing up like this?'

'No way. He'll take one look at you and realize how much of an idiot he's been, and beg you to forgive him before you can get a single word in,' Bea said, smiling.

'She's right, Faith,' Lucie said. 'He knows you're special; he just doesn't know that he's special too. He had this once and he lost it, and he doesn't want you to ever feel the way he did. You doing this, quite literally crossing borders for him, is proof that he's worth every risk.'

As the three of them huddled together and watched the white cliffs of Dover get further and further away until they were a dot in the distance, Faith prayed that her friends knew what the hell they were talking about.

Once they'd made it off the ferry, with Brett swiftly moving into the driver's seat after they realized Bea was likely to kill them all with her road skills, they began the next part of their journey. Julien lived in the middle of nowhere with only a bakery in close proximity, and the nearest super-market was thirty minutes away at least. They knew he was currently sat on a digger and wasn't going anywhere, so they had time to figure out the logistics.

Twenty minutes from Julien's farmhouse, Brett let out an angry growl and pulled over.

'What the hell is that?!' Bea looked up from her phone and bolted upright, pointing at the steam coming from the front of the car.

Brett flung the door open.

'Everyone, calm down.' Lucie clambered out and stood on the road with Brett.

'We can't drive that. We'll have to get a tow to the nearest garage. God knows where that is.' Brett threw his hands up in the air, looking like he had just been told the world was ending.

'There's that one right at the edge of Francorchamps that sells the racing merchandise,' Lucie reminded him.

'Um, you guys are racing drivers . . . Can't you take a look at it? See if there's anything you can do?' Faith didn't know why she was so shy all of a sudden. Maybe it was to do with the fact that they had come all this way for her benefit, and this threw a spanner in the works.

'Come on. Let's give it a shot.' Marco marched over and started giving orders while the girls stood on the grass at the side of the road.

Ten minutes passed, then twenty, then thirty. There were two world-class racing drivers huddled over the engine, swearing and yelling at each other.

'We don't have time! If this isn't working, move on to the next solution!' Brett snapped.

'It's no use yelling at me, Anderson. It's not going to get Faith to Jules any quicker, is it?'

Marco swatted his hand out of the way. 'Screw this.'

'What are you –' Lucie mumbled through a bite of cookie when Brett appeared in front of her, hand outstretched.

'Your phone please, Luce.'

'So demanding.' She rolled her eyes but handed it over. 'Do you need the passcode?'

'No. I've seen you type it a million times.' Brett put the phone to his ear and placed his hand on his hip, growing more and more impatient with every ring.

'Brett, who are you calling?' Faith asked.

'I'm calling Jules and telling him to get his ass out here. You've waited long enough.'

## 31

She heard Julien's car a good forty seconds before she saw it. It was a streak of red in the distance, ripping through the tree-lined roads until it was right in front of them. He stepped out in his scuffed Doc Marten boots, which were too hot to be wearing on a late-summer afternoon, and a black muscle tee. His hair was clinging to the sweat on his tanned forehead and his arms were streaked with oil and dirt. *Classic Jules.*

He blinked. 'The hell are you lot doing here?'

Once he had processed the situation, there it was again. That look. The one reserved for Faith. He zeroed in on her and she could sense that he had blocked out the presence of the four other people there. Faith, however, had not. She was hyper aware of the shuffling as their friends got in the car, Lucie and Brett hovering by their open doors in case either of them wanted out of this reunion.

'We'll be fine,' Faith reassured them.

Instead of leaving the couple stood in an uncomfortable silence, they were met with the distant notes of an all-time classic by the Vengaboys. Julien's strictly business facade disappeared and was replaced by a smile that Faith couldn't help but match.

'I take it you're here for me.'

'I am . . . I rehearsed the hell out of this.'

'Yeah?'

'Yeah. But now I don't know where to start.'

'Are you angry with me?' He looked vulnerable. Hurt, even.

'Not angry. Just frustrated. You sat there in that hospital room and made a decision without consulting me, or talking anything through with me, as normal. And I walked away because I was done with that crap, but I am not done with you. I was going to throw all of this away because I was scared. Then you crashed, and I thought I was going to lose you. I walked into that hospital prepared to lay all my cards on the table and tell you I wanted to be with you, and you took it all away from me. You chase what you want, Jules. On the track and off. It's in your nature. So why won't you fight for us?'

'You know what I love about you, Faith? You've got a fire in you. You and me aren't all that different.' He took a step closer to her. 'But I love you too much to keep you.'

'And I love you too much to let you go.'

His entire expression softened in an instant and she saw innocence flash across his features. Julien had never had someone fight for *him*. He had only ever had women desiring him for what he could offer them. She had seen the deepest parts of him. She knew what was under the surface, what gave him purpose and the pain he had endured.

'I can't guarantee that you won't lose me one day.'

'I know.'

'You might have to see me crash again.'

'I know.'

'You're honestly OK with that?'

'You think I'm going to stop being friends with Marco and Brett just because they *might* get hurt? Life doesn't work that way. I know you want to protect me, Jules. But what I need you to understand is that you're worth it to me.'

'There's no going back after this. You know that, right? You're it for me.'

'You think I just drove here from England for the fun of it?'

'Maybe. Something to do, you know? Team bonding.'

'I'm here because I know you. I can't believe I'm able to say that, but I do. I know you well enough to know that you were acting out of fear, and because you were doing what you thought was right for me. But I'm a big girl, Jules. I make my own choices, and I choose you.'

'I choose you too. I'm sorry I tried to push you away and made you think I didn't want you. Truth is, I've wanted you from day one.' He reached for her, pulling her close.

'I'm glad you came to your senses. So we're doing this?'

'Uh-huh. But I need you to do something for me.'

'Anything,' she said.

'Promise me you'll always fight for yourself the way you just fought for me. This industry is fucking hard for women, Faith. People's opinions will be fed down to you and there will be days when you want out. There will be days when this relationship will be viewed harshly, and you'll be wrongly judged. Prove them wrong. I can't defend you in every scenario, as much as I want to. It just isn't my place. You've got to show everyone what you're capable of, keep showing them who you are. Promise?'

'I promise.' Faith nodded. 'As long as you promise *me* something. *Talk* to me. You don't have to do shit alone any more. You have me. Use me. Offload on me instead of bottling things up; don't punish me with mood swings and silent treatments and shut yourself away in your trailer. I'm not going anywhere, OK? I'm here to stay. It's you and me. *We* are a team.'

'Scout's honour. And when things inevitably get hard, I still want this industry to feel like your home. It's served me well over the years, and it's given me everything I could possibly ask for in life. Including you. Every racing driver has a moment in their career that they never saw coming, and I always thought I'd had my moment. Until you. *You* were the one thing I never saw coming.'

Another inch closer, then another. Faith watched his jaw tense as he contemplated what he was doing but before he could change his mind, he was placing his lips on hers. And she could feel the fight in him reaching the surface, pulling her in and refusing to let her go. So there they were, stood on the side of a country road, souls intertwining with an Ibiza dance anthem as their soundtrack. Julien was hers as much as she was his.

Faith was in her rightful place in the passenger seat of Julien's Mustang, and she couldn't stop staring at him. It wasn't just his arms this time, it was the glow radiating from him. This guy was suddenly the human embodiment of sunshine, which was freaking her out a little.

'What made you come all the way out here instead of waiting until we saw each other at the next race?' Julien glanced at her quizzically before focusing on the road again.

'This year has been about travelling the world for what I love. I took a big risk when I took this job, so I figured what was one more? Why should we waste more time? What matters is always having faith that it will pay off in the end.'

'Having faith.' He cracked a smile. 'I see what you did there.'

'Yeah? Hilarious, aren't I?'

'One of the funniest women I've ever met.' Julien placed his hand on her thigh. 'I spoke to Jasmine about you this morning.'

'Oh?'

'She kept asking about you. She asked me if you and me were secretly dating. I said no. She called me an idiot. Her grandmother chimed in, told me that Kailani would approve and agreed I was a fool if I let you go. So I booked a flight to Athens . . . Shame you got to me first really. Greece is beautiful.'

She choked. 'You booked a what?!'

'A flight. You weren't the only one planning a grand declaration of love, you know.'

'Julien! What was that whole "I love you too much to keep you" spiel you gave?!'

'That was me trying to be all tragically romantic, a bit like Allie and Noah from *The Notebook*. Got to give ourselves a story to put in our wedding vows one day.'

'You've watched *The Notebook*?'

'It's Ford's favourite.'

'Your dog has a favourite film?'

'Ours.'

'What?'

'He's our dog now.'

Faith bypassed the wedding vows remark and the fact she now shared custody of a gigantic grey and white husky and focused on the man she could finally call her boyfriend. He watched romantic dramas alone, drove fast cars for a living and treated his dog like his second child. He was straight out of a romance novel.

Faith lay in bed that night in Julien's arms. His expensive white sheets felt a million times more luxurious and welcoming with him by her side, and instead of being drunk she was feeling lightheaded as a result of other more scandalous actions. Actions that they would repeat a hundred times over.

'I think it's time for another round, sweetheart.' Julien kissed Faith's bare shoulder and trailed his hand down her stomach, resulting in faint butterflies that she would never get tired of.

'Can you at least kick the dog out first?' Faith looked over his shoulder at the mass of fur lying next to the bed.

'Hear that, Ford? Your new mum wants you out. Go on, out you go.' Julien gestured for Ford to leave and he did, sighing as he went.

Faith almost felt bad, but she wanted to cherish the time she had with Julien before their friends joined them for breakfast in a few hours. They would be running on zero sleep, but it was worth it.

Faith kissed him, savouring the taste. His tongue slipped into her mouth and as he wrestled for control she knew where this was going.

He removed his mouth from hers and with his blue eyes locked on her own, used one hand to part her legs. Within seconds, his head of blond hair was between them and his tongue was on her clit, the sensation making her shiver with anticipation.

'You're so wet for me already.' He looked up at her and her eyes fluttered closed as he inserted his fingers, almost causing her to immediately beg him to take her. All afternoon he had dragged out foreplay until she was almost in tears because she needed more of him.

'Don't make me wait, Jules.'

'Hmmm?' He pretended not to hear her.

'I know you're already hard. You could just put it in right now, we have the rest of our lives for foreplay. Or I could let you make me orgasm from this, and then I could roll over and go to sleep and leave you lying there wide awake for the rest of the night.'

With that, Julien's head shot up and he shifted his body so she could see his boxers struggling to contain what she craved.

'You are a cold, calculated young woman, Faith Indigo Jensen.'

'But you love me.'

'I do . . .' After pausing for a few seconds so they could soak in the admission, he winked at her and took his length out of his boxers, standing up briefly to kick the material on to the floor.

'Get a move on.' Faith grinned at him.

'Ready?' Julien waited for her to respond and then he was on top of her, rubbing her clit with his thumb to open her up before thrusting into her.

She gasped as he filled her and she tightened round him, and he barely hesitated before pounding into her so hard the bed rocked with his movements. This wasn't like it had been on the camp bed. This bed provided them with a stability they hadn't had before, and the thought of all the positions he was going to put her in made it feel ten times more intense.

He pulled out and she whimpered, but he flipped her over so she was on her stomach and grabbed her ass, entering her again from behind while she took over and played with her clit.

His hand went to her head and he grabbed hold of her hair, tugging it and grabbing her breast with his other hand. He thrusted into her fast, not relenting his pace, and she could feel her orgasm building rapidly. He was letting out soft little moans behind her.

'Who do you belong to, Faith?' he whispered in her ear.

'I'm yours, Julien.'

'Say it again.'

'I'm yours.'

Julien slowed down and pulled out of her all the way, twisting her round so he could kiss her as he entered her again. And again, and again. She moaned into his mouth as he slammed into her. She knew he was close from the growl in the back of his throat.

'Where do you want me to cum? Tell me where.' Julien struggled to get his words out.

'Cum inside me. Please. Fuck, I need you to cum inside me.'

With a loud moan, he let go and released his load inside her right as she reached her own climax, her whole body writhing against him. She tightened her muscles around his dick, resulting in what he would later claim was the best orgasm of his life.

'If this is what sex is gonna be like for the rest of our lives, I might just retire from racing early and stay in bed for the next fifty years.' He placed a gentle kiss on her forehead.

'I think the outside world would miss you.'

'The outside world doesn't give me orgasms.'

'Well, not any more.' She raised an eyebrow.

'Those days are far behind me. I'm all yours.'

Faith and Julien were used to a world of fame and recognition. They were on display for the entire world the majority of the time, but in that moment the love they'd found over the last few months was the only thing that mattered. The models from Julien's past were irrelevant, fan opinions were merely that, opinions. They were untouchable.

'Thank you,' Faith whispered.

'What for?'

'Letting me into your world.'

'It's a chaotic world, sweetheart. But it's ours.'

And as she lay next to a man she never thought she would, Faith was grateful. For him, for her friends, for her job. For every ounce of chaos the universe had gifted her with.

# Epilogue

'You cannot drive this thing at this speed with a *child* in the back seat, Julien! Is this what you want to teach kids?' Faith gripped on to the metal bar in front of her as they sailed past masses of fans in the paddock. Her brand-new sapphire engagement ring sparkled over her white knuckles.

'Yeah, but she's my kid and she loves it! Right, Jas?' Julien turned to look at his daughter, who was ghostly white but plastering a smile on her face nonetheless.

'Right!' Jasmine yelled back.

'I'm just saying, I know you won yet another championship last season but that doesn't mean you're immune to golf cart accidents. This is as bad as Gabriel swerving potted plants.'

Revolution Racing were in Oyama for the fourth race of the new season, and it was the first time Jasmine had been allowed to attend. Julien had been filming an ad for a safety in motorsport campaign – ironic – and insisted that Faith go to Hawaii, personally collect Jasmine and bring her to Japan, where they had spent four days in Tokyo before joining Julien at the track.

In the last year their lives had integrated and calendars synced so that each time they had a break from racing they spent at least half of it in Hawaii or Malmedy with Jasmine. She had quickly adapted to Faith's presence, and although

Faith was still adopting more of a best-friend approach, things had gradually been shifting into parental territory.

She helped Jasmine with schoolwork, braided her hair in the mornings, told her off when she stomped mud through the house, and had a quiet word when she had an attitude about something. Not once had Jasmine rebelled against her, and Faith didn't know if it was because she was just well adjusted or because she genuinely viewed her dad's girlfriend as a maternal figure. Julien believed it was the latter and was insisting they pop out six more.

Faith wasn't so sure about *six*, but one or two would be OK in a couple of years. She hoped at least one would follow in their footsteps and show an interest in racing, because Jasmine was dead set on going to medical school. The legacy children would have to wait.

Faith was run off her feet with the women in motor-sport programme she was running with Lucie, Bea and Esme. They had promoted Esme at the end of the last season to work directly alongside Lucie and Bea as heads of social content, and asked her to come on board with their new movement. It was still in the planning stages but they had their first round of workshops in the spring at the Silverstone circuit.

'There you are! Take your fucking time!' Brett shouted across the garage and covered his mouth with his hands when he spotted Jasmine. 'Sorry, Jas. My bad. Jules, please don't hit me.'

Jasmine shrugged. 'Dad curses in front of me all the time.'

'Hey! That's not true!' Julien attempted to defend himself but it was pointless. As much as he tried to be on his best behaviour, he was a passionate man. And passionate men didn't have a filter, or so he claimed every time he was called out.

'I got you a li'l something, Jazzy. Well, Uncle Mars and I both did. We wanted your first race to be special.' Brett beckoned them into the trailer and directed Jasmine to the wardrobe, where there was a racing suit waiting for her. It had been made especially for her, and even had her name stitched on the waist in white.

'Thank you! Can I go and put it on?'

'Go and find Uncle Marco after, OK? You've got to thank him.' Julien ushered Jasmine into the trailer's tiny bathroom, leaving him and Faith alone.

Brett was already heading back into the garage, and Lucie was halfway down the pit lane talking to a group of their new interns. Jasmine began singing while she got changed, which was their cue to talk. She did this a lot. Sang so she couldn't accidentally overhear their conversations.

It had confused them both at first, until she had informed them that her friend from school did the same thing because her own parents were heavy on the PDA. Faith and Julien were much more reserved when Jasmine was around, but that didn't stop Julien eyeing the sofa and raising a suggestive eyebrow.

'Absolutely not.'

'Jas will be out of the trailer in a minute to go and find Marco, then it's just us. We can lock the door . . .' He held her gaze as he ran his hands over her hips and pulled her closer.

'Guys!' Jasmine emerged from the bathroom. 'Can we get sushi from the food trucks?'

Just like that, the moment was gone. Faith got Julien to herself almost fifty per cent of the time, so an interruption every now and then did no harm when it meant she got to enjoy authentic Japanese food in the foothills of Mount Fuji and listen to Jasmine talk animatedly about how she was going to convince her dad to be her show-and-tell next semester to score points with her friends.

Besides, Faith would have plenty of alone time with the world's favourite racing driver next month, when they spent their two-week honeymoon in Switzerland. Her first trip to the Swiss Alps would be enjoyed cosied up in a log cabin by the fire, with a gold wedding band on her finger and the name *Faith Jensen-Moretz* plastered all over her social media.

Faith's family was growing, but her definition of what family meant to her had changed drastically. She had come to the wonderful conclusion that family was complicated. Sometimes you're separated by thousands of miles, sometimes by bitterness.

It doesn't always mean that you're related by blood. It's just a group of people who fit in your world perfectly. *Your* people. And sometimes you don't need anything more than that. But in the rare cases that you do have more, or that more finds its way back to you, nothing can diminish the role of the people who landed right in your lap when you least expected it. The people who took you under their wing. The people who love you without limits, who pick you up when you're down. The Juliens, Lucies, Bretts, Marcos and Beas of the world. *Those* are your family. And they were Faith's.

# Acknowledgements

The journey from the beginning stages of this book to the traditional release has been a roller coaster. I planned it five years ago on my way home from a road trip to Belgium, where I'd just watched the six hours of Spa, and it took me another two years and a rather traumatic life event to start writing it. Since I finished the very first chapter, it's been my baby.

To see it being brought into the world of traditionally published Romance books by the publishing company of my dreams has been truly special, but there are some people I couldn't have done it without.

Thank you firstly to the team at PMJ who have helped me develop Faith and Julien's story and the world of Revolution Racing, particularly Jennie Roman, Emma Henderson, and of course Hannah Smith, who took a chance on me and opened up a whole new chapter in my life. You all seem to have understood my vision flawlessly from day one.

To the best support system I could ask for: Kez, Nicole, Dylan, Meg, Carina, Katrina, Ella and Kyle. The words of encouragement and the pride you've all expressed have meant more than you could know.

A monumental thank you to my family (and extended family!) for having an unwavering belief in me and for making sure I know I'm capable and worthy of everything

I've dreamed of (this is literally it). Sorry to all of you who have read the spicy scenes, although I did warn you. Please never mention them to me directly.

And to Hoppy, the most special Grandad a girl could ask for. The faith you had in me as a little girl has shaped me into the woman I am, and I'm not sure I would've pushed quite so hard had you not been the one to read my very first short story at the age of six or seven. What grown man wants to read one A4 sheet of paper about fairies and gemstones? But you did, proudly, and I hope you know I did this for you as much as I did it for myself.

Lastly, I want to thank the friends I've made online along the way. You all gave me a community and a platform and, had I not discovered the world of Bookstagram, I don't think that I'd have known where to start. It's because of your support on social media that PMJ found me, and I couldn't be more grateful.

I hope you've enjoyed reading *Bloodstream* as much as I've enjoyed writing it.

Lots of love,

Emilee